ABOUT THE AUTHOR

Linda writes in several genres, crime being her main one. Her gentle romances are published under the name Linda M Priestley. "Earth Magic" and "Book Lovers" are available on Kindle.

After graduating from the University of Leicester, Linda spent several years in clinical research before starting a family. Once the children were at school, Linda started writing mysteries. The first novel in the Elversford series, 'Death in Spigg's Wood' (published Dec 2011 on Kindle) was born out of a casual conversation arising from the question, "What would happen if..." The follow-up, "Death in Flitbury Marshes" followed in April 2012. The short story "Burden of Proof" and the novel "Blood Will Out" have joined these mysteries.

Linda's short stories and articles have been published in several national magazines. The short story "Wargeld" was Highly Commended in The Yellow Room Short Story Spring Competition 2009. Wargeld is published in an anthology of several short stories.

"Charlie's War" was first published by My Weekly Pocket Novels and is now available as a Large Print Linford Romance (Ulverscroft).

Linda can be found at www.lindagruchy.wordpress.com

Author's Note

This is a work of fiction and the characters have no existence outside my imagination. Any resemblance to real persons, living or dead is coincidental. Those places in Essex where the main action is based have been renamed and changed to fit the story.

Williams & Whiting (Publishers)

15 Chestnut Grove, Hurstpierpoint,

West Sussex, BN6 9SS

Dedication

To Dave, Jo and Alex

With love

BLOOD WILL OUT

LINDA GRUCHY

WILLIAMS & WHITING

Chapter 1

Angie Bain

"You're pregnant," said Dr Thomas, moving a stethoscope over my abdomen.

I laughed. "No, I can't be."

He slid the disc around again, and put on that GP expression, the one they wear when they're not sure what you want to hear. "I can hear a foetal heartbeat. You're definitely pregnant. I'll do an internal now." Gloved probing fingers, indifferent or immune to embarrassment, slithering around in my private areas. Competent. That distant look on his face.

Pregnant? Pregnant? Impossible.

"Thanks, get dressed please." He handed me a swatch of blue towelling, then helped me sit and swivel, legs dangling over the side of the couch. I stepped into my knickers and jeans, eased them up, and coaxed the zip closed, belly creasing over the denim. I took my disbelief out on my shoes, slamming my feet into them, and shuffled over to the patient's chair.

He stripped his gloves and washed his hands meticulously; a ritual. He'd been my GP for years, but I hardly knew him. He sat, typed into the computer and said, "When was your last menstrual period?"

"I can't be pregnant," I said, as if I were talking into a pillow. "I haven't had sex. At least, not with a man."

"Are you sure?" He then looked abashed at the inanity of the question.

"I think I'd remember. Especially with a man. I have never had sex with a man in my life. I'm a lesbian; the thought of having sex with a man makes me feel… ugh." I shuddered. My voice sounded unintentionally sarcastic, rude even. "Sorry; I

1

thought it was just the menopause," I added a little more gently. "I can't possibly be pregnant." I gave a humourless laugh. "I suppose you could say I'm a virgin."

"I'm sorry, Angela. I heard a foetal heartbeat, and your cervix is closed. There is no doubt. We'll book you in for a scan to determine age. Soon, in case we have to take... decisions. You must have had sex. Unless you've tried artificial insemination." He raised a brow and waited for me to confess. To what? A syringe-full of maleness? I felt my gorge rise.

"I'm a lesbian. I don't have sex with men. Never."

His Adam's apple rose and fell, eyes retreating to the computer screen. Looking to see if I'd ever been prescribed contraceptives perhaps? To check if I was lying? He scrolled idly up and down, as if the computer could tell him the answer. He pulled in a sharp breath. "Have you any recollection of a time when you perhaps got very drunk, or something? Probably about 6 months ago."

"No. I don't drink much," I said, but my fingers clenched. "Well, now you mention it. I wasn't drunk, but I was very poorly... Like really bad food poisoning... So bad, I lost a day, I mean, I can't recollect anything about it. Around Christmas. But I got better, so I didn't bother you," I added as an excuse. I hate going to the doctor's, and it's so hard to get an appointment.

"And you've had no symptoms that suggested you were pregnant? No nausea, no foetal movements, like a bubbles-inside sensation? What about your missed periods? Surely that should have told you...?"

"Well, I did feel sicky for a while, but not now. I just thought it was a lurgy, but I suppose that must've been morning sickness; how could I guess it was that? Same with the missed periods. I thought that was the menopause even

2

though I'm only 46. And I put that bubbling feeling down to wind... except just lately it happened really frequently, and that got me worried. I thought maybe I had cancer. I thought I'd better get it checked out, just in case. That's why I'm here."

Not cancer, then; pregnant.

Pregnant?

I watched his moustache moving like a hairy caterpillar. It writhed with his lips, and I heard his voice from a long way away, as if he was speaking under water in the swimming pool. Gradually he came back into focus and my thoughts stopped their discordant hurdy-gurdy screaming round my brain. "But surely I'd be a lot bigger if I were six months pregnant," I said. "I mean, there's a bump, but I just thought I was putting on weight."

"In my experience a lot of women don't show very much for the first six months. It's only in the last two or three months that it really becomes prominent. Forgive me, Angela, I really couldn't understand how you came to be about six months pregnant without getting an inkling that you were carrying, but I understand now, especially if you didn't realise you'd had intercourse."

"But I didn't..." A sick feeling settled like gravel in my stomach. "You think I was drugged and raped, don't you?"

When I left him, he had already put things in train, referred me for a scan to fix the due date (though 6 months seemed right) and find out how far gone I was, just in case I had to take...

'Decisions.'

~~~

I had no pangs of guilt about phoning up the supermarket where I work and saying I was ill, though I wasn't exactly ill, was I? They knew I had a doctor's appointment first thing that morning anyway, so it wouldn't be questioned. And no way did I feel fit for work.

I climbed into bed after I phoned, because it was suddenly cold for June, though the sun blistered the tarmac. I replayed my memories of the last six months like a tacky video ad nauseum, trying to think, to remember.

How?

When?

And what would Kim say?

~~~

There's something very off-putting about police stations. Is it a feeling of oppression built into the bricks? A field of repulsion. It even crushed me down the phone. I tried 3 times to phone but couldn't even finish diallling the number. So how come I thought it would be easier to do it this way? I mounted the steps, pushing against the force field. The door handle burned cold on my fingers despite the afternoon sun. The door swung in and I followed.

CCTV camera. I couldn't run, now, it would look too silly, too suspicious. There was a girl at the front desk. She looked up, stood with a smile. "Can I help?"

She was very pretty. That beauty was like a gag in my mouth. I chewed on it, then spat the words out. "I'd like to report a rape. I think." The blush started in my belly and creept up to my face, as if it was my fault.

"Please take a seat, and I'll fetch someone." She indicated a blue vinyl bench. I sat and looked at the notice board. 'Essex

4

Police: Making Essex Safer.' The statement seemed almost insulting in its inanity. I'd seen it on the police cars, but it hadn't struck me until now what a stupid slogan it was. I didn't feel at all safe. Not anymore. There was a poster asking for information about a horrible assault and murder. Next to that was a harrowing depiction of what crack cocaine does to you. So I looked at the leaflets instead. One slapped me in the eyes; a leaflet about spiked drinks. I flinched and shut the world away. A shred of moisture escaped from between my screwed-up eyes and I told myself not to be such a child.

I heard a heavy door swing open and snapped my eyes open. A woman came over, casual smart, about 40, on the tall side. Not pretty, not ugly. Mrs Neutral. Except for her eyes. Beautiful eyes. "Would you like to come through?" she asked, ushering me along a bland corridor and into a room, flicking the 'Occupied' sign on the door across.

"I understand you want to make a complaint of rape," she said, neutrally, as she indicated a chair. I sat, she took another chair, and picked up a pad. "My name is DC Suzy Rolfe, and I'm part of the Sexual Offences Investigation Team based here in Galchester... I'm specially trained in these matters, as are my colleagues, and we have lots of help available to you, here and at a multi-agency rape centre, Rosamundi House in Galchester—that's run jointly by the NHS, the police and other public bodies. Just take your time, as long as you need, and tell me what happened."

"I don't know where to begin."

"Well, let's start with the easy stuff. What's your name? Date of birth? Address?"

"My name is Angie—Angela Bain and I live at 34B Flitbury Road, Galchester, Essex..." She wrote it all down on a form. "Erm, I'm afraid you'll think I'm being very silly," I added.

5

Her lovely emerald eyes betrayed no opinion. "No. Carry on. I'm listening."

I told her what I thought had happened. My words sounded silly in my ears. Too dramatic. Too banal. A contradiction.

"Did you think you'd been assaulted at the time?"

"Of course not. I'd have reported it otherwise."

"No signs of intercourse in your home?"

I shook my head. "Nothing. Nothing gave me any clue that anything had happened. Until now. I couldn't believe I'm pregnant. I still can't believe it."

"Let me take you back to that night in December, the one where you suffered the memory loss. Where were you drinking?"

Mrs Neutral slowly and gently extracted my memories of that evening. They were hazy because six months had elapsed, and I'd gone out with my friends since then, the usual crowd, and one recollection merged into another, like ice cubes melting in a drink. I wasn't sure what was real any more. Sometimes she would ask a question, and I'd feel like I knew the answer, but my mind was blank, well, not blank, more covered in hieroglyphics where there was meaning, but it was hidden to me.

After a while I wondered where the box of tissues had come from, and the tea, and was surprised by the pile of sodden tissue paper on my lap. My fat lap. My gravid lap. I'd told Mrs Neutral when I thought it had happened (ish) and who I thought I'd been drinking with (ish). As ambiguity piled on vagueness, I wondered why I'd bothered coming.

As if she'd read my thoughts Mrs Neutral said, "I'm sure you can guess just how difficult it's going to be to find the culprit since we've lost most of the forensic evidence, Angie, but I really appreciate you coming forward with this. So many of these sorts of attacks go unreported. We need to talk to your partner and the friends you've told me you think you went drinking with that evening..."

I said, "Oh, I'd rather they didn't know," before I realised the absurdity of that. My eyes fell onto the bump that would tell them my story anyway. It wriggled. Not gas. Baby kicking. My gullet burned.

"We'd like to approach your GP if that's OK. Ask him about this. But we need you to fill a consent form for that." She handed it to me. I signed it, handwriting like a drunken spider. "And even though we don't know if the assault took place at your home, we could send Scenes of Crime round to see if they can find anything. You say that you don't entertain men in your home? Ever?"

"Well, no, certainly not like that. I've a few male friends, but we never have them round." My home was Kim's and my sanctuary. I didn't like to share it. "We tend to socialise down the pub. The Craven Arms in Galchester. About a mile from home."

"So if we were to find semen, for example, it could very likely belong to the perpetrator?"

"Almost certainly."

Mrs Neutral told me that there's a centre for rape survivors (which seemed a funny way of putting it) just down the road, Rosamundi House, run by the Health Service and the police, and that I might like to see what help and advice they could give me. I shook my head. "Thanks," I said, closing the door on that idea.

~~~

Scenes of Crime found nothing. Hardly surprising after 6 months, I suppose. The bed became an alien place, polluted with possibility, so I curled up in a sodden heap on the leather settee. I pulled the whisky out of the sideboard and placed it on the coffee table, which was probably a bad move, because it was easier to refill the glass.

I heard Kim's key in the door, but still stared at her stupidly when she came in. "What are we celebrating?" she said blithely until she saw my face. "Shit, Angie, what's the matter?"

"I'm pregnant," I said numbly.

"Pregnant?"

I nodded.

"Are you sure? You can't be?" Her mouth was a slack O.

"I've just been to the doctors. It's confirmed... Six or seven months gone..."

"So you've had sex with a man, you cow. How could you? You betrayed me. Who is he? Bastard. Who is he?"

"I don't know."

"You mean there's more than one? You bike! Men? I'll kill you, you tart, you bitch." Her face switched from injured bewilderment to fury. "You told me you're not bi. You lied to me. You know how I feel about men. It's disgusting. I thought you loved me."

"I do, I... Listen. I was raped, for God's sake! It's not my fault." Why was she so angry? I expected shock, horror, sympathy. Not this. I'd never seen her so outraged. It was terrifying.

She shoved her furious face into mine, her spittle flecking me. "Yeah, right, like when?" she snarled.

8

The slap echoed round the room. She reared back, cheek white and red with finger marks.

"Oh God, I'm sorry," I said. "I didn't mean it. I swear…"

Tears streamed down her face. "Don't you… ever… do that again."

I cringed at every word, hiding behind my hands. "I'm sorry, I'm so sorry. I don't know what came over me, I'd never… I won't, I won't, I promise. I never meant to; I love you. But I was raped. Don't you understand? Don't shout at me, please don't; I need your help, not… not…. It must have been around Christmas time." I went to embrace her, but she slid away from me.

"Don't you know?"

"I was drugged. I must've been because I don't remember a thing. Remember that time you came back from your Mum's and I said I'd felt bloody awful? How I…" But I'd only told Kim how I felt poorly, not that I'd woken up at home with no recollection, thinking I was sick. I didn't like to say how I'd gone to the pub when she was away up north, visiting her Mum, who hates me. "My periods stopping; well, it wasn't the menopause like we thought. It's a baby."

I saw her gaze slithering down to my abdomen. She flinched, face breaking into splinters of grief. Without a word, she turned and left the room. A couple of minutes later I heard the front door slam.

"The police want to talk to you," I told the empty space.

Chapter 2

Angie

Pregnant. I was pickling the poor little thing in alcohol, but I didn't care. I wondered if I'd have the opportunity to make...decisions. It might be too late.

I'm not used to a lot of alcohol, and my body rebelled. After a few minutes ugly intimacy with the toilet bowl, I made myself a tea, and tried to fish my brains out of the mire. Kim would come round, eventually. It was just a shock to her, as it was to me. I should never have hit her. I couldn't understand why I had. Perhaps I was punishing her for what had happened to me, making a scapegoat of her. I chewed my lips until they burned. I would have to put things right when she came home. She'd understand. Eventually.

~~~

She wasn't home by bedtime. She hadn't answered her phone, or the 'I love you' texts I'd sent.

~~~

I woke in a shiver of fright and groped for Kim but found nothing. It was dark, mid-summer, so it must have been about 2.00am. I spent the rest of the night worrying about her, telling myself that she was a tough cookie; she could look after herself. But I loved her, I needed her, and she'd never stayed away before. Suppose something had happened? Maybe she was hurt, lying injured somewhere. The thoughts jigged round my hangover like evil sprites until dawn came. I gave up on sleep, rose, and started to make lists of things I had to do.

I made a list of friends where I thought Kim might have retreated to. I would phone each of them, starting with Digby, Kim's brother. Kim adored him, would do anything for him, but he didn't seem to like me much, so we didn't see that much of him. It's almost like he was jealous of me, jealous of the attention Kim gave me. Weird. You'd think he'd be happy because we were so happy. Anyway, when he and Kim were together I felt uncomfortable; the interloper. He lived seven miles or so away in Elversford.

His voice was blurred with sleep when he answered the phone.

"Digby, it's Angie here..."

"Oh." Hostile, guarded. My hunch was right then.

"Is Kim there?"

"She told me you had a row. You hit her. How could you, Angie? That's not like you."

"I was out of my mind, Digby. I didn't mean it. Only I've just found out I'm six months pregnant."

"Shit!" There was a pause, a few pants of breath, "You sure?"

"Yes, I'm sure. I was raped. I must have been."

"Shit! Can't you get rid of it?"

"It's probably too late."

"Fucking hell, Angie, didn't you realise sooner? Shit!"

"I was drugged. How the heck could I guess I was pregnant when as far as I knew I hadn't had sex with a bloke? Kim and I just thought it was the menopause."

"Shit!"

I warmed to Digby then. He was more sympathetic than Kim, despite the awful swearing. Kim obviously hadn't even told him what the row was about, just that we'd rowed. "Is

11

Kim with you? Only she didn't come home last night. I'm worried. I love her."

"You've got a funny way of showing it."

The silence lengthened. "I know. I hate myself for that."

I heard him suck in a breath. "Yes, she's here, safe, but very upset, won't tell me what's wrong, just that you betrayed her and hit her. I don't think she wants to talk to you just now. Give us some time to get our heads round this, will you Angie. Give us a breathing space."

'Us.' Digby was going to be a big support. He'd help us get through this.

~~~

I phoned the supermarket where I work and told them I still wasn't well. I was wary of my supervisor, Ms Curtis. She was strict and aloof, and could tell when people were skiving, or lying. I had the feeling she wasn't keen on lesbians, though she never said as much.

I'd been bullied at school, as if I wore my sexuality on my forehead like a brand. The other kids treated me like a pervert. I left school left after 'O' Levels and got a job. Seven 'O' levels but no 'A' Levels. My parents were crushed. They'd planned on University for me. But I was sick of the prejudice, the innuendos and the sniggers. But it was just as ugly in the real world. Worse, perhaps.

A couple of years later, when I told Mum and Dad I was a lesbian, Mum flopped in her armchair, pale as paper, limp as a dishcloth, and wept, Dad raged round the lounge, purple and snarling. They said stop being silly or we'll never speak to you again. Fine, I said, suits me. I left the house in a storm of tears, guilt, wounded pride, anguish and fury, taking just my personal papers and a small case crammed higgledy-piggledy with a random selection of screwed up clothes. Fool that I was. I wonder if they really meant it, if they hate me still. I wonder where they are now. What would they say if they knew they were going to be grandparents? Perhaps they already were. My brother Richard probably has kids. Aunty Angie.

When I left home, I left the area, found another, better job. I bought this place just before house prices went mad. I can't afford to give up work. I can't afford to have a child minder. I've nobody but Kim to baby-sit. And she works.

What on earth am I going to do with this baby?

Chapter 3

Angie

The hospital phoned. They were keen to get me in for a scan, and there had been a cancellation for the next day. Could I make it? Of course I could.

~~~

I was alone for the rest of the day and night. Next morning, Friday, I drove myself to the hospital, and flinched at the cost of parking. The ultrasound department was full of couples holding hands. There was a water fountain, so I tanked up on water until I hoped nobody would make me laugh. I'd just got to the stage when I thought I'd have to go to the loo, when I was called.

Unzip the jeans, slide the knickers down over the bump. Baby, not fat. Gel, cool. Probe, image. Testicles. It would be. Wipe clean, tug jeans up, fasten ambitiously. Dash to loo. Huge pee. Relief.

They gave me a due date estimated on the foetus' size. 20th September. And they told me cheerfully that they could detect no gross abnormality.

~~~

Home. Still no Kim. Just an image of a baby. I was on the whisky again. It seemed to stop him kicking. Heck, I wish I hadn't known what gender. Knowing he was a boy kicking me to death in there made him real, not an "it" any more. A person. I swigged down another mouthful of whisky.

The phone went. Dr Thomas. The hospital had phoned through the results. Everything was normal, and it was too late for a termination. But he wanted to see me weekly to monitor my blood pressure and so on. How did I feel? I told him that I had reported the intercourse as rape, and he said he knew because the police had spoken to him already.

I'd barely put the phone down when it went again. My supervisor Ms Curtis. Was I still ill, only I was scheduled for work at the weekend. I told her yes, I was ill, and no, I wasn't sure when I'd be better. She asked me what was wrong. "I don't know, yet," I lied. "I went to the hospital for tests." I could tell she didn't believe me.

The phone rang again, DC Rolfe. How was I? Pissed, I told her, pissed, for the second time in as long as I could remember. Doesn't take much to get me pissed, I told her. Just rape, an unwanted pregnancy, and three glasses (big ones) of whisky. She made some bland noises about the inquiry and rung off.

~~~

Empty bed, Friday night. Just me and him, the alien.

~~~

Saturday morning. Furry mouth, wriggling abdomen. How the heck had I kidded myself for so long? My brains were slopping up against the inside of my skull, so I stayed as still as I could.

I heard the key in the door an hour or so later, and sat up so abruptly I thought my brains would spill out onto the bed. The light was bright and the day punched me between the eyes. I squinted, stood and stumbled down the stairs.

Kim.

Digby.

Side by side, the sibling resemblance was remarkable, as if the Y chromosome alone was responsible for Dig's maleness, and apart from that he had the same genes as Kim. Nonsense, of course. It was just a strong family resemblance. If I fancied men, I'd find him sexy. But he's not. He's just Digby.

Normally when Kim has been staying with Digby, or if they go to visit their Mum together, Kim comes back to me sparkling like Champagne, as if she's been refreshed and renewed. Not today, though. She looked listless and wary. She didn't exactly fall into my arms, but I gathered her to me, hugged her, kissed her forehead and she melted against me. The tears started in my eyes I was so happy to see her, and feel her forgiveness. "Sorry, sorry, sorry, I'll never do anything like that ever again my darling," I said. She raised her face to me and we kissed lightly, a loving buss on the lips, salty with our tears.

Digby pushed us inside the house. "Save that for inside," he said. "I'm off now. I guess you've a lot to say to each other." The person I'd hoped we could rely on retreated to his car, that tatty Ford, and left.

We went inside and sat down. The silence stretched before us like a pit, until I filled it with my news. I told her about the scan, and how it was too late for any ...decisions, how I'd have to go through with the birth, but how it needn't affect us too much because I would have him adopted. We could go on as before. My words seemed to drop like a bag of nails emptied onto the floor, one by one.

"Please just shut up," she said eventually, her face bleak with pain. "I can't get my head round this, and you're not helping."

I retreated into routine and cooked some lunch. We cleared up after ourselves the way we normally did when we were home together. A thought hit me. "It's Saturday; shouldn't you be at the boutique?"

16

"I've been off sick. Couldn't face it." The silence gelled around us again.

"Good of them to let you have the time off."

Silence.

I said, "Do they do maternity wear?" I would love to shop there, but the boutique was expensive and the fashions a little young for me. They looked great on Kim though, she had the sort of figure to carry designer stuff off well. Her silence was getting to me. My eyelids pricked, the sense of panic making me dizzy. "Darling…"

"Please Angie, just leave it for a bit, yeah?"

I retreated to the bedroom to put my feet up, limbs like lead, body sagging under the worries of the last few days. I woke from my nap feeling like I'd been drugged again. It gave me a moment's wild fright, then I realised it was just sleep, normal sleep, utter exhaustion sleep. I rose, went into the lounge. No Kim, so I thought she must be in the kitchen, but she wasn't. She was in the garden, on the bench. "Want a cuppa?" I called.

She looked startled. "Yeah. Please." She stood and put her mobile away, sauntered in, her eyes on my bump. The baby's foot was pressing into my side. Weird. Alien. Unwanted and unwelcome. I passed Kim her mug, she took it without a word and went into the lounge. I followed, sat down. She turned the telly on, turned it up. As soon as she'd finished her tea, she stood and went back outside. I didn't follow.

After supper she locked herself in the bathroom, had a long bath, took all the hot water. I had a shower instead. Besides, the last bath had made me so swoony I'd felt ill for hours afterwards. By the time I was dry she was in bed, and the light was out. She was dressed in her winter pyjamas, hunched up under the quilt with her back to the middle of the

17

bed. I slid in quietly, flicked my light off. "Night night, Darling," I whispered.

Nothing.

I snuggled up to her, kissed the back of her neck. She tensed. I put my arm round her. "Don't." she said. "Please don't. I don't want..."

"I just want a hug."

She rolled over, nestled in my arms briefly, then, duty done she turned away. "Love you," I said.

"Love you too," she responded. It sounded like a lie.

~~~

I woke when the darkness was fading with predawn light. Kim was lying on her back, staring at the ceiling, crying silently. I could see the grey light gleaming on the tears on her eyelashes.

"What's the matter?" I asked. "It was me that was raped, not you. I can't understand why you're being like this. I know I shouldn't have hit you, but you were right in my face and I was desperately upset, really shocked."

"And drunk." She reached for a tissue, wiped the tears away, blew her nose. "I've been thinking. Remembering. When we first met..."

"Oh yes. At the Craven Arms. You were there with Moira and the rest, just got the job at the boutique. I was there with the supermarket crowd saying goodbye to Dean. It was love at first sight. For me, anyway."

"Dean. Yes. That was his name. I wasn't thinking of that so much, I was thinking of our first date together, where we had a meal at the Chinese, you told me about yourself, and I

18

told you about me. You caught me on the rebound, didn't you?"

"Did I? I don't remember." The silence grew, so I added. "I wasn't interested in your ex-es, I expect. I was interested in you."

"Really?" There was a sniff. "So you don't remember what I said then, about how any girlfriend I had, had to be lesbian not bi?"

I rummaged through my memories. They were all joyful, and the memory of that meal was about the emotions, not what we'd actually said to each other, but of the feelings of having found a soul mate, the feelings of love, excitement, arousal. I shook my head.

"But I told you how I was let down badly by some of my previous girlfriends, how they left me for a man, and how... how disgusting that is. You agreed, you laughed, said it was OK, you felt the same and aren't men repulsive. I told you when Clair left me how violated I felt. And you said what a beast to betray me like that, and you said you're not bi, swore you're not bi. Were you lying to me?"

"No, silly. I don't remember the conversation because it didn't matter to me, you're all that mattered."

"But it did matter to me. It mattered a lot." She was silent for a few minutes as I pondered how to respond. "It didn't matter to you because you thought it was trivial... you wanted me so I bet you lied to me and said you weren't bi because you knew how I'd feel. You just wanted me and you lied to get me. Like Clair did."

I flinched with a stab of bewildered annoyance. "What the hell are you talking about? I'm not bi, I have never slept with a bloke."

"You have now, haven't you?"

19

"That was hardly my fault. I didn't even know."

"But Angie, don't you understand? Don't you see? Every time I see you now, I think of you and a man…. The physical side of things, I just can't do that at the moment. Not until I've got my head round it. I know it's not your fault if you were raped, but just now I can't…"

It was as if she'd punched my midriff. I fought to keep my voice steady, to be reasonable. "You think I'm sullied goods now, don't you? Soiled. That's so cruel."

"No, no, it's not that. It's just that…." I could feel her trembling. I reached out to soothe her, but she tensed, whimpered. "You told me you're not bi," she said, "and now you come out with a story about being raped and say it was months ago. For all I know, you… Digs said…" She stopped talking, swallowed the words back down. "I don't want to make love just now. I know it's not fair, but I can't help it. Sorry, sorry, sorry. I feel so bad but I can't just grit my teeth and let you get on with it. I'd feel violated, I just know it. I need some time to get used to this. Some space. Please."

"OK, I understand," I turned my back to her and wept on my island of loneliness, with her body warmth glowing next to me. But I didn't understand. None of it made any sense to me at all.

Chapter 4

Suzy Rolfe

"Bad one?" asked DI Gill Cheung.

DC Suzy Rolfe looked up from the computer screen, scowl disappearing in favour of a puzzled frown. "Dunno about bad, Ma'am. Weird. How does anyone get to six/seven months pregnant without realising?"

"Unusual, but not unheard of. I've known teenagers drop one before they even knew they were expecting. Sometimes they go into a sort of denial. And sometimes they genuinely don't know. Or so they say."

Suzy saw a sceptical look flicker across Cheungy's face. She shrugged in agreement. "True enough, I s'pose...." Suzy outlined Angie's case to her boss, paused, then added, "I didn't know you on duty this weekend, Ma'am. I thought I was here on my own."

"I'm not here, if anyone phones. I'm just behind with the paperwork. I've found myself extra busy just lately."

"Would you like a tea? I'm gasping."

Cheungy smiled. "Me too. Yes please. I'll read through the file while you fetch some."

A short while later Suzy handed Cheungy a steaming mug, sat down again, eyes magnetically drawn to the computer screen. "Lynne and I have caught up with all the people Angie normally drinks with, but it's so long ago..." Suzy shrugged. "Not a lot we can do at the moment."

"How's young Kirsty?" asked Cheungy, changing the subject to a more personal one; Suzy's daughter.

"Growing up fast, though she thinks she's more mature than she really is. She's taking a gap year before university to get a job and build up some funds. Or at least, that's the theory. It's been a bit difficult to get a job as all the school leavers are after one. She's got one at the pizza factory in Elversford, starting on Monday. Rotten pay, but with any luck it'll push her into studying hard for a decent job. Actually, I'll be glad to get her out of the house. It's been nothing but stressies since she finished her exams. What is it about the teenage whine that makes you want to slap them? Tell her this 'n that and it's 'I know, I know', but dare to assume she knows something and it's 'You never said…' And if anything goes wrong it's All My Fault. Kids. Love her to bits, but she's driving me nuts."

"Um. Difficult age. Sort of grown up, but very much still a kid."

"I wonder what Angie will do about the baby. I think it's too late to abort."

"Give her a call tomorrow, update her. Make sure she knows we want the baby's DNA, if she agrees. And you'd better talk to her lover. Are there males in this 'In-crowd' at the Craven Arms?"

"Yes, three or four: Steve Hasset; Derek Golding; Liam Smith."

"Any previous on any of them?"

"Liam Smith's had a conviction for cannabis possession."

"What does she look like, this Angie?"

"Handsome. Greying wavy hair, kept short. White. 5`6ish. Running to seed a bit. Well, getting quite fat-looking now she's pregnant. Beats me how she didn't twig."

"Why should she if she's not had male sex? Ask the men if they'll volunteer a DNA sample for elimination." The phone rang. Cheungy grabbed it, "DI Cheung." Then she looked vexed with herself, obviously remembering she 'wasn't in.' Suzy grinned, listening to half the conversation. "Oh. Oh I see. The hospital? OK. We'll make a job of that. You've got statements from the witnesses? We'll chase those up again once we've spoken to the victim…. The Blue Boar… Oh… B, o, r, e… are you sure? Oh, OK. Some joke, ha bloody ha." A few more details were noted, then Cheungy put the phone down. "Looks like we've got another one. Elversford. Girl suddenly loses control of her legs. Might be she's pissed but looks like she's been drugged. Keeps passing out. Good job she was with her mates."

"Has she been assaulted?" asked Suzy.

"Don't know yet. She's been taken to The Broomfield Hospital. The men in the pub where she was drinking have been searched, but nobody had anything untoward. Early yet. So she's either pissed out of her brains, or she has been drugged and the bloke's got cold feet, or she's ill for some other reason. Can you make a job of it, please Suzy?"

Suzy saved her file, closed it, threw a parting smile at Cheungy and left.

An hour later Suzy phoned Cheungy. "The Elversford lot have arrested the barman for possession with intent to supply. Ketamine. That's what he told them it was, and that's what it looks like. He says it's for personal use. Yeah right, eh? I've seen the girl. No sexual assault, but only because her friends had their wits about them. And she's coming out of it. No sense from her, yet of course. It was her friends who thought the barman was a bit dodgy. He's the only one to touch their drinks before they did. And they were careful. He's new there, apparently. He's being brought over. But he's under the influence of something, though he won't say what, so we can't interview him yet."

23

~~~

The bartender sat slumped opposite Suzy, down from whatever drug he'd taken, malodorous and dishevelled. Suzy was glad to have PC Pete Brooks next to her. Brooks looked strong and was reputed to have something of a mean streak. He seemed as peaceable as a Rottweiler. The solicitor sat next to the bartender in bland indifference.

Brooks initiated the interview and asked the bartender his name and date of birth. Suzy was surprised at how gentle Brooks' tone was, contradicting his impression of aggressive power.

"Clifford Gary Hanger, 13th April 1977."

Suzy slid a glance at Brooks, who deliberately turned his eyes away, a quirk on his lips.

"Yesterday at about 8.00pm, in the Blue Bore in Elversford, you were subjected to a search for drugs by myself, PC Brooks. I found two packets of white powder in the back, right hand pocket of your trousers, of which the button was done up."

Brooks showed the powder, in small polythene sachets, sealed in an evidence bag, and described them for the tape recording.

"Are these yours?" asked Brooks.

Dull eyes glanced at the package. "Yeah."

"We believe them to be a controlled substance. What are they?"

"Ketamine. For my own personal use."

"Both packets?"

"Yeah."

"Where did you get these from?"

"No comment."

24

"How much did you pay?"

"No comment."

"How long have you been working at the Blue Bore?"

"A couple of weeks."

"Have you worked in other bars?"

"No."

"You told the landlord you're an experienced bartender," objected Brooks, looking at his notes.

"I wanted the job."

"So you lied to get the job?"

Cliff shrugged.

"Clifford has just shrugged," commented Brooks. "Are you lying to us now, Cliff?"

"No. And call me Gaz, not Cliff. I hate the name, Cliff."

"Sorry, Gaz. I should have checked, though the landlord of the Blue Bore called you Cliff. What time did you start work on Saturday?"

"Eleven am, when the pub opens."

"And you were due to finish when?"

"Eight pm."

"OK, so what time did you get up in the morning?" Brooks took Cliff 'Call me Gaz' Hanger through his day. Gaz answered most of the questions, though sulkily, before Brooks got to the meatier questions. "Yesterday, in the Blue Bore at approximate 7.30pm, a girl was taken ill with suspect ketamine poisoning. Do you know this girl?"

"No... comment." Cliff Hanger slid a look at the solicitor beside him.

"You were the only person to touch her drink apart from herself, and she and her friends say they are very careful not to leave the drinks unattended. Did you spike her drink?"

"Wasn't me."

25

"But nobody else had access to the drinks, Gaz."

"No comment."

After a predictable number of 'No comments' Brooks terminated the interview and they took Clifford back to the cells to stew for a little longer.

"Coffee?" Suzy asked Brooks.

"Please," he said.

~~~

"Looks like the girl's going to be OK, thank goodness. She couldn't remember much when I went to see her in hospital," said Suzy. She yawned, stirred her canteen coffee, looking at it slightly suspiciously. It looked like tea. Cheungy was wise to have her own coffee machine.

"Her friends all say they were very careful with their drinks, so it must be him. But nobody saw him do it. She's in hospital, and he's sitting there saying no comment. I'd like to kick him in the place he was planning on using," said Brooks.

"Me too, wouldn't do though, would it? What did the owner of the Blue Bore say?" asked Suzy.

"Took the guy on, didn't bother checking the references, silly bugger. We approached the references, and they're Cliff's chums. Meaningless. He's got previous. Cannabis. Rather a lot of it. Couple of years back. Only just avoided being done with intent to supply because he agreed to plead guilty to the lesser charge. The landlord strikes me as the type that's not too choosy. What a fool, risking his licence like that. Well, didn't look too good last night with us crawling all over the place. We picked up a couple of men with some other gear as well, but not date-rape drugs. I hate the way the pub's called the Blue Bore, B O R E. Instead of a tusker on the sign, it has a man dressed in blue, boring people to death. Landlord's idea of a joke. Twat. That's going to look good transcribed for court. The barristers will think we're thick."

"Clifford Hanger; I could hardly keep a straight face when we started the interview."

"Yeah, when I nicked him I thought he was extracting the Michael, but that's his name. I saw your look and I had to look away or I'd have hooted. Do you think the 'Can't Prosecute Service' will run it?"

"Doubt it," said Suzy. "Bugger, I know he did it, but you can't prove it. They'll just tell us to do him for possession. Slimy toe-rag."

Chapter 5

Angie

Kim went out and stayed away all day Sunday. I stayed at home, mind grinding over the same old things. I got on with the mindless tasks, cleaning, washing. As I hung Kim's clothes on the line I was ambushed by memories of when she bought them. Most of her clothing came from the boutique, but this top was a lucky find in Clacton. We'd gone there for a silly day out, but the wind from the east had been colder than we expected. The sea was a slab of slate under a curdled sky, but that didn't really matter, not at first. We did the seaside things like eating ice creams and we'd walked along hand in hand, admiring the grey, grey sea and huge sky until the wind drove us inland to the shops. We mooched along arm in arm and found a charity shop. "I want a look at the books," I said.

"Yeah, like you haven't got enough already."

"You never knew what you might find, and anyhow, it'll be warm in there." I love charity shops because they're like Aladdin's Caves, and I can pretend I'm a dealer looking out for an overlooked gem. Never happens, of course, because I don't know what I'm looking for. But it's a good place for books. Clothing you have to be a bit careful about though; choosey, but you can still find something special. Kim fingered thorough the racks of summer tops, while I scanned the bookshelves with my head on one side.

"Oh, that's well nice," she said, pulling this particular blouse out. It was blue, pretty, and unusual. "My size, too," she said, peering at the label, and scrutinised the garment carefully for anything untoward.

"Try it on," I suggested.

28

She came out of the changing room and my heart had leapt at the sight of her she was so stunning in it. So we bought it. "Designer label," she muttered to me as we left the shop. "Real bargain."

It was showing signs of wear now, when I pegged it out on the line. Fortunately despite the designer label it was easy to wash. Next to it I pegged out some jeans, bigger than my normal size, bought because I thought I was putting on weight, not realising the reason for the gain in girth. It made me feel big and ugly.

Once I'd done the chores I sat in the lounge, moodily dissecting the conversation we'd had in bed. I hadn't remembered the conversation about her ex-es, though the more I thought about it, the more I seemed to recall something. The memory slid away from me every time I tried to pin it down. I vaguely remembered a shadow of nausea crossing Kim's face when she mentioned her last lover and how that lover had lied and turned out to be bi. "She betrayed me, she betrayed me," the ghost of Kim's anguished voice whispered to me. "It was obscene. I felt used, when I found out, and she just didn't care..." I'd taken her hands in mine, I suddenly recalled, yearning to protect her from harm. "That was wicked. I'll never treat you like that, I promise."

~~~

When Kim came home in the evening my heart sang. I hugged her, kissed her, she responded reluctantly. "I've been phoning my Mum, had a long chat," she said. "And Digby. Angie, we need to talk about this."

"I know. I know we do, love." A frisson of cold stroked my back. Kim's Mum hates me, really hates me, and I'm not sure

29

why. It's as if she blames me for Kim's sexuality, which is outrageous. She took against me from the very start, and when Kim's father died a couple of years back, I couldn't even go to the funeral when Kim needed me most. Kim worshipped her father in the same way she adores Digby and had been devastated when he died suddenly. And now she'd been talking with her Mum over the phone and I wondered what poison had been poured in her ears.

We sat down in the lounge. "Look," she said, looking into her lap, fiddling with the seams of her jeans with a well-chewed fingernail. "What I can't get my head round is that you tell me you were raped and didn't know anything about it, and then from that one single unknown intercourse, you fall pregnant. Mum says that's a likely story, especially at your age. She reckons you're bi and have sex with a man every time I go up to see her, every time we're not together. My God, you could have a man round here every time your shifts allow. Mum says it took her years to fall for Digs and me, and you must've had sex more than once to get pregnant, because you're so old." Kim's mouth shut like a trap, she swallowed hard, tears brimming.

I took her hand in mine, stoked it gently. I found my head shaking slowly like that wretched dog in the advert. No no no. "Darling, darling, that's not true. I love you, only you and I'd never do that behind your back, and you should know that. I'm not bi. I was raped. That's why I hadn't a clue I was pregnant."

She raised her eyes to mine, still full of pain and disbelief, but what more could I say? The more I protested the more false I sounded.

"Digs says it stands to reason," continued Kim. "Nobody your age falls pregnant just like that."

"But I did. Why don't you believe me? I love you. I need you, especially now." I could understand her pain, her bewilderment; hadn't I felt the same utter disbelief at the doctor's? She would have to come to terms with the truth, just as I had. Trouble is, I knew for sure I hadn't knowingly had sex with a man. Kim had to take that on trust.

She nestled into my arms the way she used to, fitting perfectly into the crook of my arm and lifted her pretty little face to me. Her eyes were still clouded with doubts, but I was beginning to see the old Kim behind the clouds. I showered her face with kisses, my tears mingling with hers. I knew she believed me now, that it was going to be all right.

~~~

The next day I went back to work. When my supervisor Ms Curtis asked what had been the matter with me. I just said, "Women's things," and hoped she'd leave it at that. She did. I was on the early shift and went home at 3.00pm, which was just as well because DC Rolfe phoned. She asked if I'd remembered which pub I thought I'd been to when the rape took place. I told her I still couldn't remember, though I expected it was the Craven Arms because that's where we usually meet.

"Is it always the Craven Arms, or do you ever go to a different pub?"

It seemed an odd question, as if she knew something I didn't. "We sometimes go to the Nag's Head or the Long Boat, but usually in the summer because they've got nice gardens."

"Ever been to the Blue Bore? B,o,r,e…"

"Don't think so. Don't even know it."

"It's in Elversford."

31

"Oh, no, never go there. Not even with Digs. He always comes to us if he's coming over."

"Digs?"

"Digby Jamieson. Kim's brother. Don't see much of him. He lives in Elversford."

"Was he around in the blank weekend?"

"Nope, don't remember seeing him. Ask the others."

"Nobody's mentioned him. Is Kim with you just now?"

"No, sorry. She won't be back until 6.00pm."

"Oh, I'll pop round at 6.30pm to have a chat if I may."

"She was away that weekend."

"I know. I just want a chat, that's all."

~~~

I didn't warn Kim about DC Rolfe. Perhaps I was punishing her for running off, for not being more sympathetic, for not believing me from the very start, for treating me like a leper. I don't know. But she blenched when, on answering the door, I brought DC Rolfe into the sitting room, and I bit my lips with guilt.

Rolfe wanted to speak to Kim privately.

Chapter 6

Suzy

Suzy waited until Angie had closed the door before smiling at Kim. Kim seemed nervous, rubbing her hands palm-down on her jeans, and not looking at Suzy. "I expect Angie's told you what's happened," Suzy began.

"Um."

It wasn't a promising start.

"I understand you were away the weekend of the 18th December."

"Um. At my Mum's. So I don't know anything." Suzy could feel hostility oozing from Kim. And defensiveness. Perhaps Kim was hiding something. Or perhaps she just didn't like the police.

"Do you mind if I ask you a few routine questions?"

"No. Ask what you like, though I might not answer." The reply had that wary cockiness, the one Suzy had frequently encountered from guilty teenage yobs.

Suzy shrugged it off with a smile. "Of course. How long have you two been together?"

"About five years."

"What sort of a relationship do you have?"

"What do you mean?" Kim frowned at Suzy.

"Sorry, I mean, is it a sexual relationship?"

"We're lesbian lovers." The tone was exasperated, sneering at the inanity of the question. And there was still the undercurrent of hostility.

"Are either of you bisexual?"

"No. I'm not. I didn't think Angie was but Digs thinks she might be secretly, lied to me about it, thinks this rape story is

33

a cover-up because she's got caught out and doesn't want to confess to f... making love to men."

"Have you ever had sex with a man?"

"Not fucking likely."

"What about Angie?"

"Well, she has now, hasn't she?" Kim bit her lip, tears suddenly gleaming. "But until this happened, no. Not that I know of. But like I said..." Her lip trembled and she clamped her teeth down harder.

"Do either of you use drugs? Please, I'm not wanting to cause trouble over this if you do... I just need to know."

"Nope, don't even smoke."

"Are you aware of anyone paying Angie attention? Singling her out?"

"What like stalking, you mean? Nope."

Suzy had been expecting a difficult conversation, but difficult because this Kim's lover had been raped. But Kim was acting like an offender in interview, begrudging every answer. Suzy couldn't decide if it was because she had something to hide or if was because she was utterly miserable.

After a little more rummaging into Kim and Angie's relationship, and questions about the In Crowd in the Craven Arms, Suzy stood. "Thanks, Kim. You've been helpful," she lied. "Here's my card, with the crime number on it if there's anything you need to talk to me about, or if you think of something."

Kim took the proffered card like a vegetarian grabbing a steak.

~~~

Kirsty Rolfe

Kirsty saw that her mother was home because her car was parked on the drive. She manoeuvred her moped past it and into the garage.

"Well, how was it?" called her mum from the kitchen as Kirsty stepped into the hall

"Shattering. I've never been so tired in my life. Gawd, I'm starved. But I'm almost too tired to eat."

"Welcome to the working world. Now you know how I feel sometimes." Her mum looked out of the kitchen with a cynical smile.

Kirsty unzipped the leathers her mother insisted she wear with her moped. "And I'm bloody baked in these. What's for eating?"

"I've only just got in myself, so it's a microwave dinner I'm afraid."

"S'OK." Kirsty dumped her leathers in the hall. "Half Ten. What a time to eat."

"Hang those up properly before you break your neck on them."

Noticing an adamant look in her mother's eye, Kirsty complied, then went into the living room. She could hear the sounds of her mum getting the meal ready, there was a ping of the microwave, and her mother came into the living room bearing a tray. Kirsty held her hands out. "No," said her mum. "This is mine. Yours is in the kitchen. I'm not waiting on you hand, foot and arse."

Scowling, Kirsty found her feet and stomped into the kitchen. Her anger evaporated when she saw that her mum had placed her supper on a tray, complete with a glass of wine. She picked it up and returned to the living room. Her mother was seated at the dining table, and the TV was off. Kirsty looked at the sofa and the blank screen but took the hint.

"Look at us, eating off trays like this was the nick canteen," said her mum.

"Saves mucking the table up," said Kirsty, immediately dropping a forkful onto the cloth. "Oops." They giggled.

"Well, how was your day, apart from exhausting?"

"OK I s'pose. They gave me overalls, hair net, hat, and safety shoes. Bloody uncomfortable, those. You have to have clean overalls on every time you go back into the production area, and wash your hands and so on. And there are cleaners squelching around in wellies all the time. It's like a bloody ant colony, with people moving around doing their thing. My line supervisor is quite hot in an old and crumbly sort of way. He must be at least forty."

"Um, way past his sell by date then..." said her mum dryly.

"There's another bloke called Eddie of about the same age. He looks angry all the time, and I saw him eyeing up my boobs."

"You be careful of people like that. I mean it, Sweetie, if you'd seen some of the things I've seem..."

"All right, all right, I know... And stop calling me 'Sweetie'. Makes me feel like I'm seven. Or off Ab Fab. Sweetie, Sweetie."

"Sorry Kirsty. Anyway, what were you doing? What's the work like?"

"Boring. So boring that they make us shift round on the line every couple of hours. We start up for two hours ish, then have a fifteen-minute break, which is just about enough time to have a drink and a pee. That's called 'line out' or something, then another couple of hours, then it's meal break. And we only get forty-five minutes for that, then a couple more hours or so. It's a production line, and each person is in charge of one process, even though it's mostly automated." Kirsty dropped another forkful on the tablecloth.

"You mucky pup."

"Sorry Mum. I'm just too tired to find my mouth." Kirsty swigged the rest of her wine.

"Sorry, Sweetie. I didn't mean to nag. It's for the wash anyway. Anyway, you were saying…."

"We do things in batches for this company or that company. I was in charge of the cheese hopper and the puree hopper today. Gawd I'm glad you didn't bring home pepperoni pizza for supper or something. Oh yeah, I can buy mis-shapes and over-bakes at a discount if you want."

"What are the people like?"

"Look, Mum, I'm really tired, and I don't need this cross-examination right now. I'm going to bed, OK." Kirsty rose, and started to walk away.

"Tray."

Kirsty turned, flinched slightly at the look of rebuffed injury on her mother's face, grabbed the tray and took it into the kitchen then started up the stairs. "And put your plate in the dishwasher," came her mother's voice from the lounge. Kirsty went back into the kitchen and did as she was told.

Chapter 7

Angie

On Monday, when Kim got home from work we sat in the kitchen and ate supper, just as we always did. She concentrated on her plate. I concentrated on her. She's altogether dainty and delicious, perfect hands holding her fork just right, spearing the food, conveying it to her beautiful mouth. How can such a simple thing as eating be so bewitching? When she'd finished I reached across, took her hand as I often did when we sat like this, but this time it was like grasping a dead branch. She slowly raised her eyes to mine, silently slid her hand away and went outside into the back garden. I didn't dare follow, though I kept looking at her as I cleared the table. She was sitting on the garden bench, shoulders slumped, hunched over herself, texting. I hadn't seen her looking like that since her father died. At that time, when she'd looked like that, I would gather her in my arms and hug the pain away. Now I just stood and watched, my heart rattling painfully in my ribcage. She must have felt my look because she looked up, looked away, then walked round the front out of view.

I made two coffees, took them into the lounge, turned the telly on but there was nothing worth watching. I left it muttering to itself because it banished the silence and I could pretend everything was normal. Baby shifted. Nothing was normal. I started to cry because what I needed most of all was Kim's arms round me, comforting me, reassuring me, and instead I knew she was probably phoning her mum.

She was gone a long time.

I found the photo album, a sparse reminder of all the lovely things we'd done together; the holidays, the days out. Each a happy memory. But we hadn't printed many photos, and only one or two were of us together, taken by one of the in-crowd or by some kindly passer-by. The best one, which captured Kim at her prettiest, relaxing seductively in my embrace, we'd had blown up and framed. It stood on the top of the bookcase. It had been taken in Majorca on a week's holiday. My mind slipped back to when the photo was taken. It was a new camera and was supposed to have a timer, but we couldn't get it to work. We'd been shrieking with laughter over the picture of my back as I scurried towards her, all out of focus, when someone offered to take a photo. I handed the camera over without a thought. The man took a couple, of snaps, then handed it back to us and we thanked him.

"You're so stupid, so trusting," Kim had laughed. "He could of been a thief, and you gave him your camera. He could of legged it."

"Well, he didn't, and that's a cool picture." It was more than cool, it was the best picture we'd ever had, so we framed it.

I remembered her arms round me, her teasing words, the fun we'd had, and I now shuddered with a moment's vertiginous panic.

Baby shifted. I watched the skin of my stomach peaking over a baby limb.

I heard footsteps, started guiltily, put the photo album away as if I'd been reading porn.

I jumped up as Kim came into the lounge, went to hug her, but she flung herself onto the settee. Her coffee was cold, of course. "I'll make you another," I said as her eyes fell on the scummy surface.

"Don't bother." She turned the telly up loud, her eyes focused into the distance.

~~~

The days slipped past. Kim kept looking askance at me, at my belly, with a troubled, hurt expression. She spent a lot of time on the garden, on her mobile. Talking to her toxic mum, most likely. I yearned to rush into the garden, grabbing the phone, throwing it away, telling her not to listen, that I was telling the truth and I loved her, only her. But I couldn't, of course. I had to give Kim her privacy, give her some space. I tried to hug her, to encourage her to make love, to recapture the magic we had between us, but every time I tried, instead of bringing us closer, it seemed to push us further apart.

~~~

I attended my antenatal appointment on Friday with Dr Thomas, put up with being weighed, my urine tested for sugar, and my blood pressure taken. He took some blood for an HIV test. If I tested positive, I'd need treatment to reduce the chance of the baby being born with the virus.

HIV positive? I might die of this rape.

I went home for a hot drink before going back to work. Kim was home, with a guilty look and a half-packed suitcase on the bed. I stared at it dumbly, wondering if this was 'Time out' for thought-gathering, or permanent. I stood and watched as she loaded the suitcase, going through the drawers like a surgeon, cutting away all that was hers: The beautiful clothes from the boutique, the jewellery I'd bought her, the perfume, trinkets. I didn't begrudge the gifts, but each of them had a pleasant memory attached. It was as if she was stealing our past.

"I can't hack it," she said eventually, turning to me with tears in her eyes. "I can't. It's all gone. You've been with a man, and you're up the duff. I know you say it's not your fault 'n all, but I can't hack it." She turned back to her case, squeezed the air from it, fastened it. Then she took the hold-all, and filled that too. Everything. Every scrap of clothing. Including the blue blouse.

"Where will you go?" I asked when my brain finally located my tongue.

"Digs'."

I followed her into the bathroom. Her towels, her toothbrush, anything and everything personal. Then down to the lounge. CDs Tapes, ornaments we'd chosen together but that she'd bought. Books. She slowly unravelled her life from mine, like a knitting pattern gone wrong.

The only thing between us now was tears. Both of us. Streaming.

Into the kitchen. Her favourite mug, her clock, the pepper grinder.

She looked through the door to our garden. I wondered if she'd uproot the plants. She went out, but sat on the bench, bent over and buried her head. "Why d'you keep following me round?" she asked, muffled against her knees. "I'm not going to take anything that isn't mine."

"I know," I whispered. I stroked the back of her neck, looking for words that didn't exist. She turned, grabbed my hand, kissed it.

"I'm sorry. I truly am. I just can't take it. I can't get my head straight. I can't love you anymore."

Digby came in his tatty Ford, with his disturbing air, and took my love away with him.

I thought she'd taken the photograph off the bookshelf, and that gave me hope. But when I put the rubbish out, there it was in the dustbin, splintered frame, shards of glass, the photograph torn into a thousand fragments.

~~~

Kirsty

"Tired, luv?" asked Janet. They were in the canteen eating a meal.

Kirsty looked up at the older woman. "I was so tired all I wanted to do was sleep all weekend, but Dad had other ideas. Busy, busy, busy."

A hand fell on her shoulder. Kirsty froze, turned. Her line supervisor with a big smile on his face. "Settled in yet, Kirsty?"

"Yes, thanks, Jimbo," said Kirsty, nodding and sitting up straighter, pushing her front out a little.

"Good." Jimbo wandered along to the other line supervisors. Kirsty watched him sit and start eating, joking with the other supervisors.

"He's got WHT," said Janet. "If it gets too much, complain."

"What's WHT?" asked Kirsty.

"Wandering hand trouble," said Tom with a snigger. "One of Aunty Janet's old fashioned phrases. He can be a bit over-friendly, but he's all right really. He's fun."

"I don't think he knows how intrusive contact like that can be," added Janet. "I think he just likes to reassure people. He does it with everyone."

"He's a good supervisor, kind," said Jordan. "He might try it on, though. He sort of gets a crush on all the new girls. Asks them out. He's got a super sports car and a great bachelor pad in Galchester. Really swish." Jordan laughed. "I've seen the sports car, but not the bachelor pad. I went out with him once, to this really expensive pub. But I saw the amount of booze he was packing away. Then he asked me outright to sleep with him, and got quite shirty when I said no. Seemed to think I owed him that for the meal, cheeky bastard. But I left him rubbing his dick. Didn't fancy a ride home with a pissed driver."

"He's a tosser," Stuart contributed. "No, really...I've seen him in the bogs. I wondered if he was gay."

"Ugly git like you should be safe enough," said Tom.

"Well boo you," replied Stuart amicably, sticking his tongue out. "He hasn't got much of a dick though. Bit on the small side. Perhaps he's worn it down with all that rubbing. I said something like that to him once, cheeked him, like, and he gave me such a poisonous look." Stuart gave a mock shudder.

"Stop it, boys. You shouldn't talk about the supervisor like that or spread rumours. And you're embarrassing Kirsty with your talk."

"You started it, with your talk about WHT," said Tom indignantly.

"I wasn't spreading rumours, more warning Kirsty what Jimbo's like. And if Jord wants to share the sordid details of her love life, that's up to her. But it's not a good idea to make slanderous remarks about him like that, you two."

"Yes, Aunty Janet..." sang Tom.

"Are you really his aunt?" asked Kirsty.

43

"She's my real aunty," said Stuart. "She just acts like everyone else's. If you've got a problem, speak to her before you speak to the Human Resources Manager. You'll likely get more help from Aunty Janet."

Jordan looked down at the paper she was reading, turned a page. It had a photograph of the latest heartthrob actor. "He's well hot," she said.

"We had a teacher who looked just like him," said Kirsty. "All the girls fancied him something rotten. But we found out he was gay and we all felt cheated."

"I don't know why you felt cheated," grumbled Aunty Janet. "It's not like he's available or anything. Teachers aren't allowed."

"Maybe not, but that doesn't always stop them," said Jordan with a snigger. "There's a girl in Trish's class with a real thing for one of the teachers. She's dropped loads of hints about how he's both ready and willing." Jordan gave a leering wink.

"Who's Trish?" asked Kirsty

"My sister. Did you go to Elversford Secondary School? You might know her."

"Ner. I live in Tiptree and went to school there."

"Roger wasn't there when I was at school," added Jordan. "Pity; he sounds hot."

"Roger who?"

"Roger-the-girls Turner."

"Will you stop it," snapped Janet. "Gossip like that could land him in serious trouble. I bet none of it's true."

"I just wish I wasn't so shattered." Kirsty hoped to change the subject because things were getting a bit strained. "I had to get up at five this morning, to get here for six. I wish it was nine to five instead of the two shifts, six till two and two till ten."

"You'll get used to it," said Janet. "It has its advantages, like time off in the afternoons on early shift."

"Buggers up your social life on a late shift, though," said Tom. "Well, every other week, that is."

"Once a week is quite enough for you, my lad. You should be saving your wages, not spending them getting steamed up."

"Once a week?" asked Kirsty,

"We go out as a group on Saturday nights often. You should come, if you can. We go to the Blue Bore," said Janet.

"Aunty Janet makes sure we don't get too pissed and the kids just go soft," said Stuart. "Got raided by the pigs last a week ago. We all got searched. Good job we were all clean," he added, sliding a look at Janet. "They nicked the barman. It was dead exciting. Blue lights 'n all."

"You'd think they'd have better things to do than nick a few people over a bit of cannabis," said Tom.

~~~

"You lazy little monkey!"

Kirsty sat bolt upright, eyes squinting against the evening sun shafting into her room. The sleep trickled away in a shiver of nausea. "Mum."

"What time did you get home? 3 o'clock at the latest. Couldn't be bothered to bring the washing in, even when it started raining. Oh, no; too much trouble, that. So it's soaked. And I bet it was dry when you got in. You lazy, idle little..."

Kirsty blinked, got off her bed and looked out of the window. The sun was dazzling against the wetness of a

45

cloudburst. The roads were slick, and dark clouds brooded ominously. As she watched, they swallowed the sun. The temperature dropped.

Kirsty surprised even herself when she burst into tears. She sat down on the bed. Her mother sat next to her, hugging. "Has someone done something? Have you got a problem at work?"

Kirsty shook her head, trying to force the words round the sobs. "I'm... just... so... tired... that's all. I'm sorry Mum. About the washing. And I brought some pizzas home because they're cheap, and I know how tough..." 'things are since Dad left,' she finished in her mind but not with her mouth. Her mum seemed to have heard the unsaid words and turned away for a moment.

Then her mother said, "I know it's been hard. Just you and me. Was he OK with you this weekend?"

"He wanted to do lots with me, so of course we had to, when I was so shattered all I wanted to do was rest. But he did buy me a new top."

"It's going to get tougher, now you're eighteen. That's why I'm so glad you've got a job. Don't jack it in just because you're bored or fed up, will you? You'll get used to working. And I'll have a word next time you're due to visit. Make sure he understands."

"It's like he has to fit a month's worth into two days. He tries too hard, sometimes. Bribes me with presents and tries to buy my love. He's got that anyway. Oh, sorry Mum. I love you too."

"I know you do, Sweetie. I know."

Chapter 8

Angie

I thought it would get better as the days slipped by, but it didn't. The worst was when I cooked for two, or when I found Kim's undies forgotten at the back of the airing cupboard. I didn't know whether to send them to her, throw them, or keep them as a memento. Kim had been so thorough in her removal of all things Kimberly that they were the only things I had left of her. That and a few photographs.

I didn't know why I was torturing myself by thinking about her, but I did. Buried memories bubbled up like gas in a swamp, though they were mostly pleasant; like a year after we met and we'd gone out to celebrate. She bought me a bracelet, and when I opened it, I found I had bought exactly the same one for her. "You're amazing," she said as we laughed over the coincidence. "You're the best thing that ever happened to me." So it made her leaving me now all the harder to understand.

I yearned to phone her. I sent cards to her at Digby's. "Please phone, just to chat. No pressure," I wrote. I received the first one back with bold black felt pen scribbled on the front. "Leave me alone." The second one came back unopened.

One of the long-forgotten memories that bubbled up was of when I was at the hairdresser's a couple of years ago, yakking with the stylist as she trimmed my hair. She asked me how Kim was, and the girl in the seat next to me caught my eyes in the mirror. "Pardon me, but would that be Kim Jamieson?" she'd asked. When I said yes, she told me she was Kim's ex. Clair. She seemed like a really nice girl, but I

47

remembered how Kim said she'd betrayed her by lying to her, then leaving her, and not caring that she'd lied. I was trying to square up this attractive girl in the mirror with the treacherous bitch Kim had told me about, and I couldn't.

We'd chatted in front of that mirror until our hair was done, like two leaves floating down a stream briefly coming together, spinning round, then parting. But Clair told me she was bi, yes, though she hadn't told Kim, but someone else had, and it was Kim who had broken the relationship, pushing and pushing Clair away with hurtful, snide remarks until Clair got tired and left, carrying the blame with her. "I've been thinking," said Clair earnestly to my reflection. "She was always afraid of rejection, of being abandoned, so I think she did the pushing to get the stress of it all over and done with. As a way of staying in control. Or something."

At the time it had just seemed like a coincidence and a trivial conversation, but it came back to me now with renewed significance.

~~~

By the end of the week my blood pressure was stable, my blood sugar normal, and the baby was kicking me in one place in particular.

When I dressed on Monday and I pulled my knickers up (sensible, comfortable, un-sexy knickers, the ones I generally wore during my period because I used to feel very un-sexy then) my skin felt crinkled. Puzzled I stood naked in front of the mirror, looking, really looking at myself for the first time in ages. It was as if my skin had unravelled into bumps and troughs. Stretch marks, purple against the white. There was a brown line cleaving me left from right. My breasts hung full, the veins an echoing blue under the skin. The nipples were full, engorged, maroon, and that belly swelled, almost ballooning as I watched.

My smart trousers didn't fit. I tried to pin them shut, but the zip gaped like a cry of pain. I put on my tracksuit trousers, phoned in sick, then went shopping for maternity wear. Smart trousers, good enough for work. They also sold me some support bras, like I'd escaped from a Wagnerian Opera.

The next day my supervisor, Ms Curtis called me in for a telling off. I'd been seen shopping. Well, seen in the high street. The snitch hadn't seen which shop I'd been in.

I looked at her smug face, and I wanted to howl. Instead I said, "I've got a problem. A big problem. And I'm going to need some new staff uniform."

Her eyes scanned my belly, the work blouse taut against it, then studied my face. "You're pregnant," she said, more a statement than a question.

I nodded. "Seven months." My voice died.

"But." She looked at the wall, then the clock, then me. "But…"

"Until a few days ago, I didn't know. That's what I went to the doctor's for." I waited for the sneers, the sarcasm, the vitriol.

"But. I thought… I'm sorry. Er Congratulations. I think." She examined my face for the right thing to say. "Seven months," she said. "Didn't you know?"

"We think my drink was spiked, and I was raped. December."

I'd caught her out so badly her thoughts were plain. Horrified. She couldn't hide behind her usual aloofness. "That's awful," she breathed. "What will you do? How will you cope? Seven months, you say, and you only just found out; too late...?"

"Too late."

"You'll need time off for antenatal appointments, and maternity leave and all that. And I'll get new uniform ordered straight away, and we'll see if there's anything in the second-hand cupboard." People who left had to return their uniform. It was stored for the use of temporary staff, or in case someone had an accident. Like me.

She bit her lips. "It's not 'congratulations' is it? I can't believe I said that. I'm so sorry. Look, if there's anything I can do to help, or anything." She looked as if she meant it.

She found me some old uniform normally three sizes too big, but it fitted. Sort of. "You are going to stay on, aren't you?" she asked, folding up the blouses which didn't fit. "But how will you cope? With a baby and all, I mean."

"I... I'll have it adopted. I can't have that sort of a reminder. I'd hate him—the baby, I mean. I hate him already." It was easier talking to this woman who I'd been scared of until now than it had to Kim.

"I s'pose it'll be for the best," she agreed in a low voice. "But you'll find it hard."

~~~

Whispers at work. Speculative looks. Nudges. Ms Curtis saw. The innuendos stopped.

My abdomen, once so neat, seemed bigger every day, as if the foetus was making up for lost growth. I made a remark like that to Ms Curtis, and she laughed. "I was like that. Almost flat for six months, then suddenly, like a mushroom." She thrust her hands out as if holding a bump. A shadow crossed her face. "How's it going?" she added casually.

"OK," I said, unsure how much to say. "They keep a close eye on me because of my age. My feet are swelling up a bit. I had to buy new shoes."

"Um," she agreed. "I went up a shoe size. I got terrible indigestion, too. Both times. And one was such a fidget. Like a spinning top. You wonder if it's worth it. Oh sorry, Angie, tactless of me. Um. Are things OK here?"

"Better once everyone got over the shock and after you had a word. Thank you. I mean that. Thank you."

How could I have thought her cold and unapproachable? Why had I disliked her so much?

~~~

Until that point I'd kept myself fit and strong. I had a good body for a 46-year-old, well-toned. Attractive, sexy. Now it was bloated with a baby that I didn't want. This intruder kicked me, weighed ever heavier inside me, gave me stretch marks, dragged at my breasts, gave me slack joints and indigestion. It was as if the baby had tipped me forward into old age. I hated it.

Chapter 9

Suzy

"Hi, it's DS Fiona Connor. Is DI Cheung there, please?" Suzy handed the phone to Cheungy, and went to move away, but Cheungy signalled her to stay and listen in.

"Oh, hi Fiona. I hope you're phoning to tell me you're going to join my team at last. I need a sergeant like you." Cheungy laughed.

Fiona laughed in response. "Not likely, Ma'am. H would never forgive me. Or you. Tell you what, I'll join you when he retires."

"Tell him he's getting too old for the job."

"No thank you. I like my head just as it is, firmly attached to my body." Fiona abandoned the old joke. "I've got some intel here. I think we've got a paedophile in Elversford, preying on girls, using date rape drugs. But I've got no evidence, no coherent story. Nothing. And it could all be 'alien abduction syndrome'." Suzy could almost hear Fiona chewing her lips. "And this is on top of the sporadic date rape reports and victims we've already passed on to you, including that one where the girl was drugged at the Blue Bore.

"You know PC Kat Davies? She was giving a talk on the dangers of date rape drugs, and even the dangers of getting rat-arsed, to a bunch of fifteen-year-olds at Elversford Secondary School as part of their PSE lessons, last day of term. As she went on, Kat saw one of the girls go very pale. Kat's very good with kids, knows a lot of their names, so at the end of the talk, seeing Trish hanging back, she said, 'OK Trish?' And this Trish Dale just burst into tears.

"Kat took her to the medical room, and the nurse sat her down. Between them they coaxed the story from her. She was very reluctant at first, because it involved her going out underage drinking with her sister. Kat said that a bit of make-up and it would be hard to tell, but I think we'll have a word with the proprietor of the Blue Bore. Again. Anyway, this girl said she got completely rat-arsed. So rat-arsed she can't remember anything. She said she woke up the next morning, in bed, knickers on inside out, and her sister was in the same sort of state.

"Her sister Jordan swore her to secrecy, blackmailing Trish with threats to reveal some sort of trivial information. So Trish said nothing. Until today. And worse, Kat had barely got back to the nick when the phone goes for her. Another one, similar story. And then another."

"It could be alien abduction syndrome, as you said... suggestion; everyone thinking it's happened to them."

"It smells real to me, Cheungy. But you're right, it could just be that these girls got pissed, and now feel they may have been raped just because Kat's talk suggested it. They are pretty suggestible types. Dear God, we can't win, can we?"

~~~

"Where is everyone?" asked Suzy, looking around Elversford nick. "It's like the Marie Celeste."

"Busy. This is the thin blue line," said Kat. "Far too thin for comfort. I've told the girls we're coming, but couldn't tell them when. You're sure you don't want them to come to Galchester?"

"Unless the assault is certain, and recent, I don't see much point. I thought I'd have a chat first, see if it rings true. If it

53

does, we'll have to take them to Rosamundi House to give video statements etc, but from what Cheungy told me, you're not even certain they were attacked."

"We're seeing Trish first, if that's OK. Her sister works at the pizza factory, 6 until 2 this week, but has a dentist appointment, according to Trish's mum. She should be back at 4.30ish."

"Kat, could you change into plain clothes for this, please? I don't want curtains twitched."

~~~

Suzy estimated that Trish's mother was about her own age. Her hair was lank against her scalp as if flattened by bad news. "Mrs Tracey Dale?" asked Suzy, and showed her warrant card.

"Come in," said Mrs Dale. "Into the lounge."

Trish was perched on the sofa as if it were a bed of nails. Kat introduced Suzy, just saying she was CID, and to tell Suzy what she'd told Kat.

It was a rambling account, with repetitions and omissions, but Suzy was patient. The basic story was that Trish and her sister Jordan had gone with a crowd to the Blue Bore and had a few drinks, but she could remember nothing more before waking up with her knickers on inside out. She'd felt sick, and strange, but just assumed she'd got drunk, though she didn't actually remember drinking much. Careful coaxing with seasonal triggers established that this was about the beginning of May.

There was a sound of a key in the front door. Trish's mother jumped up as if her nerves were crashing like discordant wind chimes. "That'll be Jordan."

Jordan barged into the sitting room. "Hi, I'm home. My teeth are great. What's...." She stopped abruptly when she saw Suzy and Kat, Trish in tears, and the haunted look in her mother's eyes. "What's up?"

"You might well ask..." began her mother.

"We need to talk to you, Jordan. It's OK. You're not in trouble. Thanks, Trish, we need to talk to Jordan without you," said Suzy amicably.

Jordan pulled a sneering scowl. "Let me get through the fucking door..."

"Jordan!" The scolding in her mother's voice had an undercurrent of exhortation.

"Well, I'm fucking shattered, and I want a drink."

"I'll get you one," said Trish, with a sniff.

Jordan watched her leave. "What's up? Is she in trouble? What is all this? Who are you?"

"In a minute," said Suzy. "Have your drink first, since you're 'fucking shattered'."

Jordan, blushing slightly sat in a strained silence with her mother for a couple of minutes. They could hear clattering of crockery, a crash, a curse, then Trish appeared with a tea tray and four cups. "I've just bust a cup," she grizzled. "I'll clear that up then I'll be upstairs."

"Oh, thanks Trish. That's really thoughtful of you," said Kat.

Trish's mother poured. The cups clattered as she passed them round, then offered the box of tissues to blot the slops. "Sorry. Can't seem to pour straight."

Suzy showed Jordan her warrant card, as did Kat. "Trish thinks something untoward happened to her, and to you, which is why we need to talk to you. Now Jordan, it's important that you tell us the whole truth, even if you've done something you shouldn't have. We're not interested in you buying alcohol for Trish, though you must know that's a criminal offence because she's under age, so don't do it again. No, this is something far more serious. And we need to have your version, so we can work out what's happened, if anything."

Emotions flickered across Jordan's face like firelight.

"Jordan, do you recall…."

~~~

Half an hour later, Jordan went up to her room, sullenly angry and miserable. Suzy and Kat were left confronting Mrs Dale. She looked as if she'd forgotten how to breathe.

"Mrs Dale, we had hoped that when we spoke to your daughters, it would turn out that they had both got a bit tipsy, nothing more than that, but on the face of it, it seems possible that one or both your daughters have been assaulted in some way, and they both knew something was amiss, but kept quiet."

Tracy Dale's face broke into splinters, she heaved in a mouthful of pain, then shuddered.

"We'd like you to bring them both to Rosamundi House in Galchester. It's a sanctuary run in conjunction with the NHS and other partnership agencies. I expect Kat told you that I'm part of a sexual offences investigation team there, specially trained in this sort of thing. We have rooms where we can take video statements from vulnerable witnesses like your girls. And you can also get any help and support they need. A lot of time has elapsed since the suspected offences took place, and we don't know exactly what happened, and probably never will. But this incident should be recorded, and any help and support needed for your daughters will be made easily available. Are you agreeable to that if the girls consent to it?"

Tracey Dale made a tight noise, and nodded her head, eyes anywhere but on them. She rocked on the sofa, stifled sobs escaping.

Suzy decided to leave the advice about sexually transmitted diseases until they were at Rosamundi House.

~~~

"You OK, Kat?" asked Suzy as they got back in the car.

"Yup," said Kat. "Do you know, I wonder if my talk hasn't done more harm than good, bringing all this to the surface."

"Who knows? But they might have been secretly fretting about it, or been infected with an STI… better supported in the long run. I hope. No easy answers."

~~~

Kirsty

Kirsty barely looked up from the telly when she heard her mother come home. She said nothing. She assumed a look of insolent indifference when her mother came into the lounge. "You're very late home," she offered at last, in a resentful tone. "You could have phoned."

Suzy said nothing.

Startled by the lack of response, Kirsty looked up at her mother, sat herself up, and looked again. "Mum? What's up, Mum?"

Her mother's eyes were haggard, and she looked exhausted. She seemed to be talking through ice cubes. "Don't…. Don't you ever get so drunk you don't know what you're doing. Don't you ever let your drinks out of your sight. Never, ever have so much to drink that you assume you're drunk not drugged. You hear me?"

"I won't, all right, all right, don't go on."

Her mother, with a couple of sinuous bounds, closed the space between then. Kirsty found her mother's hands digging into her shoulders, shaking her as she shrank into the sofa. "I mean it, I mean it. Never, you understand." Her mother's face filled her vision, fierce, furious, weeping.

The tears shocked Kirsty more than the anger. "Mum! You're hurting."

Her mother let go, backed away, contrition flaring across her face. Kirsty jumped up and hugged her. "Mum. Mum, what's the matter?" Kirsty wondered where to put her cheek, now they were the same height. It seemed wrong, somehow, to be holding her mother like this, rocking her gently. Until now it had always been Mum hugging her pain away; the bleeding knees; the cat dying; Dad leaving. And always, until now, her head had rested on her mother's lap, or on her chest, cheek absorbing comfort as she was rocked, soothing the sadness away.

Her mother broke the clinch, then held Kirsty's shoulders again, gentler now. "I can't tell you. I shouldn't tell you. But I... They were your age, Kirsty. I'm glad you went to school here in Tiptree or you'd probably know them. You might, anyway. In fact... And when I saw you sitting there, same age, same look, same oblivious insolence, I... I can't say any more."

Kirsty shook her head, wanting to block the thoughts. She knew, in the way a child in England understands the hazard of a lion, the sort of work her mother did, the sort of people her mother dealt with. But work was work, another planet, never touching her, never touching them. Until today. "You sit down, Mum, and I'll get the supper ready."

As soon as Kirsty entered the kitchen she regretted the generous impulse. It was a simple enough supper, chicken in a cook-in sauce, rice, and salad from a bag, and she could have cooked it earlier instead of sulkily waiting for her mother to come and cook at 9.30 at night. As she tipped the chicken pieces into the pan, Kirsty mulled over the last few minutes. There had been a subtle power shift, a change in their relationship, a readjustment. Her mother was more of a friend, now. But less of a mother? Mum crying? Mum vulnerable?

And what the hell had happened to some kids her own age? And did she know them?

Chapter 10

Kirsty

"Jordan's off sick, today, so I'm relying on you to have learned the ropes, Kirsty. But if you have any problems, give me a yell, and I'll give you a hand, OK?"

"Yes, Jimbo. Did she say what's wrong?"

"No. And remember if you have a tummy bug, you're not to come in. But tummy bug isn't the same as a hangover."

"I've never had a hangover."

"No? I can soon cure that, if you like. Only on a Saturday night, not a Sunday. I like you bright eyed and bush tailed on a Monday. Ready for action." He gave her a suggestive wink.

When Jimbo had wandered off, Janet rolled her eyes at Kirsty. "He's after you," she whispered. "Interested?"

"Ugh. Don't be soft. He's old enough to be my Dad. Has he really got a Lotus?"

"Yes. I've seen it. But he usually drives an old heap. Says he daren't risk the Lotus in the car park."

~~~

Angie

I was told I had to go to antenatal classes held at the maternity hospital. I parked, mentally tallying up how much in parking these classes were going to cost me. I hoped they were worth it. I asked at reception and was pointed to a room with a circle of chairs in it. The door was open, so I stuck my head round.

"Come in, come in, you're…" said one of two women in medical uniform.

"Angie Bain."

The women examined the space behind me, then invited me to sit. I watched as couples came along, timorously peeping round the doorframe in the same way as I had. They sat down, the women gravid, the men nursing beer bellies. Every other mother-to-be had the (presumed) father with her, except one. It transpired her husband was in the Navy and would be away for the birth. There was a whisper of sympathy round the room as she told us this. Her sister was going to be her birth partner. Her sister was the only person in the room, barring the midwife and the physiotherapist, who didn't look pregnant.

Everyone looked at the vacant space beside me, but I told them nothing.

As the first class went on, I was more and more an interloper, immune to the feeling of anticipation and excitement. The men looked irritatingly cocky, and the women nervous but pleased.

We all giggled at the bunch of grapes and breast analogy, but my laughter sounded empty. We promised to buy maternity bras and take care of our breasts.

Milk? Oozing out of my breasts? Breast-feeding? What a disgusting thing the human body is.

~~~

Kirsty

"You all right, Jordan?" asked Janet the next day, as they were on their meal break.

"Yeah," said Jordan.

Kirsty thought she didn't look all right. She looked worn out, pale and ill. Eddie was gazing at Jordan with a rather hungry look, Kirsty thought. Creeped her out a bit.

"You look like shit," said Tom. "What was wrong yesterday? Period pains?"

"Tom, don't be so personal," said Janet.

But her admonishment was drowned by Jordan. "Shut the fuck up, nosey bastard, nobody asked you."

"You shuttup," said Tom, face flushing. "You tarty slag."

Jordan aimed a slap at Tom, but he swayed back and she missed.

"Stop that!" said Janet. "How dare you. I don't know what's got into you, Jordan. You're acting like a four-year-old. And Tom, you behave as well."

"Nobody calls me a bastard," growled Tom.

"What, just because you are one?" said Stuart with a sneer.

"Well, don't call me a tarty slag," said Jordan, bursting into tears. "I wasn't. I was drugged. We both were. And that stupid little brat of a sister went and told, didn't she?"

Kirsty sucked in a breath. "You were drug-raped?" she asked in a horrified whisper.

"I don't know. I don't know," said Jordan. "It happened a while back. To Trish and me. You know she tags along on a Saturday, sometimes. Well, we thought we'd overdone it one Sunday, 'cos we felt like shit, had the most humongous hangovers. We must've got in before Mum and Dad, though, or there'd have been a row, but we both woke up fully dressed. Only it wasn't fully dressed. Trish's knickers were inside out, and messy, and I didn't have any on under my jeans. I made her promise to say nothing, or we'd not be allowed out again. But the stupid little twat told, and I spent all yesterday telling the police what happened with them videoing it."

"You shouldn't have said," said Kirsty.

"That's what I told Trish."

"No, I mean, just now. You shouldn't have told us what you just did, because it's confidential. You shouldn't tell us about Trish. And you should have told your parents straight away, and the police. You should have reported it instead of trying to hide it. People like that need stopping and they'll never be stopped if people don't come forward. And what if you got a disease, or fell pregnant?"

"You shut up too, you fucking know-all. None of your fucking business."

"That's the whole point," said Kirsty. "It isn't any of our business. Now everybody knows and will gossip about it. Trish doesn't deserve that. And you shouldn't have put yourself and her in that sort of position."

"You fucking self-righteous cow. Nobody asked your opinion." Jordan stood so abruptly her chair fell over.

"Jordan, that's enough. I think you ought to go home. You're obviously not well."

Jordan's face dissolved. "Home's awful just now. My mum blames me for making Trish not tell. And we're being tested for... oh, fuck."

Tom looked intrigued. Stuart just stared at the table chewing his lips. Eddie was examining his hands. Kirsty saw his tongue flick out like a snake's.

Janet took Jordan to the loo, then Jimbo drove her home. After the meal break, the line started again, one person down, Jimbo standing in, and everyone very subdued.

~~~

After work, Kirsty was just putting on her helmet when Tom came up to her. "D'you wanna coffee at Snack-a-Randy's with

63

me?" Kirsty thought he had a cute smile and a fit body too, muscles outlined under his tee-shirt. He was wearing trackies and a baseball cap and looked exactly the sort of boy her mother had warned her about.

"Yeah, all right," she said. "Where is it?"

"Just round the corner, not far. You can wheel your moped if you want."

Kirsty slung her helmet on her handlebar. "OK."

"It's on my way home," said Tom. "I walk. Someone nicked me bike. Hey, talking of bikes, what did you think of what Jordan said? Fuck me... I wonder if it was that creepy teacher she was talking about the other day. Roger-the-girls." He sniggered.

"She shouldn't have said," said Kirsty, brusquely. "And if that's all you want to talk about, I'll go home now."

"Noooo," said Tom. "I won't mention it again."

"OK."

They walked along in a slightly embarrassed silence until they got to a parade of shops. "The Chinese is good," said Tom, indicating the takeaway, "but I like Randy's better. And it's open."

Kirsty parked her moped on the side of the road. Tom told her to take her helmet in with her.

"Can I have a hot chocolate, not a coffee, please?" she said. She seated herself at one of the Formica topped tables.

"Course," said Tom, going to the counter. He returned with two hot chocolates and some biscuits. "Who are you texting?"

"Mum. Tell her I'll be a bit late."

"Do you have to tell her your every move?"

"No. But she gets twitchy if I'm late home. She won't be home herself, but I wouldn't put it past her to ring home, expecting me to be there, and then to worry when I'm not."

"My mum doesn't worry about me."

"How old are you?"

"Twenty-two."

"And a dude. I'm only eighteen, and a girl. Of course Mum worries."

"What about your dad? Or haven't you got one?"

"My parents are divorced. I have to stay with him some weekends, him and the bimbo slut who stole him from my mum. I hate her."

"I haven't got a dad, either," said Tom. "I never knew him, neither. Not my real dad. I had a couple of others, but they buggered off too, and mum said she'd had enough of men."

Another customer sat near them, attacking a plate laden with sausage, egg, chips and beans.

Kirsty looked at it enviously. "I'm starved. I can't believe I ate at ten, and now I'm hungry again. I think I'll order something like that. I really fancy some."

"Yes, lets, but we'll have to go Dutch."

"Of course," said Kirsty. "I'll let you stand me a hot choccy, but not a meal." They ordered a meal each and chatted until the plates arrived.

"I find my stomach doesn't know what my head's doing on early shift. I can't face breakfast, then I'm starving come ten o'clock, then I'm starved again like now," said Tom, squirting rather a lot of ketchup over the chips.

"I'm kinda used to meals at weird times," said Kirsty. "I used to have dinner at school, then a snack when I got home, and then supper when Mum got in... and that can be any time.

Now I'm working, it seems even worse. Ate supper at half ten Tuesday night. Half six yesterday. Then I was hungry later."

"What does your mum do?"

"She's a... nurse at the hospital."

As they ate, the conversation warmed until Kirsty found they had a similar taste in music, and that she thought Tom was pretty fit, really.

Chapter 11

Angie

A couple of days after the antenatal class, DC Rolfe came to see me. "Look," she said, perched on the semen-free settee. "I'm sorry I haven't been back before now, but we've been busy with your case. We've spoken to all the witnesses we can find. Most people don't seem very clear, it was so long ago, but the consensus is you didn't drink more than a pint of bitter at the Craven Arms before having soft drinks or coffee. Everyone else left you at about 11.00 pm to go on to Janger's Night Club. You said you'd stay at the pub and enjoy another coffee before going home. They left you in the corner near the fire. You'd said you were a bit tired. The pub was busy, nobody saw you talking to anyone, or leave the pub with anyone. That's not to say you didn't, just that nobody saw you. The pub only keeps the car park CCTV for three months, so we've got no idea about cars. The town centre CCTV has picked nothing up either so it's probable that you were taken from the pub straight into a car, but unless there are witnesses, we'll never know. Unless we catch the culprit through a different crime.

"There is one more thing we can do, and that's take a sample of umbilical cord blood from the baby, or a cheek swab, when it arrives. The father will have contributed half his DNA and we might get some evidence that way. Will you consent to your baby's DNA being taken in that way?"

"Yes, of course, especially if you might catch the bastard. He's ruined my life," I said.

She couldn't take the case further at present. So much for justice.

67

When she'd gone I went to the sideboard where I keep the whisky. "I think that deserves a toast to justice, don't you, you little bastard?" I said to the lump. My hand paused on the bottle. He never asked to be created. He never asked his father to drug and rape me. Why was I punishing him? Where was the justice in that?

I made a mug of tea instead.

~~~

Suzy

"Why do I get all the Elversford jobs?" moaned Suzy.

"I like a bit of continuity," said DI Cheung. "You know you don't really mean it; you're just moaning because it's Saturday."

"OK, what's the story, then?"

"This girl Ellie went missing last night. The mother and father, Mr and Mrs Warrener phoned Elversford police last night when Ellie didn't come home from a night out with her friends. They were expecting her home by midnight, but she didn't come back. She's never done this before, so at 1.00am they phoned the friend she went out with. That friend said she thought Ellie was at another friend's, so they phoned there. This friend said that Ellie had been with her that evening, but she hadn't seen her since ten o'clock, when she left Ellie at the Blue Bore in the company of some other girls. The Blue Bore seems quite the place to be if you're young and feckless. Definitely worth keeping an eye on. Ellie's fifteen but looks eighteen."

"Anyway, the parents phoned round all her friends in case Ellie was with them. No luck. So they phoned Elversford Police, reporting her missing."

"Did they not try her mobile?"

"At home, no credit. Too much texting, apparently. Anyway, we alerted everyone to be on the lookout, but expected her to turn up at someone's. Brooks went round to see the parents. The Warreners were adamant that something must have happened because this sort of thing was completely out of character, so Brooks went to the pub, the Blue Bore, which was just shutting up. 3.00am by now. The landlord remembered the girls. They had got quite tipsy, but he says they all left together about 11.00ish, and there were a couple of lads with them. That's the last he saw."

"No dodgy barmen this time, I take it?"

"I bet the landlord was shitting bricks when Brooks turned up. Not in the nicest of areas, that pub. Near the old industrial area with that bloody horrible derelict warehouse. Can you imagine walking home past there at 3.00am in the morning?"

"Oh, don't. Kirsty works in the pizza factory nearby."

"Well, make sure she knows how dodgy that area is then. Anyway, no sign of the girl, so Brooks asked if he can have a poke around in her room, find a list of friends perhaps; someone they've overlooked or don't know about. And they found a diary. Featuring some pretty lurid teenage ...well let's hope, just fantasies, about a teacher."

"Ah… and?"

"Of course, Brooks went round to the teacher's house immediately. 4.37am. Roger Turner answered the door in his pyjamas and dressing gown. Brooks said Turner seemed puzzled, but not furtive or worried. He invited Brooks in. Brooks told him that a girl had disappeared, and that a diary had been found mentioning him. Turner knew or guessed who it was straight away. Laughed, according to Brooks. Said Ellie has a teenage crush on him. Seemed nonplussed and a bit

69

cross that Brooks should think the girl was there; invited them to look all over the house. Then he says, 'but please knock on the bedroom door as Jane's still in bed.' His wife. Only she isn't by this time; she's put a dressing gown on and is halfway down the stairs. Turner outlined the problem to his wife, who laughed at the idea the girl was there. Then her face went pale, and she said, 'I hope she's OK.'" Cheungy frowned. "But something struck Brooks as odd. The wife, Jane Turner's a real looker, but looks like an older version of Ellie from the photos Ellie's parents had given him. Not dead alike, but reminiscent. And Jane Turner could have been Mrs Warrener's younger sister. Striking resemblance.

"Brooks had a good look round, but the girl's not there. When Brooks got back to the nick he's well pissed off because he should have finished at 4.00am and it's getting on for 6.00am, and he hasn't found the girl, but had an embarrassing time with a teacher and his wife. But Brooks said he thinks something's amiss, but he's not sure what.

"Anyway, the girl turns up safe and well at a newly-made friend's house. Turns out she went with some of the pub crowd to a party, and bumped into someone she knew vaguely, got talking, didn't notice the time, and decided to kip on the floor of this acquaintance's house. She didn't phone and tell her parents because, wait for it; she thought they'd be angry about being phoned at 2.00am in the morning. Kids!"

"Was she assaulted at the friend's house, then?" asked Suzy.

"No. Her parents, having nothing better to do than fret, read her diary, cover to cover, found some dodgy stuff in it, and have made a formal complaint against the teacher, Roger Turner. Could you go and see them, please, and if they'll let you, seize the diary and read it, see if there really is something dodgy going on."

~~~

The Warreners lived in one of the better districts of Elversford. The open-plan front garden was reasonably well cared for, and there were two cars on the drive. Mr Warrener opened the door to Suzy. He looked grim. He ushered her into the lounge, where Mrs Warrener was standing. There was no sign of Ellie. "Please sit down," Mrs Warrener invited.

Suzy perched on the edge of the sofa, skewed so that she could see both Mrs Warrener on the sofa and Mr Warrener who sat down in what was obviously his (and only his) armchair.

"I understand you wish to make a formal complaint against someone," said Suzy.

Mrs Warrener launched into a rambling account of the previous evening, how they had phoned round her friends, starting with Trish Dale, who was in her class and one of her best mates, but whose mother had answered frostily and said that Trish was grounded, and no, she didn't know where Ellie was. Mrs Warrener said they then went through all the friends they knew. And how PC Brooks had come, and they'd gone up to Ellie's room, found the diary, and then Brooks had left with some photographs. Mrs Warrener stopped mid-gabble, drew a breath, and continued. Then Ellie had walked in, cool as cucumber that morning. But by that time, they had read the diary.

And they weren't happy.

"Look," said Mr Warrener, passing Suzy the diary. He had put Post-it notes on various pages.

Suzy looked at the highlighted pages. It read like some of the badly written erotica drivel she had read on the internet. It was very explicit.

"He must have led her on," said Mr Warrener. "Ellie's far too young to know about that sort of thing. She denied it, of course. She's been sent to her room, the bad, bad girl. But this teacher. If he's done anything to her, I want his balls nailed to the blackboard."

"May I take this and read through it; see if it looks as though any offences have been committed. If so, we can crime it, and then we'll need to do a vulnerable witness interview to video camera with Ellie. You say she denies it? Denies what?"

"Doing... that..." Mr Warrener indicated the diary with revulsion. "Doing any of that with him."

~~~

Back in Galchester nick, Suzy took the diary and opened it. There was an entry for every day. 'Saw him three times today. He was doing athletics with the boys. What fit legs. Didn't get much Maths done.' A bit further on; 'He smiled at me... He said hello. My heart just flipped. I am in lurve.' There were hearts in all the margins, initials, RT 4 E. There was a photo at the school disco. A girl was standing so close to a teacher, she was as near as she could be without touching him. The girl looked aroused, and the teacher looked very handsome, but oblivious to the girl, though the teacher was slightly older than Suzy had imagined. About her own age. That was confirmed a little further along when Ellie had put down his personal details, such as his date of birth, and his address. How had she found that sort of information out? 'I sent him a valentine. At home.' And 'I sent him a birthday card, from a secret admirer.'

"It's a bad schoolgirl crush. She shouldn't bother him like that," said Suzy, aloud to herself.

Cheungy came over, having made some real coffee, her private indulgence in the nick. "Here," she said, passing Suzy one, and a chocolate biscuit. "I think we deserve a treat for working at the weekend, yet again. Anything like an offence yet?

"Thanks, Ma'am, and no; looks like a swooning girl with a crush fantasising about her teacher."

Cheungy turned her attention back to her paperwork.

A while later, Suzy swallowed. "Bloody hell, Ellie should write steamy novels. But this is mainly fantasy, apart from where she says he put his hand on her shoulder and brushed against her breasts on the stairs. But if you look at Ellie's description of the lead-in to the breast part, she contrived that."

Cheungy took the diary and read it. "I see what you mean. I think we'll have to talk to Ellie about this, though; one to keep her parents satisfied, and two, to stop her stalking him like this. Carry on reading, though, and see if there is anything amiss."

A little later, Suzy said, "Oh."

"Found something?"

"Maybe; 'I was down by the river today when he ran past. He's well fit, he is. He stopped, came over and said hello, and we started chatting. I think he fancies me.' Well, that means the erotic stuff up to this point is all fantasy, then." Suzy flicked through the next few pages. "But she keeps bumping into him along the river. And he stops, and chats. And look here. 'He ran past today with a wave. He was wearing very short shorts and his legs are cute. He stopped a bit further on, bent over, and wiggled his arse at me. And I saw them; his bits. He let them fall out. I'd like to give him a blowjob.' Uh-oh, she says she told him it was she who sent the valentines. He blew her a kiss, and told her to wait until she's older. She writes that she said she was old enough. And he said, no; she's still at school and not yet 16. And he's told her he always runs this way, Mondays Wednesdays and Fridays. If I were a teacher being sent valentines by a pupil, I'd change my route and go out of my way to avoid her. And notice that he knows her age... I wonder why."

A little later, Suzy said, "This reads like grooming. Nothing overt, but... But the problem is, how much of this is in Ellie's head, and how much really happened? It would be awful to arrest let alone charge a man who was nothing more than the subject of a child's fantasies, since even the arrest will stay on his record as he's a teacher and could ruin his career."

Cheungy read some of the pertinent paragraphs. "He's not doing anything to put a stop to the accidental meetings, though, is he? I think we will crime it and have a word with Ellie."

~~~

Suzy sank into the hot, fragrant water with a sigh. This was supposed to wash away the stresses of the day, to switch her from copper mode to human mode. But today it wasn't working. Perhaps it was because usually when she conducted a Vulnerable Witness interview, there was clear evidence of wrongdoing, or an obvious misinterpretation of events. Here though...

Ellie had been furious about the diary, had at first refused to have anything to do with the police. Her father had become angry, threatened to go round and 'sort the teacher out',

74

which Suzy had had to object to. The mother had cajoled until Ellie, perhaps realising that she had to do something to appease her worried parents, had agreed to the Vulnerable Witness Interview.

It had taken a long time, but Suzy was used to that. As she'd suspected, the first part of the diary was just fantasy on Ellie's part. Suzy asked Ellie where she got the ideas for such explicit ideas from. Ellie had told her; the internet.

No; Turner had not had sex with Ellie (despite the fantasies otherwise). No; Turner had not touched Ellie intentionally except twice, when he put his hand on her shoulder briefly, and when she had brushed up against him in the corridor and he accidentally touched her breasts. But yes, they did see each other out of school when he said hello during his runs. And yes, he had flashed his genitals at her by bending over, when wearing shorts. And yes; that conversation about her age had taken place—she thought. But couldn't swear to it.

Suzy submerged herself in the bathwater, rinsing the shampoo from her head. A vision from years back slapped her in the face; a child the same age as Ellie, discarded in an alleyway like a broken doll, sweaty from ecstasy, cold with death. Raped and dumped. It had been a pivotal moment in Suzy's career. She exploded out of the water, raking in a breath. Something had given her the heeby-jeebies, but she couldn't think what. She wiped her face clear of water and slicked her hair away.

It was difficult to know how truthful Ellie's answers had been, though she seemed suddenly mortified and seemed to be telling the simple truth. Yet when Suzy had asked about the valentine's cards, Suzy had said, "How do you think his wife feels about that? He's a happily married man."

"No he isn't!"

"What d'you mean?"

"He told me..." Ellie's's face had shut down, blanking them. Suzy knew that look; Kirsty used the same expression.

Chapter 12

Suzy

The house was seedier than Suzy was expecting; not as run down as the houses near the old industrial estate, but not as up-market as she would have expected for a teacher aged forty-one.

For a moment Suzy had to blink and look for her voice when a woman answered the door; the similarity to Ellie was startling, as if this woman was Ellie's elder sister. She was about twenty-five, glowing in one way, yet haggard in her expression. Suzy and Lynne Alderton showed their warrant cards. "We're looking for Roger Turner, please. Is he here?"

"He's out. Down the gym. As usual."

"Oh, any idea when he'll be back?"

It wasn't a difficult question, but Jane Turner took her time answering. "No. No idea. I don't suppose he'll be that long, though."

"Can we come in and wait, please? It's important."

"Please do," said Jane Turner, stepping back and inviting them in. "Go through to the living room."

Smiling her thanks, Suzy entered. The carpet had a pattern reminiscent of the Eighties, and the leather sofa was cracked, sagging uncomfortably as Suzy sat.

"Did you find the girl?"

"Turned up safe and sound, thank goodness," said Lynne.

"Sorry. I didn't mean to be rude just now. Only it's a bit embarrassing, having police come round."

Suzy shrugged. "No problem," she added, with a smile, "We often get quite a hostile reception. I didn't think you rude so much as taken aback. Was it a shock when the officers knocked you up in the middle of the night?"

"Of course it was. Where was the girl?"

"Turned up safe and well, at a friend's." Suzy echoed Lynne's words.

"But you found a diary?"

"I'm sorry PC Brooks had to trouble you."

"And you've come back. So there's something in it?"

"I just need to talk to Mr Turner about it."

Jane sat down in a decrepit armchair. She swallowed, bit her lips, wet them. "I... I think I'd like to tell you something."

The silence solidified. "Go on, then," prompted Suzy.

"About eight years ago, I was just doing my 'A' Levels. Roger was teaching. He was our form teacher. I thought he was wonderful. But he was married. And a teacher. He knew I had the hots for him. Shortly after I left school, he found me. And we started an affair. I was eighteen, no longer his pupil. It was all above board. Apart from the fact he was married, of course. He ditched his wife and kids, he moved to a different school, and we got married a couple of years later once his divorce came through, though I moved in with him as soon as I could. My parents weren't happy, but tough, I thought. And it's been great, until recently.

"I'm pregnant. It's what we both wanted. I thought. But now I wonder... Things haven't been good since I fell pregnant. I've not been well and I haven't felt much like...anything." Jane paused. Blinked. "Strange, isn't it, when I ousted Gillian from his bed, he joked that he was trading up to a newer model. I was flattered at the time. Made me feel special. I never dreamed I'd become last year's model. This girl... Is she pretty? Does she look like me?"

"I can't tell you anything."

78

"Is she screwing him?"

"No. I'm sorry, I really can't discuss this."

There was a noise at the front door. Jane looked startled, jumped up, and said, "He's back... Please don't..."

Roger exploded into the room. "Some stupid pillock's parked in my place. Oh."

"I imagine I'm that stupid pillock," said Suzy, delighted with the heat that suffused his cheeks. She showed him her warrant card.

No wonder girls had a crush on Roger. He was outrageously handsome. Suzy found herself responding to him. He was built like an athlete and his face graced that poise. His hair was just the length to make you want to run your fingers through it, the colour of honeycomb, damp at the roots from a shower. The embarrassed glow added to his allure, making him seem at once manly yet vulnerable.

"Are you Roger Turner?" asked Suzy.

"Yes," said Turner, suddenly wary.

"An allegation of indecent exposure and abuse of a position of trust has been made against you, and as a result of this, I am arresting you on suspicion of indecent exposure and abuse of a position of trust." Suzy watched the blood drain from his face as she gave him the caution. Jane Turner burst into tears. "I'm sorry, but I'm going to handcuff you," added Suzy, applying her cuffs to Turner such that his hands were stacked to the front. "Have you got a jacket or something to put over them so that the neighbours don't see?"

Jane Turner fetched Roger's fleece, and Suzy arranged it so that it hid the cuffs.

By the way Roger walked to the car and got in it, it was fairly obvious that his movement was restricted in some way, but at least they weren't in uniform, and it was an unmarked car. Lynne drove whilst Suzy sat in next to him and watched her prisoner like a lioness observing a gazelle.

Roger Turner just studied his lap.

~~~

"He had an answer for everything," said Suzy. "And do you know, I'm not sorry. I think it was worth following up the complaint, to satisfy Ellie's parents, and I suppose it's shown Ellie that her behaviour is out of order, but I don't think any offences have been committed."

"Perhaps she'll have the decency to phone and inform her parents where she is, next time. If there is a next time. I'm not sure I'd want my two out like that when they're older," said Cheungy.

"I'd kill Kirsty if she did that to me," agreed Suzy. "And she is older."

"So what did Turner say about the frequent bumping into Ellie on his runs?"

"Said it was entirely accidental, and she was a bit of a nuisance."

"Did you ask him why he continued to use that route if she was there, swooning at him? He's a teacher. He ought to know how careful he needs to be."

"Well, if he didn't he does now," said Suzy, with a rueful laugh. "He said that he uses that specific run because he can tell good days from bad days, he knows where he should be by what time, so he can pace himself. It's a run he's been using for years and doesn't see why a simpering school kid with a crush on him should spoil his training. He came across as quite contemptuous of Ellie. Thinks she's a bit of an airhead. He didn't remember any incident on the stairs, and never put his hand on her shoulder."

"What about the flashing incident? The one where he bent over and showed his knackers to her?"

"Do you know, he blushed. He said he remembers bending down to retie his laces once, which had come undone. He was wearing some shorts which were a bad buy. Most of his running shorts have an internal gusset which helps support the testicles when he's running... apparently there can be quite a bit of jiggling. These shorts were poorly designed, and his goolies had slipped out on running on a couple of occasions. But not the whole kit, just one testicle, which apparently, is bloody uncomfortable, and needs putting back in place. He was aware of his slipped testicle when he tied his laces but could hardly fiddle with it when she was watching. He had no idea the testicle was visible when he bent over and seemed quite mortified when we discussed it in the interview. He said the shorts were rubbish and he chucked them the next day."

"If he was aware that his testicle had slipped out of the gusset, why didn't he crouch down as opposed to bending over, I wonder. And why didn't he wear Y fronts as well as shorts?

"Chafing, he says. And Y fronts get sweaty and nasty and will add to the rubbing. Seems a bit odd, but not enough to charge him with anything, I don't think."

"Run it past the CPS, though they seem to only want dead certs nowadays."

"Yes, Ma'am." Suzy found herself frowning.

Cheungy noticed. "You're not happy, are you?"

"Not really, but I think I'm just being cynical. Why am I so cynical about everyone and everything? It comes out in my home life too... all the time I'm questioning people's veracity and motives. Why? Why do I look on everyone as a potential offender?"

"Police personality, I think. It goes with the territory."

Suzy smiled. "Yeah, maybe that's it; I'm so used to seeing the bad and the ugly, I think everyone's bad and ugly.   "I think the whole thing's a storm in a teacup. Poor bloke. Not sure I like him though."

"He teaches PE, from the remark in Ellie's diary."

"That's not his main subject. He teaches chemistry, but does some PE too, and has an interest in sports physiology. Coaches under sixteens' footie on a Saturday morning, as well. A lot to lose if he were to do anything untoward. I really can't see it."

"Or deliberately placing himself in a position of trust and interacting with kids," said Cheungy.

"Now who's being cynical?"

"That's not cynicism, it's a copper's nose."

"Same thing, perhaps. OK, how about this for a bit of copper's nose twitching...." Suzy repeated the story Jane Turner had told her. "I'd love to know what the original wife looks like."

"You think he might start grooming look-alikes to take over when the present model gets old or won't perform in bed?"

"It's possible."

Cheungy took the file for a good look. A little later she took the phone and called DI Hedley who was in charge of CID at Elversford. Because it was Sunday, she phoned him at home.

"Hal, have you got time for an unofficial chinwag?"

"For you, Cheungy, of course."

Cheungy explained what had happened so far, particularly about the trading up. "Thing is, Hal, this girl does look awfully like a younger version of his present wife, and I wondered what his previous wife looks like."

"Go camp outside her address, then."

"Good idea. Except that takes a lot of time. And it's hard to justify in work time, and under RIPA, and I'm pushed... I know it's a long shot, but Turner used to work at the same school as your wife does now. I wondered if she had any old school photographs with his ex-wife in tow... like a staff Christmas Party or something."

Hedley laughed. "They don't have a party, exactly, though they do go out for a meal. It's just possible that I took a photograph or too. But you're talking eight, ten years ago, aren't you?"

"Yes. That's the point. I'd like to see whether the then Mrs Turner looked like the now Mrs Turner, then. Bugger; that sounds silly."

"I know what you mean. I'll look through my photos. Fortunately, I keep them catalogued and in order."

"Now why doesn't that surprise me?" said Cheungy.

~~~

"I'd have scanned it and emailed it to you, but this seemed to be a bit on the sly," said Hedley on Monday morning. He passed Cheungy a photograph. "My fee is a coffee," he added.

Cheungy looked at it, then showed it to Suzy. "Which is Turner?" Cheungy asked Hedley.

"Him," said Hedley, pointing.

"Hnm, he is good looking. OK, Suzy... can you spot the then Mrs Turner out of that crowd?"

Suzy took the photograph. "I reckon that's her," she said, pointing.

"Correct," said Hedley.

"She's very pretty in this picture," said Cheungy.

"Six months later, he's walked out on her, leaving her holding the babies, and shacks up with this school leaver, Jane. Pretty dastardly thing to do. Frankly, there's an element of poetic justice if this present wife is facing being similarly traded in." Suzy scowled at the photograph. "This makes me uneasy, because I can't see a school leaver jumping into a relationship so soon after leaving school, unless there was something going on beforehand. The timing doesn't seem right. You don't just fall in love with your ex-teacher and jump into his bed in a matter of weeks. Do you?"

Cheungy shook her head. "You're judging people on what you yourself wouldn't do. Having read the diary, do you think, given half a chance, Ellie wouldn't have jumped into his bed?"

"My wife says Turner left their school a little after, because of the embarrassment factor. But she says there was something that didn't smell quite right about him, and although what he had done wasn't illegal, or even justifying disciplinary measures, it was frowned upon."

"Like now; there's something not quite right about all of this, but there's no evidence of wrongdoing that would give a dead cert conviction in court. Thanks, Hal," said Cheungy. "Does that answer your curiosity, Suzy?"

"Yes Ma'am, though it's just made me more uneasy. Thanks, Guv; that's really helpful. Your wife won't gossip about Turner will she?"

Hedley glared at her with his piercing eyes. "Of course not."

Chapter 13

Angie

I started my maternity leave on 30th July. Several of the girls gathered in the coffee room after work, 9.00pm. Giggling. They had a good luck card, and a gift. I glanced at Sally Curtis when she came into the room. She took the scene in, sucked a breath over her teeth, but said nothing.

"Open it, open it," urged the girls. I pulled at the paper and unwrapped a lovely two-piece baby outfit. Unisex. And a rattle/teething ring.

I smiled to make my tears seem joyful, though my face was cracking. "It's lovely," I said. "Thank you so much. It's so kind of you. I don't know what to say."

"Good luck, hope it all goes well," they said, variously repeating the sentiments. They trickled away until just Ms Curtis and I were left like flotsam.

"I'm sorry, Angie. I didn't know they were going to do that. I know you told me you plan to have him adopted, but I treated that as confidential, of course. They don't know."

I looked down at the baby outfit. Until that moment I hadn't thought of the lump being a living, squalling baby. A Lump, scientifically gendered 'him'. The fruit of rape.

An abomination.

Not a baby.

In my mind I filled the baby outfit with a wriggling scrap of humanity, and for the first time wondered if I was doing the right thing in having him adopted.

~~~

Sally Curtis phoned a few times during my maternity leave to see if I was OK. I was, though I wasn't sleeping well. I'm a restless sleeper at the best of times, and the summer heat was getting to me. Every time I woke, I needed to turn over, and that was getting harder and harder. The belly grew huge, not like a pillow as I'd imagined, but a rucksack of fluid, heavy and awkward on my front. The baby wriggled and shifted.

They made sure that I really wanted him adopted. Did I? Apart from that one spurt of maternal instinct I felt nothing for the baby. He might be half mine, but the other half belonged to my assailant. Blood will out, and I believe in bad blood. I tried to be logical about it. I even drew up a list of pros and cons. The cons; he was a baby from a rape, and every time I was angry with him, this fact would rankle. Con. I hadn't any help and on my wages I couldn't afford childcare. Con. I was nearly 47, not that old, but I didn't want, couldn't face a lifestyle change at my age. Con. It might stand in the way of me forming another relationship. I hated the last two cons, they seemed so selfish. But I was trying to be realistic. And the pro? I was almost 47, a lesbian, so lesbian the thought of sex with a man made me feel sick. This was my one and only chance of motherhood. Presented to me, on a plate, without the hideous sex involved. How big was that pro?

Big, but not big enough. I opted for adoption and booked an elective Caesarian for 5th September.

~~~

There was a couple missing from the next maternity class. They'd had a lovely baby boy, 6lb 4 oz. in old money. Lucky old them.

The next day it was my birthday. I didn't celebrate. Nobody sent me a card.

The next maternity class another couple had had their baby; the Navy lass with the help of her sister. Another boy. 6lb 10 oz.

The following week two other couples were missing, and the midwife made a joke about them just wanting to avoid the classes.

~~~

Suzy

Suzy looked up from her computer as Lynne Alderton entered the CID room noisily, with a gusty sigh. Lynne threw down her notebook, looked round. "Anyone want a coffee?"

Suzy said, "Shall we nick some of Cheungy's or go to the canteen?"

"I need a break. And you shouldn't spend all day staring at a screen either."

"Not getting me anywhere fast anyway." Suzy shoved herself backwards, stood, stretched and went with Lynne to the canteen.

Lynne sat stirring her coffee morosely. "D'you ever wonder if we're being used in marriage breakdowns as a source of vengeance?"

"I do wonder sometimes. Why? Something get to you today?"

"I went to see that family in North Street, Galchester, today. The one where the mother phoned up a couple of days back and made a complaint about the father. The Priors. The mother, Sylvia is living with her two daughters Katy, aged nineteen and Emma, seventeen. She said that Emma recently let on that the father, Edward, had been touching her intimately for years. So Sylvia asked Katy outright, and Katy said the same.

"I asked to speak to Katy first as she's not a juvenile. And she told me that the first time she remembered being touched was when her mother was away at a conference and Katy remembers her father opening her pyjamas and looking at her chest, peering at it. And another incident where she was getting dressed and her zip stuck. He touched her breast then, and a couple of similar incidents. But this was several years ago. Their marriage broke down last year, and the father has moved out.

"I then spoke to Emma in the presence of her mother. Similar sorts of incidents, like when Emma wanted a tee shirt, her dad measured her up for it, tape measure round her breasts. Seemed a bit odd as it's the sort of thing you'd leave to the mother or the sister, you'd think, wouldn't you. And little, intimate sorts of things like 'playing puppets'."

"What the hell is 'playing puppets'?" asked Suzy.

"Where someone comes up behind you and grabs your bra straps and pulls. Here, let me show you…" Lynne went behind Suzy, grasped her bra straps through the clothing and pulled.

Suzy felt her breasts jigged up and down. She burst out laughing, wrapping her arms over her chest protectively. "Stop it! That's horrible."

"It's a bit intrusive, isn't it? I can't imagine my dad ever doing that to me."

"I can't imagine my dad ever doing that to my mum," said Suzy with a laugh. "But then, he's the stiff upper lip type who never demonstrates affection, let alone saucy behaviour. Carry on…"

"I took a statement from Emma. Then I took one from her mother, Sylvia. And she told me that both girls had told her that the touching had been far more intimate. Then I asked Sylvia a bit about her relationship. You know, how had it been between them, how long ago had they split up, was it an amicable split. She told me it was amicable, about a year ago, just that they didn't like each other anymore. However, it turns out Sylvia's earning about twice as much as Eddie, she's upwardly mobile and he isn't. And I don't think the split was as amicable as she makes out."

"You think she may be exaggerating what happened to get at him?" suggested Suzy.

"It's possible. It's very possible. I mean, what have we got; a few touching incidents plucked from over the years. No penetration alleged. What makes me a bit suspicious is that Sylvia's reactions were a bit, well, not horrified at what had happened to her daughters so much as gleeful that there was something to pin on Eddie." Lynne shook her head, then sipped her coffee, scowled. "We should have nicked Cheungy's coffee."

"People are affected on different ways, I suppose. It may be that Sylvia isn't the type to beat her chest in sorrow. Or it could be vengeful. But vengeful or not, doesn't mean something didn't happen."

"Yes, but I wouldn't be surprised if it was wildly exaggerated. But we'll have to follow it up, I suppose."

~~~

"The lying bitch." Eddie slammed his hands into the table top.

"Why d'you say that, Eddie?" Lynne asked calmly.

89

"She's put them up to this. I can't believe she's doing this to me. Oh, the cow. Listen, that time I opened Katy's PJs, I was looking for a red rash on her tummy. She was ill, really hot, running a temperature and the light hurt her eyes. And I was dead frightened for her. And the other things, well, I don't remember half of them. No; I don't remember any of them except the helping her on with her dress. Like any dad would do. There was nothing in it. Oh, God, I can't believe she's doing this to me. Well, yes I can, actually, because she really is a vindictive cow, but the girls. I can't understand that…"

"Neither can we, Eddie, which is one reason why you're here."

"I wanna talk to the solicitor."

~~~

More questioning gained no admissions. Eddie ended up a sodden, crumpled heap over the desk. "My girls, my girls. She's poisoned my girls against me. I never did those things, or if I did, I never meant them to be pervy. I can't even remember them. If I did them at all, it was all innocent, I tell you."

~~~

"We're going to release you on bail until a decision is taken on where to go with this. The conditions are you're not to contact Sylvia or the girls in any way, and you're to report once a week on Friday evenings between 5.00pm and 6.00pm."

"I can't do that! I work a shift pattern. At the pizza factory. 6.00am till 2 pm or 2 pm until 10pm."

"OK, well give you a bit more flexibility. From 10.00am until 4.00pm."

"And I can't see my kids?"

"No, sorry. Not until this is sorted."

"I don't believe this. She's won, the bitch. She's using you and you're letting her."

~~~

Lynne and Suzy watched Eddie walk out of the nick. He looked like a cat, stiff with rage. "He might be right, you know," said Lynne.

Chapter 14

Kirsty

Kirsty spooned a bit of the froth from the hot chocolate into her mouth. The bubbles rested briefly on her tongue before vanishing into sweetness.

Tom's eyes opened a little wider. "I've got something for you," he said. "A little pressie."

"Why? It's not my birthday."

Tom shrugged. "Just because." He fumbled in his pocket and pulled out a small box. He pushed it across the Formica table to Kirsty. She opened the box. Inside was a pretty, heart-shaped silver locket. "Open it," he urged.

Kirsty pulled the halves apart. Inside was a note. 'Please go out with me.' "That is so romantic," she said. Part of her was screaming, no, no; you don't fancy him, not really. You're only having a drink with him because nobody else has taken any interest in you, except Jimbo. Nobody fancies you. They thought you were a les at school, or hated you because you're a copper's kid. Don't tell Tom that. That Jord has poisoned the others against you a bit, told them you're a les. Why does everyone think you're a les?

And you fancy Jimbo, don't you? But he's a bit old and crumbly. He'd want sex and nothing else.

Part of her was screaming, Tom's not bad looking. He's twenty-two, past the scrawny, spotty-pillock stage. More your age than Jimbo. He's a chav. But he's nice. And he sticks up for you at work. And you need the practice in having a boyfriend. That's mean, to just use him to practice on. Say no. Give him back the locket and say no. But that's mean too, and he might cause problems at work. Go on. What harm can it do?

Tom seemed to assume that was a "yes" because he took the locket, stood, and fastened it round her neck, then kissed her full on the lips, not the inexpert snog one boy at school had given her (for a dare, she later and hurtfully found out), but a soft buss full on the lips, and a little flick of a suggestive tongue suddenly slipping between hers, just enough to surprise and arouse her.

"You look beautiful in that," he said. "You're worth it."

"Thanks. It's beautiful," said Kirsty for want of anything better to say. "Do you want another chocolate?"

"Ner, thanks. I thought we could go for a walk by the river."

"Cool."

They stood, and when they walked towards the river, Tom put his arm round Kirsty's shoulders, pulled her in close to him. She could feel his hip working against hers and seemed to fit snugly against him. When the going got a bit tricky, he held her by the hand. By the river, he stopped, pulled her to him, and kissed her again, his hands pulling on her buttocks so that she was crushed hard against him. There was something hard in his jeans which she was a little too shy to think about, because if she did, she was swamped with odd feelings.

"Have you ever had a boyfriend before?"

"No. Not really. All the boys at school were immature pratts and I never really fancied any of them. I prefer older…"

"But you fancy me, right…?"

"Um, Tom. I think I should say I don't want to get too involved too quickly. I'm not just a cheap fuck, you know."

"I know that…" said Tom. "Or you'd of had it off with Jimbo by now. I know he fancies you, but you don't give anyone the come-on. You're a nice girl."

93

A surge of relief flooded through Kirsty. Tom didn't expect her to drop her knickers to pay for the locket then. Though she wanted a boyfriend, she didn't want sex. Not yet. Not until she was ready. Despite what her loins were telling her.

"It's more exciting to take things slowly, anyway," said Tom.

~~~

Angie

I was in the supermarket shopping when I felt a gush of warm wetness between my legs. I'd been having Braxton Hicks contractions off and on but had been reassured it was just the body gearing up for labour. The baby's head wasn't engaged when I last saw the midwife, and he hadn't turned. I still had a week to go, and was just stocking up, last minute, in preparation.

I thought I'd wet myself and dashed for the public loos. But the trickle of liquid that continued to drain told me I was wrong. I stood in the cubicle, amniotic fluid pooling by my feet and burned with the heat of humiliation on my face. I heard the Tannoy ask for the store cleaner, and the heat worsened. The outer door swung open. "Angie, Angie, are you there?" said Sally Curtis.

I was going to say yes but groaned as a contraction hit me. Someone had pulled a rope tight round my abdomen and pulled it so tight it cut in like cheese wire. I grabbed the cubicle wall, swayed and gasped until it subsided. I unlocked the door and confronted Sally. She had an incontinence pad and some knickers obviously just grabbed off the shelf. "I'll sort this later," she said. "Put this on, and let's go..."

I binned my soaking knickers, did as she said, and allowed her to take me to her car. There was a gauntlet of curious people, but I didn't really care at the time. Another wave of pain. She stood and supported me. "Rock with it," she said. "Breathe."

I belted up, and she drove off, fast but competently, not like a maniac. "Are you timing those?" she asked, as another wave hit me.

"No." I said. A moment later I added. "I've left my trolley. And my car. What about an ambulance?"

"I'll sort it. I'll sort everything. Don't worry. Shit, not another one."

It was the first time I'd ever heard her swear.

"Mr Willis won't be impressed, you leaving your post like that."

"Stuff him. I was near the end of my shift anyway, and we have a new trainee supervisor. She'll have to manage. Baptism of fire."

Sally dropped me off at the main doors of the maternity unit and went to park the car. She caught up with me once I'd been admitted.

"You're not as far advanced as we first thought," said the midwife "You're dilated by about a centimetre. Plenty of time. You were booked in for an elective Caesarean, weren't you?"

I nodded, pain stealing my voice.

"Breathe," she said.

"I would if I had any lungs," I said.

"Are you her birth partner?" the midwife asked Sally Curtis.

Sally's mouth opened as if she could suck the answer in from the ether. She released her breath. "I wasn't planning on it, I'll stay for a bit, though."

They assigned me a bed, and I lay on top of it. But I couldn't settle. "I found it easier if I kept moving," said Sally. So we wandered round the ward, stopping at every contraction. She supported me, swaying against the agony. Then the midwife found me. The consultant wanted to see me. She swished the curtains around, banished Sally, examined me, and told me that a Caesar was probably the best option under the circumstances. I agreed. I had no wish to go through birth, all that pain, and possible complications just for an unwanted baby I was giving up for adoption.

Childbirth flipping hurts, let me tell you. And I wanted no more part in it.

I signed the consent to do the Caesarean, and consent to take some cord blood for genetic analysis, and a cheek swab from the baby, for the same, because that's what they usually used. The police, that is, when testing DNA from a suspect. I'd forgotten they wanted it, what with the pain and the desire to rid myself of the baby, but it was in my notes.

The medical staff clustered around me like termites round the gross, gravid queen, and took me to theatre.

Chapter 15

Angie

My stomach was like a deflated balloon, all wrinkles and puckers. There was a cut just below the bikini line where they'd pulled the alien out. I was healing well, apparently.

They'd offered me an epidural as it was safer than a general, and most women wanted some part in the actual labour, even if it was a surgical labour. Stuff that; I wanted no part in it, none at all. Take the fruit of rape away. Let me wake up whole and well. Curse the rapist, curse him to hell. I looked at my belly, wrinkled, cut, horrible, ugly. Curse him, curse him.

~~~

Breasts. Beautiful breasts. How I loved Kim's. Just the right size. Not like mine, now, when the milk came in. The midwives gave me something to reduce it, but I still swelled up with colostrum. It revolted me, almost the colour of pus. This hideous process was still happening to my body, even though the baby was gone. I hoped he'd be happy. I hoped when he was old enough, he would forgive me. I cried and cried, with pain and humiliation, until they moved me into a side room, on my own. I was upsetting the other mothers in their contentedness. Yes, they were sore, doddering on unsteady legs, breasts oozing, and looking stupidly bovine, but they were happy. I could see the competitiveness starting, the my-baby's-better-than-yours, the little victories over the gain of an ounce in weight, the smug superiority of the woman who'd had no pain relief.

And I hated my tears as much as I hated theirs. The post-natal blues. Two days in and we were all weeping. Some went home, smug men gloating over the sprogs. Like they'd been clever or something. And the clusters of doting friends and relatives. I turned my face to the wall and thought sour thoughts, glad to be alone, away from them.

Sally came with grapes. She listened as I told her a summary of my time, then gave me a hug. She flinched back, a thought slapping her. "That was a sisterly hug, by the way…"

"I can't understand why you've been so kind," I said. And I couldn't. Not really.

Her eyes fell onto the bedclothes, onto the milk-sopped nightie, then found the window. "I don't know…I hope this doesn't sound condescending, but… well, you've got nobody, and it just panned out that way. I brought you some clean knickers and a fresh nightie," she added, making me cry.

~~~

Sally took me home on Friday. The midwives seemed glad to be rid of me, saying how well I was doing, considering my age, and how much better people recovered at home. I just think they preferred it quiet at the weekend. I left empty handed, slithering out of the hospital, almost in shame. When the others left, they took with them the paraphernalia of parenthood. I took my dirty washing.

"Oh, damn," I said. "My car. It's at work."

"No, it isn't," Sally said. "I got a special insurance and drove it home for you. We didn't like to leave it in the car park overnight in case it got vandalised."

"But the keys…"

"With your house keys. Or don't you remember?" I sat in puzzled silence for about a minute before she added, "You know, Monday. I took your keys. You gave them to me. Don't you remember?"

"No."

Sally drove competently. The world slid by. "You won't be able to drive for a while. You will tell us if you need anything, won't you?" I choked on her kindness and started to cry. "Um," she hummed sympathetically. "Childbirth gets to you like that. Emotional, I mean. Look," she added seriously. "You might find you're a bit down, for a while. If you do, promise you'll get some help, won't you?" When I didn't answer, she said, "Won't you?"

"Thanks Ms Curtis. Sally, I mean."

We reached home, and she fished out my keys and handed them to me. "I won't stop, if you don't mind. John and I are going out tonight and I want a wallow. I'll bring your bag in, though. 'cos you've got to take care of your back and your tummy."

She took the bag into the kitchen and left it by the washing machine. I saw her to the front door, thanked her, then went back into the kitchen, put the kettle on, filled the machine with the dirty linen, and had made the cup of tea before I wondered where the milk had come from. There was a fresh loaf in the bread bin, some fruit, some cold meats and hard cheese in the fridge. And a vase of flowers in the sitting room with a card from the girls at work.

~~~

I suppose most new mothers have something to occupy themselves; learning to cope with baby. All I had was my thoughts and they didn't make very good company. After a few days fretting, I thought the least I could do was let Kim know. Now the baby was gone perhaps she'd come back. So I phoned Digby, holding the phone in a slippery grip.

"Hello," he said cheerfully.

"Hi Digby."

Frost. Reservation. That odd quirkiness I found so disturbing in him translated into silence. "Hello," he said eventually.

"I had the baby."

"Congratulations."

"I put it up for adoption."

"Probably for the best. Can't see you as a mother."

Why, why did I resent that observation so? I gripped the phone tighter. "Is Kim there?"

"She doesn't want to speak to you."

"She didn't know I'd phone. Why don't you ask her? The police believed me it was rape. Why don't you?"

"Was it?"

"Yes it was, I keep saying. And one day they might catch the bastard. They've taken the baby's DNA to test against their database, but I haven't heard back yet."

There was a silence.

"Just fetch her to the phone, Digby."

I heard a clunk, footsteps, mumbled words. Heart slamming against the rib cage. Kim.

"Don't do this to me, Angie. I told you it was over. I'm seeing somebody else."

"No. No, you can't. It's me you love."

"Not any more. Not since..."

"But that wasn't my fault. I was raped. Can't you understand?"

"Yeah, so you kept saying, on and on, like you thought the more you said it the truer it was. Well, I don't believe you. It doesn't make sense. How could you fall pregnant just like that at your age? Stands to reason. You let me down Angie, spoilt it all by going with men. You're bisexual and you lied to me. You lied from the very start."

"I didn't. I don't. I love you, please come back. We can make it all right."

"I don't think you ever loved me, really loved me for me. You fancied me, and you lied to me to get me into your bed. How do you think that makes me feel? Dirty. Used. Violated."

"What d'you mean? Of course I love you, I always have. We had so many happy times. You can't throw all that away."

"You lied to me from the start about not being bi, and now I feel dirty, dirty, thinking back to the times we made love when you were up the duff, when you'd been screwing men behind my back. It's disgusting. If you really loved me, you'd never of done that to me. It's all lies, Angie, lies."

"What? What? I don't understand. What are you talking about? What lies?"

Kim's voice turned gravely with tears. I heard her sobbing over the words. "You never loved me. I was just your, your, your fuck-buddy. I can see that now. I've got some new. Someone who really loves me, doesn't go with men the minute my back's turned. Someone who respects me and loves me for the person I am." The phone went dead.

Like my heart.

"She doesn't mean it, she's confused... she can't mean it about the lies," I said to myself. "She's been poisoned against me. She'd have come back if it wasn't for her mother, I know it. She did love me, she really did. But now..." I was rocking to and fro, hugging the pain like a lump in my midriff.

When the tears eventually came, they didn't stop for two days.

~~~

The only person I saw over the next few days was the midwife. That was OK. I didn't want to see anyone else. I didn't really want to see her but was reassured by her. I got better daily, saw Dr Thomas, who said I was doing very well. I'd warmed to him and didn't detest his moustache like I had before. He'd been sympathetic but business-like over the situation. He asked how I was coping mentally, leaving a big silence for me to fill with admissions of depression. But I felt OK, despite Kim abandoning me. Once I'd got used to not having her around, I knew I'd be fine. Or so I kept telling myself.

Chapter 16

Kirsty

Someone was coming along the footpath, so Kirsty pulled her hand out of Tom's pocket where she had been pleasuring him through the cloth. He pulled his hand from down the back of her jeans. They continued walking along like any other courting couple. The passer by barely glanced at them. Tom looked over his shoulder, said, "OK," and they resumed their activities.

On the weeks where their shift was 6.00am until 2.00pm, it was easy to meet up after work for chocolate and, weather permitting, other activity like petting. They didn't bother on the shift 2.00pm to 10.00pm, because Kirsty's mother expected her home soon afterwards. Kirsty knew her mother would want to know the whos and the whats if she said she wouldn't be home until much later in the evening, just as Saturday nights in the Blue Bore were the subject of close questioning. Her mother seemed to want reassuring that it was a group she was going out with, not just one boy. Often Kirsty was with her father and the bimbo slut his new wife and couldn't go out on the Saturday anyway.

Kirsty decided that the less she said about Tom, the better.

The other advantage of daylight was the whole world acted as chaperone. She could go so far, but no further.

~~~

"Like it?"

"Tom, you've got to stop buying me presents. I can't afford to do the same for you because my mum takes most of my money in rent."

"Nick some back."

"Don't be silly."

"My mum lets me keep all mine. And I want to spend it on you. Put it on, go on..."

Kirsty clipped the bracelet round her wrist. It suited her, and she liked it, but she was beginning to find Tom's lavishness with gifts a little awkward. She couldn't afford to reciprocate and didn't feel it was altogether appropriate to be given so much. There was also awkwardness at home. Her mother had noticed the locket and asked where she had got it from. "The market," Kirsty had lied, and refrained from wearing the other frequent gifts from Tom in front of her mother. Her father didn't notice, but the bimbo slut did, so Kirsty stopped wearing the jewellery except when going out with Tom.

"I have another present for you," said Tom as they were walking along the river arm in arm. He had his hand up her blouse and was tickling her back. "It's in my pocket. Put your hand in and find it." Kirsty slipped her hand, which had been resting on his hip, round a bit further into his pocket.

Then pulled it out fast. "You cut the end off your pocket," she said incredulously.

Tom grinned. "Yep. I know you don't want to go all the way yet, but heavy petting's OK. So, well, I... Go on; do it." His voice was husky. "This way, people won't see."

Kirsty slipped her hand back into his pocket. His penis was full, warm, silky to the touch, not quite as she'd been expecting. The feel of it sent a jolt of desire through her.

Half a mile later, Kirsty was wondering if it was worth losing her virginity to Tom. But what if she fell pregnant or caught something? And screwing out in the open seemed both uncomfortable and sleazy. Besides, Tom seemed happy enough to take things slowly.

"Up here," said Tom, pulling her along a different path from their usual. The path was oppressed with stinging nettles and overhanging branches, but after a couple of hundred yards they found themselves under the shade of five pine trees. The ground was thick with old pine needles, there were a number of logs scattered around, and even an old bench. A tarpaulin was draped across one of the lower branches and fastened to the ground to make a rather scruffy but effective tent. Inside were some more old plastic chairs and an old sunlounger.

A couple of lads were there already. "All right Tom," said one, a runty looking boy with spots. "Want some gear?"

"Yeah," said Tom, fishing out his wallet. "This is me girlfriend, Kirsty." He took out a fiver and passed it to the runt. "This is Glyn, and that's Toby," he said to Kirsty, carelessly. The runt passed Tom a package. Tom looked inside, smiled, then went over to a log and sat down. He took out some tobacco and papers, then carefully wrapped himself a cigarette, including some of the cannabis he had just bought.

Kirsty frowned and said, "I didn't know you were a smoker."

"I don't much," said Tom. "Not cigarettes, just a spliff or two a day, and not at home or Mum'd kill me. Want some?" he offered her the spliff. "You have this one. I'll do myself another."

"No thanks." Kirsty stared down at Tom as if he had just regressed to a twelve-year-old snotty boy. She sat down on the log next to him, trying to pluck up the courage to leave. There was a rustling of vegetation and two more people arrived. A boy and a girl, both in school uniform. They made their purchases of cannabis, and the boy brought out a bottle of cider.

"Who sold you that?" asked Glyn the runt.

"Nicked it," said the schoolboy, passing it round.

Kirsty declined. "I'm on my moped," she explained. The others laughed at her, which almost, almost made her accept a swig.

"Ellie, are you gonna give Andy one?" asked Toby.

"What, with you lot here? Fuck off."

"Tell you what," said Glyn, "Why don't you and Andy, Tom and his girl have a fucking competition. I'll give a prize for the best fuck." He held up a packet of cannabis.

"No way," said Kirsty with a laugh. She knew he was joking, but even so…. She grinned but she could feel the smile cracking. Get me out of here. Mum'd kill me if she knew, she thought

"Sod off," said Tom. "Kirsty's not like that."

"Aw," said Ellie, frowning. "I could do with some of that."

"Some of what?" teased Toby. "Some of Andy's cock or some of Glyn's skunk?"

"Both," said Ellie. She stuck her tongue out lasciviously, which Kirsty found very shocking, even though it was just a joke.

"OK, give us a blowjob and I'll give you this skunk," said Glyn.

"Hey," said Andy indignantly.

"Are you his girlfriend?" Glyn asked Ellie.

"No exactly," said Ellie. "He wants to be, but…"

"Give me a blowjob and let Andy fuck you and you'll get the skunk," said Glyn.

"No way." Ellie sat down and accepted the bottle of cider, took a long swig. Andy rolled up a spliff and shared it with Ellie.

"I gotta go," said Kirsty.

"Why, Babe? You a prude or something?" Tom's tone was contemptuous. He'd probably tell them all at work that she was a snob, a prude, frigid, a les.

Kirsty shook her head, said nothing, but made no move to go.

Ellie had a silly grin on her face as she smoked the spliff. Andy had his hand up the back of her blouse. Kirsty saw Glyn lick his lips as he took out the bag of skunk and waved it at her, wafting it before Ellie's eyes. She reached out to grab it, but Glyn whisked it away. "You want it, you know how to get it." He pointed to his groin. "Go on babe, you know you love it really. You're just playing hard to get."

"Two packets, then, and I'll do it, but I won't swallow."

Glyn looked round with a knowing grin. "She's hot," he said.

Kirsty stood up. "I've got to go, see ya," she muttered, barging back through the stingers, tears surprising her. She glanced back. Tom had started after her but kept looking back as if he couldn't make up his mind. Ellie and Glyn and the others formed a tableau that looked just like the scenes from the porn sites Kirsty stumbled across on the internet. Ellie seemed to be enjoying herself, seemed to know what she was doing. Tom still had his back to her as if he was enjoying the spectacle. Kirsty turned away walked away, fists clenching, stomach churning. She heard Glyn give a yelp.

Kirsty continued away from them, snivelling slightly. She heard footsteps running behind her. Tom. "She's a right shagbag, Ellie."

"That was disgusting. I can't believe you took me there. I can't believe she did that. It's like she prostituted herself for a handful of cannabis."

~~~

A couple of days later, Kirsty was stirring her hot chocolate moodily. Tom was in one of his hungry phases and was munching his way through an All-Day Breakfast. He seemed to eat with an economy of movement which Kirsty found both fascinating and repellent. It was as if he had to eat within a certain time limit or lose his meal. There was no placing his knife and fork down to pause for a moment and make conversation. It was all slice, spear, mouth, chew, and whilst he was swallowing, the next slice was being cut and moved towards his mouth. He carefully manoeuvred the half tomato to the edge of the plate.

"Don't you eat any vegetables?" Kirsty asked. "I've never seen you eat anything except baked beans."

"They're a vegetable," said Tom. "And I eat tomato ketchup. That's a vegetable too. It says so on the bottle."

"They don't count."

"They do."

Kirsty looked out of the window. It had started to rain. "I don't fancy a walk in this," she said.

"It'll be dry under the pines."

"I'm not going there again. That tart might be there."

"Ellie? Yeah," said Tom with a look that Kirsty didn't altogether like. "She's good for a laugh, Ellie is."

"More than just a laugh," said Kirsty acidly.

"You could have what she was getting any time, babe. Just ask." Tom opened his lips and flickered his tongue.

"Sod off. And Ellie's just a slag. I bet she'd part her legs for anyone."

"Noooo," said Tom. "She wouldn't for Jimbo. Mind you. She was younger then." Kirsty frowned, so Tom continued. "She did her work experience at the pizza factory a while back. Jimbo had the hots for her, but she was well underage then. Mind you, she's still under age now, but boy..." He ground to a halt.

"I'm not going there. It's disgusting. And there are used condoms everywhere. Ugh."

"You wanna go bareback, then?"

"What?"

"Oh, forget it."

A couple of minute's disgruntled silence later, Tom said, "Look, promise you won't look down on me or nothing. But if you like, we could go back to my place. Have a drink. I'll show you my Xbox. Only, our house isn't very posh, and Mum works long hours down the old folk's home and she's knackered when she gets back. But I s'pose your mum's knackered from the hospital."

"Eh?"

"Being a nurse 'n all."

"Oh... yes."

"It would be nicer than biking home in this. I wouldn't touch you, honest. And you can meet my Mum."

"OK then."

Chapter 17

Kirsty

Tom took her to the humble little street where he lived with his mother. The houses were terraced, many were shabby, but basically, they were sound enough homes. Tom lived on the end of one of the roads into the old estate. A ruinous old industrial unit overshadowed the area. Tom's front garden was filled with three dustbins and an old mattress. He took her to the front door, which opened went straight into the living room. "Hi Mum," he called. There was no reply. "She's out," he said unnecessarily. "Sit down and I'll get a drink."

"Not alcohol," said Kirsty. "I've got to ride home, remember and I don't drink anything if I have to do that."

"I know, I know. Bitter lemon?"

"Yeah, thanks."

Tom disappeared into the kitchen and Kirsty was left alone in the living room. The dining table was groaning with a huge basket of ironing. The ironing board was abandoned with a blouse half ironed on it. The flat screen TV dominated the lounge area, and the sofa she was sitting on had seen better days a long, long time ago. There was a tacky painting of a lion and cubs on the wall. And no books. There were a couple of magazines, though, with real life stories, and a TV guide.

Tom came back in with a beer and her bitter lemon. "Cheers," he said, passing the glass to her.

She took a sip. "That's really nice," she said.

Tom put on some music, tossed back his lager. "Another?"

"Let me enjoy this one first," said Kirsty, taking a long swig. It was the best bitter lemon she'd ever tasted. She passed Tom the empty glass. "I need to use your loo."

"Through that door," said Tom. "There's some cake. I'll get that out."

Kirsty went through the door indicated. It was to a staircase on one side and the loo on the other. The plumbing was stained and very old. She'd thought her own home scruffy; this was very shabby, though clean enough. There was what looked like a spliff on the windowsill. So much for not smoking at home or his mother would kill him.

She went back into the lounge and flopped down on the sofa.

"It's still pissing down outside," said Tom. "Here." He passed her another bitter lemon and a slab of fruit cake. He lit a spliff and smoked it, offering it to her.

"No thanks," she said. "It's illegal."

"Ner, it's legal now."

"No, it isn't."

"It's as good as… go on, have some." He blew a breath of smoke in her face.

"Don't or I'll leave right now."

"Moody." Tom finished the spliff, then he got out his Xbox. Soon they were playing and laughing, and the minutes slid by easily, as did the lager and the bitter lemon. Then Tom slid his hands into her blouse and undid her bra. He undid the buttons at the front, fumbling slightly, then removed it and the bra. He stroked and suckled at her breasts and she did nothing to stop him. "Touch me," he said, taking her hand and guiding it into his trousers. It was awkward, and she took her hand out. "Go on," he urged. Then he stood, undid his belt and

111

top button, unzipped his jeans. His penis flopped out. "Do it," he said. Kirsty tentatively took it. "Touch it. Suck it. Go on."

She rubbed gently, unwilling to put her mouth over it, the vision of sleazy oversexed Ellie putting her off, but she was willing to do more than she thought she would have earlier that day.

"Let's go all the way," said Tom.

"OK, but what about your Mum?"

"She's at work, and won't be back for hours," he said. "I've got some condoms upstairs." He tugged his jeans back up, did up the button, and walked awkwardly to the door to the stairs.

He seemed to be taking a while, so Kirsty thought she'd have a glass of water. She was tired of bitter lemon, and it sat acidly in her guts. She picked up the empty glass and empty lager can and went into the kitchen.

The kitchen was a mess, a pile of breakfast things in the sink. The fridge was grumbling to itself, and there was washing in the washing machine. Kirsty was surprised how tired she was. The recycling bin was stood in the corner. It looked unsavoury with a bird dropping smeared on the outside. Inside were four empty alcopop bottles and three empty lager cans. She picked up an alcopop bottle. It was bitter lemon based, and as strong as a lager.

"Do you want another, babe?" asked Tom. He was wearing nothing but a condom.

"This is alcohol." Kirsty's anger drowned the shock she felt at seeing a man naked.

"Ner. Not much anyway."

"You stupid idiot. It's enough to put me over the limit. How can I get home now? Mum'll kill me." Another thought penetrated Kirsty's brain. "And you said your Mum would be here and I could meet her, when you knew full well she'd be at work. You lying little scrote." She dashed the water in his face, pushed past him, grabbed her blouse and her jacket, and fled the house. Night had fallen and she hadn't noticed, but it was still raining, sheets of cold wetness which soaked her instantly. She struggled into her blouse, snagging her arms on the wet cloth, gave up trying to put it on properly, and just put her jacket on over the top. It was cold and she started to shiver. She looked back. Tom was standing in the doorway of his house, utterly naked except for the condom. "You stupid tosser," she yelled. "I never want to see you again." Tom stepped out of the house, and she whimpered, got ready to run.

He yelled, "You fucking prick-tease lesbian," then turned and stormed inside, slamming the door.

Kirsty strode through the slick streets, not feeling very drunk, but knowing that she probably was over the limit. She was sobbing and shivering. The Snack-a-Randy was still open, glass streaming with condensation. She slipped inside and turned her phone on. There were eleven missed calls. Mum. She dialled home.

"Kirsty, oh Thank God. I was doing my nut."

"Sorry, Mum, I've been a bit stupid. I went for a drink with the works, and I asked for soft drinks, but they bought me alcopops instead. I'm over the limit, I expect. Can you come and fetch me, please? I'm in a café called the Snack-A-Randy near the pizza factory."

"I know it," said her mother. "I'll be over soon as. Don't move from there. It's a dodgy area."

"OK. Thanks Mum." Kirsty hung up, looked round. Several people were looking at her, one or two very curiously. Especially a scruffy bloke who looked in need of a hose down

113

with disinfectant. She stepped outside into the rain, and remembered her badly buttoned blouse, She spent five minutes sorting it out, and hoped her mother wouldn't ask too many questions.

The rough looking man came out, and came over, a miasma of foul odour clinging to him. "Got a light, luv?"

"Piss off," she said. "My mum's a copper and she'll be here any minute.

The scruffy man stepped back and walked off hurriedly. Kirsty moved back to the café doorway and sheltered from the rain. A couple of cars went past, one slowing right down, the occupant eyeing her up. She looked away. He speeded up and drove off.

Then she recognised her mother's car splashing through the puddles. Her mother indicated, stopped, and Kirsty jumped in, yanking the seatbelt over.

"You stupid girl, whatever possessed you," began her mother. Kirsty just burst into tears. A couple of minutes later Kirsty asked if she could put the heating up as she was cold. The warm air blasted into the car but did nothing to thaw her mother's frost.

"Where's your moped?" asked her mum suddenly.

Kirsty's stomach lurched. At Tom's. Shit. "It's at a girlfriends'. I'll take the bus in tomorrow."

"You'll be lucky, that time of the morning. I'll have to take you in, you utter idiot."

Kirsty hoped the moped was safe. Tom wouldn't take his anger out on it, would he?

When they got home, her mother said in a kinder voice, "You don't seem too drunk... go and have a nice hot bath, we'll talk about this another time. But don't lock the door."

Kirsty went upstairs, peeled her wet clothes off, whilst the bath was running, then sunk into it, washing herself. The effects of the alcohol had worn off, and she found herself picking over what she had done. She had nearly given her virginity to a dope-smoking ignorant scrote.

~~~

Next day her mother dropped her off at work. A minute later Tom wheeled her moped into the car park. He parked it and walked past her, avoiding her eyes. He didn't say a word.

Chapter 18

Angie

Six weeks after the birth, I had to see the consultant to check I was mending after the Caesarean. I wasn't sure if I was allowed to drive, though I felt fine, so I asked for transport. Gawd, the fuss they made, but they did send someone. The ambulance wasn't an ambulance, it was a volunteer and his car. A retired chap, he was reminiscent of my father; in mannerisms rather than looks. I hadn't seen Dad for years, not since I'd stormed off as a teenager. Then I had a shocking thought; my Dad must be this chap's age. It was well-nigh 30 years since I'd seen Dad. He'd be in his early seventies. Like this chap. For a wild moment I wondered if this man was my father.

"Thanks Mr Er…" I said as I struggled from the car.

"Mr Jenkins," he supplied, which both comforted and saddened me. I'd like it to have been my Dad, thrown up randomly at me, after all these years.

~~~

Kirsty

"Muuum! There's a documentary you might want to watch," Kirsty yelled. Her mother had gone up to her bedroom for a lie down and a read.

"What's it about?" shouted her mum from the bedroom.

"Date rape drugs. And how people aren't taking them seriously enough. I'll make us a coffee."

Her mother appeared downstairs, swathed in her dressing gown after a long bath. "Can't say I really want to watch it, Kirsty. Get enough of that at work."

Kirsty bit back a feeling of disappointment. Of course her mother didn't want to watch it; she wanted to escape that sort of thing once she left the nick. And neither did the programme appeal to herself particularly. So why had she yelled for her mum? Kirsty picked over the possible reasons. Was it to please her mother? Show her that she was a responsible and thoughtful daughter? Or was she hoping that her mum would let something slip about Jord? Had they caught the rapist yet? The memory of Jord's reaction made her frown.

Her mother responded to the frown. "Thanks, sw… er love, I will watch it. Useful to know what they've said."

When the programme finished, her mother said, "See why I get so frantic at the thought of you not taking care of your drinks? See why I worry when you go out? Every time you go out with that crowd from work, I worry. Ten minutes after you're supposed to be home, and I'm getting frantic, wondering if some filthy little sod has drugged you, or if you've been stupid enough to get so drunk you don't know what you're doing. You realise that alcohol is by far the most common drug used in drug-assisted rapes? That's why I freak out if your phone's turned off. Eleven times I tried to call you that time you were tiddly. And your stupid phone was off." Her mother didn't seem angry so much as anxious.

"It happened to Jord and her sister Trish, didn't it?"

"What? Who told you…? I can't talk about…"

"Why not? She did. Thank God she didn't twig you're my mum. (I told them you're a nurse.) And when I told her that she shouldn't be telling us, and that she was stupid to have got herself into trouble like that, she was really horrible to me.

117

And she's been nasty and sly about me ever since. Says I'm a les behind my back."

"You told them I'm a nurse? Why?"

"Because they don't like coppers. A lot of them smoke skunk. If they thought I was a copper's daughter, they wouldn't invite me out with them. Like when I was at school." A few old memories turned over in their sleep, making Kirsty blink.

"Oh, Sweetie, you'd better tell me about it." Her mother's eyes were big with concern, and Kirsty warmed under a rush of gratitude. She recounted the incident in the canteen.

Her mother sat very still for a few minutes. "This must go no further. Is that clear? I could get into serious trouble for discussing this with you. Serious trouble. Like lose my job and go to prison type trouble. So do I have your word?"

"Course."

"Even if you're very angry. Provoked. You must say nothing. And not let things slip by accident? Do you understand?"

"Um."

"Jordan sounds like a right little idiot. She led her sister into trouble, and it could have ended in tragedy. Suppose they'd fallen pregnant? Or got HIV? Or died? You saw from the program that sometimes these drugs are fatal. And you were right; she had no right to tell the girls at work about her sister. That's appalling. But she's still a victim, Kirsty. And we'll never know exactly what happened to them, just that something did. Probably. The perpetrator's impossible to find if we don't have any forensic evidence. As you told that silly little girl. If they'd come to us straight away we might have stood a chance."

~~~

Suzy

A couple of days later, Suzy was sitting staring at the computer screen. Her tea was so cold that there was a brown scum on the surface.

"You won't get the answer just by staring at the blank computer screen, you know." Cheungy sat down next to Suzy.

"Why not? They do on the TV. By a wild leap of serendipitous logic, the villain jumps out of the screen in a blinding flash of inspiration. On the sketchiest information I should be able to tell who he is and what he likes for breakfast. Profilers can do magic." Suzy could hear the bitter sarcasm in her tone. If anything, it worsened her mood.

"Who who is?"

"The bogeyman… After that TV programme a couple of nights back we've had eight people phoning up and saying they think something's happened to them, including one young lad, Stuart Bracknell, who works at the pizza factory—I bet Kirsty knows him. Only they're not sure. And that's just the ones who've rung. There are probably others. I've plotted these new ones geographically, and look…" Suzy brought up a map on the screen. It had various colours, getting warmer until two areas were highlighted in red. "OK, it's very sketchy, but there seem to be clusters. One in Galchester, and one in Elversford. The shabbier housing estates."

"That could be a reflection of some of the people living there. Prostitutes and junkies, people who are likely to not take enough care, for one reason or another. It would be naïve to think this shows we've got just two perpetrators working in their comfort zone."

"Well, maybe, but there are no reports from Woodham Parkway at all, and they have a deprived area with more than its fair share of problems, including a lot of drugs." Suzy brought up some more images. "I've been having a rummage round the old reports. Not just rapes, or presumed rapes, but other sexual offences as well. We've had a number of reports of a flasher, or indecent acts and a few indecent assaults over several years. I've mapped those. If I include all of them, I get more specific foci. The Blue Bore in Elversford. The Craven Arms in Galchester; yes thought that might ring a bell. And in the streets near the old industrial estate in Elversford, near that derelict building. And someone has recently been flashing near the school again. I wonder if that's Raphael Smith, now he's out of prison. He's incorrigible and ought to be locked up forever, or preferably put down. Ugh. He's on the sex offenders' register and he's supposed to tell us if he changes address, but he's disappeared.

"Also, look where the two pubs are in relation to the two shabby estates..." Suzy pointed the pubs out on the map, sliding to one side to let her boss have a look.

"Close enough. And there's the reports from several girls at Elversford Secondary School," Cheungy frowned, looking pensive.

Lynne Alderton added, "There's another connection between several of the girls; the Pizza factory." She too stared at the screen as if hoping for a TV miracle.

"Including Jordan, who works there, and her sister, still at school. And the boy, Stuart. Is that where your Kirsty's working?" asked Cheungy. "Does that worry you? It would me."

Suzy's heart skipped. "I think she's too sensible. But she goes out with the crowd some Saturdays. I don't like it, but she's eighteen now. I have to rely on her common sense. Bugger it."

"It's all too woolly at the moment. These attacks may be unconnected, each by a separate perpetrator, or there may be several predators, responsible for one or more offences..." Lynne said.

"Or one predator, with a connection with all these places." Suzy twiddled with the mouse, frowning, mind escaping to her daughter, working in one of the hotspots, and still naïve and not that streetwise. How could she not have realised the drink was alcopop, not just bitter lemon? Idiot girl. Still, at least she hadn't lost her licence over it, and perhaps it would make her more careful in future.

"Oh, incidentally, anything back on Angela Bain's baby's DNA?" asked Cheungy.

"We've got the results back, but nothing in the DNA database matches," said Suzy.

"So her rapist isn't anyone we've nicked recently then... Pity. I'd like to nail the bastard that did that to her." Cheungy scanned over the new drug-rape reports. "Interesting; this woman thought something was amiss when she found a used condom in her toilet. So why the hell didn't the silly woman contact us sooner? This could explain why there haven't been more unexpected pregnancies like Angie's. Either there is more than one predator, or the rapist has twigged for some reason that leaving sperm might give us more to go on."

"Well, seems a bit silly just chucking the evidence in the loo where it can be found, then. Or maybe it just didn't flush away properly," said Lynne.

"By the way, Clifford (call me Gaz) Hanger has skipped bail. He was due in court for his trial this morning." Cheungy grinned a nasty smile. "I've sent some feet round to invite him to explain his absence. And, naturally enough, make sure he's got no chance of skipping bail again. I'm not having pervs like him on the loose if he's given us an excuse to remand him in custody... Providing the Magistrates don't listen to some glib-tongued defence solicitor and let him out on bail again."

"I bet they will," said Suzy. "You know what they're like nowadays, sod the victim's rights."

"His DNA doesn't match some of Angie's baby's, does it? He's not Angie's baby's dad?" said Lynne.

"No. He's not guilty of that, at least," said Suzy. "So I suppose that shows there's more than one predator. I'd like to have a rummage through some of the old evidence, now we've better DNA techniques. See if he's implicated in some unsolved sexual assaults from years ago."

"Good idea," said Cheungy, "but it takes time and it's expensive. Have a look and see if there are any likely ones first. Ask at the Craven Arms if Cliff Hanger ever worked there. Hopefully that TV programme will make people come forward when they've still got some evidence on them."

The phone went. Cheungy answered it, took some details. After she'd finished the call, she turned to Lynne. "Job for you..." and briefed her.

Once Lynne had gone, Cheungy looked again at the maps. She shook her head sadly. "It's too woolly. Not even sure if real assaults have taken place with some of these reports, though put all the data together and it's interesting how we get a focus on that awful old building, and the pizza factory and those two pubs. I think I might suggest to Elversford that they step up patrols in that area, and stop-and-search anyone but anyone looking sus."

Chapter 19

Kirsty

"I'd rather you didn't go out tonight, Sweetie."

Kirsty stopped mid-stairs and decided on all-out attack. "You still can't stop calling me Sweetie, can you? Like I'm five. Well I'm not. I'm eighteen, and I can do what I want."

"Not while you're under my roof, you can't. My roof, my rules. I don't want you going out tonight. Not with those people, not to that pub."

"What? What is it with you? You take most of my pay from me in rent, and now you won't even let me go and spend what pissing little you leave me."

"You idiot girl, that's exactly why I take your money from you. You're supposed to be saving it for university, not spending it down the pub with your low-life friends."

"They're not low-lives. How dare you. Jord comes from a good background, and Aunty Janet's really nice."

"Aunty Janet?"

"See how little attention you pay to me. I've told you about her before. You're so damned taken up with your fucking police work, you don't give a flying fuck about me."

"Don't you use that language on me."

"Why not? You do on me."

"I don't. Well, only when you drive me so hard it's either swear at you or hit you, and I'd rather swear."

"Same here. You try to run my life and treat me like a six-year-old."

"That's because there are times when you act like one. What's got into you? Can't you see I'm worried about you, especially after that little escapade the other day when I had

123

to come and rescue you. That pub's got a bad reputation. It's where the new barman spiked a girl's drink." Kirsty saw her mother flinch, clamp a hand over her mouth. "Shit. You mustn't repeat that, because we couldn't prove it was him, and he left, so he's not there now. Don't repeat that. And there's a link between the pub and other assaults. We think. And there's a link to the pizza factory. We think. But we don't know. Not for sure. And I shouldn't be telling you this, I could get into serious trouble, but I don't know how else to get into your thick skull."

Kirsty watched her mother's fury subside into despair, voice dropping with every revelation. She was shocked at the glint of tears glinting in her mother's eyes, just like the time when Mum come home from speaking to Jord and her sister.

Kirsty retreated into the living room, neutral territory. She flopped into the sofa. Her mother followed her.

"I want to go out. Please, Mum. I know Jord's a bit of a chav. And so's Tom, for that matter. But Janet's OK, she looks after us. And Jimbo's great. He takes care of us too."

"Who's Jimbo?"

"Muuum! I told you before. He's the line supervisor. He looks after us when we're at the pub. He's very nice."

"And Janet?"

"She's old. Like you..."

"Thanks."

"She's Stuart's aunt."

"Stuart?"

"Stuart Bracknell. He's one of the boys on the line. Don't worry, mum. I don't fancy any of them..."

Kirsty watched as her mother went to the drawer and pulled out a building society book. Without saying anything, she passed the book to Kirsty. Inside were substantial monthly payments. The rent she paid to her mother. The name inside the book was Kirsty's own. It was a savings account she had had for years but forgotten about.

"Sometimes," said her mother, "Sometimes what you say really hurts."

"Sorry Mum." The book shook in Kirsty's fingers, and she found herself regretting the cruel remarks. She handed the passbook back. "Better take it back. Look after it for me. Thanks, Mum. But what d'you mean about the pub and the factory?"

"I shouldn't have told you that."

"But you did, so you'd better tell me what you meant by it."

Her mother sat down next to her, throwing a comforting arm round her. "Not much to tell, really. We've just had rather a lot of sex attacks reported recently, like after that programme. And Jord and her sister before that. And one or two other things. Like the girl allegedly poisoned by the ex-bartender in the Blue Bore. And we don't know if it's lots of people using date rape drugs or just one or two people. But these attacks have happened in clusters, or there are connections. The Blue Bore is one connection. The pizza factory is another. A pub in Galchester is another. But it's all anecdotal evidence. Nothing firm. So there's nothing we can do. And that worries me, because the attacks'll keep happening. But what worries me most is you going into the danger zone for a night out with your mates. The pizza factory is near a very shabby part of Elversford. Not exactly Red Light District, but I wouldn't want to walk there after dark. Not past that horrid old derelict building."

"But Mum, I'm careful. Especially after all you've told me. Especially after... the other night. And I'm with people. And because I'm on my moped I don't drink and I'll buy my own drinks from now on to make sure it's not laced with anything or an alcopop. So I won't get pissed and I won't get spiked. But now you mention it, I'll keep my eyes peeled for things in the pub. Or in the factory."

"Don't you go getting involved. It's dangerous. And you might ruin things if we decide to do a surveillance. OK, go out, but please, please be careful."

~~~

It must have been around midnight when Kirsty quietly inserted her key in the front door lock. She turned it carefully and swung the door open. The hall and landing lights were on, but the living room and kitchen lights were off, which meant her mother was in bed. Kirsty shut the front door carefully and tiptoed up the stairs. She couldn't avoid making a noise in the bathroom. When she came out, her mother was on the landing, swathed in her dressing gown.

"Nice time?" she enquired.

Kirsty burst into tears.

"What's wrong… you didn't get drunk and get nicked or anything?" Her mother's voice was full of concern, but with an underlay of accusation.

Kirsty shook her head at her mother, her mouth working silently.

"Something happened?"

Kirsty nodded.

"What?"

Kirsty shook her head, the words jumbled in her brain like jackstraws.

"Someone hurt you?"

Kirsty felt her head shaking again, still no words.

"What then?"

Eventually she squeezed out, "Sorry, Mummy, I just can't talk about it. It wasn't me. Nothing to do with me."

Kirsty saw her mother's temper slipping, then, miraculously, a calmer face took over. "All right, Sweetie. Maybe another time." Her mother enveloped her in a strong, safe hug, then turned and retreated into her bedroom.

Chapter 20

Angie

I went back to work a week after I saw the consultant. I was fine at first, pleased to be out of the house, but I found things harder than I'd anticipated. After a few days of finding myself in tears for no good reason, Sally Curtis said I should see my doctor, and sent me home.

Post-natal depression. I'd been warned about it. But I felt OK most of the time. It was just little things that got to me. I was tired, that's all. And upset about the rape. That was all. I wasn't depressed. And I certainly didn't want any of those nasty antidepressants. Taking those was like admitting a weakness.

I phoned the Doctors' anyway. It rang. It wasn't engaged; no excuse to hang up. I nearly gave up, but it was answered. "I'd like to book an appointment to see Dr Thomas, please," I said quickly, before the words died in my mouth.

There was an awkward silence. "I'm sorry, that's not possible."

"Oh, I..."

There was a sound like a stifled sob. "Who are you, please?" It sounded like Deirdre, one of the receptionists. I'd got to know them quite well with my antenatal visits.

"It's Angie Bain here. Is that Deirdre? What's wrong?"

"Dr Thomas died yesterday, suddenly." Deirdre said it rapidly, as if it made it bearable. A bucket of snow fell on my head and trickled down my back.

"Oh." What an inadequate word.

"Would you like to see somebody else?" asked Deirdre, professionalism rescuing her.

"Look. I'll phone back another day. It's not urgent, at least not that urgent. I, I need to think about this. Bye." I squeezed the last word out as a gasp. The phone seemed to tingle with the news as I set it back in its cradle.

Dr Thomas. Dead? How? Why? How could he die? He was a doctor. Doctors don't die. They self-diagnose and make themselves better. They don't get ill. They don't drop dead. I'd built up a relationship with him during my pregnancy. He knew how bloody awful it was. And now he was gone.

The poor sod hadn't even retired. All that dedicated slog and no reward.

I cried myself to sleep, though I wasn't sure for whom, and phoned in sick the next day because the quilt was too heavy to lift.

Strange how you can lie in bed and watch your thoughts drifting by like clouds. You can see them, but you can't touch them. They waft slowly past as you gaze at them, noting the contours, the fluffiness, until they disappear from view, and you turn your eyes on the next thought. And you can do this without any emotion, as if your passion has hit neutral, and the engine is idling. Idle. Idle hands, idle thoughts, idle eyes. The far-off sounds of traffic, the school children, the starlings squabbling in the garden, are all just images, concepts hitching a lift on the clouds. Your body has no meaning, a vacuum lies between you and the world, as if you're dead, the bed your coffin, and life moving on around you, away from you. You wonder if you should jump up and run after the world before it drifts away from you forever, but the bed is so safe, so secure, and there is no need to leave it.

~~~

I went to work the next day. I didn't bother the doctors. I thought they'd have more than enough to do now their number was depleted. Sally Curtis asked if I'd gone to the doctor's, so I told her what had happened, but that I would go as soon as it seemed decent. She said nothing, though her eyes spoke. The word they said was 'Concern.'

~~~

I struggled for a fortnight. Then something happened. A phone call. DC Rolfe. Mrs Neutral. "Can I come and see you?" she asked.

She stood on the doorstep, framed by the evening November sun. It was still warm, though people were promising a cold winter. She looked tired, but excited. She wasn't alone. "This is DC Lynne Alderton," she said, indicating a dainty and rather delicious looking woman beside her. Alderton smiled. I invited them in, and they sat on the settee, not very comfortably, prim, not relaxed. I took the armchair. "How are you keeping?" Rolfe asked. How full an answer did she want?

"OK," I said. "I had a Caesarean and it took a while to get over that. I had the baby adopted, but I expect you know that. And the first HIV test came back negative, if you're interested." My thoughts ran aground.

"Angie, are you OK?" Rolfe's eyes sought mine. They're the loveliest shade of emerald I've ever seen.

"Yes, yes sorry. I was just thinking back, that's all."

"Look. Can I just double-check a few details about the alleged rape? Have you remembered anything else?"

"OK," I said. Alleged?

I told her what had happened to me. The same story. How I hadn't a clue I was pregnant until Dr Thomas told me. And

130

how the blank-out Friday fitted with the due dates, so it must have been then, because I was sure as damn-it sure it hadn't happened any other time.

"Now look, Angie, we are one hundred percent behind you on this. Can I ask, are you prepared to go to Court over this? Bear witness that you did not consent to sex with the father of your child?" she asked.

"You got him? You found him?" My head spun with a surge of blood.

"We've got a match, a DNA match from someone we arrested a couple of weeks back, on a separate matter."

"What?"

"I can't tell you. We haven't arrested this man for this yet, because we have to be absolutely sure that you did not consent to sex with this man. If you consented, there's nothing we can do."

"I didn't consent. I'd never consent. He's a man!"

"Are you prepared to face this man in Court and swear that you did not consent to sex with him?" Her emerald eyes stripped me to my soul. Beautiful, startling. Compelling.

"Of course I will. He deserves prison for what he did to me. Oh, well done for catching him."

"Are you sure? The defence barristers will try to show you consented. The whole thing can be pretty daunting. You must be prepared for that. We will support you every step of the way, but you need to know that it's not easy."

"He can't say I led him on or anything, because I never would, so yes, of course I'll go to court. We have to stand up for what's right."

"You also have to bear in mind the possibility he might be acquitted."

131

"But he did it. I'd never consent to sex with him; I'm a lesbian. If you've got a DNA match, I can't see how he can possibly wriggle out of it."

Chapter 21

Angie

The police were back the next day, showed me a photograph of the man whose DNA matched part of the baby's and asked if I knew him.

Digby.

After I'd been sick, hideously sick, I staggered back into the living room, mouth tasting of acid and minty from a rapid brushing with toothpaste.

Digby.

"Do you know him?" asked Rolfe, again.

"He's my ex-lover's brother." My brain seemed impervious to the news. It kept bouncing off my understanding. Digby?

"Ex?"

"Her name's Kim Jamieson; you know, you spoke to her when I first reported this. I'd been steady with her for five years. Thought we were set for life, but she walked out shortly after I found out I was pregnant." The room was stifling, and the carpet was made of marshmallow.

"I have to ask you, did you ever lead Digby on? Flirt with him. Not intentionally perhaps?"

"Yeaugh, no. I didn't, I wouldn't. Quite apart from the fact that he's a man, there's something...odd...about him. He actually gives me the creeps a bit. And he doesn't like me, but I put up with him for Kim's sake. The bastard. I'll kill him. How could he? It's like he betrayed both Kim and me. Are you sure it was him?"

"We're sure. It's unequivocal. He is the father of your baby."

I know now why they call it a stiff upper lip. I could feel a spasm in mine, a bit of whalebone keeping me from screaming. I waited until they'd gone, heard the car drive away. Then I flung myself onto the bed.

Later, in that washed-out calm, the aftermath, I changed the sheets, throwing the torn sheet away, and the quilt cover. The quilt itself still smelled faintly of vomit. I didn't bother putting a new cover on it, as I would buy a new quilt in the morning. The bath was so hot it left me swooning, I didn't even look at that empty baby-bag of a stomach, pitted with stretch marks that would never disappear. I just went to bed, swaddled in towels.

~~~

Suzy

Suzy did her seatbelt up. "Well, I thought that pretty convincing, didn't you?"

Lynne Alderton nodded. "Came as one helluva shock to her. She obviously didn't consent. I think we've got him. I really can't see how he can wriggle out of it even though we've no forensic evidence supporting the actual assault."

"I'm glad she's sure about going to court. All too often these rapists get away with it because of the anguish. Mind you, it should be better nowadays since there are strict rules about the trial. I hope she's going to be OK. She doesn't seem to be accessing any help, but maybe she doesn't need it."

"Or feels she doesn't need it." Lynne moved the car off. Her attention focussed on the traffic. "It's been a busy day."

"Um," agreed Suzy, fishing her mobile out. She phoned Cheungy. "Angie was so shocked she was sick, physically sick. But she's confirmed that there was no consent and she'll testify in court. Can we deal with him tomorrow Ma'am. Only if we nick him tonight...we're both knackered."

"You don't think Angie will spill the beans or do anything stupid do you?"

"Shouldn't think so."

"OK, I'll sort it."

Suzy hung up. "Thank gawd for that..."

"Amen. I'm knackered. How's Kirsty? You said she's been in a funny mood lately...?"

"Um. She went out Saturday couple of weeks back and came back really upset and couldn't tell me why. I felt myself getting so angry with her but managed not to lose my rag; weird how I can cope with rape victims who are unable to say what happened, but when it's my own daughter... anyway, I said to tell me when she could... but she never did. That must have been the same night Digby Jamieson was arrested. Shit. Jimbo? Jamieson? I wonder... Where does Digby work?"

"I don't know offhand. It was Elversford who nicked him; Bully Brooks, I think. Why the sudden alarm?"

"D'you know, Lynne, there are times when I feel bloody stupid. Kirsty's been talking about a 'Jimbo' off and on these last few months, and I never twigged that Digby Jamieson might be him. If they are one and the same, that connects one drug assisted rape and the pizza factory, where another suspect drug assisted rapes victim works; Jordan Dale."

"And another; Stuart Bracknell. I think you should have a chat to Brooks, get the low-down on this man. Sounds a right minger."

"That minger could be my daughter's boss. And the way she goes on about him, well, it's a bit like a teenage crush. Dear God, no, please. She seemed devastated that Saturday. I hope she hasn't...."

135

Chapter 22

Angie

They're very quiet, the couple in the maisonette above. They work long hours and I hardly see them. They never use their half of the garden, except as a dumping ground for the bin bags prior to putting them out on a Wednesday. Today, though, it sounded like they had a horse up there. I hid under the pillows. I'd not slept, so thought I'd try to catch up, but the galloping penetrated the pillows. I got the broom to whack on the ceiling. I'd never done it before. I aimed, and the phone went. The broom clattered to the floor, and I slipped as I grabbed at the phone, cursing the dressing table's bruising edge. "Yes?"

"Angie, it's Ms Curtis. Are you coming to work today? It's just that we're a bit short staffed, it being Saturday 'n all." She was Ms Curtis at work, Sally when she was running around for me.

"Drat! I... I..." I stuffed a sob back down my throat.

"Angie, are you OK?" Her tone was warmer, now, concerned.

"I'm not well, no. They've found the rapist."

"Well, that's good, isn't it?"

"Yes. And no. It's... It's difficult. Do you mind if I don't come in today?"

"You stay at home, Angie, and get over the shock. We'll manage."

I made a tea, and put some clothes on, but retreated to bed in them, feet up, snuggled in. The window looks out onto the fence; dreary, but that doesn't matter in a bedroom. My living room looks out over the tiny front garden, and the bathroom is tacked onto the kitchen as an afterthought. I get the sun in the kitchen in the morning, and the sunset lights up the living room. But the bedroom gets no sun at all, because the gaps between the houses are narrow. The bedroom walls are painted blue. Kim's idea. Her favourite colour. Matched her eyes.

Kim.

Digby.

Sicked-on quilt.

I went out and bought a new one. And new sheets. But my card was refused in the DIY store when I tried to buy some paint. I transferred some money from my savings and told myself to be careful. The walls would have to wait.

~~~

When I got in, I dropped the new quilt and covers on the bedroom floor, grabbed a tea, then went to put my feet up. In bed. I felt...wrong.

The doorbell. I grabbed the bed to stop it rocking. The bell rang again. I stumbled out of the bedroom, through the gloomy hallway, through the kitchen, with the floor fragile beneath me. I saw DC Rolfe through the glass, and her sidekick, Ald-what Aldrich? No, Alderton. I opened the door. "Come in." I could feel my face smile with an alien grimace. They crowded into the tiny lobby. There's enough room for two coats and one person, so we spilled into the kitchen.

Something was amiss. Something was different. They seemed uneasy, wary of being friendly. "We'd like you to come to the station," Rolfe said.

"What, now?"

"Now would be a good time."

"Er... OK. What for?"

"We've got some questions we have to ask you."

I got the feeling that I didn't have much choice.

~~~

They took me in through the front door of the police station, to the same bland but friendly room as before. Rolfe sat me down, and made sure I was comfortable enough, whilst Sidekick Alderton fetched some tea. They shut the door and gave me a look that seemed both compassionate and stern.

"You recall when we spoke to you last that we had managed to get a DNA match indicating the father of your child. You told us that you did not consent to sexual intercourse with this man. You alleged rape. We have since arrested and interviewed the suspect, and what he told us means we need to talk to you again. And we would like to tape-record what you say. Now you're not under arrest, and free to go at any point. If we're to progress with this case, we need to ask you these questions. Is that OK? And if you want, you can have the duty solicitor."

I tried to wrap my mind round what she was saying. I hadn't done anything wrong, so I didn't need a solicitor, and I presumed they knew what they were doing. And I wanted to land Digby in the manure, where he deserved to be, the evil git. Of course I would answer the questions, and of course I didn't mind it taped. So I shrugged my consent. "Go ahead."

Rolfe loaded up the tape machine with two tapes and read some words off a card. The words included the 'You do not have to say anything' business, which puzzled me. "You said I'm not under arrest..." I said.

"That's correct. You are free to leave at any time, but anything you do say to us now may be given in evidence. And if I ask a question and you don't give me an answer, but then, if it gets to court, then you give the court an answer, they may wonder why you didn't just answer that question now."

My brain stumbled over her words. It was almost as if they suspected me of something criminal. I shrugged away my confusion. She gently asked me loads of questions about how I'd found out I was pregnant, the blank Friday, and everything. She knew the answers from before, but I thought they must need this interview for evidence in court or something. It may be that I remembered a couple of additional facts; I don't know. I was unsure what I had and hadn't told them by this time.

"We have interviewed the male whose DNA shows him to be the father of the baby you allege was the result of your rape. Do you recognise this man?" Rolfe showed me the picture of Digby looking awful, a police photo.

"That's Digby Jamieson, my ex-lover's brother." Memory of sickness tugged at my guts.

"What's your ex-lover's name?" She knew already, but I suppose she had to ask, just like before, when they were trying to help me remember things. Going forwards scene by scene, then back from the end to the beginning again. Memories. Fogged by drugs. Fogged by time. Fogged by that dopiness that pregnancy brings with it. Mind-blanks. Missing words.

"When did you split up from your lover?"

"The day I found out I was pregnant."

"Which day was that?"

"Oh, I can't remember." All I could hang the memory on was that it happened the day I found out. I couldn't remember which day, because motherhood had swapped my brains for mush. "The Doctor will know," I added helpfully.

"Why did you split?"

"She couldn't hack me being pregnant. Actually, she didn't exactly move out then. It was a couple of weeks later. But that's the day we had a row. I think. And nothing was quite the same after that."

"We'll now read to you part of the interview material from when we interviewed Digby Jamieson." Rolfe and Alderton picked up some typed pages. They read through them, Rolfe being herself, and Alderton reading what Digby had said. They'd asked him about having intercourse with me, and he freely admitted it, but he said that I'd consented to it. He said that Kim and I had wanted a child, that he was Kim's closest living relative and so it would seem more like her child if he was the sperm donor. We had intercourse the weekend Kim went to visit her Mum because we calculated it as the most fertile time. I'd come on strong, told him I fancied him, longed for his baby because he reminded me so much of Kim. We'd both got drunk together afterwards. I had fallen pregnant as we hoped, and everything was great until Kim and I rowed. I said I was going to abort the baby and had gone to the Doctor's. Kim had left. When I found it was too late to terminate, I had obviously decided on revenge by alleging this rape nonsense.

"Do you have any comments to make on what Digby has said?" asked Rolfe.

"He's lying. I never consented. I never even knew I was pregnant until it was too late. He's lying. He did that to me, drugged me, raped me, put that, that baby inside me and I had to carry the poor bastard until I gave birth, No I didn't consent. I'd never consent to that. I don't want a baby. I'd never want

140

a baby. They're disgusting, all sick and pooh...." I recollected the tapes turning quietly in the background. I studied my fingers, one to ten. I looked up into the lovely emerald eyes. "You don't believe him, do you?" I asked, pleased my voice was normal again.

Rolfe produced a photograph. "Who's this?"

"Kim Jamieson. My Ex."

Rolfe took out another sheaf of paper. "We'll now read to you what Kim Jamieson said in a statement." Kim had told the police that we had been lovers for 5 years (true) and how we wanted a baby between us (outrageous), and how I (yes, I!) had suggested that Digby be the father as he was related to Kim, the person I really wished to have a baby by. She told them that she had gone to visit her mother the weekend we decided to try for the baby because she couldn't bear the thought of a man having sex with me, even though it would produce a baby. When they asked her why we hadn't tried artificial insemination if sex between Digby and myself was so distasteful to her. She had replied that we didn't know how, and that to get the semen for artificial insemination would have required Digby to commit the sin of Onan, against his religious principles. I laughed at that; an explosion of bitter mirth.

Rolfe looked up, which stifled my laugh, then continued. Kim told them how we rowed, how I'd hit her, how I vowed to get rid of the baby, and had sought revenge by alleging rape. They asked her what had caused the row, and she said I'd turned a bit weird with the pregnancy.

Rolfe asked me if I had any comments. I thought of Digby and his sin of Onan. Pompous twit. I started to laugh again. "Digby is the biggest tosser on the planet," I said. "I've seen him jerking off outside the pub before now. Sin of Onan? Oh, the ..." The manic giggles got louder. I wanted to shut her up, the person making that noise, except that person was me, gulping out guffaws that crossed the cusp between laughter and grief, until I'd sobbed myself to silence.

I never thought to deny the reason for the row.

"Do you understand why we must ask you about this?" asked Rolfe. "It's not unusual for people to consent to sex and then accuse the other person of rape. Especially after a row. Or when a relationship breaks down. We have to be satisfied that a crime took place before we take this further."

"But he's lying. They're lying. They've cooked it up between them. You can't believe this baby nonsense."

"Kim and Digby haven't spoken to each other since he was taken into custody. Kim was at Digby's when we came to arrest him, and DC Alderton here took this statement from her straight away. They haven't conferred over this. They made their statements independently."

I found myself rocking back and forth. The marshmallows were back in my brains. "Well they must've talked about it beforehand," I said eventually.

"That doesn't seem very logical, does it? If Digby did, as you allege, rape you, he'd want to keep it from Kim. He didn't know we were going to match up his DNA with that of the baby's, so why would he confess to Kim out of the blue?"

"Maybe he guessed when you arrested him," I hazarded.

"But how would he know we had the DNA from the baby?"

"Because I told him. Before I knew it was him. I phoned him so he could tell Kim that I'd had the baby. I hoped she'd come back to me. But she didn't. But he knew that you had the baby's DNA, so if you arrested him, and took his, he must've been wetting himself afterwards. Maybe he'd thought you'd realise he was the rapist, and he told Kim to come up with this story. That'd make sense, wouldn't it?" I listened to myself. It sounded as if I were trying to wriggle out of an unpleasant truth with a plausible explanation.

"You told him?"

"Yes. After I came out of hospital. Shortly after I had the baby. Can't remember when, exactly. I thought it only fair. So when you arrested him he must have twigged, got worried, and told her then. And another thing, if we had wanted a baby like he said, I'd have gone to the doctors straight away. I'm not stupid. I'd want to make sure everything was OK from the start. And if I wanted revenge, why not tell you it was Digby from the start? You know; when I first came to see you. See; their version doesn't make sense."

"Why did you think it 'only fair' to tell Digby about the baby?" Emerald eyes probed mine, and I felt guilty.

"I wanted him to tell Kim. I wanted her back."

"So you didn't think it only fair to tell Digby about the baby because he's the father?"

"Of course not. I didn't know he's the father."

"No?"

"No!"

"If they contrived a lie between them, though, surely he would have said you'd done this with artificial insemination? That way he wouldn't have penetrated you at all. His explanation seems plausible. At the moment it's their word against yours." Rolfe sounded reasonable.

"You believe them over me? Maybe they never thought the lie through properly." Why should the police believe me? The dismay lay like glass in my guts. The police weren't going to do anything because Digby and Kim lied successfully. They were going to get away with it, rape and lies. And Kim, how

143

could she betray me so? Acid burned my gullet and the coppers blurred before me.

"I didn't say that. We have to see if a crime has been committed in the first place, or if, as they allege, you've been wasting police time with false allegations. We also have to see if we have enough evidence to secure a conviction. If it's just your word against theirs, it's more difficult. We've got to be realistic."

"You're going to let him get away with it?"

"There's no point in going through all the grief and trauma of a trial if he's going to walk at the end of it. How will you feel if you give all your evidence, go through all that, and he's acquitted? You have to understand what's involved. It's not easy giving evidence in a rape case, as I've told you before. We'll have to see if the Crown Prosecution Service think it's worth taking this to trial."

"But he raped me. He planted his baby inside me, and now he and Kim are lying. I want him to go to jail for what he did to me. You can't let him get away with it. You can't."

Evil bastard. Treacherous bitch. The enormity of their crimes against me crushed me over my lap, and I wept into my knees, whilst Rolfe tried inadequately to comfort me. She didn't touch me. Perhaps she didn't dare.

Chapter 23

Suzy

Brooks had a slightly cocky look about him, as if he'd guessed Suzy found him rather sexy. He had a good body which she found herself responding to, but he had a forcefulness which was both stimulating and slightly off-putting. It was mid-afternoon on the Monday after Digby's arrest, and the stress of the busy weekend was catching up with her.

"Well?" asked Brooks, looking up from the computer and leering at her.

Suzy dumped herself in a chair beside him. She was off territory, and slightly at a disadvantage because of it. "Smarmy bollocks from the defence sol, but no nonsense from the Mags. Digby's pleaded not guilty, but he's been remanded in custody. Good job too. The defence sol squealed a bit because Digby has only the Sec 5 caution in the way of previous, but I'm glad to say he didn't get bail.

"You found nothing when you searched, then?" she added.

"What a shit-hole that estate is," said Brooks. "Digby Jamieson's house backs onto the car park of that terrible old building. Should have been torn down years ago. Good solid Victorian 'dark, satanic' factory. His house is a semi, with a long garden and what used to be the privy built into the wall at the back of the property, ie the wall round the factory. That wall is ten-foot high, and it's got broken glass cemented into the top of it, stopping anyone getting into the factory grounds. Not that you'd want to.

"We went for a poke round the garden. Gawd, what a shambles. And that old privy at the back of the garden. Stunk.

And falling down. We pushed the door open, and there was the old bog, cacced up with something. Sheets of corrugated iron, weeds, dust, filth. But we thought we'd better check, so the dog team came over. Dog was interested in a hole, but we think it was just a rat hole, because we found nothing in it. And the whole thing looked like it was going to collapse, so we left it.

"The drugs dog went a bit loopy in the house. I reckon Digby's had gear in there, but we found nothing."

"How come you nicked him that first time?" asked Suzy. "That was a bit of luck."

"Saturday night, a couple of weeks back, and he's rollicking down the street, drunk as a skunk, possibly because that's what he's been smoking. He's with a group of people, kids mainly, and he's showing off by being a pillock. Sees us in a patrol car and turns round and walks away down a side street, with a guilty look. So, of course, we follow and stop him. He's unsteady and starts shouting at us. I can smell the cannabis on him, so I tell him to pipe down, and that I'm going to search him. Bloody hell, the language! I found a couple of spliffs. He'd have got a street caution if he hadn't been such an arse. But he was noisy and uncooperative, aggressive, swore a lot, pushed me away, stupid sod, so I nicked him. Good job too, as it turns out. We let him stew till morning, then released him with a caution."

Suzy didn't hear the next remark, wondering who had been with Jimbo when he was nicked. Was Kirsty with the group? This could explain why she came home upset that time. Was this why she'd been so odd the last couple of weeks? The amount of upset seemed disproportionate to the event… unless she had some sort of relationship with Digby/Jimbo. "Pardon?"

"I said, what did Angie Bain say in response to what Kim said?" Brooks repeated what he'd said whilst Suzy was wool-gathering.

"Oh, stuck firmly to her story, and offered a good explanation as to how Digby and Kim knew to cook up a story about consent. Angie told him we have the baby's DNA, so he's had a couple of weeks since you arrested him and took cheek swabs for his DNA, to come up with that bunch of fibs. Not the best fibs he could have managed either. If he'd said he'd used artificial insemination, we'd have a much shakier case. I wish I'd asked him about why he hadn't tried AI, to see if his reasons matched what Kim said, but it's a bit late now, bugger it. There's always something you don't get right. But I don't believe a word they said.

"Anyway, I'm off now. I'm going for a drive round the area, get a feel for the place."

"Gut instincts?" Brooks' smile was bordering on a sneer.

"Maybe, maybe."

~~~

Suzy drove down the hill from Elversford nick, crossing the river via the bridge. (The ford was long gone and even the elvers were disappearing.) It was as if the river were a barrier guarding the posher end of Elversford from the shabbier housing and the industry. Like the elvers, the industry was dwindling too. The derelict building fronted onto the main road. All the possible entries were sealed off with sheets of steel to prevent junkies and kids trespassing. It gave the building an uncared for look. The 'For Sale or To Let' sign was falling apart, as if the owner had given up hope.

She turned an abrupt left at the roundabout and found herself on the mean estate built to house the artisans who had worked at the factory in its heyday. When first built, she supposed, they were probably avante garde, especially if they had privies and enough room to grow a few vegetables. But now after more than a hundred years, the deterioration showed. Yet with a bit of money, and a revamp, these old dwellings could be doubled in value. What it needed was an investor with a few million to spend. Several of the houses showed valiant efforts to renovate but these too looked as if the apathy had sapped the will of the owners. The front gardens had bins in, and other rubbish like old mattresses. Some had knocked the walls down to squeeze the cars off the road. The whole area oozed seedy despair.

She passed Digby Jamieson's house. Shabby like the rest, curtains dated, paintwork fresh, though, and the front garden better than most. Kim's work perhaps? Suzy hadn't paid much attention to the dwelling when they'd nicked Digby a couple of days previously. She regretted that now.

She had intended just to drive past, to get a feel for the place, but on impulse she turned right at the crossroads, taking her further into the estate. These houses looked a little better, perhaps because the view was over the water meadow. All it would take was someone to wake up to the potential of the view... Suzy found herself regretting that she didn't have the money to be a property developer.

The road swung round and met up with the road where Digby lived. She parked up and sat staring at the houses. The daydreams about property impinged on her thoughts. She blinked and shook her head. Digby. 'Dirty Digby,' the name fell into her mind uninvited. Why had he drugged and raped his sister's lover? How, and where? In his house? Car? And why, above all, why? And why hadn't he taken basic precautions? Had he chanced the pregnancy, or had he just thought her too old? Or had he just not given it a thought? And did he make a habit of it? He was connected to Jordan at the pizza factory, and so to her sister. Was he the perpetrator there? That was a question they couldn't resolve. Or was it the ex-barman at the Blue Bore who had drugged Jordan and Trish? A bit of digging had discovered that he, too, had worked for a week at the pizza factory (obviously an unreliable type, to be 'let go' after one week.) So he knew Jordan. He'd skipped bail and was still missing.

Suzy frowned. She unclipped the seatbelt, slid from the car, locked it with a furtive look round, wondering if it would still be there on her return. She wandered up the road, eyes into the front gardens, wondering why poverty should mean squalor. Never used to. She remembered her Gran, scrubbing the front doorstep, her house almost painfully clean.

Bother, it looked like someone was at home in Digby's house. Kim Jamieson perhaps. Any thoughts of a surreptitious snoop round the garden were abandoned.

She did cast a glance down the path as she sauntered by, though, past a reasonably tidy front garden, segueing into an unkempt back garden, grass high and falling over. The tree fighting for survival still had its leaves; autumn was late this year. She caught a glimpse of the disgusting old privy, roof slumping, glass broken, door hanging half off, half rotted. The privy was built into the boundary wall, ten-foot of shabby brick, with broken glass snagged and jagged along the top. A buddleia clung to one crevice, seed heads blackened. As she went past, she cast her head over her shoulder at the monstrous derelict building hogging the skyline. Brooks was

149

right; it was darkly satanic and should have no existence in the twenty first century.

Suzy wandered along until she was at the back of the derelict building, windows this side also sealed with metal sheets. There was a smell of old urine, fag ends, and a used condom littering the pavement. At the crossroads she carried straight on to a cul-de-sac, discovering that she was yards away from where Eddie Prior, the father of the two girls in the divorce case lived. Had he offended against them? Or was it some vengeful invention or exaggeration from the mother? Perhaps it was a ploy to ensure he didn't have access to the girls. If so, the mother had succeeded. At least for the moment. If he were innocent, he must be suffering hellishly. And to have to live in a dump like this whilst his ex-wife and kids lorded it up in their fancy house: If he were innocent, it sure as hell wasn't fair. But if he was guilty, then he deserved all he got.

At the end of the road, Suzy turned back, suddenly anxious for her car. A girl was coming towards her, pushing a buggy. The girl was podgy, hair dyed black with punky red streaks, earrings which jiggled as she walked. The bare midriff where her all too short skirt didn't meet the jumper was unbecoming because it oozed out over the top of the skirt. The face, though pallid and indicating a need for more fresh vegetables, was far healthier than the last time they'd met. A one-year-old child gurgled and smiled out of the oversized coat. As they approached, Suzy's eyes met with the girl's with a clash.

"Hello Shannon. Glad to say I haven't seen you for a long time."

"Hullo." Dull, guarded, ready to flare up in anger and resentment.

"You look really well," added Suzy, scanning Shannon's face for tell-tale signs.

"I've been off it for two years now," said Shannon, proudly.

Suzy found her face splitting with an unexpectedly huge grin. "Really? You chucked the habit? Oh, Shannon, that's such good news. Oh, I am glad," Her tone was so obviously genuine, Suzy saw the girl relax a bit, allow herself a wistful smile.

"Yeah well, got tired of the game. Hated it even. It's no way to live. Got myself a boyfriend, moved out here, away from Galchester. Better here, and then there's me kid. Couldn't do that to her. Not when I found myself pregnant, I couldn't."

"Do you still...? Sorry, I shouldn't ask."

"Not now. Did at first. Better here, or at least, it was."

"Was?"

"Um." Shannon shoved the buggy to and fro. "I've got to go, now."

"Shannon, just off the top of my head, now... You haven't heard of anyone being date rape drugged round here, have you?" Suzy blinked in surprise at herself.

Silence. Buggy jiggling. Contemplation. The answer was yes, then.

"Someone you know?" hazarded Suzy. Then, as the silence shouted at her, "Not you, Shannon?" She heard the dismay in her voice and wondered if Shannon noticed.

"No. A friend. Here. He drugged her, had his way, took her money. She was in a right state for a few days. She couldn't get a hit, not with her money all gone, so she... never mind. Don't say I said... I've got to go now, please."

"Oh, Shannon. Look, he shouldn't get away with that. Ask your friend to give me a ring. Here's my card. If she wants to make a complaint."

"Don't be stupid. What's she gonna say?" Shannon pushed the buggy like a battering ram. "I've got to go now, please."

Chapter 24

Kirsty

When Kirsty went into work, 'Aunty' Janet told her that Jimbo was ill, so she was acting supervisor. During a spell out, over coffee, Kirsty asked "What's up with Jimbo, then?"

"Don't know. The woman wouldn't say. But she sounded very upset."

"Woman?" asked Kirsty.

"That sucks," said Tom. "He's got a wife. Disappointed Kirsty?" Kirsty said nothing. "She is," crowed Tom incredulously. "Kirsty fancies Jimbo!" He stuck his tongue out suggestively.

"No I don't," protested Kirsty. "And shut up."

"He's not worth it, luv," advised Janet. "He's far too old for you. And a lech."

"I know, I know. I don't fancy him. That's Tom. He's jealous."

"Not half, you prick-tease," jeered Tom. "Wonder what's up."

"Just a cold, I should think. Or he's smashed out of his brains and nursing a hangover," said Aunty Janet dismissively. "Right, let's get that line rolling again."

~~~

Kirsty was on the cheese hopper, mind chewing over Tom's words. Did she fancy Jimbo? Yes, sod it, she did, ever since she'd seen him arrive one Friday in that gorgeous Lotus of his, in his schmexy jacket. He'd climbed out of his car with a lithe, sexy wriggle, grabbed his jacket, flashed a dangerous smile at her, and stolen her heart. 'Silly,' she told herself. 'It's only a teenage crush. Probably, but who cares?' She'd found herself acting like a blushing schoolgirl, aiming to be in a certain place at a certain time, just to smile at him.

She wasn't in love with him. Didn't even fancy him in a sexual sense, she just found him intoxicatingly dangerous, like the whisky she used to nick from her mum when she was younger. She didn't much care for whisky, but the spice was the danger, and the tipsy feeling. It was much the same now.

Jimbo had made his attraction to her no secret, either, the night they all went on the town. He'd brushed up against her a couple of times, patted her bottom, seated himself next to her in the Blue Bore; made eyes at her. But he hadn't asked her out that night, just shown off, then got himself nicked. Gawd, that had been frightening; bad enough to be with someone kicking off like that, but for a minute, Kirsty had wondered if she'd be nicked as well. The thought of facing her mother over something like that was sickening.

Was Jimbo married? He never mentioned a Mrs Jimbo. But then he wouldn't, would he, if he was hoping for a quick fuck on the sly. And he had screwed around, according to Tina on the ovens. She'd been in the car, to his wonderful bachelor pad. They'd had lobster or something posh. And then he'd screwed her on a king-sized bed. Or so she said.

On the next spell out, the meal break, Tom poked her and said, "Stop daydreaming about lover-boy. I bet he's got a dose of clap, that's what's wrong."

"Fuck off," said Kirsty.

"Oy, less of that, madam," said Aunty Janet

"Sorry," muttered Kirsty.

"If you're that worried about him, why don't you call in on the way home? He lives down the road near that derelict building," said Tom.

"No," disagreed Kirsty. "He's got a posh flat in Galchester. Tina said."

"That's a fib. He lives just round the corner from me. Number 8, Tindale Street. Honest."

"But Tina said…"

Tom laughed. "You believe her…?"

"But I've seen the Lotus."

"Yeah, I've seen the Lotus. But not parked up outside his house. Not that you'd leave anything like that parked up outside your house in that street."

Kirsty was quiet for the rest of the shift. As she left the building, Tom caught up with her. "Look," he said, "I'm sorry I teased you earlier. Only… well, I'm a bit jealous, that's all. I know you chucked me over the spliff 'n all, an' the misunderstanding, but I'm sorry and I really fancy you. And I respect you; I thought you wanted to, so I…Why go for a dirty old man like him? 'Cos that's what he is. A dirty old man with Wandering Hand Trouble. He does live near me. Honest. All this talk about a posh flat. It's bollox. Walk home with me and I'll show you."

Kirsty's mind shuffled like a pack of cards, each thought flicking momentarily before her. Jimbo. Lotus. Tina. Tom. Tom fancied her, really fancied her. She fancied Jimbo. No; she fancied a fantasy. The real Jimbo was the sort of pillock who got himself nicked. She didn't fancy that Jimbo. But did she fancy Tom? Nice Tom, Tom the chavvy kid, but interesting, and slightly dangerous? He wasn't really her type, but he was fun. And she had enjoyed experimenting before, until he gave her that drink when she was supposed to be riding her bike home, and then tried it on. She giggled over the memory of him naked except for the condom. But she also felt aroused.

155

"OK I s'pose. Let's just be friends for a while," she said. "I'm not sure I'm ready for that sort of thing. Anyway, Tina said she'd been in that flat. He took her there in his Lotus and… she says he's good. Experienced."

"Yeah, right. He's the fashionable fuck, you know. Good job most of the girls in the factory are on the pill."

"How do you know that?"

"I can hear you lot talking in the changing rooms. The wall's thin, you know."

"You're kidding…"

"S'true."

They set off along the main road, the November sun already dipping. There was little traffic, the lull before the school run. Tom made no moves to hold her hand or anything, and Kirsty found herself relaxing.

"That's where he lives," said Tom, pointing out Digby's house. "The telly's on. I wonder if he's really ill, or if he's got a woman in there."

"Let's find out, shall we?" said Kirsty. She wanted to challenge Jimbo, embarrass him on the doorstep. Fancy flat indeed. She remembered his hand on her shoulder, briefly dropping, fingers brushing oh-so-subtly over her breast. She shuddered. She marched up the path to the door and rapped loudly. Kirsty turned to Tom. He'd vanished.

The door opened. A woman, petite, tight with pent up aggression. Mrs Jimbo?

"Er, er, does Digby Jamieson live here?"

"Who's asking?" Kirsty noticed bags under the woman's eyes, and a drawn look. The eyes were angry, wary.

"Kirsty from work. We heard he's ill, Mrs Jamieson. I just called by to see how he is, that's all."

156

"You nosy little moo. Ill, yeah? Yeah, he's ill all right. Fuck knows when he'll be better, so you piss off out of it, Kirsty-from-work, and leave us alone, yeah. Go on, piss off. And I'm not Mrs Jamieson, OK."

Kirsty turned and fled, fearing that the woman was about to hit her. At the gate, she turned back, the door was slammed shut. She closed the rusty gate, shuddering, snivelling, wishing Tom hadn't disappeared.

"Ill? That's a joke."

Kirsty jumped, turned. Jimbo's next-door neighbour, leaning on her gate, a bag of garden refuse testament to her reason for being outside. "Aw, pet, don't let her get to you. She's got a right tongue on her, that one, when she's a mind to it. That's his sister. Nice enough on the right side of her, but when she's riled, phew, what a bitch. And she's well riled now, him being nicked, 'n all"

"Nicked? Jimbo's been nicked?"

"Yeah, Saturday, early like, they came for him. And they took his car away. And searched his house. Didn't you know?"

"No," said Kirsty tightly. "No. We were told he was ill. I've made a bit of a fool of myself."

"Don't worry pet. I'd leave him well alone, if I was you. He's trouble, and no mistake."

"Um, pardon me, but is his car a Lotus?"

The woman laughed. "Lotus? You've gotta be kidding. It's a clapped-out Orion. Has he been leading you on? He's trouble. Leave him." The woman retreated indoors.

Kirsty turned, frowning. Tom jumped out of a gateway from behind a shrub. "Gotcha."

Kirsty stepped away defensively. "Fuck off."

"Sorry," said Tom. "Come here and I'll give you a hug to make up for it."

157

Kirsty looked at him dubiously. "Just a hug, then."

Tom pulled her into his arms, hugged her, then passed a suggestive hand over her buttock. She didn't pull away or demur. She could smell a spliff in his shirt pocket.

"Let's go for a walk," she said. "I wonder why he's been nicked."

"For being a tosser," said Tom. "You should hear him talk about what a good fuck he is, but..." Tom sniggered. "He's got a tiny dick, and he's ever so sensitive about it."

~~~

Suzy sat in her car, mouth gaping, wondering why her daughter was gossiping with the neighbour of a rape suspect. Then worse, snuggling in the arms of a chavvy little runt.

~~~

Kirsty had barely shut the front door, when she heard the key in the lock. "Mum! You're home early."

"Yes, I am. With good reason. I think you have some explaining to do, my girl. Like what you were doing in Tindale Street today at 2.30 this afternoon?"

"You were there?"

"I was. In a car. Parked up."

"Watching? You never said about Jimbo."

"None of your business, is it? Or is it? Tell me, has he done anything to you?"

"No. No."

"Don't lie to me. How far has he got?"

"Nowhere. Though I... He's got a bit of a reputation. And Tom lives nearby. When he didn't come to work, we were told he was ill and went to see how he was."

"Tom? The lad you wrapped yourself around, went for a walk with?"

Kirsty nodded.

"You told him Digby has been arrested, didn't you?"

Kirsty nodded, heat seeping from her ears over her cheeks. "His neighbour told me. I didn't know."

"See why I didn't tell you… Suppose we had to release him… suppose we had the wrong bloke?"

"It's not like I found out from you, is it? Stop blaming me. You blame me for everything. I can't do anything right, can I? But I wish you'd told me he's crooked… What's he done?"

"Drug assisted rape… Shit, child, sit down!" Her mother's face was suddenly filled with concern, worse, with fear. "Has he, has he…?"

"No, Mum. But if I'd known. I'd never have gone out with him and the others from work Saturday nights. Blimey, Mum. D'you think he's done it more than once…? Like Jordan? And her sister?"

"I don't know. I just don't know. We've no evidence that he's done anything to anyone other than the victim. But it's possible. But you mustn't say, you really, really must-not-say. Because there's no evidence, and it could easily have been someone else. And he might have targeted you at some point. Were you there when he was arrested that first time? Is that why you came home so upset?"

Kirsty nodded. "I hid, I was that frightened. He went loopy. Kicked off. I was terrified he'd hurt someone, or I'd get nicked too."

"Lucky for us; we got a match with his DNA that way."

"Oh." Kirsty found she was sitting in the living room, her mother's arm comfortingly around her. She burst into tears.

"It's been a shock, that's all. He never tried it on, though I think he might have... he..."

"I think you'd better tell me what you know."

Kirsty told her mum about Jimbo's reputation, and what he was like at work. She didn't mention the Lotus, though, ashamed that she should fall for a sleazy man just because he had a schmexy car. Nor did she mention the mythical bachelor flat. But she did tell the mum about Stuart who'd said Jimbo's dick was tiny, and the poisonous look; and about Eddie who was supposed to be good for a spliff if you wanted that sort of thing; and about Ant and Chelsea who had both been sacked for having sex in the loos.

Then, just as the emotional turmoil was calming down, her mother said, "Who's the chavvy boy?"

"What?"

"The boy you were all over, after going to Digby's house."

"He's Tom. He's nothing."

"It didn't look like nothing, the way you let him paw you. Has he tried it on?"

"No," lied Kirsty, forgetting her mother was an expert detector of lies.

"You're not to go out with him. You're too good for him. He's a chav."

"He's nice."

"Don't cheapen yourself. He's only after one thing. He's probably on drugs, a waster, probably got some STDs. For God's sake, Kirsty, where's your common sense?" Her mother froze, sniffed, came closer to Kirsty. "Cannabis, fucking cannabis. Have you been smoking, my girl?"

"No."

"You're lying. I'll get you tested, God help me. I will: Did. You. Smoke. A. Spliff?"

"No. Not all of it. I just had a puff to try. I didn't like it much."

Her mother raged at her then, face distorted and terrifying, but Kirsty found her own anger mounting, and instead of backing down, which would have calmed the row, she said, "I'll go and live with Dad."

"Do that... do that for more a weekend, and find out what a slime ball he really is. You stupid, idiotic, childish, immature little brat."

~~~

Angie

Monday, DC Rolfe phoned me to say that Digby had been charged, taken before the magistrates, and was now remanded in custody for a week. But I wasn't to contact Kim in any way.

Chapter 25

Suzy

"Ma'am, I can't come in today. I'm knackered."

"Oh, I quite understand," said Cheungy down the phone. "It's been a bit of a weekend. Are you OK? You sound really down."

Suzy could imagine Cheungy's face, full of care and concern. "I had the most awful row with my daughter and I didn't sleep a wink. I found she's going out with someone totally unsuitable." Suzy sighed. "Isn't it odd how we can treat suspects carefully, interview using the peace model, yet when it comes to our own flesh and blood, we end up shouting at them, confrontational, finding out nothing. She's lied to me, and I can't stand that."

"Too close, too emotionally involved," agreed Cheungy.

"She says she wants to live with her Dad. That hurts. That hurts so much, because he left us for another woman, just when she needed him most. And the things he said to me and about me in self-justification. Said I was a rotten parent, thought more of the Job than of him or Kirsty. He wanted custody of Kirsty, you know, but that slag of a girl who stole him from me was a right bitch to her. So glad I…. And now Kirsty…"

"Lots of things are said in anger, in the heat of the moment, which aren't meant," said Cheungy. "You're tired, overwrought, and you've worked hard on this and the other cases, including working on rest days. Take a couple of days off. We'll manage, now Digby Jamieson is in custody."

~~~

Angie

Tuesday, I tried to work. I thought working might distract me from it all. But it was hard, smiling with lips of glass at the customers' inane chit-chat, praying that nothing would go wrong, no abusive customers. Or screaming babies. But of course, I got a rotten customer. The small man, small-mind mentality, the man who feels inferior and makes up for it in unpleasantness. It was over a bag of reduced apples. They should have been sold or binned the day before but had been overlooked. The till noticed. "I'm sorry, these are out of date. I can't sell them to you."

"Phough! Nonsense, they're perfectly edible."

Of course they were, but they were dated as if apples slump into globes of toxin overnight. "I'm sorry sir, I'm not allowed to let you have them." Normally, I'd have made some witticism about the absurdity of the use-by rules, especially regarding fruit and so on, but today all I could feel was the fragility of my face as the tears hammered like pickaxes at the back of my eyes. I rang the bell for the supervisor as if I were pressing the alarm at a bank raid.

Sally bustled over, looked at me, and told the queuing customers, sorry, this till was closing. There were mutterings as the two people behind wheeled off, but their vitriol was directed at Mr Pompous. Sally told him firmly he wasn't having the apples. He muttered something about writing to complain to head office as Sally finished his load. He stalked off like an angry cat.

"I can't do the tills," I whispered, my distress pulling the occasional curious glance. "Can I do something else?"

"You could give Tim a hand with the fruit and veg. Check the dates, if we're getting stuff like that overlooked. But give

yourself a couple of minutes. Have a coffee or something."
This was strict Ms Curtis telling me to slope off for an
additional coffee break. Unheard of.

Someone hadn't been doing their job, and there was
more out-of-date fruit and vegetables to be pulled from the
shelves. "Don't blame me," said Tim, as we tossed the bags of
apples, carrots and potatoes onto the bottom of the trolley.

It was mid-afternoon, so the majority of customers were
mothers and babies. I found myself looking at the babies,
wondering what mine looked like, and if he was OK. Then I saw
one wearing an outfit like the girls had bought me, and for a
stabbing moment, thought he was mine. I must have made
some noise, because the mother glanced at me, then moved
on, as if some sixth sense had warned her about me.

"You OK Angie?" asked Tim.

"Oh, er , yeah, sorry."

"Can I go for a break? Only I've not had one yet."

And I'd had two. "We've done the heavy stuff, so of
course. Tell Ms Curtis, though, OK?"

It's a world of isolation, checking the dates. I went
through the mushrooms. Most in date, some on the edge and
needing to be reduced, but some which should have been
reduced and/or chucked the day before. Blip of scanner, whirr
of reduced tickets. Stick the labels over the bar code.

People treat you like you're a machine, a robot. They
reach in front of you as if you're not there, rude in their
eagerness for a bargain, especially for things like apples,
which, contrary to popular belief, don't self-destruct at
midnight on Use-by Day. What they do with the stuff once
they've bought it is up to them. But of course, we can't sell if
out of date. That stupid arrogant old git. The anger rattled
around me like static.

My friend Moira passed me, pushing a laden shopping trolley, Toddler in the trolley. That baby must be well over a year old, now. I hadn't seen Moira for ages. Not since she showed her baby off to us, before... She was one of the crowd, the Craven Arms bunch. "Hi," I said, maybe a tad too enthusiastically.

"Hello." Guarded. Hostile, even.

"How are you?"

"OK."

The question wasn't reciprocated, but I supplied an answer anyway. "I'm OK. I don't know if you heard, but I, I, I had a baby. I was raped. And Kim and I have split."

"I heard. The police came round to see me." Deadpan tone.

Perhaps that explained the frost, the hostility. "Oh of course, sorry about that." I remembered now, giving DC Rolfe Moira's name as a possible witness. "So you sort of know the story..."

"Oh, yes, I know the story all right."

"I thought I'd come to the pub on Friday, say hello to the usual crowd."

"You reckon?" Moira spluttered a sneering laugh, as if I was stupid to think I'd be welcome.

"Yeah," I said, the devil in my mouth. I should have left it there, taken the hint. "Why not? I've done nothing wrong."

"That's not what I heard. I heard you beat Kim up."

The memory hit me. Venom, spittle, slap. "I didn't beat her up..."

"That's not what I heard. I saw the mark on her face. And it's not all I heard. You vicious, lying bitch. Don't come to the C. Never. You won't be welcome. We don't like your sort." She edged away.

165

"What d'you mean?" I said, panic flavouring my voice. "What's she said? She's lying..." I sidled after Moira, forcing myself not to grab her arm.

She gave me a look of withering contempt. "I think you know," she sneered, and moved away.

The world went out of focus, the customers like blurring shadows, noise muffled by my misery. I didn't cry. Not on the outside. The vegetables seemed very real, but I was attenuated, ghostly amongst them.

Sally ('Ms Curtis') found me and manoeuvred me into her office. I don't know if she pulled me, or commanded me, the world was too dissociated from me. "You're not well," she told me. "I can't have you working like this, Angie. You're a liability." That last comment was a knife in the guts. "To yourself as well as the store. I can't have you on the edge like this. You'll have to go long term sick until you're better. You been to the doctor's yet?"

"No. I keep meaning to, but..." Dr Thomas's ghost smiled at me, breaking my heart.

"See?" said Sally when I had sobbed to a halt. "Angie, this needs treating. It won't get better on its own. Believe me. You've got to go to the doctors. And you're not working till you're better. You need to get yourself signed off, for Statuary Sick Pay and so on."

~~~

I nearly crashed the car on the way home. My fault. The offended car punished me with a blare of horns that ripped across my wounds like fire.

~~~

I was out of milk. I plunged my hands in my coat pockets. 'Don't think, don't think.' Walk. 'You didn't lock the front door. A burglar will get in. Go back, go back.' I walked on. The rain teased, gelling from a sodden sky. Air-sweat. It keeps people indoors, safely out of the way. I didn't want to see anyone. Talk to anyone. Be seen by anyone. I walked, mind screwed up like eyes against the glare, telling myself, 'Don't think. Thinking means feeling, and feeling is dangerous. Feeling means pain.'

The corner shop. Sanctuary turned dangerous. Bought milk. Left. The world, the huge empty skies crowding round, trees shrunk against the vault of grey, the houses hunched aggressively over me. I looked down at the grey dull pavement. A leaf. Gold and red. Beautiful. Emotional connection. I ran, a stilted skip, not daring a jog like I used to enjoy, breasts still huge and wobbly despite the Wagnerian bra, insides threatening to slither out from between my legs.

Front door. Locked. Key fumbling. In. Slam. Lock. Heart staccato. Tears. Over milk. Not even spilled.

~~~

Moira's words festered. So I phoned Danny. Left a message.

~~~

Friday. Sod Moira. I'd go, smile and tell them what a bastard Digs was. And what a liar Kim was.

Bloody jeans were still too tight. Found some joggers that fitted. Jumper. Hair sorted. Door impossible.

~~~

167

Saturday. Phoned Danny again.

"How dare you phone me, you poisonous bitch. We heard what you did to Kim. And Digs. You lying cow."

"She's wrong. She's confused. I need to talk, give my version of events."

The phone went dead.

I knew had to go to the pub, to explain. It wasn't fair. This time I made it through the front door, and managed the walk to the pub. All the time I was fighting the urge to run home and lock myself away. But when I got there I couldn't force myself to go in, so I turned, started to walk home, compelling myself to walk, not run. Turned the corner. Kim.

We both froze. She moved to one side. I blocked her. "You lied, lied to the police about the baby."

"No I didn't. Not exactly. Digs told me what really happened that weekend. Told me how you'd come on strong when you were pissed after a good night out the Friday I went up to Mum's. You started pawing him, saying as how you wanted a baby by him, like Moira's, and how you wanted one to look like me, how you fancied Digs because he looks so much like me, and that time was running out. And worst of all, you liar, you told him I knew you were bi, and told him I knew you wanted a baby and was happy to have one with you so long as I didn't have so see you with a man. And you were fiddling around with him so much he was ready, and gave you one, and you enjoyed it, said you wanted to see him again, but by that time he was feeling ashamed, he said. He said he was dead embarrassed because a bloke doesn't fuck his sister's lover. It's just not on. And you got what you want, didn't you; a baby. But you never asked me, never gave a thought as to how I'd feel about it. And then you lied to me again about the menopause and all."

"That's lies, lies. When did he tell you this?"

"He told me he knew you were bisexual years ago, but I didn't believe him, didn't want to believe him, because you'd told me you weren't. And he told me about you wanting the baby when we split."

"Are you sure? Are you sure he didn't tell you when he knew he was going to be found out?"

I saw a flicker of doubt cross her face. Kim shook her head. "He told me pretty much straight away about you wanting the baby."

"And when did he tell you he was the father…? Straight away or when it was obvious it was going to come out because the police had his DNA?" I went to grab her hand, to make her think, think, see things from my angle, but she dodged, said nothing, shaking her head. "And that's not what you told the police, is it? You told them we'd planned it together, the three of us."

"Yeah, same difference. Just like the lies you told Digs about me wanting a baby too. You leave my Digs alone. I don't know what I ever saw in you."

"Kim, darling, for God's sake, think this through. Digby's lying. He drugged me, he raped me and he planted the baby inside me, and now he's lying to you so you'll side with him. Why believe him and not me?"

"No, no. He always saw through you, but he put up with you for my sake. He tried to warn me what you're like, just like Mum did, and Dad for that matter. But I never listened until now. I wish I'd never met you. You broke my heart."

"I'm telling the police you lied to them."

"Oh yeah, like hell you will. You're not supposed to be talking to me. They'll do you for witness intimidation. I never want to speak to you again." She walked past me, and I saw the tears in her eyes, tears that once I would have kissed away. I followed her round the corner, back towards the pub. A gorgeous looking woman maybe a few years younger than me got out of a car in the pub car park. Kim fell into her arms, laid her head on the woman's chest. I could tell Kim was crying, shoulders shaking as those arms comforted her.

The sky was falling down on me, so I scuttled home and slammed the door.

Another lost weekend. I don't remember it. I don't remember eating, I don't remember sleeping. I don't remember anything.

~~~

Monday. I phoned the doctors. Engaged. When I got through, they told me all the appointments had gone for the day. I would have to phone again tomorrow. Reality crumbled. It wasn't Deidre. Pity; I could have explained to Deidre. I sat for hours by the phone, as if I was planning on staying put all night, like someone at the sales camping out for the best bargain. Waiting for morning, and the surgery to open.

The phone rang. Sally. "Go your certificate yet? Only I need it for your SSP."

It took me a while to pull the answer from my brain. "No appointments," I said, a thin whisper.

"Angie, this is important. Phone them back. Tell them you have to see someone."

My mouth no longer worked. My thoughts piled up in my brain like a derailment.

"Angie? Angie are you there?"

What?

"Angie… Angie. Oh, shit, Angie."

~~~

The doorbell. So far away. Insistent. Ignorable. Sally at the window. Banging. Angry looking. "Let me in, Angie, or I'll break in!"

Muscles of wood. Immobile. Splinters as I rose, through the dim corridor to the kitchen. Door open. Sally burst in. "Who's your doctor?"

Voiceless. I pointed at my address book. She looked under D. And phoned. And phoned again, with cajoles, and threats about phoning ambulances, needing someone now, this was an emergency.

Red suffused my face. I wasn't an emergency. I wasn't dying.

Dying. Easier than living, sometimes.

~~~

Dr Galton. Young. Pretty in a strained sort of way, as if her beauty had been tempered with grief. She didn't section me, though in hindsight, I think she came close. But she did prescribe medication. Which Sally fetched. And I took.

~~~

Sally came the next day, just to see how I was. Samish. The tablets had filled my brains with fog, which was better than the clamorous noise of before. The noise was still there, but muted, and I no longer jumped at every new sound. I made us a pot of tea. It seemed more civilised than tea bags in mugs, somehow. And I broke open a packet of biscuits because there was an emptiness inside. I wasn't sure if it was hunger, but since I had no recollection of eating, I supposed it must be.

If I'd known Sally better, as a friend before all this business happened, we could have sat in companionable silence, and it wouldn't have mattered.

The silence reached a crescendo. Sally broke it. "Would it help to talk?"

"Thanks." I could manage that. No more.

The tea drained away into the silence, the noise of the cup in saucer cymbals against the hush.

She took the sick note with her.

~~~

My home is the ground floor of a Victorian house which has been divided into two maisonettes. It didn't divide that easily. The old front door belongs to the upstairs maisonette. It opens onto what was originally the tiny hallway. Before the house was split, there were doors leading to the lounge off one side and the dining room off the other. Beyond what was originally the dining room is the kitchen. Those doorways were now bricked up, and the old front door just leads to the stairs for the upstairs maisonette. Originally the dining room, the middle room, had the under-stairs cupboard in it. This was knocked through into the lounge, and the dining room converted into a bedroom. The bedroom was closed off with a thin partition wall, which had windows at the very top to let a glimmer of natural light into the dingy corridor to the kitchen. It was hellishly claustrophobic, and I had wondered whether to knock it down, make the bedroom the lounge/diner, and the lounge into the bedroom. But I liked my lounge to have a view, and the bedroom didn't need a view.

The bathroom was tacked on like an afterthought. It was a flat roofed bit at the back, and the flat roof kept leaking on the couple above. But they let the bath overflow once, so I had the same effect downstairs.

There's a gap between the kitchen and the bathroom, giving us the necessary two doors, and space for a washing machine. The old back door, through a cramped lobby, is my front door. Not bad. Habitable. And mine. Paid for, thank goodness. One less worry, though things were tight enough now.

~~~

I couldn't warm to Dr Galton. Perhaps Dr Thomas's ghost stood between us. But she did her job, and the medication did its job. Sort of. Though there were times when I thought it wasn't easing the depression so much as making me less able to voice my thoughts, even to myself.

~~~

Sally. Heterosexual. Aloof. Snobbish? I never liked the way she wears her makeup. I never liked the clothes she wears or her perfume. Nothing appeals to me, yet the whole of Sally, made up of an amalgam of undesirable parts, is very likeable. Once you get past the reserve.

She came again, a week later, ostensibly to pick up this week's sick note. I had managed to get myself to the doctors, laid Dr Thomas's ghost partly to rest with a burst of condolences to the other staff, and come away with another note, and another prescription refining the medication, new instructions, and a feeling of encouragement.

"I feel such a nitwit, taking these, I said to Sally. "Humiliating, really. You'd think I could snap out of it." I gave a wan smile.

"Don't you ever let anybody tell you that!" she said, astonishing me with her vehemence. "Postnatal depression is incredibly common. It's from the effort of carrying the baby, the birth and all that. It's biochemical. Something to do with the brain chemistry. It's not a matter of weakness..." Sally looked away, out of the window, but I was too wrapped up in my own misery to wonder why. The drugs that fogged my brain stopped me thinking, guessing. Thinking was an effort. And dangerous.

The teacups didn't clatter like they had the week before. The noise was normal, comforting even. Sally shifted uneasily. "D'you mind me asking how thing are with the er..." she said.

When I didn't answer straight away, Sally seemed to find the view very interesting. But I wasn't angry, or embarrassed. I was thinking. With woolly brains. Kim had obviously told all my friends that I had lied about Digs. Time I had an ally. "Sally, can I tell you things in confidence. I mean, really in confidence? Like, not tell a soul?"

There was a long moment before Sally said, "Um."

So I told her about Kim, and Digs, and that he was the father, the lies they had told, the poison they had spread, and how I was impotent to rebut the lies; not even the lies Kim said to the police because I shouldn't have spoken to her near the pub that time. Sally just sat and listened and thanked me for sharing it with her. She said it helped her understand the hell I was going through a lot better. "Maybe Kim isn't lying so much as confused. Maybe she believes what she said, even if it's not true," she suggested.

I froze at that, wondering if I'd lost Sally too, but then I remembered Kim's tears. Maybe Sally was right; Kim was confused, and Digby's lies had taken root until they looked like the truth. But it didn't change anything.

Sally seemed on the verge of saying something else, but then switched the conversation down more trivial paths. I made more tea, and counted it as an achievement, progress. We talked, and that was progress, too.

"Well, I must go," she said. "My son's coming home from university for the weekend, and I have to get his room straight."

I thought I ought to make an effort with Sally's family. I remembered her saying how she had suddenly mushroomed at 6 months. Both times. Or both babies had been fidgets, or something. "Do you have two sons, or is your other one a girl?"

The words fell on the ground and shattered. Sally sat down, no; sagged into the chair, as if her bones had melted. Her eyes unfocussed, she swallowed, breath soughed out over her teeth. I rummaged around for something to say, wondering what the hell I'd said to warrant this reaction. I opened my mouth to burp out a trivial inanity but thank goodness it stuck in my throat. The silence crystallised.

Sally spoke first. "If I tell you something, it must go no further. Really, in confidence. Just like you have, with me. Sort of balances things out I suppose."

I could feel my eyes owl-wide and serious. I nodded.

"I was OK first time round. With Drew, I had the usual, the sickness, the aches, the slack joints, the pain. And after the birth, the sore nipples, the feelings of inadequacy, and the blues. Two days in, the blues came in with the milk. Same for you?"

I nodded.

"Second time was much like the first. Difficult birth, though. Not turned properly, and they say the second's easier. Not for me, it wasn't. And you forget how it hurts, until you're back in labour again. Then you remember. Same as before, aches, sore nipples, the milk coming in. The blues. Only things got worse. Much worse. Felt like a wall. Smashed into it. They weren't so aware of things in those days. Or at least, not so open about it. And they were busy. Very busy. Mini baby boom. And I'm a quiet sort. Not likely to make a fuss. Keep things inside..."

She understood herself; better than we did at the supermarket, where we took such reserve as snootiness, snobbery.

"I, I thought the nurses were out to kill me. I was terrified if they tried to give me pain relief. I refused it. And the vitamin K for Anna. Because they were trying to poison us. And I wasn't the only one. I saw them stop someone else from wheeling her baby down the corridor, and shortly afterwards, she disappeared. So I knew they were going to kill me, and the baby. I picked up Anna, wrapped her in a bath towel to hide her, put my belongings in my sponge bag, and told the midwives I was going for a shower.

"I made it outside before anyone noticed. They have gardens round that hospital, and patients often go out in their dressing gowns; it wasn't unusual to have a woman in a dressing gown wandering around the place. Then I saw the nurses coming towards me. I ran. My knee went; my ligaments were slack, of course. Over I went, dropping Anna, and then falling on top of her.

"The post mortem showed she was already fatally injured by the fall, though the crushing meant I killed her through and through. They sectioned me. Puerperal psychosis. They treated that, OK, eventually, but they couldn't treat the grief or the guilt.

"The Inquest returned a verdict of misadventure. At the time, I almost wished they'd tried me for murder, because that's what it felt like. At the time."

A chasm of silence opened. What can you say to a story like that? This explained it, Sally's attitude, her helpfulness, her unexpected sympathy, her fury at the Doctors' receptionist (not Deidre).

"And actually, a lot of people treated me as if I'd done it deliberately. A baby killer. But it was an accident. I never intended Anna harm. I just panicked, dropped her. Killed her. Nineteen years ago, and it still hurts. Funnily enough, Post Natal Depression became a big thing shortly after that. The Health Visitors round our way started to really look out for it. Perhaps I misjudged the midwives, and they did notice most of the time, but just missed me. I don't know. I know I blamed them for not diagnosing for a long time afterwards. And Drew was only two, and it made things difficult with him, too. But in the end, I had counselling, and it helped me turn the corner. I'm still in contact with my counsellor. Like Christmas cards, and things. I've got her card here, in case you need it." Sally fished the card easily from her purse. She had obviously intended I should have the card, though maybe not the accompanying confession/explanation. "I can't understand why your doctor didn't suggest it. Or the police, considering what you've been through. I'll see myself out," she added, then she fled.

I put the card on the mantelpiece above the gas fire. Not really my thing; counselling. But I didn't like to throw the card away.

Chapter 26

Angie

The day of the presumed anniversary of the rape, I got a phone call, DC Rolfe, to tell me that Digby had been committed to Crown for trial by Jury, but that he had requested bail. He'd said he stood a chance of losing his job and home if he were not released on bail. So the magistrates let him out. No thought for me. Rolfe reassured me that he had bail conditions; a curfew which meant he had to be in by 7.00pm on early shift weeks and 11.00pm on late shift weeks, and not to leave the house before 5.00am. And he wasn't to contact me in any way, or ask Kim or his friends to.

They had let him out. My rapist.

Rolfe could tell I was upset, because she told me if I thought he was doing anything like phoning me, to make a note of it and they could do something.

I changed the locks on my doors and made very sure I used them.

~~~

Kirsty

"Jimbo's back," hissed Tom as Kirsty walked into work Monday morning. She was cold from the ride in and it took a moment for Tom's words to register.

"You're joking," she said. "Has he been tried and found not guilty then?"

"Dunno. He says he wants a five-minute meeting before the line starts up."

Jimbo had lost weight, which made him seem older, Kirsty thought. He still looked suave and cocky though.

"Right," he said. "Just to scotch any rumours before they begin, I'm sure you saw in the papers that I was falsely accused of rape and arrested. Worst luck, I was remanded in custody, though that wasn't fair, so they have let me out on bail. This means I can work.

"I gotta tell you that I'm not guilty; the woman involved has done it to spite me. Often happens, I'm told. And it looks like I'm going to have to go to court to clear my name.

"Just make sure that you don't gossip about this. I am innocent, not guilty, and you'd better remember that. Any false allegations and rumours will be dealt with. OK?

"OK?" he asked a second time, this time louder, demanding a response.

"Yes Jimbo," said Janet meekly. "Good to have you back."

Chapter 27

Angie

I was gradually getting better, days since the birth melting into weeks. Then I hit a plateau just before Christmas.

By that time, I'd got to know Dr Galton quite well, but never managed the same doctor/patient relationship as had developed between me and Dr T. I hadn't realised how much I'd grown to like Dr T, to respect him, until he wasn't there anymore. Galton didn't seem to warm to me, to like me that much. Homophobic, maybe? Or scared of her own sexuality? Or perhaps she was just intolerant of mental problems. Who knows. She did her best for me, I'm sure, but in a perfunctory way. Distanced. I asked if she thought counselling might help. She said it might, then told me there was a six month wait on the NHS waiting list. I was still too lacking in self-confidence to ask for her recommendations, or if the practice could refer me.

A couple of days before Christmas I phoned the counselling woman on the card Sally had left and left a message.

Petronella returned my phone call later that day. Her voice was like gravel in a wooden box, as if it had been all talked out years ago. I found it vaguely comforting. I made an appointment to see her in two weeks' time. Seemed a long time away, but a helluva lot better than six months for an NHS appointment. Then I got jittery. "Er… er… can you tell me a little about what to expect," I asked. "Only I'm not sure if it'll help. And the cost. I need to know that…"

"Well, the initial consultation is free, but I charge £40 per session after that. I do it that way so that you get a feel for the sort of counselling I offer and see if you feel it's right for you. Basically, I offer a chance for you to talk through some of the things that are troubling you, teach you some relaxation exercises and so on. I tend to work in an eclectic way, with you, finding what works for you."

"You mean like a sort of agony aunt."

"Not exactly. It's more that I help you to become your own agony aunt. Put you back in control. It's difficult to explain, and easier just to experience."

"Oh, OK, I understand," I fibbed, suddenly finding the phone too heavy. "See... See you..."

Why? Why did I get that rush of inadequacy and self-loathing washing over me like a cold wave? I could feel the undertow, tugging at my feet.

~~~

I spent Christmas Day and Boxing Day pissed out of my brains. I knew it was wrong, very wrong to mix alcohol and my tablets, but if I'd died then, I wouldn't have cared.

~~~

The public car park was full. January Sales. I was panting over the injustice of it, when someone left and I grabbed the space. I fed the machine for a couple of hours' worth. My hand was shaking as I fumbled the ticket onto my windscreen. I wandered towards the High Street, then went back to the car to check that I'd locked it, and that the ticket was stuck on the windscreen OK.

The Healing Centre was a shared facility. Aromatherapy and massage on Tuesdays and Fridays. Reiki on Wednesday. Chinese Medicine, hypnotherapy, weight loss, help with smoking, Counselling; all for the ills of a modern society. I rang the bell, and a voice came over the intercom, in and to the right, please. The door unlocked and swung shut behind me. My hands tingled. I knocked a timorous rap on the door.

Five foot two ish, punky hair, face like crumpled tissue paper. Smile. Warm, real smile. "Angie, come in. Have a seat. I'm Petronella Woods but call me Peter." A smile, an emanation of warmth.

I perched on the edge of the seat and wiped my hands down my jeans. She poured some water into a glass, and placed it on a coffee table, near a box of tissues, and flung herself into the other chair at right angles to mine. The coffee table was a comfortable reach away from us, somewhere for my eyes to rest, a neutral space. There was a third chair but tucked out of the way.

It was easy to look at her when I wanted to, but restful to look away when I needed to examine my thoughts. I took a sip of water, hiding behind the glass, surprised at how cold and soothing the liquid was on my throat.

The first thing she did was tell me a little about herself, her professional self, her qualifications. (I never found out anything about Peter the person, though I wondered.) And she reassured me that anything we discussed was confidential.

I told her my story in begrudged sentences. Hard, so hard to squeeze them out. The room was swaying, or so it seemed, but it was me, rocking. I slid backwards, deeper into the chair. Very comfortable, like a hug in leather. The room steadied. "I've found it... Difficult."

She waited for more, but that was enough for starters. "Sounds like you've had a really tough time. It's been hard for you, but I feel that counselling could help you work through this."

"Yes. Sally thought I should try counselling. She said about her, um. And how you helped. And she made me see the doctor." The grief made me stumble. "Did you happen to know Dr Thomas? Only he died. Suddenly. So I have to see Dr Galton now." The unsaid words swarmed round like bees. Bereavement. Loss. Distrust. I wondered if Peter heard them, the word-bees. I took a sip of water to ease the words. "She put me on medication for postnatal depression. And it's helped. But I seem to have stopped making progress."

"Um. It can take a year to get over postnatal depression. Don't expect too much too soon."

"Well, yes. But I think there might be other… issues."

"Yes, Angie. Sounds like you've already got a good insight into the root cause of some of your problems. I feel we could do a lot of work, don't you?"

How the hell should I know? I didn't know my own mind half the time, not now. The simplest decision seemed to take mind-boggling thought, and the fear that I had made the wrong decision would poke me awake at night. "It's worth a try," I said at last, the phrase betraying my scepticism.

Peter asked me details about Dr Galton, the medication, and asked permission to talk to Galton if it was necessary. Then I told her a little about how I felt as a person. She hardly said anything. Perhaps it was grief that made her voice so gravelly, not overuse. It was as if I were carrying bin-loads of grief and tipping them into her, and she absorbed it all.

I told her about Kim, and how betrayed I felt, and about Digby and how disgusted I was, and about me, and how I loathed myself for hating an innocent baby.

At the end Peter said, "You've done really well today Angie. I would recommend at least a further six sessions. It you'd like to continue, we do offer a reduction for advance payment if that helps."

I mentally raided the moneybox, and said I'll have to see.

~~~

DC Rolfe came to see me with her startling emerald eyes and asked if I was prepared to give my evidence face to face or whether I'd prefer to do it via a video link or hidden by screens. Rape victims often do, nowadays, apparently. "Look, she said, hooking my eyes with hers. "It's tough giving evidence in a rape trial. The prosecutor will ask you questions, though he mustn't lead you. You answer those questions and it tells your story. But then you're cross-examined by the defence barrister. He's not allowed to ask you about your sex life, or badger you, but it's his job to show that you're exaggerating. Or lying. In rape cases this often means showing that the defendant thought you had consented."

"But I didn't consent. I'd never consent."

"Digby and Kim both said you did. You must be prepared for that."

"You don't believe me, then."

"If we thought you'd consented, no way would we be taking this further. It's a matter of convincing the jury. In the case of, say, a rape where the defendant used violence, quite apart from protecting a vulnerable witness, there are advantages in giving evidence by videolink. Looks bad on the defendant if you're too afraid to face him in person, as well as being easier for the rape survivor. However, in your case, you have no memory of the actual rape. So the videolink isn't quite so justifiable, might look a bit contrived. And the jury may think you're too afraid to face them in person. But it's up to you. Which would you rather do?"

A decision. She was asking for a decision. "I don't know. Can I think about it?"

"Well, OK, but can you let me know ASAP. By Friday at the latest, as it's Digby's Plea and Directions Hearing soon and we'd prefer to know by then so we can formally request it of the Judge."

"Oh," I said, wondering if she'd suddenly slipped into Greek. "I'll phone you Friday afternoon."

There; a decision. An assertion. Progress?

Chapter 28

Kirsty

"You might at least knock before barging in," yelled Kirsty, rather more aggressively than necessary.

Her mother, carrying a bundle of Kirsty's clean clothes, immediately looked contrite, then flabbergasted. "What are you wearing? Is that what you got in the sales?"

Kirsty preened and did a twirl. "Great isn't it? They were really reduced."

"I can see why. Shall I change the outdoor light for a red one?" Her mother's tone was dry and disapproving.

"Muuuum, it's not that bad." Kirsty looked down at her new ensemble. She looked rather good in it. It was a red tee shirt with a football on it and the words, 'You've scored', and a blue miniskirt which clung to her bum because it was slightly elasticated. The knee length boots really set it off.

"F me, F me," said her mother in an aghast tone.

"What d'you mean?"

"Follow me, Fuck me. That's what that says. It's an open invitation to being approached."

"Don't be silly, Mum. You're over-reacting as usual. People will know it's only a joke. And everyone's into footie tee shirts just now. Don't be so.... old."

"The tee shirt is bad enough, but that thing round your bum is a belt masquerading as a skirt. Don't you realise your knickers will show every time you sit down. You take them back, exchange them. The boots are OK but the rest stinks."

"I bought it with the money Dad gave me and I'll spend it on what I like. Bimbo slut has a skirt this short." It was time

Mum realised she was an adult and could do as she pleased, thought Kirsty.

"She is just a bimbo slut and she's not exactly a good role model. She stole your father from us when we needed him most by flashing her knickers at him, the cow." Her mother pulled in a breath. "What kind of message do you think that gear says about you? It says, 'cheap screw'. You should be looking for someone who'll support you through thick and thin, be loyal and faithful. You won't get that by acting like a tart. You'll end up with some ignorant little cannabis-smoking scrote like that chav Tom."

"He's not a chav, he's nice, and he respects me."

"Rubbish. I've seen his sort before, usually on the wrong side of a cell door."

"You don't know him, you're just prejudiced against him because of where he lives. Coppers shouldn't be prejudiced like that."

Her mum snorted. "That's true enough, but that doesn't get away from the fact those clothes are trashy."

"So, I should dress like a frump like you do and attract a bloke like you did, yeah right; he really hung around didn't he, my Dad."

Kirsty saw the hurt flair over her mother's face. When her mum replied it was as if she was talking through splinters of glass. "That just goes to show what fuck-heads most men are." She broke off, storming out of the room, mouth crumpled like an old paper bag, but not before Kirsty saw the remembered pain in her eyes.

The memories of the divorce rocked Kirsty too, like the wake from a boat, leaving her dizzy and nauseated. Mum didn't normally use the F word in her presence, either. She undressed, put the tee shirt and the skirt back in the bag, carefully, found the receipt, and put that in with them. Then she threw herself on the bed and wept. She wasn't quite sure why.

When Kirsty went downstairs, her mother was attacking the potatoes for supper, peeler shredding off huge slices of skin. "I'm sorry, Mum. I'm taking them back. And I've been thinking: I think you're overprotective because of your job. I'm not stupid you know. I know better than to walk down dark alleys at night wearing that sort of thing, but I want to fit in with everyone else, and everyone's wearing footie stuff just now. And anyhow, men shouldn't rape women just because of the clothes they're wearing. That's wrong, and I'm shocked that you think women are asking for it just because of what they're wearing."

"Well, get some footie stuff then. A nice footie tee shirt and jeans is fine." Her mum frowned but more with indignation than anger. "Besides which how dare you; I don't think women are 'asking for it' just because of what they're wearing, we ought to be able to wear what the hell we like, but it's like leaving your front door open and being burgled. The burglar is still a criminal, you're still a victim of crime, but the insurance company won't pay out. And yes, maybe I am over-protective, but that's because you're so naïve."

"I'm not."

"You are; you've just shown that with your remarks about dark alleys. Stranger rape is far less common than being raped by someone you know; a friend, a relative, a boyfriend. And that sort of rape is very hard to prove."

"I don't see why. If a girl says no, and he carries on, then he's guilty. No means no."

Dropping the mutilated potato and peeler into the sink, her mother dried her hands then gave Kirsty a long mummy-hug. "True, but sometimes proving rape is hard. I haven't really discussed what happened the other night, and I don't propose to go on about it, but I'd like you think about this. I had to come and rescue you because you'd been drinking and couldn't ride your moped home. Someone you trusted had slipped you alcohol, the date rape drug of choice. Luckily you realised in time and phoned me. Luckily, I was off duty and able to come and pick you up. But supposing someone had offered to drive you home, and then raped you in the back of the car? You allege rape, but he says you were willing – how do we prove otherwise? Or he drives you home, you offer him a coffee by way of thanks, which he then assumes is an invitation for something more. He rapes you, and, when arrested, says you were keen for it. How do we know who to believe?"

"If a girl says no, it's rape, end of." Kirsty flounced towards the door.

"I haven't finished with you yet. Obviously, I'd believe you, but would a jury? And worse, if you'd been raped, that would have stayed with you for the rest of your life. I know what a god-awful effect rape has on its victims, because I see it every working day. I don't want you to ever be a victim, understand. Never."

Kirsty was shocked to see her mum's eyes filled with fear, and it made her think. Supposing that revolting man outside Snack-a-Randy's who'd asked her for a light, had instead just grabbed her and dragged her off? She shuddered. "I don't want to talk about it."

"OK, let's not talk about you, let's talk hypothetically. Let's say Mary and John meet up on a night out and go back to her place for coffee. He starts kissing her and she responds.

189

He says, 'I've a condom,' she says, 'It's OK, I'm on the Pill,' and they have sex. Is that rape?"

"No, because she's consented." Obviously, duh.

"What if they're a bit drunk and the same thing happens?"

"Then it's rape, because she's incapable of giving consent because she's drunk."

"Is it? She wasn't so drunk she didn't know what she was doing, because they'd discussed contraception, so maybe she was capable of giving consent, despite having had a drink or two. But suppose she's so drunk she doesn't know what she's doing. Then there's no consent, and it's rape. But how does the jury know who is telling the truth, beyond reasonable doubt? How drunk does someone have to be before they can no longer consent?"

Kirsty's thoughts went back to the horrible time by the pine trees. Ellie had been reluctant to give Glyn the blow job at first, yet wasn't totally pissed when she acquiesced, just more chilled out after the cider and skunk. In fact, she seemed to be enjoying it when Kirsty had flounced off in disgust. So that was consented to... but they were under age and so sex was illegal, as was the alcohol and the cannabis, so did that make it rape?

"At this rate I'll never get the supper cooked. I think you should go to the Essex Police website, and under where it says, 'Be Safe' you'll find a section on rape. You'll also find a link to an organisation called, "Rights of Women". They do an excellent PDF about rape and other sexual offences. It explains things very well. I can see by that closed-off expression you're not really listening to me."

Kirsty fled upstairs. Gawd, her mum could be patronising sometimes. What a lecture! Like she was ten and didn't know anything. She lay on the bed and studied the ceiling, thinking back to Tom and his alcopops, and how she'd been willing to go all the way. Would that have been rape? She'd been tipsy, not drunk, and aroused, wanting sex. It hadn't seemed like rape at the time, it had seemed like a good idea. Thinking about it, she wasn't so drunk she couldn't give consent, so it wasn't rape, was it?

But would she have agreed to sex if she'd been stone cold sober? Unlikely. He'd given her alcohol without her knowing, and then tried to have sex. Had Tom nearly raped her?

Better do as her mum said. With a sigh, Kirsty opened her laptop and started browsing. She learned that a lot of rapes were by someone the victim knew.

Like Tom perhaps? Or Stuart? Or Jimbo?

She read about husbands who forced their wives, about serial rapists, and about predatory people who had got away with date rape after date rape because each allegation was tried separately and without reference to the past. This was the sort of thing her mum dealt with, and Kirsty had never really appreciated how hard it must be.

~~~

Suzy

Suzy went back to the potatoes. Supper would be late. Again. But the conversation had been worth it. Maybe Kirsty would understand how important it was to stay safe, not get drunk, not put herself in a vulnerable position, because you never knew who might take advantage of it. Maybe at last Kirsty was beginning to truly comprehend what Suzy meant, rather than just, 'I know, I know.' The thoughts rumbled round Suzy's head until supper was ready.

"Grub's up," she yelled as she dished up.

Kirsty came into the kitchen with a strange expression on her face. "I've been thinking Mum. I don't want to go to university after all. I want to join the police."

Suzy gasped as if Kirsty had hit her. "You can't." A gestalt of visions from the past dropped into her mind, the horror, the filth, to sordidness of the lower human existence. Not Kirsty dealing with that, putting herself at risk. No way. "No."

"Why not?"

"Because…." Why not? It was a bloody rewarding job. There were times when Suzy knew it was the best job in the world. "Because you're not old enough."

"I am nearly. Eighteen and a half, I can apply."

"You haven't the life experience. They'll turn you down."

Kirsty's face puckered. "You always say that, you say I'm not grown up enough, you say I'm still a child. Well, I'm not. I'm an adult and I can do as I want," she wailed.

"Will you listen! I said you haven't the life-experience. It's hard to get into the police, can take a couple of years, and only when they're having a recruitment drive. And they might turn you down anyway, after all that waiting, and you'll have chucked your university place for nothing, spend the rest of your life making pizzas. If you're serious about this…"

Kirsty nodded her head vigorously. "I am."

"Then what I suggest is that when you get to university you volunteer as a Special Constable. Get a feel for the job, get some experience. It's not all blue lights and glamour, you know. Far from it."

Suzy watched Kirsty simmer down to a sullen glower. They ate in near silence. If Kirsty was serious, then perhaps she would make a good copper, but not when she was still so young, so naive, so willing to believe people, so easy to fly off

192

the handle at the least provocation. Suzy had her doubts about Kirsty's seriousness, though, because until an hour ago she'd never shown any ambitions to join the Job. Maybe the idea would die a death. Suzy hoped so.

~~~

Angie

When I saw Peter again, I told her about the forthcoming trial, and the fears I had about giving evidence. As I told her about the videolink problem, I decided, yes I decided that I'd prefer to give evidence in person. Stand up and tell them all what he'd done, and how he'd damaged me. Hell, I ought to be able to sue him for my treatment.

Talking about the trial meant I started talking about Kim. "She did love me, you know, and I loved her. Five years, five happy years. But she took against me when I told her I was pregnant, when I needed her most." I told Peter about Kim being let down by previous bisexual lovers and her insecurities. "I had completely forgotten the conversation about bisexuality on our first date. I think it didn't matter to me because I'm not bi... the thought of penetration by a man leaves me cold... more than that, it leaves me feeling a bit revolted—I, I can't help feeling that way," I added in case Peter thought it was an outrageous way to feel.

"Do you think Kim feels the same way?"

"She made out that she left me because I'd lied to her about being bi, that I'd betrayed her by having sex with a man, but I think there's more to it, like being raped meant I was disgusting. She really hurt me, you know, her reaction when she found out. I needed love and hugs and reassurance and all I got was her telling me she didn't want any intimacy. That made me feel worthless." I sniffed into some tissues for a bit, and sipped the cooling water. "She seems to think I'd leave her for a man like her ex did. And I wouldn't, never. She seems to push people away in case they dump her. Like standing on a cliff and jumping off because you're afraid you might fall off. So she left me and now she's lied about me to the police, she's protecting her brother because he's manipulated her until she believes I came on strong to him when her back was turned, that I lied to him as well. It doesn't make sense, his lies, but she believes them. It's almost like she wants to believe them to justify the way she's behaved towards me."

"Do you hate her now?"

"Yes…. No. I just don't recognise her any more. She's not the Kim I loved for five years. And of course, now I know Digby is the rapist, it explains why he said all those things about me being bisexual just after I told Kim I was pregnant—I can see that in hindsight. He knew her weaknesses and he played on them, got her on his side, and now I don't know if she knows she's deliberately lying, or if she really believes what she's saying.

"I can understand it, but it doesn't lessen the hurt. It makes me angry and frustrated because there's nothing I can do about it. I miss her. I want things to be the way they were before the rape. I really miss her."

Peter didn't agree or disagree with my analysis of Kim, the just let me talk the hurt out into the open. Then she said, "We need to accept people for who they are, not who we'd like them to be. Kim has her own issues, her own problems, and the way she behaved to you is as a result of her past, nothing to do with you or your sense of self-worth. She couldn't help it. We can't afford unrealistic expectations of people or we'll always be disappointed."

194

"You mean the way she's behaved to me isn't my fault? Well, I know that, in my mind. But in my heart it makes me feel worthless. I want her back."

"Is that a realistic hope?"

I thought for a long, long time, though I knew the answer. But acknowledging it was hard. "No."

"If she came back to you tomorrow, how would you feel?"

"Wonderful."

"Are you sure? With all this between you? Or is it that you want to go back to the past, back to the way things were before the rape? The rape can't be undone. Going back is impossible; you can only go forward. Perhaps you could get back together again, work through all these problems until you have a resolution and live happily together. Or perhaps you could look on what happened as a wonderful time in your life, acknowledge the relationship is over, grieve for it and move on."

I pondered this for a while, silently. The silences never bothered Peter. It was as if she hit neutral while I sorted things through in my mind; waiting ready for the next dose of grief and hurt to be revealed to her. "I don't think I can think this through at the moment. I'm not sure what I want, except for none of this to have happened, which is impossible. I can't forgive her yet. Though I know it's not really her fault, any more than the rape was my fault. But do I really want her back? I'm not so sure right now."

"We have to grieve for broken relationships in the same way as we grieve over a death," said Peter.

That took the conversation round to the swamping grief over Dr T dying, and how bad I felt that when I cried, I wasn't sure for whom it was. I'm not sure it helped, because I ended up crying all over again.

~~~

That night as I lay restless, I thought about this. I tried to conjure up some of the joyful memories of Kim. It was hard, as if her treachery had contaminated all that was good. And that in itself made me angry, not with her, but with Digby. I rose, went into the kitchen to make myself a hot drink. It was dark outside, with just a glimmer of the streetlight finding its way round the back.

"We ought to do something with the back garden," Kim had said about six months after moving in with me. We were snuggled together on the settee and we'd just watched one of those garden makeover programmes. "It's just a lawn and a few scratty flowers, and all we ever do out there is hang the washing out." She jumped up, dragged me up. "C'mon, let's have a look, see what we can do with it."

When the house had been divided into two maisonettes, the back garden had been divided too. I owned the front garden, which was tiny, and the first part of the back garden. The upstairs maisonette owned the rest. The entire back garden was surrounded by six-foot fences, there was a concrete path which led down from the front gate to the very end of the entire garden. Originally there had been a washing line stretched down the whole length of the path, and one green metal post remained like a fossil at the far end. There was a low picket fence dividing my half from Upstairs' half, and against the path, making it a passageway past my garden to Upstairs' garden. My front door, the original back door, opened straight out into our back garden, and there was a little picket gate between the garden and the path. That meant that sometimes people like the postman didn't realise it was my front door, and pushed my post through Upstairs'

(No. 34A's) letterbox. But it meant I got the better bargain with the more convenient garden.

Kim was right, though. It was just a small patch of utilitarian grass, with uptight one-foot borders with a few plants shoved in willy-nilly to survive or not. It was just like my father's garden. Utterly conventional and uncontroversial.

The rotary washing line was beginning to rust. Kim yanked it out in a fit of zealous enthusiasm. "There, that's better. Look, we could have a patio like on the telly, a courtyard garden, a water feature, somewhere to sit…"

"And soggy washing," I said, laughing at her. "They never think of the practicalities, these garden makeover programmes."

Kim looked in dismay at the washing line. She tried to shove it back into the ground, but it had rusted at lawn level and had broken off. She looked so chastened and unsure of herself I kissed her. "Why don't you draw up some plans and we'll see what we can do? That old line was past its sell by date anyway. We'll get a new one and get one of those socket things so we can take it out and put it away when we don't need it."

Kim applied the same design flair that made her such a wow in the boutique, and she came up with a lovely plan. But designs on paper are all very well, and the makeover programmes make it all seem so easy. After a couple of days' frustrated lawn scalping, I grabbed her lovely hands, now ravaged by the rather inadequate spade. "I'll get a bloke in to do the hard landscaping," I told her. "I'm not having you wreck yourself over this."

"But I want to do it myself. For us."

"I'll get the patio laid, you pick the plants and we'll do the planting together."

We had a couple of quotes, and a bloke came and laid the Indian sandstone Kim had picked, and put a socket for the new washing line in the middle of the patio.

We went to the garden centre. I'd paid for the landscaping, but Kim was paying for the plants. "Aw that's well nice," she said, grabbing a well-grown clematis covered in huge blue flowers. They matched her eyes.

"If you like it..."

"But do you like it? I'm doing this for you, remember. For us."

"I love it."

She put it in the trolley, which I pushed. "We'll need some soil conditioner and fertiliser," I reminded her. "And a watering can or a hose and stuff."

She'd set herself a budget but by the time we'd put the compost, bagged manure and a few well-grown plants into the trolley, the budget was spent. We took it home, the manure stinking the car out, and put the plants into the three generous borders. When we'd finished we brought out the kitchen chairs and sat and admired our handiwork. "It's not quite how I thought it would be," Kim said mournfully. "It looks half empty."

"We'll go to the garden centre tomorrow, and buy some more plants. I'll pay," I promised, taking her hand. "And we need something to sit on. We can't keep taking these chairs out."

Next day, we went round the garden centre again. "Can we have this?" Kim said, picking up a peony. "Mum has one of these and they're well nice."

Of course we could have it. My love could have whatever she wanted. We planted the garden up and it looked beautiful, softly feminine, just like my girl. I bought a bench which we sat out on in the evenings...

...The bench which Kim had sat on so much before she left me, texting, texting that evil brother of hers.

~~~

After my sleepless night remembering our garden makeover I went outside and sat down on the bench in the wan chilly sunshine, with a coffee. The washing line was closed up, the clematis a dead-looking tangle against the fence. The climbing roses needed a prune, should have been cut back in the autumn. The herbaceous plants were a mass of blackened stems. The garden had been Kim's province and was redolent with memories, most of them happy, but I had a sudden urge to pull up all the plants, destroy the patio, obliterate the reminders of our past. I couldn't obliterate the past any more than I could realistically dig up and destroy the patio. I would have to learn to live with it.

The roses really did need pruning, and half the clematis looked dead. It was getting top heavy and tangled. I went inside and fetched the secateurs.

Chapter 29

Angie

I was getting really frumpy. The baby was gone, now, but my tummy still felt wobbly and my joints not quite my own. I wondered about a postnatal exercise class but the thought of being in with a load of smug mums filled me with dread. And anyhow, group things aren't really my thing. Kim and I used to go for walks, sometimes ending up at a pub for a meal, though Kim's not really much of a walker, more a town girl, trendy girl. Thinking about her sent a pang through me but hurt less than I would have expected. Peter was right. It was over, and I needed to move on, and get through the grieving over what we'd lost. I wasn't sure I could forgive Kim yet, though. Maybe after the trial and Digs was in jail, perhaps then I could come to terms with her treachery.

It was all very well deciding to go for walks but the agoraphobia which had gripped me in the autumn still lurked like an undertow, despite the medication and relaxation exercises. The stronger side of me said this needed exorcising too, and that if I gave into it, it would be with me forever. I tried to analyse why I was afraid of outdoors. Part of it was the fear of bumping into people in Kim's gang. Part of it was a desperate feeling of vulnerability.

I phoned DC Rolfe. "This might sound a bit daft, but I'm scared to go out in case I get raped. Tell me I'm being stupid." I explained the problem.

There was a short silence, "I could say you're 'being stupid' but it would sound flippant and disparaging. A lot of victims feel like you do; it's understandable, and sometimes makes them prisoners in their own homes. The fear of crime often outweighs the chances of being a victim, but if you've been a victim, it magnifies things, makes you feel vulnerable. Did you enjoy walking before all this? I mean, did you feel vulnerable before?"

"I loved walks. And I felt safe enough. Never gave it much thought."

"Your rapist is known to you. Most rape victims know their rapist. So nothing has changed for you, except yourself. The chances of you being assaulted now are the same as before, it's just your fear has magnified."

"True. Where can I get some CS spray, please? That might make me feel safer."

Rolfe sucked in a breath. "You can't carry anything like that! That's classed as a firearm. It's illegal for you to carry it. You can't get it in this country and don't even think about ordering it over the internet."

"That's not fair. Women should be able to carry something like that for their own protection."

"If it was freely available every mugger and yob would carry it."

"I'll take a knife with me then."

"No. Angie, sorry, you can't. Definitely not. If you are found carrying a knife without good reason—and self-defence is not a good reason, you will go to jail. Carrying a knife usually ends up in a custodial sentence."

"What, even a pen-knife?" I asked, thinking about the tiny knife on my key ring.

"That depends. If the blade is shorter than 3 inches and doesn't lock, it's OK—providing you're not carrying it intending to use it for anything criminal, but if the blade locks in place, doesn't matter how short the blade is, you're breaking the law."

"That's not fair."

"Helps stop knife fights by yobs in town centres. Angie, honestly, you don't need to carry anything like that. Please don't carry a knife; it won't make you any safer and it could mean you end up in jail. Look, are you getting help with all this? Like counselling?"

"Yes, yes, I am, thanks. Thanks, DC Rolfe, you've put my mind at rest. A bit."

~~~

I sat in my car in Tiptree Heath car park telling myself there were no rapists on the heath, telling myself that Kim's gang wouldn't be there, and not to be so silly. There were several other cars parked there. As I sat, another car drew up, the driver got out—a woman, and let a greyhound out the back. She set off, the dog following her at a gentle lope.

I got out, put my boots on. They felt odd because it was ages since I'd worn them... must have been May last year, when they'd got soaked. Kim and I had gone for a walk at Tollesbury, on the salt marshes there. It had been a beautiful day, the sky a huge vault of blue above us. We'd walked hand in hand along the footpaths of the marina. The tide was out, I remembered, the glasswort like miniature cacti on the mud, not quite big enough to pick and eat. As we'd walked, the horizon across the marsh had turned ominous, grey as slate, and we'd watched in awe as a storm approached. The sun behind us picked out the masts of the yachts, bright against the grey wall of cloud. There was nowhere to run, nowhere to hide, so we stood still as the rain swept over us. We were instantly drenched through. We stood laughing and shivering as the spears of water lashed our bodies. Kim had been wearing that lovely blouse. It clung to her body, moulded round her breasts, and I longed to rip it off, cup those breasts, nuzzle her and tell her how much I loved her. But it's open there, and not at all private, so I just clung to her, and she to me, laughing as the rain beat down.

Thinking back now, it was like a premonition of the storm that had hit our lives a few weeks later; my pregnancy, this rape, our heartbreak. Another memory, another ghost. The tears filled my eyes. One day maybe I'd be able to remember the good times without wincing in pain every time I thought of her.

I'd never been to Tiptree Heath before. Driven past it loads of times, but never stopped, so I had no haunting memories of walking there with Kim, which made it emotionally safer than Clacton or the marshes. The trees were bare, pointing fingers at a grey sky. It was cold, the wind penetrating the layers I'd swaddled myself in. I walked between a gap in the gorse bushes and found myself in an open green sward with a choice of directions between the trees, gorse and brambles. I had no map, no idea where I was going. In the middle of the clearing there was a huge oak tree with a woodcarving lodged in the crook of its trunk. I was so surprised I just stared at it.

A golden retriever came and sniffed at my ankles. "Misty! Here!" A woman called the dog off. The dog gave me a doggy grin and a wag of her tail. The woman gave me a second glance. "You look a bit perplexed," she said.

"I haven't been here before and I can't make up my mind... I don't want to get lost." I glanced back at my car with sudden yearning.

"I'll show you round if you like. I'm a Friend." She smiled, then added, "A Friend of Tiptree Heath. FoTH. We look after it. There's a warden and volunteers and everything."

"Oh thanks, that's kind," I said.

We walked round together, and I felt safer for the company. And it was just companionship, no undercurrents, no questions. She told me a bit about the Heath, about the rare Wasp Spiders, and the ponies brought onto the heath in summer to eat the scrub back, the heather which was fighting against the invasive silver birch. When we got back to the car I was tired, but refreshed, as if I'd had a few minutes' normal life again. She got into her car and left, the dog smiling out of the rear window.

Though I walked there often after that, on my own, without fear, I never saw her again. I saw lots of other people, mainly women walking their dogs, and everyone would nod, say hello, exchange some trivial but friendly remark. I was blessed with the kindness of strangers; a place of healing.

~~~

In the next session with Peter, I was able to tell her about Mum and Dad, and what I'd done to them. And I went further back, to the bullying at school when the other girls saw where I was looking in the changing rooms after PE. But they knew about things like homosexuality. I didn't. I wish my parents weren't so innocent; had told me about such things. Then I might have known, might have understood those savage emotions. And then, when I finally did understand what I was, what I am, Mum and Dad didn't. Couldn't. How I'd punished them. And me. Just because they didn't, wouldn't understand.

Thirty years. Heavy bonds of iron. Like annual rings in wood. Ingrained. The first few years I maintained a stubborn silence. And then, when I finally realised how much I missed them, when I finally grew up, it was too late and they'd vanished.

"Do you think the way you related to your mother has had an effect on the way you felt about the baby?" asked Peter.

"No," I denied. "No. I hated the baby because he was the fruit of rape, not because of my Mum. I hated the way being pregnant wrecked my relationship with Kim, and the way it wrecked my body. In fact, I realised just what Mum went through. I suddenly wished that... I suddenly realised just how much I... miss her." The thought lay there on the table beside me, like Pandora's Box, full of potential. Peter just watched as I opened the box, tentatively lifting the lid just an inch. I understood that cliché now. Slam it down. Breathe. Wait for the heart to return to normal. Then look again. At the hurt I'd caused. And the pain it had caused me. Brought to the surface by my own pregnancy.

"Let it go," she said. And I did.

~~~

Fears are like wasps. Hold them tight, and they sting you. Let them go, and the hazard is still there. They can sting but hold them tight and they will sting. Again and again.

~~~

I went back to work, and it was OK. But I couldn't discuss my counselling with Sally, apart from asking for time off to attend the appointments. She didn't seem to want to know, respecting my privacy. All I said was that I was receiving the help I needed.

~~~

Peter helped me change, to accept me for who I am. To not feel guilty over the feelings of hatred, to recognise them as natural. To forgive myself.

The feelings of regret took a little longer to exorcise.

I have a son. Somewhere. I found myself looking into prams and pushchairs, wondering if that baby was my child, knowing (really) that the answer is no. I had, on occasions, even had to resist a compulsion to steal the baby.

"I don't understand why I feel this way," I grizzled at Peter, eyes awash. "I had advice about the adoption. I thought about all the issues, logically, and I know it was for the best. For baby and for me. I'm not a mum. I can't be a proper mum. So why do I feel like this?"

~~~

At the end of the six sessions, a void opened up in front of me. I had a vertiginous stab of agoraphobia, but from a counselling sense, not an open space sense. So I said I wanted to see her again. After a month, if that was OK.

I found I liked me again. In fact, I liked me better than I have done in years. I liked me better than I've ever done since I grew breasts and found I liked looking at the other girls'.

Still missed my Mum, though. And there was nothing I could do about it.

~~~

The people in the flat above me had left, apparently. I thought it had gone quiet up there. The first I knew was when someone came knocking on the back door, which is my front door, and handed me a wad of post. "Hello," he said. "I own the flat above. You don't happen to have a forwarding address of the young couple who used to live here, do you?"

"No, sorry. I never saw them, heard them occasionally." The flat above was rented, which meant quite a high turnover of tenants, some pleasant, some not.

"Only they stopped paying about four months ago, and now they've done a bunk, leaving the place in a right mess. I'm afraid some of this post is a bit old. It was in a box in the hall full of junk post. I sorted through in case I could get some idea of where they've gone. They owe me. I hope it wasn't anything important."

"I doubt it," I said, taking the bundle from him. "I haven't noticed anything missing, and I don't get that much post."

"Lazy sods," he added. "Couldn't be bothered to walk twenty feet and give you your post."

"Thanks anyway." I closed the door absentmindedly behind him.

Most of it was junk, there was a get well soon card from work, and an A5 envelope with leaflets in it. There was a covering letter from DC Rolfe, saying she thought I might find them useful, and if I needed any help at all, to contact her or the Rape Crisis Centre at Rosamundi House. It was dated a day or two after I'd seen her at the police station. The leaflets were about the help available for rape victims, including counselling, information about STDs.

If I'd known, I could have got help this way, not waited until I was ill before seeing Peter and paying money privately.

But then again, when I thought about it, counselling and crisis management had been mentioned to me early on. I'd just been too stunned to take any notice; not my thing. Or so I'd thought.

Chapter 30

Angie

I invited Sally Curtis to dinner and extended the invitation to her husband John as well. Over the last few weeks, Sally had seemed a little distant. At first, I thought her confidences about her accident with the baby lay between us, but the problem was more worrying than that. Big John was jealous, or so she told me when I timidly asked her if I'd upset her somehow. He thought I was trying to seduce his wife away from him. As if... Sally just wasn't my type. So I thought the best thing was to get to know John too, show him I'm not a monster.

Big John really is big. Huge. Brian Blessed style huge. And burly, with a deep voice, like a bear about to hibernate. Huge appetite, too. He just ate everything that was put in front of him like a combine harvester. He's actually a very sweet man. Cuddly type. I liked him a lot, but not in a sexual way. Like a brother. I wondered if my real brother was as nice.

Sally was driving, so she didn't drink, but John had her share. He didn't seem to get drunk but mellowed as the evening went on.

The conversation slipped into the scary place, the forthcoming trial. I don't know how the conversation got there, but suddenly we were talking about it, and how scared I was beginning to feel. I didn't identify Digby or even go into any details, as I wasn't prepared to trust Big John yet. I told them how the Witness Service people had been helpful, showing me an empty courtroom and telling me what to expect.

"The person who showed me round asked if I'd been in touch with Victim Support and gave me a booklet about rape trials and what to expect. The embarrassing thing is, DC Rolfe gave the same thing to me at the beginning, it's really useful, but I was too hung up to read it then and just put it to one side," I told John and Sally.

"That's a shame. What do Victim Support do?" asked John.

"Well, as I understand it, there's a coordinator or somebody who puts you in touch with a trained volunteer, someone who isn't family, isn't police, who you can talk to. In confidence, knowing that they're not there to judge you, more to act as a pair of sympathetic ears."

"A bit like Peter then," commented Sally. "If you'd contacted them perhaps you wouldn't have had to..." she trailed off, recalling that my seeing Peter was confidential. But of course John filled in the unsaid words; so easy to breach a confidence. A few relaxed words, a minor indiscretion, and the truth is out. But I didn't really mind, not now I realised there should be no stigma attached to seeking that sort of help. The reverse, in fact; it shows a certain intelligence.

"Peter's been enormously helpful," I said, "So in some respects I'm glad I saw her first. But I will contact someone because they're more knowledgeable about the trial and things, you know, they've tons of experience."

"I'd be willing to bet that Peter has experience in that field as well," Sally said.

"I asked Peter about it, worried that it might put her nose out of joint, but she was quite happy for me to contact Victim Support, because they can offer extra help and expertise. A sort of back up. Belt and braces. Thank goodness I've got better before having to give evidence. I don't think I could have hacked it a few months ago."

~~~

I got in contact with Victim Support again, asking for help. They said a trained volunteer called Bea would be in touch. She came to visit me, and she was great. I hadn't realised just how much the thought of going to court was preying on my mind. Bea went over what would happen in court. I told her that I was going to give my evidence in the witness stand, and how I was beginning to regret saying I would. I was also scared that I might meet Digby face to face in the court building. Or Kim. Bea said that they could find somewhere quiet for me to sit, and even have someone come into the courtroom with me, though, Bea said with a smile, I'd have to go into the witness stand on my own.

Bea said to phone if I had any questions, or she'd visit again if I wanted. Did I want to make an impact statement to be read out in court? It wouldn't be used as evidence but was a way of expressing how I felt about the rape, and the sort of effects it had had on me. That could be used to help the Judge in his sentencing. She promised to pop by to see me just before the trial.

~~~

I started writing an impact statement, but it turned into an account of what had happened to me. It helped to write it down, though I wasn't sure I wanted other people to read it. Not the unexpurgated version, anyway.

Chapter 31

Suzy

"Everything seems a bit frenzied," commented Suzy, looking round that Friday when she arrived.

Lynne looked up from her computer. "Misper. Elversford. That girl Ellie Warrener didn't come home last night, but that's not the first time she's led her parents on a merry dance, if you remember, which is why we've been involved. Her parents have phoned round all her friends, and she's not there. So they reported her missing this morning. They didn't like to trouble us too soon after the last time.

"Ellie's about to do her GCSEs, and there was some tension at home because she's not revising like she ought to. She's in the same class as Trish, the girl who may have been date raped. In fact, they're part of a pack of kids who go out together. Trish, her sister Jordan, a lad called Tom, Stuart (both also from the pizza factory), to name but a few. Or at least, they used to go out drinking together, to the Blue Bore until the landlord found himself in deep shit over the barman Cliff Hanger, and the younger ones are banned from that pub. The thing is, they're all known to each other.

"And the kids have got a drinking, smoking den in the pines near the river. The local PCSO knows about it, has nicknamed it Camp Cannabis 2nd, and sometimes goes to the area with the beat officer to confiscate the alcohol, and seize any cannabis and report it. Tom and some other kids say Ellie was there yesterday afternoon, smoking, drinking. They say she was texting someone. Then she got all excited and left. That's the last reported sighting. Let's hope she's either fetched up in someone unknown's house. Or if she's drugged or drunk out of her mind, let's hope we find her before she dies of hypothermia."

Suzy looked at her watch. "Kirsty's at home with dreadful period pains, poor kid. I'll give her a ring, see if she knows anything. She knows Jordan and Tom. She's even been out with the crowd. And Tom, unfortunately. He's a bit scrotey looking and not my choice as a boyfriend. I hope she shows more discernment at university. Oh how tempted I was to do a PNC check on him."

"And lose your job and end up Inside, like as not, and even then not persuade Kirsty of his unsuitability," said Lynne in a rueful tone.

"Yes. Quite," agreed Suzy, staring into space.

"You were going to phone Kirsty," said Lynne, nudging Suzy.

Suzy jumped. "Oh, yes, so I was." She dialled.

Kirsty answered rather abruptly. "Yeah?"

"Do you know an Ellie Warrener?"

There was a silence. Was Kirsty thinking about the question, or just deciding whether to lie? "Sort of. Vaguely."

"How?" asked Suzy, stifling exasperation.

"She used to hang out with the crowd from work. I only met her the once, when she tried to come to the Blue Bore with us. The Landlord told us all to leave. So we said she couldn't come with us anymore. And I haven't seen her since."

Suzy thought there was a lie somewhere in what Kirsty had said but decided to overlook it. "Look, this is important. I want you to write a list of all the people you go drinking with. Including those you remember from that night."

"Muuum! I'm knackered. My period's hurting badly.... And it was months ago..."

"Now look, you stupid little girl, Ellie's gone missing. So you get your worthless, self-centred brain working on that, and email it to me as soon as you can. You hear? Ellie's missing. And we need to find her."

Suzy heard a gasp. "Missing? Oh. Sorry Mum. I'll do it now."

Suzy put the phone down with a sigh, and cradled her head in the hands, fingers combed into her hair. "Gawd, why did I snap at her like that? She wasn't to know about Ellie, but she's just so... oh." Suzy looked up, gesturing with her hands, like claws. "It's just such hard work talking to her. Grr. Yet underneath she's a caring sort of girl. Oh, I wish I hadn't been so horrible to her. She just touched a nerve."

"I shouldn't worry about it. Water off a teenager's back," said Lynne.

"They do grow up, you know," said Cheungy. "Eventually."

~~~

Kirsty

Kirsty made the list, and emailed it to her mother, sniffing the feelings of inadequacy down. Her mother held her in contempt, that was clear. And no wonder; she was a pretty worthless person, really. No good at anything. Useless.

~~~

Suzy

A little later, Suzy phoned Kirsty, this time on her mobile, and not observed by anyone. "Thanks for the list, Sweetie, and sorry I snapped at you earlier. Elversford are doing house-to-house enquiries, starting with that horrible estate, basically because it's close to Camp Cannabis, which is the last place Ellie was seen," Suzy told her daughter. There was a sullen silence. "You know about the drinking den in the woods behind the supermarket?" Suzy added.

There was a further silence except for breathing, then Kirsty said, "Yes."

"Do you go there?"

"No!" Suzy was shocked and partly reassured by Kirsty's vehement denial.

"Brooks tried a couple of other places where, according to her friends, she might have fetched up, and not want it known to her parents. No luck."

"You think she's dead, don't you?"

"Don't tell anyone, Kirsty, Sweetie, but yes. Yes, I think she is."

~~~

Suzy returned to the nick after a hastily snatched sandwich lunch. Cheungy looked up as she entered the room. "Ellie: We've found her…"

Suzy scrutinized her boss's face for joy. Found none. "Where?"

"Ebbed dry on the river mudflats, spotted by Air Support, DI Hedley's at the scene just now. Scenes of Crime and the pathologist are on their way. Dr Shaw's attended already. Life extinct. Can you come with me because this may end up our job."

~~~

215

They parked in the Supermarket car park. The footpath to the river was taped off, guarded by police officers, and they had to sign in. The log keeper asked them to put paper suits on. There were shoppers nearby, some pretending to ignore the police cordon, some gawping blatantly. There were stepping plates along the footpath down to the riverbank. They had to step from plate to plate, rustling with every step. A swan hissed at them and raised his wings.

"I'm surprised they took this route in—I hope we haven't lost any evidence," commented Cheungy. "It's most likely the route any murderer would have taken in, if we are looking at murder and the poor child didn't just get drunk, fall in and drown."

"Maybe there's a problem with the tide," suggested Suzy. "Maybe scenes of crime have to hurry so we can get the body out before the tide turns."

The inner scene was further taped off, and one of the Elversford officers was keeping the log of this scene. Ellie was lying like some broken flotsam on the tidal mud flats, caught up round some jagged spars of wood from an ancient shipwreck. The waters had receded, though the River Galwell still cut through the middle of the channel.

Hugh and his Scenes of Crime team were already busy, one eye on the tide. A tent was being erected over the body to hide it from the onlookers who were gathering like blowflies on the opposite bank. Some onlookers were taking photographs.

"Maybe that's what all the hurry was about, Ellie being on public display like that. I seriously hope some tabloid doesn't splash photographs of the body all over tomorrow's papers. If they do I shall consider doing murder myself." Cheungy sounded like she meant it.

Terrant the pathologist was talking to DI Hedley. Suzy and her boss joined the group. Hedley turned. "Hi Cheungy," he said without enthusiasm. He nodded to Suzy, "Hello DC... Rolfe, isn't it? Looks like the tide just left her high and dry." He frowned, compressing his lips and shaking his head.

Dr Shaw must have seen Cheungy's frown at the trails of footprints, because he said, "I needed to go straight in because there was a possibility that she wasn't dead, poor kid. Forlorn hope, though. And anyhow, the tide will have washed away any evidence. Though I suppose I may have screwed up something from the footpath to the shore. But I went in at this angle...." He pointed to a route in, now covered by footplates. "It's downstream of where she is, and she's most likely to have gone in upstream of here, I'd have thought."

"I hope you kept to the stepping plates on the way up here," said Hugh Lampeter, the head SOCO, coming over to Cheungy and Suzy.

"That's a nice, friendly greeting," replied Cheungy teasingly.

"I've got a niece her age," growled Hugh. "And did you have to bring Uncle Tom Cobbley and all," he added, glaring at Suzy. "We had to get the tent up in a hurry. Bloody public. Vultures. If we've lost evidence because of their prurient interest..."

Suzy avoided the glare, looked at the crumpled heap of arms and legs, seeing not Ellie but Kirsty. She forgave Hugh his rudeness. And he was right; she felt superfluous. She felt a sense of relief when the tent cut Ellie's body off from idle scrutiny.

Hugh continued, "We're pushed for time because the tide will be turning soon. From my knowledge of the way bodies behave in water, the only reason we've found her before she bloated is that her hair got snagged on that wood and she ebbed dry when the tide went out. Because of the timing, she won't have drifted very far, I doubt, so she most probably went in fairly close to here, and from this bank, not the other. But that's guesswork at the moment.

"It's not just a matter of looking for crushed vegetation, though, because this is a popular fishing spot, so there are numerous paths down to the water."

"I see she's naked," said Cheungy. "I assume that suggests a sexual assault and why this might be our job."

Terrant the pathologist shrugged. "Maybe, though not necessarily. I can't see any signs of violence on her, such as I might expect if she had had the clothes ripped from her. Another explanation might be that she had been drinking, became hypothermic. When that happens, often the sufferer feels hot rather than cold, and takes their clothes off to cool off. They then get very confused. She could easily have fallen in and drowned. Or maybe she thought skinny-dipping would be a good idea. I have a very open mind; all this is speculation."

"Well, if she took her own clothes off, we ought to find her clothes at the point she went in," said Suzy.

"Indeed," said DI Hedley. "And we haven't, yet. So, either we haven't found where she went in, or the clothes aren't there anymore. But even that might not mean anything suspicious, because they may have been taken by the tide and lost separately."

A seagull circled overhead, yelling mournfully. More joined, wheeling oppressively.

"How long before the tide becomes a problem?" asked Suzy.

"Not long," said Hedley. "Three, four hours to record everything, and get the body. Hugh's a bit twitchy." Hedley flashed a teasing grin at the scenes of crime officer. "He likes to take his time."

Hugh nodded. "The body's the priority just now, of course, but I also want to take a good look at the supermarket car park in case she was brought in by car, parked near the footpath and her body carried in from there. Hence the stepping plates. Though I think it's less likely."

"Suicide?" asked Cheungy. "It's coming up to GCSEs and I understand there were pressures at home."

"No evidence of that yet," said Terrant. "Though it's possible."

One of the white-swathed scenes of crime officers left the body, came up and spoke to Hugh, who then nodded. "Do you want to view the body in situ before we move her?"

"I'll take a look," said Cheungy. Hedley nodded. They rustled down the designated path. Suzy saw a glimpse of Ellie as they entered the tent. So young, young as Kirsty. Suzy stifled a sob.

"Don't drip tears on the scene, now," said the log keeper.

"Fuck off," she said. "That's just not funny."

Hedley and Cheungy came out of the tent. As they walked back, Suzy heard DI Hedley say to her boss, "I bet it's at times like this you wonder why you do this job."

"No Hal, it's at times like this that I remember why I do this job. Just as you do, I suspect."

Hedley nodded in reply.

"Suzy," said Cheungy. "Can I ask you to see the parents immediately, please, because the media have sniffed this out already, and I want the family told before they see something on the news. Would you mind taking on the role of Family Liaison Officer. DI Hedley will fix up someone for you to go with. Leave me the car, would you."

Chapter 32

Suzy

"So how come it's you again?" asked Suzy.

"Because I'm the only one who does any work round here," said Pete Brooks with a grin. "For some reason I always end up going to the misper reports or babysitting the FLO. I'm FLO trained myself, but I prefer the roughty toughty stuff."

"Shit, Pete, I'm not looking forward to this."

Brooks parked up on the road near the Warreners' house. Their drive was crammed with vehicles.

A woman answered the door and blenched. "Come in," she said. "My sister's through here."

The TV was on, turned down low, as if to obliterate thought. Mr and Mrs Warrener sat welded together in misery. They looked up at Pete Brooks and Suzy Rolfe with knowing eyes. "Please sit down," Mr Warrener invited.

"I'm afraid we've found the body of a teenage girl matching Ellie's description," said Suzy. "On the tidal flats near the supermarket. We're moving the body soon. And we'd like someone to identify her, please."

Mrs Warrener's fingers bit into the sofa as her face broke. "My babee, my babee," she said between her teeth. Her body convulsed and the tears fell unheeded. Mr Warrener pulled her to him, but she resisted, then acquiesced. Suzy knew she'd seen the first signs of alienation, vituperation and blame that might cleave this couple apart.

The surge of fury at the death of this young girl left Suzy swooning for a moment. 'If it's not suicide, I'll find him', she swore silently. 'I'll find him and I'll make him pay.' Pay what, though? No price could pay for this, buy back a life.

~~~

They got back in the squad car. "Fuck!" said Suzy. "Fuck, fuck, fuck. Sorry Pete." A minute later she asked, "Where's this Camp Cannabis, then Pete?"

"There's a copse of pine trees behind the supermarket. The kids have built it there out of what they can nick and scrounge. I wish those kids were as inventive and constructive in other ways. It's their second den, so I call it Camp Cannabis 2nd. I don't like it, but if we close it down, they'd find somewhere worse. Like that awful derelict building, perhaps."

"Can we have a drive round there? Past that derelict building and the shabby estate. D'you mind, Pete…. I want to see how close that estate is to the river."

"There's a footpath through to the river from the estate."

"Really?"

"We've got lots of footpaths and alleyways. There are ways down to the river, footpaths from a lot of the town, so put your copper's nose away." Brooks swung the car down to the shabby estate. They parked up, and Brooks led Suzy down the path towards the river. He pointed upstream. "Follow this and you get to the Supermarket, which is where Hugh and Co closed the scene off. Then of course, the footpath goes to the scene itself. The pines… you can see the tops from here, are where Camp Cannabis the Second is, and that's accessed by a footpath from the river, though there's lots of stinging nettles in the way. It's not that far really, but you'd never walk from here to the scene with a body. Much easier to ditch it in the river at this point."

"I understand Ellie was at Camp Cannabis yesterday afternoon. I wonder where she went after Camp Cannabis, and who was texting her," said Suzy. "I suppose the others support what young Tom said?"

"Yup. They all say she left them just as it was beginning to get dark, after getting some texts. Unless they're all lying..."

"Could be. They might have bullied her to death, or it might be a prank gone wrong," said Suzy.

"Maybe, but I didn't get that feeling when we interviewed them. Though now we've found her, I s'pose you'll want another word." Ellie's ghost walked between them.

Brooks drove past Digby Jamieson's house. "That's another suspect," said Suzy nodding at his house, "Though he's on doorstep curfew from 7pm to 5am on days when he's working six till two. And I know that's his shift because he's on the same shift as Kirsty."

"He was in last night," said Brooks. "You know that dozy pillock of a PCSO we're lumbered with, that wannabe who's too dim to pass the selection for the real police? Well, sarge sent him to check on Digby Jamieson last night. Just knock on the door and see if he was in, then this PCSO was supposed to go on foot patrol over this estate because there have been complaints of antisocial behaviour and criminal damage. He knocked on Digby Jamieson's door at 7.00pm, and Jamieson answered. Then the dozy twat sat on the wall of the house opposite like he was staking the house out. He must've looked like a bag of shit doing that, and of course Jamieson's not going to leave with that twat sat outside. Complete waste of time. Shows you what a useless idea PCSOs are. Get rid of the dross like him and swear the good ones in as proper coppers, I say. And train them properly. Bloody wannabes. Sarge gave him a well-deserved bollocking, but fact is, Digby was in his house until quarter to tenish, when the dozy pillock of a PCSO decided to wander back up to the nick because it was home time."

Suzy laughed. "I take it you don't like PCSOs."

"Too bloody right. They swan around joined at the hip, pretending to be coppers, and giving us a bad name. The good ones do a good job, I s'pose, whatever that's supposed to be. But the bad ones are complete disaster."

"That only gives Digby Jamieson an alibi until 9.45 though," said Suzy. "We don't yet know when Ellie died. It could have been after that."

"Yeah, well, maybe, but the kids said Ellie left when it was just starting to get dark, which must've been getting on for eight o'clock. I can't see her hanging around the riverbank in the dark for a couple of hours. It doesn't make sense. Much more likely she responded to a text inviting her to go and meet with whoever, which means Digby was at home when Ellie was meeting someone."

"Um... unless the timing's a bit out, and the PCSO knocked after Digby had told Ellie he was on his way, effectively putting the kybosh on any meeting until the PCSO went home," suggested Suzy.

"Well, in that case, Ellie would have felt stood-up and gone home, not hung around waiting for a couple of hours, or more likely he'd have texted her and said he wasn't able to arrive after all. Or postpone it until later. Maybe that's what happened. So much for alibis. Even pillocky PCSO alibis.

"Anyway, let's go back to the nick for a coffee," added Brooks. "Where are you meeting your boss?"

"Dunno." Suzy shrugged. "But let's sneak back for a coffee anyway. It's been one hell of a day.

"Who's that bloke over there? It looks like Raff."

A down-and-out figure turned abruptly and vanished down the next road. "That's Raff all right," agreed Brooks. "He's moved without telling us, cheeky bugger. He's on the sex offender's register, isn't he?"

"I think we need a word," said Suzy. They drove around the corner, Raff was running. Brooks gunned the car down to the end of the road on blues, and they leaped out after him. Brooks brought Raff down.

"You can't arrest me, you can't, it wasn't me, I haven't done nuffink," said Raff, eel-like in Brooks' grip. Brooks pinned him down with a knee, roughly dragging Raff's arm back, slapping the cuff round. Suzy grabbed the other hand, shoving it into the cuffs. She looked up into Brooks' eyes, aware that they had used a little more force than was justified, venting their anger on Raff the derelict.

"Now then, Raff, I'm nicking you because you didn't tell us you were moving. You know you should tell us. And we're going to search you for gear. You got anything sharp in your pockets? Anything that might hurt me or my colleague?"

"Fuck off!"

"Well, I'm going to search you anyway. Hold him Suzy, while I put some gloves on. Don't kick." he added to Raff. Suzy grabbed the legs. The trousers looked cacced up round the bum, and smelled like her suspicions were correct.

"Shit, Pete; I think you've got his needle already!" She pointed to Brooks' chest.

Brooks looked down. A one ml syringe was buried in his stab vest. Brooks blenched, and slipped open the vest, relief flooding his face as he found his body armour had done its job. He gingerly removed the needle and put it by the wall. "That's Assault Police, Raff. And I'm nicking you for that 'n all. I'm calling for transport. I'm not having this douch bag in my car, he'll probably shit in it."

Suzy glanced up at the needle on the wall. She wasn't wearing body armour. And Brooks' body armour didn't cover all his body. She wanted to stamp on Raff's head until it burst.

~~~

"How did you come by those injuries, Raff?" asked Suzy. She was well into the interview with Raff, but getting nowhere, possibly because, unlike previous times, he had a solicitor next to him. So far all he had said, apart from incomprehensible mumbles, was, 'no comment.'

"Bloody PC Plod gave them to me, didn't he?"

"No, he didn't Raff. The doctor told us those injuries are a day old. They were done last night. The scratch on your face, the bruises on your body. Who did them, Raff?"

"Nobody. Er... No comment."

"Where d'you get your gear from, Raff?"

"Nobody... No comment."

"When you were searched yesterday, you had a packet of white pills and packets of white powder in your right trouser pocket. What are the pills, Raff?"

"'Hypnol, ennit."

"Rhohypnol? What do you want that for?"

"Own personal use, ennit," said Raff with a sideways glance at the solicitor.

"And the white powder?"

"GHB, only it's crap."

"Crap? What d'you mean by crap?"

"Dirty innit. Dunno. No comment."

225

A bit later, during a break, Brooks said, "Bugger it, he's hardly making sense. I'd swear he's still high except the doctor said he's fit for interview."

"He still smells high… smells to high heaven that is… Are you sure he's washed?"

"Poor Bob. He'd shat in his trackies. Raff, I mean, not Bob. And we've gotta keep them as evidence. Gawd I'd hate to be in Custody."

"Me too," giggled Suzy. "I'd hate to be in custody."

Brooks looked at her, then smiled. "You know what I mean."

~~~

"Yeah, I done it. It was me." Raff beamed at them. The solicitor sat up, jolted out of his torpor, and stared at Raff.

"How?" asked Suzy, wondering what he'd done.

"I raped her, then I strangled her, then I chucked her in the river."

The solicitor whimpered and looked through his disclosure sheets.

"Where did you do this, Raff?"

Raff pondered for a moment. "Near the river." He grinned, teeth rodent like. Just the two incisors. Yellow.

"Did you use a condom?"

"Ner."

"Did you drug her?"

"Yeah, with the dud GBH." Raff absentmindedly rubbed a bruise.

"Did you take her clothes off?"

"Ner. She took them off."

"What was she wearing, do you remember?"

"White jacket wiv fur on a split hood, like, black skirt."

"What colour were her knickers?"

Raff was silent for a moment. "Can't remember."

~~~

"I reckon he's lying," said Suzy to Brooks later. "It doesn't ring true. Though he got the clothes right, except for the knickers. And the location, though I suppose that's not hard to guess after the scene was taped off. I wonder what the PM'll show."

"I tell you what," said Brooks. "I wouldn't put it past the crafty bugger to say he did it, then lie about the details, just to wind us up. Make it look like he's stupid or mad and get off the Assault Police charge that way. Or he might just want to get back inside, though inside isn't good for sex offenders. And didn't the solicitor moan about non-disclosure until I pointed out this was an off-the-cuff cough from Raff, not something we were intending on asking him?"

"I've had enough, and I want to go home," said Suzy. "We'll carry on questioning him in the morning. And I'll see if we can ask for more time now that he's coughed to rape and manslaughter."

They went up to Elversford CID room. It was in turmoil. Cheungy was there with Hedley. "Ah, Suzy. How's it going? We're setting up an incident room here for the moment, at least until we know a bit more about how Ellie died. Prof Terrant is kindly going to do the PM immediately so that we know what we're dealing with, which is good of her."

Suzy stared blankly at Cheungy, waiting to be told to go to the PM of a child almost the same age as her daughter. She clamped her jaws tight over the moan she wanted to voice, blinking rapidly.

"Cheungy, I think it would be better if I went to the PM and reported back to you," said Hedley, quickly. "Suzy... well, if Suzy is FLO, it's probably best if she isn't exhibits officer at the PM."

Suzy let out a grateful sigh. She was tempted to fling her arms round Hedley, until she remembered his forbidding reputation.

"Thank you," said Cheungy. "I think we'll have a debrief then take things forward in the morning."

Chapter 33

Kirsty

"Mum, it said on the news that a body's been found." Kirsty looked at her mother through sore eyes. She had been weeping, though she wasn't sure for whom. "And you've got someone in custody."

Her mother nodded. "Don't," she said, backing away as Kirsty went for a hug. "I'm filthy, really filthy. Let me shower and change."

Fifteen minutes later she was back downstairs, shoving her clothes straight in the washing machine. Kirsty handed her a glass of wine and waited for the praise. It didn't come, and Kirsty was a little crushed. "Mum. Is it her?"

"Ellie? Yes, who else would it be? Her father ID'd her this afternoon."

"Is it murder?"

"Don't know yet, could be an accident, suicide, anything, and I shouldn't say anyway."

"Was she raped?"

"For goodness' sake, Kirsty. I can't tell you."

Kirsty looked away and sniffed. She was startled as her mother enveloped her in her arms and held her close. "Oh Sweetie, promise me you'll never put yourself at risk, promise me you'll be careful at work, at university. I could never bear it if I was given the news I had to give to the Warreners today. Thank God I wasn't asked to go to the PM."

"OK, Mum. I promise," said Kirsty, her mouth muffled by the crushing embrace.

~~~

"Ellie was dead before she went into the water," said Hedley to the assembled team the next morning. "She died of respiratory depression and had been drinking because there was still alcohol in her stomach, along with the remains of some food which looked like a pasty and some salted peanuts or something similar, ingested shortly before she died. Prof Terrant has sent various tissues off for toxicology, with a specific request to look for drugs like ketamine and GHB, as well as cannabis and alcohol.

"There is a snag with GHB since this is naturally occurring in the body anyway, so it's the amount which will tell us if that's what caused death, probably in conjunction with alcohol, rather than just its presence. Even if we do find GHB in the body, Ellie could have taken it voluntarily, since she was a drug user, though she is said to only take cannabis and alcohol, not any other substance, according to the kids she hangs out with. Used to hang out with," Hedley corrected himself with a rueful look.

"But Guv," said Suzy. "I doubt she just took it and died, because she was found in the water. That suggests that someone else was there and dumped her in the river to get rid of the body. Surely it's much more likely that we're looking at an attempted rape or rape which went wrong."

"I think that's much more likely too, especially as we haven't yet found her clothing," said Hedley, "but we mustn't become blinkered to other possibilities. Incidentally, though Ellie wasn't a virgin, there's no evidence that she had had vaginal intercourse recently; no semen or anything."

"What about oral sex?" asked Suzy.

"Yes please," said Brooks.

"Sod off, Brooks. That's not funny," said Suzy.

"Brooks..." said Hedley, giving Brooks a wilting look.

"Any other signs of violence?" asked Cheungy. "How about signs she was stripped after death, or dragged to the water? Anything like that?"

"No," said Hedley. "We'll have to hope the possible rapist left some other cross contamination on her. But the problem is, in the sorts of quantities we're looking at, we're talking needle in a haystack, And possibly other sources of contamination. We may not be able to rely on such evidence alone.

"What have we got so far from Scenes of Crime, Hugh?"

"A huge quantity of information, most of which is probably irrelevant, as usual," said Hugh. "We have found a possible entry site, where it looks as if something was dragged down to the water's edge from a secluded picnic spot, flattening the vegetation, and there are some fleece fibres from that part of the scene, snagged in the vegetation in the side they have been flattened from. No clothes, as DI Hedley said. Nor any drinks bottles from the scene itself, though plenty to look at along the footpath and in Camp Cannabis. And lots of used condoms. Sometimes I just love our job.

"Air Support took some photos of the scene, which I've got here in this PowerPoint presentation," said Hugh, projecting them onto the screen. They were out of focus, as usual, so there was a minute's adjustment before Suzy could see the scene from the air. Hugh pointed out where they had found the possible entry site.

"Where's Camp Cannabis? Is it under those pines?" asked Suzy.

"Must be," said Brooks. "You can just about make out that tent thing they've erected."

"Where's the footpath from the river to the camp?"

Brooks looked at the photograph for a moment before standing up and pointing with his pen. "It runs along here and joins the river footpath at this point."

"Ah. Downstream of where Ellie was found," said Suzy. "So, after leaving the others at camp cannabis, she walked to the river and turned upstream when the others went home a little later, having been texted by someone as yet unknown. When did she die?"

Hedley checked his notes. "Not easy to place, but most likely before 11.00pm. And of course, since it was getting dark around eight o'clock, that gives us a time of death between 8.00pm and 11.00pm, approximately."

"High tide was at 10.12 yesterday," chipped in Brooks. "Mr Lampeter, wouldn't you expect to see some signs in the mud if the tide was on the ebb when she was dumped?"

Hugh pulled a face. "Pockmarks? Well, yes, probably, because though it's tidal, there are no waves to pound the mud smooth again. Though when we come to close the scene down, I might make a few marks in the mud and see how long they remain visible. Incidentally, at the point where we think she was dumped, the bank drops quite steeply away, so the tide may well have been full. If you had to drag her into the river lower than high water mark, you'd surely find a shallower bit to drag her down?"

"Ooh, I don't know; just roll her off the bank onto the mud, then drag her down to the water," said Hedley. "This is all speculation..."

"But it's very useful," said Suzy, "because we've got a cough, but Brooks and I don't believe it. These discussions are giving me plenty of ideas about what to ask Raff the Derelict when we interview him again. We think he's just attention seeking after we nicked him for not complying with his sex offenders' registration. But he knows what Ellie was wearing, though he says he strangled her, so that's a contradiction with the PM evidence."

"Probably saw her before she met her end," said the PCSO.

"That only makes sense if Raff knew her, and knew she'd died," said Hedley.

Brooks nudged Suzy and rolled his eyes when she turned to him. "Twat," he mouthed.

"Anyway," said Cheungy. "Even though Raff says he dun it, I think we treat this confession with a great deal of scepticism. There are others who are potential suspects. There are the kids who she hangs out with, or there's Cliff (Gaz) Hanger the erstwhile barman suspected of drugging a girl with ketamine. He's skipped bail. Ellie had a crush on the chemistry/PE teacher at school, Roger Turner, who happens to have a history of trading up to a look-alike younger version of his wife. Maybe Ellie decided to put some of her pornographic diary into practice. Digby Jamieson is also another possible. He's on bail for drug-raping his sister's girlfriend. He's a cocky beggar and shows some psychological characteristics of a serial offender, but that's the only offence we can nail him for."

"Yeah, but he was in his house that evening," said the PCSO. "I know that for a fact."

"You know he was there at 7.00 when you checked on him, but after that you assume he was there because you didn't see him leave. Perhaps you were dozing and he tiptoed past you," said Brooks, rather more rudely than was necessary. "Oh, and it's customary to address a DI as Ma'am or Sir or Guv."

"Thank you Brooks. I trust you'll remember that yourself," said Cheungy. "Anyway, today I'd like someone to go through the kids' witness statements and look for anomalies. I'd like house to house to continue, and I'd like the friends at school who are not camp cannabis devotees asked if they know anything. Suzy, as FLO, can I ask you to update the family on progress, ie, that we haven't ruled out suspicious death, and say unfortunately the body can't yet be released to them. Could you also ask if Ellie's phone is at home, just in case the kids were fibbing, and get the phone number. In fact, do that ASAP so that we have time to ask for a warrant to get a copy of her contact numbers and texts from her phone company. Ask if we can have the dreadful diary, and her computer to see if she was being groomed by anyone. If they'll let you have it, bring it back, then interview Raff. We'll ask for more time since he's coughed, even if we don't altogether believe him." Cheungy carried on assigning people with jobs, then closed the briefing.

"You treated yourself to a coffee machine, yet?" Cheungy asked Hedley when everyone was getting ready to set about their allotted tasks.

"No," said Hedley ruefully. "I like to lead by example, and if I have coffee stuff up here, the others would, then they'd never mix with the uniform. I don't want to encourage a them-and-us situation. But now the canteen's DIY, I've made sure there's some decent coffee and a cafetiere and an honesty box down there. Would you like some?"

"You really have to ask? Aren't you afraid everyone will take liberties if you leave it there for all and sundry?"

"They wouldn't dare," growled Hedley with a fierce look. Then he winked.

~~~

"It's a barely coherent story, Ma'am, but he says he did it. Some facts tie in, but some don't," said Brooks. Suzy saw Cheungy's eyes twinkle over the 'Ma'am'.

"Crimestoppers just had a phone call. Concerning Raff. Do you know where he's been dossing? In that old derelict building," said Cheungy.

"No... Ma'am," said Brooks. "With respect Ma'am, that building's secure."

"Not according to this source. The front might be, and the walls look impossible, but there's a couple of ways in to those in the know, according to this source. Tocky. (What a name). Tocky squats there regularly. As does Raff, has done for years. Can't understand that; he has a perfectly good place to live. Wants to take drugs unobserved I suppose and keep his gear for trading there. Tocky says that Raff deals. Just enough to sort himself out. He has a regular customer for date rape drugs and cannabis. But this customer comes to them, so he knows his way in. His face is always covered, though. Yesterday, this man comes for Raff, beats him up. This man told Raff the GHB he sold is crap; the girl died. So Tocky says it wasn't Raff who killed the girl. He just supplied the gear but didn't kill her. There's the description of the person who bought the dodgy gear." Cheungy handed Suzy a sheet.

Brooks read it with her. "5' 10ish. Dark trackies, white trainers, black hoodie, Blue NY cap, black scarf. Great. We'll go a long way with that."

"Beats me how Tocky knew Raff was in custody," said Suzy.

"Well, it's been on the news that someone is in custody, and these people have more contacts than we give them

235

credit for, what with mobile phones and the like," said Cheungy. "I've arranged with the building's owner to have a look round. Can you two go and see what you can find? I think Raff knows something, but he's got some details wrong, and this makes me think he's carrying the blame for someone. God knows why, especially if that someone beat him up."

Chapter 34

Suzy

"You'd have to be bloody desperate to get over that wall," commented Brooks as they met with the factory owner, Trowbridge.

Trowbridge looked stressed and tired. "I pay for this to be kept secure," he said. "I'm trying to sell it, but nobody wants it. Not for what I think it's worth. It's brown field, and you could put a very decent sized housing estate on here." He tussled with a padlock which proved obdurate. "That's odd, I can't get the key to turn," he said, swapping the keys until he had tried them all. The last one didn't even fit in the padlock.

"I think you must have brought the wrong keys, Mr Trowbridge," said Brooks.

"No," said Trowbridge in a vexed tone. "Look." He showed them the bunch of keys clearly labelled "Elversford Cotton Mill".

"Well, then someone must have changed the padlocks," said Brooks. "I've got some bolt croppers in the car." He went to the squad car, rummaged in the boot, which was stuffed with cones, tools, and other paraphernalia. He brought out some bolt croppers. "Do I have your permission, Mr Trowbridge?"

"Too damned right you do."

Brooks cut through each lock and they swung the gates open with a graunching noise that set Suzy's teeth on edge.

The parking area was breaking up, with weeds which looked as if they had spent several years struggling until sufficient wind-born detritus had given them the rudiments of soil. The car park echoed forlornly. The perimeter wall showed serious damage on this internal side, bricks missing, pointing cracked and falling out, weeds growing. In one place there was a large hole in the wall showing a sheet of corrugated iron covering the gap on the other side. Brooks studied it, pushed it gingerly. It moved.

"I think I know where that goes," said Brooks. "Looks deliberate."

"I'll have words with the security company," muttered Trowbridge. "They're supposed to inspect regularly."

They walked up to the building, examining the metal shuttering covering the windows and doors. It looked secure enough. In a shady, hidden corner, there was a pile of discarded bricks underneath the sill of a shuttered window, and a gap big enough to squeeze through.

"I don't believe it," said Trowbridge. "They've dismantled the wall to get in. The buggers."

"If you can't get through the door, try the walls," joked Suzy.

Brooks knelt down and flashed his torch. "Any other way in?" he asked.

Mr Trowbridge nodded. "The door." This was secured with a metal roll down shutter which responded to Trowbridge's key, revealing a proper front door, which opened. A musty, shitty smell hit them. "Take care," added Trowbridge, a little unnecessarily. "Now you're in, I'd like to get some new padlocks, hire a different security firm, and hire a bricky quickly to make this secure." Trowbridge paused, staring. "What the hell?"

There was a squatter's notice on the glass of the receptionist's office. It said they (the squatters) were legally entitled to stay and threatened legal action if they were forced out. It also said that there was, at all times, at least one person on the property. It stated the laws under which the squatters laid their claim, and was signed Tocky and Raff

Trowbridge went to rip it off. "Don't, Mr Trowbridge. At least, not yet," said Brooks.

"I'm off to see my solicitor, and the rest," said Trowbridge. "Bastards. Bastards." He turned to leave. "Please don't leave before I get back," he said. "If there's nobody here, I'm going to lock them out and make sure they can't come back." He seemed to be almost in tears.

A few minutes later they were looking at Raff's and Tocky's nest. Rank sleeping bags. Needles. Sooty metal. A bong. "Shit!" said Suzy.

"No," said Brooks dryly. "That's in the room next door."

~~~

Brooks and Suzy asked for back-up, so they could leave the site and go and question Raff. Tocky, it seemed, had gone; one good bit of news for Trowbridge. Before back-up arrived, Brooks and Suzy went outside to the hole in the perimeter wall. Brooks gave the corrugated iron an experimental shove. It flopped back against the wall with a clang. Then he slid it to one side and it stayed put.

"Yuk," said Suzy. "What is it?"

"All these houses had a privy attached to this wall at the back," said Brooks. "Originally these were built to house the workers. Probably quite forward thinking at the time. Oh gawd, the things I do to protect the public." He gingerly stepped through the gap. "Coming?"

Suzy wrinkled her nose. "Strictly speaking... Oh hell, OK."

Brooks held her hand as she stepped through. "Bugger," he said. "This is Digby Jamieson's property. I wish I'd moved that sheet before, when we searched his property. But I thought it was holding the place up. I wonder what he charges in tolls."

"He doesn't need to if the squatters have got keys to the padlocks. But it does mean he has possibly secret access to Raff, and we know Raff supplies."

Brooks and Suzy walked down Digby's backyard, and out of his front gate.

"I want to ask his next-door neighbour something," said Suzy. "Bear with me a minute. She knocked on the door of the neighbour who had told Kirsty Digby had been nicked. "Sorry to trouble you," she said, showing her warrant card. "But is it only ever just Mr Jamieson and Ms Jamieson who use his garden?"

"Funny you should say that," said the woman. "I have seen one or two people just walking up the back to his shed. Pikeys most likely, looking for something to nick."

Thanks," said Suzy. She and Brooks started walking down the road to the entrance of the factory.

"Pikeys my arse," said Brooks with a grin. "If they were Pikeys, the chances of that corrugated iron still being there would be zero."

Suzy laughed. "Don't say that in front of Professional Standards or they'll dump you in it for being racist."

They turned the corner. Their squad car had been joined by another. "Good, said Brooks. "Can you go and ask a neighbour or two if people ever use this gate, while I brief the others."

Suzy knocked on a couple of doors before finding someone in. "Yeah," he said suspiciously, and looked worried when Suzy showed her warrant card.

"Does anyone ever use that factory gate?" she asked. "Or do you ever hear in creaking?"

"Yeah."

"Why didn't you report it?"

"Why should I? I mind my own business, me." He shut the door in her face.

~~~

Suzy

"You're fibbing, aren't you, Raff? About killing the girl. We know that now. Who gave you the bruises?" said Suzy quietly.

Brooks brought out some evidence bags containing child porn photographs, and some drugs. "Look what we found in your squat, the old factory. You supply, don't you, Raff, but it wasn't you that killed her, was it?"

"Ner, wasn't me. It was him."

"Who?"

"The geezer wot bought the gear. He came and beat me up because of it, but it wasn't my fault it was crap."

Suzy said, "What was crap, Raff?"

"The gear. He came back Thursday night and beat me up because she died, and he had to ditch her into the river. Wild he was."

"Who?"

"Dunno."

"How do you get into the derelict building, Raff?"

"Through the gate."

"Where do you sell your gear, Raff?"

"At home. In the yard."

"Is that where he beat you up?"

"Yeah."

241

"How does he get into the yard... does he have a padlock key?"

"Um... Ner... he comes in through the hole in the wall... The outside wall that is."

"Do your other customers do this?"

"Some. I'm going down, ain't I?" Raff didn't seem too bothered at the prospect.

"Does the home owner know?"

"Dunno. Doubt it."

"Does Tocky know this geezer?"

"Wot geezer?"

"The one who buys the gear from you."

"Ner."

"How often does he get gear from you?"

"I'm not saying... I can't remember. No comment." Raff glanced at No-Comment Cowley, the solicitor.

"Once; more than once; like a few; lots. Give us some idea, Raff."

"Quite a few, but not like once a week. Once every month or so. Apart from the cannabis. He has that more often."

"Is it always the same gear? C'mon, Raff. You don't owe him anything; he beat you up."

~~~

"Have you got any pain killers?" asked Suzy, pressing two fingers to her eyebrows and grimacing. "If not, I'll have to nip out. He is driving me nuts. It's obvious he didn't do it, though. I wish he'd tell us who he gets the gear from and who he sells it to. Those descriptions he gave are naff, deliberately naff."

"I think he wants to go back inside. Gawd knows why. Knowing the Criminal Protection Service, though, they'll say there isn't enough evidence to get him for supply, even though he's as good as coughed. And as for the Assault PC, well, of course they won't bother with that charge, the tossers."

"They ought to. That could have been fatal if he's HIV positive."

"Tell me about it," said Brooks.

"At least we've got more time to question him. And now we know for sure that Ellie's death was an attempted drug assisted rape gone wrong. And that bugger knows the killer but he's not saying. I wonder how he knew what she was wearing."

"You know what... I reckon he knows a helluva lot more than he's letting on," said Brooks. "He's such a perv, I wouldn't put it past him to tag along and watch."

"Pete, I think you've hit the nail on the head. I bet he knows what happened and is getting off on knowing something we don't."

Chapter 35

Suzy

"Oh, it's you. I was sort of expecting it. But he didn't do it, if that's what you're thinking." Jane Turner stood at the door, big bags under her eyes. A wail suggested a reason for her tiredness. "You'd better come in," she said over the crescendo of infant screams. "He's out running as usual. Excuse me while I get the baby. Look, can you see yourselves into the living room. Oh, bugger."

Suzy and Brooks went into the living room, as invited, but they didn't sit down. It was a bit of a shambles with ironing in several baskets, and the dining table was covered in school exercise books. Jane Turner returned with the baby covertly plugged onto one of her breasts. Suzy remembered when she breast-fed Kirsty, how simple it was to quell the baby rage, and how some people seemed offended, even though they could never have even glimpsed her breast.

"Can we all sit down," said Jane. "Are you going to arrest him?"

"In view of the past history we have to, to eliminate him from our enquiries," said Suzy. "We can take a statement from you too, if you wish."

"Gladly," said Jane.

Suzy took out a form, filled in Jane's name and address, then asked Jane what she was doing from midday that Thursday. Jane looked puzzled but complied readily enough. She couldn't remember much about the day until Roger came home at 5.15 as usual. They had supper at 6.00pm. then he went for a run at 7.00pm, coming back at about 8.00pm, as usual, except that it was unusual for him to run on a Thursday, but he'd had a lot of urgent marking the day before.

"Well, he went out so how do you know, it 'wasn't him?' since you weren't with him all evening?"

Jane burst into tears. "I just know…. If something awful like that had happened, he'd have given it away when he got home. I'd know something was up. I just would. But he was cool as a cucumber, had a shower, then did some more marking. If he'd just killed Mrs Roger Turner mark 3, I'd have known. He's so regimented with his runs, he takes almost the exact same time every time. I reckon he'll be home in…" Jane looked at the clock, "…three minutes."

They were a long three minutes, with the baby dropping off the nipple into a bloated slumber, mouth working in her sleep. On the dot, Roger Turner's footsteps were heard on the path, he came through the door, then stopped. "Oh," he said. "Am I to be nicked, or can I just help with your enquiries?"

"Sorry," said Suzy. "We're arresting you, so you can be eliminated from our enquiries, and we'd like to seize your computer, mobile phone, and trainers, please."

"These ones?" asked Roger, seemingly more upset over the loss of his trainers than of being arrested.

"Yes, please. A good excuse for some new ones, perhaps."

"It would be, except money's a bit tight," said Roger Turner bleakly. "Do I get a chance of a shower?"

"Sorry," said Suzy.

~~~

"Looks like he was home before the critical time," said Brooks when they had released Roger Turner without charge. "Pity he didn't actually see her on his run. Maybe he could have been a witness rather than a suspect."

"Digby Jamieson hasn't got an alibi as such, apart from Nitwit watching until nearly 10 pm. Digby says he watched telly then went to bed," said Lynne, joining them. "He said it wasn't fair to suspect him just because he'd been maliciously accused of rape. But of course, that's the rape we know about, and he has a connection to Jordan and her sister via the Pizza factory, who might be victims. And Stuart, who pissed him off by teasing him about the size of his willy. And one or two others via his connection with the Blue Bore, and the Craven Arms. Funny how those two pubs are in hot spots for this sort of offence, and how Digby Jamieson is also linked to these hot spots.

"But Roger Turner is also linked to Ellie and Trish, and to some of the other girls... and possibly Stuart. He's a teacher, and those kids are youngsters. We can't assume that there's just one offender either." Suzy rubbed her face. "I'm so goddamned tired. That's another weekend ruined, and I expect I'll be asked to update the family tomorrow."

~~~

At the evening debrief, Cheungy told Suzy to see the family first thing in the morning, then rest for a couple of days.

~~~

On Monday Suzy was delighted when Raff was remanded in custody. She thought Assault PC was a bit feeble for what Raff had nearly done to Brooks. Raff was Hep C positive, and she thought attempted murder would have been more appropriate. Brooks morosely said that he was surprised the

246

CPS were running it at all since they seemed to regard assaulting a police officer as an everyday hazard. Then he said a lot of other very rude things about the CPS, most of which she agreed with.

When she got home, Kirsty had gone to work. Suzy wasn't sorry. She wanted to be on her own, have a long soak in the bath, and read a trivial novel.

~~~

The news report was bland and empty of factual material, but the TV stations still managed to waffle meaninglessly and speculatively for ten minutes, as if the gravity of a case should be measured in footage length, not content. One useful thing that Suzy hadn't been involved with was the publication of pictures of clothes similar to what Ellie had been wearing and a request from the police for members of the public to look out for them.

~~~

Angie

In my next session with Peter I told her what was going to happen, how much more confident I felt about everything; and when it came to booking the next appointment, there was an awkwardness between us, as if we both knew the counselling had run its course. I could tell that Peter was waiting for me to say I didn't need her any more. And I knew that those unsaid words spoke the truth.

"You have my phone number," she said. "If you need me, you know where I am."

As I left The Healing Centre, the door swung shut, severing the umbilicus between us.

~~~

Suzy

Suzy looked up from her computer as Cheungy came over. "We've got the initial Toxicology results back," said Cheungy. "Ellie had been drinking heavily, and had smoked cannabis. She also had much higher than average levels of GHB in her body, so, since she died of respiratory depression, it was probably the combination of those which killed her."

"GHB can be fatal on its own," said Suzy dully. "And that fits in with Raff's story about the duff GHB. I don't suppose you'll prove it was the GHB, but whoever gave it to her is responsible for her death. Poor idiot girl."

"Suzy, are you OK?" asked Cheungy.

"Yes. No. Sort of, Ma'am." Suzy raked her fingers through her hair. "Do you remember a while back I mentioned that Kirsty was going out with the crowd from the Pizza factory, and then that she seemed to be going out with a rather unsuitable chav? I saw him all over her when I parked up to have a look at Digby's house a while back, when we first arrested Digby for the rape. I thought this kid looked like trouble. Well, guess who Ellie was texting the night she died? This chav Tom. Lynne ran a PNC check on him and he has previous."

"For sex offences?" asked Cheungy with a vexed glance at the HOLMES2 computer. The indexer imputing data didn't feel the look.

"No, Ma'am. A TWOC of a motor vehicle a couple of years back. Took a car for a joy ride but brought it back undamaged.

248

Cautioned for that. Cannabis possession. Cautioned for that too. Probably thinks he'll get away with being cautioned for every new offence."

"Probably will," said Cheungy glumly. The phone rang. Cheungy grabbed it, listened, then smiled. "Good, excellent." A few more words, and she hung up. "Ellie's clothes and phone have been found in someone's dustbin, someone on that shabby estate. They've been picked up, and we'll send them for forensics."

"Dumped on the way back to Tom's house, then. Not a very bright boy. Shall I pick him up, Ma'am?"

"Yes. No, actually. He'll keep. It's Good Friday tomorrow and I'd like to wait until we have a bit more on him. After all, he may have just been texting her, and it may just be coincidence about the clothes being dumped there."

"Yeah right... Ma'am, he's a danger to the public. Well. Women anyway."

"Who? This lad who may have just been texting the murdered girl and happens to live on an estate close to the murder scene? On the present evidence, if we lift him, as soon as he tells us that, yes she was just texting him, so what; that's that. You'd have to release him. Then what? If he's guilty, we want to keep him remanded in custody. I want a bit more evidence against him before we show our hand."

"But Kirsty..."

"Tell her to leave him alone. But don't, for God's sake, don't tell her why."

~~~

Kirsty

Kirsty arrived home just in time for the local news. She flopped onto the sofa next to her mother. "I'm shattered," she said. "Everyone's talking about..." she indicated the muted TV, where there was footage of the path down to the river. Mrs Williams the head teacher at Elversford Secondary School was talking silently to the reporter. The TV cut to scenes of Ellie's friends weeping and hugging each other. Numerous bouquets of flowers were laid at the start of the footpath. The camera silently focused on a few.

"I do hate that," said her mother. "Good for the florists though."

"Don't be so horrible," said Kirsty. "It's people's way of coping. Just 'cos you're a tough, unfeeling copper doesn't mean the rest of us are."

"I'm not unfeeling," said her mum. "I just don't like it, with those silly little messages of sentiments which they probably never felt. Hypocritical, I call it. They'd be better off spending the money on the Rape Crisis Centre."

"You are in a mood."

"Well, what do you expect? It's horrible dealing with something like this, with the family blaming me because we haven't yet found the killer. And the workload.... All the data needs to be input into HOLMES 2, and we're short of indexers, and I'm sat there, fretting over you, feeling bad because Ellie was younger than you, and now she's dead."

"I knew her, you know... How do you think I feel?"

Instead of the sympathy Kirsty was expecting, her mother suddenly stopped as if struck by a thought. "You said you hardly knew her. Look, Sweetie, I have to ask you not to join in the discussions at work, and not to mix with the crowd, at least until this is over."

"You think it's one of them." Jimbo, Kirsty thought, she has to suspect Jimbo. But he said he never went out that night. Just 'cos of that awful old bag making false allegations of rape.

"No. No. It's not that," said here mother, quickly, which made it sound like a lie. "No, the reason is, I don't want people trying to extract information from you just because you're the copper's daughter."

"I told them you're a nurse, so I don't suppose they would," said Kirsty. "I think you're just saying it to get me to stop doing out with chavs."

"Talking of chavs, are you still going out with that gormless looking lad I saw you all over that time?"

"Yes, but we're not doing anything. He respects me," said Kirsty quickly. That, too sounded like a lie to her own ears, and judging from the look her mum gave her, her mum thought she was lying too.

"Looking forward to going away with your dad?"

"You have got to be joking. Four days with Bimbo Slut Tart. I don't see why I have to go."

"Because he's your father, they've offered; Paris is interesting, you need to spend some of your time with him, and, to be honest, I think you need to get away for a short time. Just forget your dislike of the bimbo slut and try and have fun. If you're not careful, you'll drift away from your father entirely."

"I don't have to go at all now, never. I don't know why I still do."

"Because he's your father, and despite what he did to us over the bimbo slut, blood's thicker than water."

Chapter 36

Suzy

Easter Tuesday, and everyone had overdosed on Easter Eggs brought in by Cheungy. Suzy was feeling slightly hyper from the overindulgence. She answered the phone and found herself talking to Jane Turner.

"Look, I don't know whether I should be telling you this, but Roger's been awfully odd since you questioned him. Twitchy. And when a report about the murdered girl came on the news, he suddenly put his hands to his face and started weeping. I can't understand it. Maybe he did fancy her after all. Maybe the diary wasn't all fantasy. Maybe he..." The voice died away to silence.

"Oh, thank you, Jane. Can I come and talk to you about it?"

"Um. I'd rather you didn't. I'd rather come to you. Only it's a bit awkward if you really have to talk to me... it's the Easter holidays. And I don't want to... Oh, look, forget it, will you. No statement. Nothing. I just thought you should know. But I feel so bad about this now. Bye."

~~~

Kirsty

"What's up, Tom?" asked Kirsty, newly returned from Paris. He had been moodily stirring his chocolate and not drinking any of it.

He shrugged. "Just thinking."

"About Ellie?"

252

A guilty look washed over his face, then disappeared. "How did you know?"

"Not hard. Everyone's talking about her."

"Except you. You're pretty schtum about it."

"You all knew her better than I did. I never figured out how come you lot at the Pizza Factory knew her."

"She did her two weeks work experience with us last year. Yeah, it was about this time last year. She was fun." A tear stole down his cheek.

"So I saw in the camp," said Kirsty a little tartly. Another tear followed the first, and Kirsty blushed with contrition. "God, I'm sorry. I didn't mean it like that."

"You know I respect you, Kirsty. I'd never ask you to do anything like that. Unless you wanted." He swallowed hard, his Adam's apple rising almost painfully. "I heard Mrs Renshaw found her clothes in her bin. Do you reckon the police will think it's me? They asked me questions when she disappeared."

Kirsty laughed. "Why on earth would they think it's you?"

"They found her clothes."

"Loads of people live in your estate. Why pick on you?"

"Because I was one of the last to see her. Actually, Kirsty, I think I might have been the last." He grabbed the mug and swigged the now-cool chocolate down. "Come with me. Please Kirsty. And remember that I love you."

"Well wait for me to finish my chocolate, then." Kirsty drank hers down. The mug had barely stopped rattling in the saucer when Tom stood and pulled her out of the coffee shop. He walked on with her to the supermarket, "Wait for me by the footpath," he said, going into the shop.

Kirsty went to the start of the footpath. The forlorn heaps of flowers were fading. The scene had been re-opened, and

253

there was a narrow gap between the swathes of bouquets. There was a pong of mouldering flowers. Tom appeared.

"Got what you want?" she asked.

"Yeah, c'mon."

They wandered down the path in silence. Then Tom turned towards the den. The stingers had arched over the path so Tom went first, treading them down. "I hope nobody's there," he said.

Me too, thought Kirsty. But at least I won't see Ellie giving anyone a blowjob. It was such an uncharitable thought, she felt herself blushing. Then she wondered if that was why Tom was taking her there. She stopped. "You needn't try it on. Let me make it clear; I do not want sex with you. You touch me and that's rape."

Tom looked away, shook his head. "S'not what this is about." He sniffed.

The den had a desolate and deserted feel about it. "Sit down," said Tom. He didn't wait for her, but sat on one of the logs and took out a carrier bag with a cheap bottle of whisky. He unscrewed the cap and offered the bottle to Kirsty.

"You know I won't; I'm on my bike."

"Oh, yeah, sorry. I just thought it seemed rude to drink in front of you." He took a sip. And another. He was pale, and the flush on his cheeks contrasted unbecomingly. "You know I respect you. And after that time at home, I... Well, I haven't tried it on, have I?"

"True."

"Well, it's all very well not going the whole way, but I'm a man, Kirsty. And a man has... needs."

"You brought me here to tell me you're dumping me?"

Tom took another swig. "No... no. I..." he took another swig, a bigger one.

"You'll get pissed."

"Yeah, I know. I want to. To give me courage…"

"Courage for what?"

"Kirsty, I'm afraid. If they've got Ellie's clothes, they can tell all sorts of stuff from clothes, can't they, with DNA and all that stuff?" Tom took another swig. A fifth of the bottle had gone.

Kirsty took it from him. "Give me the cap." Tom did as she bid. She screwed the lid on. "I'm tempted to chuck it, but I hate waste. Now tell me what you're afraid of and why. 'Cos yes, if you did it, the police will be able to tell." Kirsty held the bottle by the neck, just in case she needed to turn it into a weapon.

"She gave me a blowjob the day she died," said Tom in a rush.

"She what? You dirty, two timing chavvy little low life."

"It's all very well, but you won't… and I respect you… but I wanted… you don't understand. It didn't mean anything."

"You screw her and it doesn't mean anything?" Kirsty jumped up. "Was it here? Is that why you brought me here, too, so I could suck your nasty little cock, but it doesn't mean anything? You scumbag. Did you kill her? Did you fill her full of drink then rape her?"

Tom sat down on the log, crying. "No, no I didn't. We went to my house 'cos Mum was out working. It was after school. And yes, I gave her a drink, and some skunk, and then she sat on the sofa, and she gave me a blowjob. I gave her a pearl necklace, and that's the problem."

"You gave her a necklace?" Kirsty clenched her fists. He was giving her little presents, too, the two-timing git.

"Yeah, all round her neck, and it dripped down into the top she was wearing. Then we came here, met up with the others and talked and drank until it started to get dark. And she was texting loads, looking all excited. Then she went, but I followed a bit later, and I saw her a bit further up the path, and she looked like she was waiting for someone. But I didn't kill her, honest."

"Did you tell the police this?"

"You're fucking joking."

"You have to."

"They won't believe me."

"They might. You don't want to wait until they pick you up."

"I can't tell them because Ellie's underage. Was, I mean. But it wasn't rape; She liked it. Sexy, always good for a..."

"The little tart," said Kirsty in wonder. "Always good for a blowjob, when you boys have your needs. Oh you disgust me. Here." She thrust the bottle back in Tom's hand. "That's it. I'm finished with you. Completely. And for that matter, it was technically rape, you stupid nitwit, because she wasn't old enough to say yes. You're a sex offender Tom. How does that feel?" She walked back down the path, cursing over the stinging nettles. When she looked back, Tom had opened the bottle again, and was drinking. She had a moment's qualm. If he drank the whole bottle, he could die. But she couldn't tell her mother, or she would know Kirsty had disobeyed her. In the end, Kirsty texted Stuart and told him to make sure Tom didn't drink himself to death.

~~~

Angie

Sally and John invited me to dinner. They lived about a mile away, past the supermarket where we both work. Nice house, one of the better areas in Galchester. Where I live is nice enough, not rough, but shabby with age. Sally's house was a well-loved house in middle class suburbia.

John gave me a kiss on my cheek, and it was fine. Natural. Sally did the same. And it was fine, natural. I felt at last that I had come to terms with my sexuality. After all these years. After several relationships. After Baby.

I told them about Bea and told them I was still worried about the forthcoming trial. It was to be held in the Crown Court near the Cathedral, in the middle of Chelmsford.

"Do you need someone with you?" asked John.

"I've asked to have Bea the Witness Service volunteer to sit with me," I said.

"John and I have booked annual leave to get the garden sorted, so if you do need us, just phone, OK."

"You'll do that? For me?"

John reached a paw over and put it on my hand, a warm sheaf of comfort. "Course we will."

Chapter 37

Suzy

"Tom, are you sure you don't want a solicitor?" Suzy asked the boy in front of her. The investigation's incident room had been shifted from Elversford to Galchester and they had taken Tom to Galchester nick. Suzy felt more at home in this interview room; home territory.

Tom had answered his name readily enough and seemed to have understood the caution. She knew that he had been offered a solicitor when he was booked into custody. He'd probably previously been talking with friends who had been arrested many times, who said solicitors were bad news if you were guilty because if you 'fessed up to them, they told you to cough. He'd refused a solicitor on both previous arrests, but still admitted his guilt after a few futile 'no comments'.

He looked afraid, he looked guilty. His hands were shaking and he had a sheen of sweat beading his forehead. He looked so scrotey that Suzy was angry that Kirsty should even give him a second glance. He stank of fear.

"Tom, I'm going to start by reading through what you told us when we were looking for Ellie. This was volunteered to us, wasn't it, as a witness?"

Tom said nothing.

Tom's story was that he had gone to the den, Ellie had been there, texting, chatting away, drinking, and then she left as it was beginning to get dark, and that was the last he saw of her.

"I don't think you're told us the whole story, have you?"

Tom said nothing.

"What's your mobile phone number, Tom?"

"Dunno. I never dial it."

"Is it this one?" Suzy read it out to him.

Tom frowned for a minute before saying, "Dunno."

"You were texting in the den, weren't you?"

"No. Comment."

"Tom, Ellie was texting your phone. We have transcripts of your conversations." Suzy read through the series of texts. "Quite intimate, isn't it?"

Tom shook his head. "No. That wasn't me. Honest to God, that wasn't me."

"That phone is registered to you, Tom."

"I lost it."

"When?"

"Ages ago. Months ago."

"Where did you lose it?"

"Dunno. It was nicked, that's what."

"Was Ellie your girlfriend, Tom?"

"No... comment."

"Did you ever have sex with Ellie, Tom?"

"No. I mean, no comment."

After a stream of no comments, Suzy decided it was time for a break. Tom was returned to his cell. A little while later, perhaps when he realised he was out of his depth, Tom asked for a solicitor.

"Don't call in No-Comment Cowley, please," said Suzy to the custody sergeant. "Because he'll just tell Tom to go No Comment, whatever."

"I'll see if Stan Otterbury is available," said the sergeant.

~~~

A couple of hours later, Tom was again seated in the interview room, this time with Otterbury the solicitor beside him. Tom still looked sick, but not quite so worried. After Tom had been reminded that he was still under caution, Suzy asked if he had anything he wanted to tell them.

"Yeah, about Ellie. I had oral sex with her the day she died."

"OK, Tom, thanks for that. When was this?"

"After school."

"Did you text her or phone her to meet up?"

"Ner.. we bumped into each other. She wanted some..." Tom trailed off and looked hunted. He glanced at Otterbury beside him.

"Why didn't you tell us this before, Tom?"

"Well, 'cos she wasn't quite sixteen, and I gave her some skunk in exchange. I thought I'd be in trouble."

"OK, Tom, what I'm going to do is ask you some questions about your whole day. Please try and answer them honestly. If you don't know something, say you don't... don't invent something just to give me an answer, OK?"

~~~

"Do you think he's lying?" asked Cheungy, back in the SOIT team office.

Suzy frowned, sighed. "I don't know. It's obvious they had sex, from the semen stains that match his DNA on her top, and the way he described giving her a 'pearl necklace' —yeuch—is consistent with the stains. He wouldn't necessarily know that. But... it's interesting how this story came out after he's had a couple of hours thinking time, waiting for the solicitor to arrive. And there's the phone. We know from a couple of witnesses, that Tom spent a lot of time on his phone too, as well as Ellie, when they were in the den. He now tells us he was playing games on the phone. That sounds like another glib lie thought up whilst he was sweating in the cell. And it doesn't quite make sense with the theft business."

"He had another phone at home, but not the one for this number," said Cheungy. "He had a couple, actually. They do like their toys, these kids."

"Anything else turn up in the search?"

"Some porn mags. Some porn DVDs, some of which are a bit hard-core. Skunk, a bit of ketamine and some E's."

"Oh," said Suzy. "Interesting. But we think it was GHB that Ellie died of. Not ketamine. But I wonder if he's responsible for more than Ellie's attempted rape. He's in the right location, has association with the Blue Bore, the Pizza factory, the derelict building... he knows the people who have made complaints, like Jordan, Trish, and now Ellie. He's as good a suspect for serial drug assisted rapes as Digby is."

"We have some evidence of Digby on her clothing," said Cheungy. "And Roger Turner, for that matter. "But only traces like fibres and DNA, not semen, and they could have been from Digby's hairs being picked up on Tom's clothing, then crossing onto Ellie's, and from Turner at school. Or both of them might have been a bit more intimate than they are letting on. She seems to have put it about a bit, this Ellie."

"I hope Kirsty didn't... If Ellie was promiscuous, she could have been HIV positive, or something. And given it to Tom, though he said it's the first time... and if Kirsty... Oh dear God, after all I've taught her." Suzy clamped her lips together, then added, "Would Otterbury the solicitor suggest the blowjob story to Tom just to get him off?"

261

"I shouldn't think so. It's not worth his while, protecting a scumbag rapist. But it's possible. Tom doesn't strike me as that bright. See if he's consistent with his next session, or if he re-jigs the story and embellishes it," said Cheungy.

"He lied in his previous interviews over the TWOC and the cannabis before coughing."

"OK, see how consistent he is now, and I think we'll bring in psychologists to monitor his answers and his comfort zone."

~~~

"Nothing, Ma'am," said Suzy after a few hours of exhausting interview. "He's consistent, and if he's our serial rapist (if indeed there is one) his personality doesn't match the profile. He's just a normal, not very bright boy who will take sex when and where it's offered. Or at least, that's what we think. But he may have done it. He was at the right place, at the right time, his semen is all over her top, he was texting her very intimate messages, she was getting excited, and he obviously knows where to get drugs if he had ketamine."

"Did he tell you his supplier?"

"Raff."

"Ah. So he had a potential source of GHB, then. But he's given reasonable responses over the questions. I think we'll have to release him on bail."

"Oh no, Ma'am. Kirsty..."

"Kirsty will have to leave him alone. Won't she listen to you and do as she's told?"

"She's a teenager, so no. I'm not happy with his story. I don't like the way he didn't tell us straight away... why not? And the phone business is damning. Haven't we got enough to charge?"

"No. Well, possibly. We could certainly do him for under-aged sex, since he's admitted that, but I doubt we have enough to nail him for the rape and killing. Not yet, anyway. I'd like to charge him and have him remanded in custody, but to be honest, I'm not sure he did it. He says he and Ellie did the blowjob business at his mum's house. I think we should look for evidence of this. So we need to ask him if he's taken her there often." Cheungy made a couple of coffees, handed one to Suzy. "Something which might sway us is this new information. Roger Turner's computer has been looked at. He has visited various sites on how to make GHB. I think we should search his house for drug making ingredients and equipment. If he's the guilty party, then Tom is innocent."

Suzy gasped and slapped her forehead. "He's a chemistry teacher. He'd be able to make it, easy. Though he might not make it at home in front of Jane. I wonder... can we get a warrant for the school labs?"

"Good idea, excellent idea, Suzy. But I don't think we need bother with a warrant. DI Hedley knows the head teacher very well... I'll phone him and see if he can help. I'm sure Mrs Williams will be happy to oblige."

~~~

"Spot on, well done to Suzy." Suzy could hear Hedley's voice even though it was Cheungy who took the call. "Turner is actually head of Chemistry. I'm sure you know that dangerous chemicals and poisons are locked in a poison's cupboard. Well, the other teachers and the technicians have access to every cupboard, except two, the poisons cupboards. The contents are listed on the outside of the cupboard, and nobody ever needs the contents of one of those cupboards, so it's never unlocked. The poisons cupboards have to be double locked... and the deputy head of chemistry has a key. And two people have to be present when either of these cupboards is unlocked. This works OK for the one with the poisons which are used in class sometimes. But the second cupboard has never been opened as long as the deputy head can remember. It's only listed as having a couple of items anyway. Mrs Williams holds duplicate keys in one of the safes. When she tried to unlock this particular cupboard, none of the keys fitted the second padlock, though the mortise lock opened OK. So we cut off the padlock, and there was the drug making equipment, ingredients, and even some GHB. Furthermore, the caretaker says that Roger Turner often works late getting ready for the next day's work. The caretaker doesn't like it because of health and safety issues, but values his job so doesn't make a fuss. The items have been seized for forensics, of course. Do you want us to nick Turner for you and see if he has a key which fits the padlock?"

"Oh, yes please, Hal, because we're rushed."

"Well, so are we, but this is important. Await incoming scoundrel."

~~~

"Yes, I made the GHB which probably killed young Ellie," Turner sobbed into the table in interview. "Oh Ellie, poor Ellie, it's all my fault. I never meant this to happen. I've been making it for ages, just a bit at a time. Finances are tight with my ex-wife leeching maintenance out of me."

Suzy gave him a jaundiced look, thinking that if he hadn't traded the old model in, he wouldn't have had to support two families. She felt sorry for Jane, the next model up, until she realised that Jane had had a hand in the first betrayal. She hardened herself against the tears. These weren't tears for Ellie. They were self-indulgent tears of fear, guilt, loss. They might even be tears designed to disarm her, manipulate her into thinking he was just a chemistry teacher who made GHB to sell on. But he could be a chemistry teacher who used the drugs to drug his more attractive pupils, like Jordan, perhaps. Trish, or the other girls who feared they'd been raped. Or Ellie, who had a crush on him and had died.

~~~

"'I never meant this to happen'. What a tosser. OK to make a substance used to abuse and rape people, but now one of his victims has died, he's all tears and remorse. He makes me sick. So glad we were able to lift him for you," said Hedley, sniffing gratefully at the fresh, fragrant coffee. "It's not often someone makes me really angry, but I'd like to kick his balls in for him. Oh well, let's see if it's just manufacture and supply he's guilty of."

~~~

After a tedious interview going over old ground, they had nothing new about what Roger Turner was doing the day Ellie died. He was consistent in his story, and the timing placed him at home at the time Ellie most probably died. So Suzy just charged him with possession with intent to supply and being concerned in the manufacture of GHB, and bailed him to appear before the magistrates the following Tuesday. "Yes: gotcha, you bastard," she said as she and Hedley returned to the CID room.

"He's not our killer, though, not directly," said Cheungy.

265

Chapter 38

Kirsty

"Have you nicked Tom?" Kirsty asked the next morning.

"None of your business. I asked you to keep away from him. He's a first class scrote and that just proves it." Her mother winced over her words. "Bugger. See? This is why I wish, really wish, you didn't work there."

"It's true then. But Mum, he didn't do it."

"And how do you know that? Because you 'love' him and he'd never do a thing like that?" her mother said in a deeply sarcastic way.

Kirsty knew she was going red. "Mum. Sorry. Tom told me something. But it's OK because we've split and I'm never talking to him ever again. Except at work. It's like this…." Kirsty watched her mother's face clamp down into neutral as she recounted the conversation with Tom about Ellie and the blowjob. "See… that explains away any evidence of semen on Ellie's top."

"You believe him?"

"She's given someone else a blowjob. I saw. It was revolting so I left as soon as she started."

"What? For goodness sake, what…" Kirsty saw her mother pull herself back under control. "Sorry, Sweetie. I think you'd better tell me and I'll try not to get cross."

Kirsty recounted the first time Tom had taken her to the cannabis den.

"Why am I shocked? I shouldn't be shocked; not after all my years in the police. But I am. Possibly because it's personal. So, Ellie was a bit of a tart. That doesn't clear Tom, you know."

"Yeah, but the point is, she's such a tart, all he'd have to do is pay her, not drug her. It doesn't make sense."

"Unless he wanted to do something she didn't. Sweetie, I know much more about this than you do. You shouldn't even know this."

"But can't you see he's innocent?"

"No. He could have had the blowjob with 'consent'… even though she's under age and strictly speaking unable to consent. And then wanted more. Don't you see that? Because he's been intimate with her on her last day, he has to fall under our radar. Look, I want you to have nothing to do with him. He's possibly dangerous. And if you talk to him I could be in the shit. But we've bailed him, it's going to be hard not talking to him. And I could hardly make it a condition that he doesn't approach you. Just brush him off if he does."

"Don't worry, Mum. I will. Two timing scumbag."

"You were still going out with him?"

"Sort of. But we never did it. He says that's why he asked Ellie."

"Oh, thank goodness; he might have STIs. You're not lying to me, are you?"

"Oh for goodness sake, Mum." Kirsty flounced upstairs, slammed her bedroom door, except it caught on some discarded clothing. She kicked it aside, slammed the door effectively this time, then flung herself on her bed.

~~~

Suzy

Suzy rang the doorbell of the Warreners' house. Mr Warrener answered it, and ushered her into the living room. Everything was immaculate, as if they spent all their time cleaning,

cleaning, cleaning the place, because cleaning meant not thinking. Ellie had been their only child. All they had now was each other, but even that could fall apart so easily. The blame. The recrimination. The little disagreements over upbringing and freedoms which would be magnified, and the re-writing of history until the blame lay firmly with the other party. "You'll have a cup of tea," Mrs Warrener commanded. Suzy didn't refuse. She updated them on developments as much as she could (which amounted to waffle and not much substance) and she helped them with some of the miserable technicalities. She told them the body couldn't be released just yet. She pitied them in their in-limbo state.

"I've been thinking," said Mrs Warrener. "Why would anyone want to do that to my baby? She was a good girl. I know she wrote that awful diary. So I wondered if it was that teacher who did it... to get back at her for getting him into trouble. For revenge."

"He's not our main suspect," said Suzy carefully. "We obviously considered him, but he has been excluded from our enquiry on this matter."

"She always was a one for having crushes on people," said Mr Warrener. "A year back she did her work experience at the pizza factory. Had a crush on Jimbo, the line manager. Soon cured her of that, though. Told her we knew him from school. Wee Willy Wanker, we used to call him, begging your pardon. Because he had a wee willy and was always... anyway. We told her that and she stopped going on about him."

"He tried it on with me at school when we were kids," added Mrs Warrener. "I told him where to get off and warned all the other girls about him. He told me he'd get me back one day... you don't suppose he did it to Ellie to get back at me?"

~~~

"It's an interesting motive," said Suzy to Cheungy, later at the nick. "I refreshed my memory over Jordan and Trish, because I remember Jordan saying something about rebuffing Digby's advances, and laughing about him in the girls' changing room. And I remember Kirsty saying something about how the boys could hear through the walls, which embarrassed her a lot. And there's Stuart, who teased Digby about the size of his todger (according to Kirsty who heard the story) who also thinks he was raped anally. Maybe Digby is sexually inadequate, not well endowed, and seeks revenge for every perceived sexual slight. That would fit in with his profile."

"Maybe, but I don't like to pay too much credence to offender profiling," said Cheungy. "Useful tool so long as you don't rely too heavily on it. Only don't tell the psychologists I said that. Mind you, rape is sometimes about power over the victim, more than it is about sex, so you might be right. Can't prove it, though. Especially as that under-trained PCSO spent time watching his front door and gate during the critical time."

"And if Digby left his TV on, went out through the back door, through the hole in the back of his old privy into the derelict building's car park, then out through the gate? Sticking his two fingers up at the system like that would be in character, too." Suzy looked down at her pocket notebook, flicking through the pages idly.

"Why rape his sister's lover, though?"

"Maybe she made him feel inadequate in some way? I don't know. Angie never said anything like that, but I bet she'd never encourage any advances. Or maybe Digby was pissed off with Kim and decided to get back at her secretly. I wouldn't be

269

surprised if he was responsible for Ellie's death, not Tom after all. Tom smells like a normal little scrote. Digby... Digby's odd."

~~~

Angie

Bea phoned up the Wednesday before the trial to check I was OK about it. I asked her then if I could stay and watch the trial after I'd given my evidence. I wanted to see Digs get what he deserved. I can't believe the courts let him out on bail. He's a rapist. It made me jumpy, knowing he was out. Especially at night. So I wanted to watch the trial, see him go down for what he did to me, and to make me feel a bit safer.

And I wanted to look my erstwhile friends in the eye whilst they testified on his behalf as Defence witnesses. But I didn't tell Bea that.

Bea said I could, but to double check with the Usher. And she reminded me that once I'd had my say, that was it.

~~~

The trial was scheduled to start on the Monday. I dressed carefully. Smart, but not too butch. For all I knew, the jury might be a bunch of homophobes, and I didn't want their prejudices to get in the way of justice. They would know, of course, that I'm a lesbian, but no point in shoving the concept in their faces.

Sally and John took me in. We parked in the Riverside Retail Park car park because it was close by, and they walked the short walk to the Crown Court with me. I could feel my heart trying to escape from my ribcage. John pulled the heavy front doors open for us. It was comforting to be looked after.

Nobody's ever done that for me, except perhaps my father, so many years ago.

Searched. My bag was examined and we had to walk through a portal, just like at the airport.

Bea was there. She reminded me that she couldn't give any legal advice and was there to help with practical things like form filling if I needed it, or just to sit with me to make things seem not so scary. She whisked us to a small room to sit and made sure the Usher knew where we were. She told me the Usher wanted to know if I wanted to give my oath on the Bible or just aver. I said I'd take my oath on the Bible.

While she'd gone to tell the usher, Sally turned to me. "Look, Angie, this evidence you're giving. It's kind of private. We'd rather not hear it, if you don't mind, as we know you as a friend. If Bea's here to look after you, would you mind if we left now? We can pick you up later. We'll be at home, in the garden. You've got a mobile, haven't you?"

"Just remember to switch it off when you go into court," said John with a laugh.

Such good friends, I'd felt reluctant to tell them I didn't want then actually listening to the trial, but they'd guessed. I didn't mind Bea watching, listening. She was part of the system. I'd never have to cross her path again, but with Sally it was different. I'd see her every day.

"Thanks," I said. "I'd rather give evidence alone. Bea'll take care of me."

Chapter 39

Angie

I tried to concentrate on the book I'd brought along but couldn't get into it. I'd brought along a magazine as well, but it was no good; my eyes slid over the words without understanding. "What's happening?" I asked Bea.

"The Jury'll be sworn in. Digby can object to anyone he thinks he knows. Then the prosecutor will introduce the case, tell them what it's about. It's a bit like telling a story in as simple a way as possible. As you're giving your evidence very early on, you can see most of what happens, if you really want to stay. Are you sure about that?"

"I'm still in two minds. I want to face him while he tells his lies. Shame him."

"You won't be able to say anything. If you do, you'll be asked to leave. Be careful of your body language, even. And check with the Usher that it's OK." Bea's teeth flashed a startling white smile. I turned back to my magazine. A few minutes' futile scanning, and my eyes slid back to her face to look at it unobserved. A dark sheen, like polished wood, rich, but with darker blemishes betraying her age. She must be about 50. She'd straightened her hair, but it rebelled with a becoming, glossy crumple that made her hair stand out from her scalp. She was comfortably plump. Motherly.

I went for a wee. Moira was in the concourse. Our eyes clashed, then we moved round each other in bubbles of isolation, stiff-legged like dogs. She had her back to me when I returned to the little room I was hiding in.

Then the Usher came and fetched me. Kim and co were in the concourse, including her mother, who gave me a look of pure hatred. I walked past, pretending I was in blinkers. They ignored me. We went through the first courtroom door into a hallway. I saw a room off to one side, caught a glimpse of police uniform, Mrs Neutral Suzy Rolfe, and Dr Galton. The police were gossiping in a hushed way, relaxed. Dr Galton looked as if she were made of glass.

Through the second door and into court.

Gowns. Wigs. OK, I'd expected it; I'd been shown round this very courtroom when it was empty. But now it was busy with the trial. Before it had just been an empty room, innocuous. Now the menace was present.

Eyes on me, watching me enter.

Police in the Public gallery, sitting at the front. A copper in uniform. And some other people just sitting, with notebooks.

The carpet had turned to mush. I waded across it. The Usher took me to the Witness Stand. She handed me the Bible and I took the oath, thinking back to when I was last in church. With Mum and Dad, next to brother Richard. I had a poignant stab of yearning for them, so unexpected it made me blink.

Twelve faces turned to me. Expectant. Faces sombre. Like birds on telephone wires.

The prosecutor flashed a smile at me. "Can I ask you to cast your mind back to Wednesday 29th June last year. Can you remember anything special about that day?"

I told them how I'd gone to the doctors, how my pregnancy had been diagnosed against all expectation. With his help I told the court how I'd reported the rape, and how I'd decided it must be a drugged rape because I'd never consent to sex with a man knowingly. And how one Saturday had been blank, so I concluded it had happened then.

273

The jury were a ragbag of faces, clothes, some smart, some casual, all sworn to give Digby justice according to the evidence. Their expressions were clones of intense concentration. Some made notes.

I wasn't sure whom to address; the judge, jury, or the prosecutor who was the one actually speaking to me. I found my eyes roving over them all, seeing none of them, like playing a role in the Nativity at school; don't focus on anyone, especially not Mum and Dad, in case I lose my nerve.

Mum and Dad; if they could see me now, what would they think?

Had I ever had sex with a man? I denied it, of course.

The prosecutor asked me how Kim had taken the news, and I said badly, and told them of the row. He asked if I had hit her, and I said yes, I had, a slap, once, when she put her face so close to mine that I felt threatened. He asked if I had ever hit her before or since, and I said no, of course not. He asked me when Kim had left. Had we rowed before my diagnosis? How were we as a couple up to that point? So I told him how I'd loved her and had hoped to be with her forever, but that the baby had changed all that.

My eyes watered in mourning for all that I'd lost, all that Digby had stolen.

The prosecutor asked me about the birth. Had I consented to the blood and cheek swabs being taken, and why? "So they stood a chance of catching him, whoever he was."

"How did you react when the police informed you they had identified the father of your child?"

"Well, I was pleased because it meant he could be brought to justice."

"And when you found out it was Digby?"

"I was sick. Physically sick. I couldn't believe it."

With his careful questioning, the Prosecutor showed the jury that I hadn't consented, I would never consent, that the blank weekend happened at about the time of conception. For some reason he emphasised the phone call I had made to tell Kim I'd had the baby and had told Digby about the DNA samples. He showed that I was appalled when I found out who the father was. And how I'd suffered.

I could see the jury gazing with revulsion towards Digby.

When the prosecutor told me he had no more questions, the Judge looked at the clock. As near to one o'clock as made no odds. "A good time to break for lunch," he said. "Can I remind all witnesses and jury that they are not to speak to each other if they should happen across each other in town, and that the identity of Ms X is confidential?"

I fled back to the room where I'd hidden. Bea suggested some fresh air. As I left the court building. I caught sight of some jurors in the distance. It seemed a perilous walk, like a nightmare where every step you take there's a demon in your path. The oppression was bearing down on me, and the temptation to flee home was crushing.

~~~

"This could get tough," warned Bea, "But it's the job of the defence barrister to ask hard questions, though she shouldn't bully you or ask the wrong type of questions. If it gets too bad, the Judge should stop it, or the Prosecutor will object."

When I took the stand again, I was reminded that I was still under oath. The Defence Barrister stood, threw a scanty bow at the judge then smiled at me. "Ms X, let me take you back to the blank weekend in December. Friday 17th. You say you have no recollection of the events of the evening?"

"All I remember was going to the Craven Arms, having a pint of beer. Then a coffee when the others went off to Janger's Night Club. The next thing I knew I was home, in bed, in the morning, feeling rough. I slept for most of the weekend. I thought I'd got food poisoning."

"Did you go to the doctor's?"

"No."

"Why not, if you felt so bad?"

"I don't like going to the doctors unless it's a real emergency. It's impossible to get an appointment, anyway." I saw a dismay flicker over the prosecutor's face, and I wondered what I'd said wrong. But I didn't have long to ponder, because the Defence barrister asked, "You say you have no recollection of the night of 17th December after you'd drunk the coffee."

"None at all."

"I put it to you that you cannot say with any certainty that you did not consent to sexual intercourse with anyone."

"Well, I wouldn't. Not with a man. Never. It's just not in me. I'd find it disgusting."

"What about if you were tipsy. Drunk, even?"

"I wasn't blind drunk. I never drink that much."

"What about the day you say you found you were pregnant? 29th June. Did you get drunk then?"

"Yes, I did. A bit. I was so shocked."

"So though it's not a habit with you, you cannot say that you never get drunk?"

"I didn't drink on 17th December. I was drugged. I know I didn't drink. I had a pint of bitter. That's all."

"How do you know?"

"I only remember…"

"Just because you don't remember, doesn't mean you didn't get drunk. You tell us you can't remember anything that happened. Can you?" The question hissed like a lash across the courtroom.

"It's just not something I do," I said lamely. I could see the prosecutor scribbling a frantic note to himself, looking slightly predatory.

"I put it to you," said the defence barrister, "That you were indeed somewhat drunk on 17th December. I'm not suggesting that you gave consent when drunk," she added, shooting a look at the prosecutor, "I'm suggesting consent was already given for the ultimate aim of obtaining a baby genetically related to the woman you love. Being slightly tipsy was a means of facilitating this intercourse, and that the main consumption of alcohol took place after the intercourse and resulted in your memory loss."

"No, no, that's not true. I never wanted a baby. This wasn't planned, consented to in any way. It was a sneaky, drugged rape." I swallowed, took a sip of water.

"Can you remember what happened on 17th December?"

"No. I can't. I was drugged."

"How do you know you were drugged? Were you tested?"

"No. I just know I felt weird that weekend. And I can't remember what happened. I'd no idea what happened until I found I was pregnant."

"That could have been the effects of alcohol, not drugs. Or food poisoning, as you first thought."

"No. I don't drink enough to get drunk, so drunk I can't remember."

"But you've just told us you got drunk the day you came back from the doctors."

"That's different. I was shocked. Amazed. Depressed."

"About what?"

"The baby. Finding I was pregnant, not menopausal."

"I put it to you that you got drunk because you'd decided to terminate and found you might be too late."

"No."

The Defence barrister cast a look at the jury, took a sip of water, scanned her notes, looked at me. "Before your relationship breakdown with Kim, you say you'd been together 5 years?"

"Yes."

"And you hoped to be together for the rest of your lives?"

"Yes. I hoped so. I loved her."

"Enough to want to bear her a baby?"

"No. The thought never entered my head. I don't like babies. I'm not like that." The jury looked a little disconcerted by my obvious revulsion. Good, I thought, until I wondered if that might feed any homophobia.

"Not once?"

"Never!"

"Do you know the man in the dock?" Digs was sitting there with a neutral expression.

"Of course. That's Digby Jamieson. Kim's brother." My rapist.

"Is there a strong family resemblance?"

"Yes."

"Have you ever felt sexually attracted to Digby?"

"No." I'd told them once already. The prosecutor had asked me.

"Even though he looks so similar to Kim, your lover?"

"No. I can't have sex with men. It's disgusting."

The jury were examining their note pads.

278

"Do you ever remember discussing with Kim and Digby how you'd like a family?"

"No, we never did."

The defence barrister looked as if she'd come across a particularly stupid child. "Let me run through something and see if it triggers any memories. If it doesn't you must say so. Beginning of November. Had one of your friends had a baby?"

"Moira." Toddler in trolley in the supermarket. Near the fruit and vegetables. Vehement repulsion of friendship. Lies. The emotions slammed into me, rocking me.

"Moira Stevenson. You all met up in a particular coffee shop. Do you remember?"

I riffled through the memories. November. Autumn day. Moira, glowing cheeks. Baby in the buggy, tiny, cute in her little garments. Appropriate cooing admiration from all of us. Me included. Baby passed round, dandled. I wouldn't hold her, worried about baby puke, but everyone else did.

"The Singing Kettle," I admitted.

"Did you all admire the baby?"

"Yes."

"You included?"

"Yes. I s'pose."

"Do you remember a conversation about babies?"

"Not really."

"Do you remember expressing the wish for one of your own?"

"Certainly not!"

"You don't remember saying you wished you had one, that it's the one problem with being a lesbian?"

"No!"

"You don't remember saying that?"

"I didn't say that. I never would."

"Perhaps you've forgotten."

"I never said that."

"It's a long time ago. I put it to you that you did say it, and you've forgotten."

"No."

"Perhaps it was in jest."

The Prosecutor jumped up. "Your Honour, I think My Learned Friend is badgering the witness."

"Agreed," said the Judge. "Please move on, Ms Seton."

The Defence barrister bowed, turned back to me. "Let me take you to a date, mid-November, where you're sitting in the Craven Arms with Digby and Kim. Do you remember such an occasion?"

"Which time?"

"Sometime in mid-November. Memories are hazy with the passage of time. But just you, Kim and Digby were there, none of the others."

"I don't remember."

"Do you remember a conversation about wanting to start a family, like Moira. Only how impossible it would be to have a baby by Kim, yet she was the one you wanted one by?"

The courtroom spun. A blunt 'no' would make it sound as if the conversation had taken place, but I'd forgotten. The silence grew, treacherous silence.

"We never had such a conversation. I know we didn't because I never wanted a baby." I looked at the Judge, then the Jury, trying to will them to believe me.

"How's your memory, Ms X?"

"Pretty good. Unless I've been drugged." I threw a venomous look towards Digby.

"What did Kim give you for Christmas last year?"

"Oh, er, er... A book."

"What was the title of the book?"

I could see the book in my mind's eye, but I could not remember the title, or who it was by. My mind groped. Nothing. "I don't remember," I confessed, when the silence had already told them that.

"And what did you give Kim?"

"A tee shirt," I hazarded.

"Are you sure?"

"No," I admitted. "But that's trivial. I know I never said anything about wanting a baby."

"When did your relationship with Kim break down?"

"As soon as I told her about the baby."

"But your relationship had been a bit rocky before that, hadn't it?"

"No." I looked at her, wondering at the question. "No. We'd been very happy. It was the pregnancy itself that wrecked it. When she knew I'd had sex with a man. She couldn't hack it, even though it wasn't my fault and I didn't remember it. We were very happy until I found I was pregnant. That's when Digby started telling Kim I was bisexual, made Kim doubt me. That's when it all started to go wrong."

The barrister went over my relationship until the Judge told her to stop badgering me again. I was a punch bag for words. In the end she backed down and said she had no more questions. I was glad because I could feel the tears poking at my eyes like needles. She'd made me seem unreliable. Not a liar as such, just unreliable, with a poor memory.

The prosecutor stood again. "When you say you don't remember the conversations about wanting a baby, is it because you just don't remember, or because they never happened?"

"They never happened. I saw Moira's baby but I never held it, though I said the sorts of things you say to a new mother. I never said I wanted one. I never would, because I don't. And I certainly never had a conversation about wanting to have a baby by Kim. That never happened."

"Had you any clue, any inkling you were pregnant before you went to see Dr Thomas?"

"No, none, why should I? As far as I was concerned, I'd never had sex with a man, so I couldn't be pregnant."

"People might find it hard to believe that you got to 30 weeks pregnant before realising something was wrong."

"I didn't see much outward sign over the first few months. I thought my periods had stopped because it was the menopause. I'm 48, I was 46 at the time, nearly 47 when I found out. And the weight gain, well, I just thought I was overeating. And the sickness, well, that I put down to the menopause."

"If you had thought at any time that you were pregnant, would you have gone to the doctor's?"

I didn't quite grasp the question. I frowned at him.

"Ms X. if at any time you knew you were pregnant, would you have gone to the doctor's?"

"Of course. I mean, if I'd realised I'd been raped I'd have gone straight away. I'd have gone to the police straight away. I'm not stupid. A first pregnancy at my age is no picnic." I twigged why he was asking that question. "I don't trouble the doctor about trivial illnesses. I went because I was frightened that something was seriously wrong, like cancer. If I had known I was pregnant earlier, I would have gone sooner. If I'd wanted the baby, and known I was pregnant, I would have gone to the doctor as soon as I thought I was pregnant."

"How did you feel when Dr Thomas told you, you were pregnant?"

"I didn't believe him at first. I thought he must have made a mistake."

"Thank you. I have no more questions," said the prosecutor.

The defence barrister bowed. "I have none," she said.

The judge turned and said, "Thank you Ms X. It's always difficult giving evidence in a case like this. You may leave the witness stand but remember if you bump into any of the witnesses or jury, you must not discuss the case with them. If you wish, you may remain and watch the rest of the trial, or you may leave. The choice is yours."

"Thank you, Your Honour," I said, with a nod, and went and sat in the public seating. The Judge scrutinised the clock as if wondering whether to finish for the day, but after some discussion with the prosecutor and defence barrister, decided to press on after a short break, as the doctor's time was valuable.

Chapter 40

Angie

Dr Thomas was dead, taking with him any recollections of my shock, disbelief and horror when he'd told me I was pregnant. All that remained was what he'd written down in my notes. Dr Galton went over them. All that was left of the disbelief, the upheaval of emotions was where he'd written "Unplanned" and "Father unknown" and that I'd had an HIV test because of that. If he'd lived, he could have told them how I'd felt, confirmed that I'd had no clue that I could possibly be pregnant. If he'd lived.

~~~

When court finished for the day, the Judge told the court that not only was I to remain anonymous, 'Ms X' but that in any reporting, Digby and Kim were to be anonymous since identifying them would make it easier to identify me. I'd seen people in the front row of the public gallery scribbling away on note pads. Until that point I hadn't realised they were reporters. Outside the courtroom, I had a slightly panicked conversation with Bea about this, but she reassured me that the Press could not publish my name unless I consented. Then she said she couldn't be with me the next day. Did I intend to come to watch? If so, would I be OK?

"Thanks for your help," I said. "I've done the difficult bit with your support; given my evidence. It was the court I found intimidating, and the thought of giving my evidence, not Digby himself. I think I'll be OK. And anyhow, if it gets too bad, I can always leave."

"Remember not to talk to anyone," she said as parting advice. "And if you need to talk later, we're still available."

I clattered down the stairs to the front entrance. Balked. TV cameras outside, a stakeout. What were they for? I dithered on the inside, wishing I was still with Bea. I wondered which important trial was going on to justify the TV cameras there. I fished my phone out and asked the security guard if I was allowed to phone from inside the building. He nodded, with a look of sympathy.

"Sally, it's Angie. Can you come and pick me up please?"

"We'll pick you up from the Waterloo Lane car park, if you like... it's nearer. By the loos."

"Oh, yes, I s'pose."

"Give us about half an hour or so. How was it?"

"Awful. I told them about it, but the defence barrister made out I'm a liar, well, not so much a liar, more that I'm a dippy woman who can't remember things. But I know what happened. Except, I s'pose, I don't because of the drugs. And the Doctor's evidence was a bit dry, y'know?"

"We're getting in the car now."

"OK, I'll start making my way over." I pushed through the swing doors, sidled out of camera shot. I walked down Waterloo Lane, fearing bloodhounds on my scent. At least if they were following me, it was a dead end for vehicles. Nobody spared me a glance, nobody followed me, but I was exposed and vulnerable. I hung around by the loos, feeling like some sort of perv, and wished they'd suggested picking me up in the retail park where I could have run into a shop if necessary. This was Chelmsford, 5.00pm ish, daylight. Why the hell did I feel so scared?

Galchester isn't that far from Chelmsford, just down the A12, but perhaps they'd be caught up in traffic. I dithered for a bit, looking at my watch while minutes crawled past.

John and Sally drove up, turned into the car park. I jumped in the back and belted myself in.

"There must be an important trial or something," said John. "We've just driven past a TV reporter do a piece to camera outside the courts." The reporter was still talking when we drove past again. Nothing to do with me. Of course. Even so, I felt a sense of relief as I realised this.

I watched the news. It was a murder trial involving some minor celebrity whom I knew nothing about. I was a bit shocked to see myself flit though the corner of the shot. I vowed to be more careful next time.

~~~

Suzy

Suzy slumped into her chair and swivelled. "Gawd, I hate court, but at least it has the decency to start and finish at a reasonable time."

"How did it go?" asked Cheungy, coming out of her office.

"Good. Good. I think," said Suzy, gratefully taking a mug of coffee that Lynne had made. "It was OK, wasn't it, Lynne?"

"Apart from the headache I always get in court, fine." Lynne swallowed a couple of tablets. "Do you know, I took some painkillers in anticipation, and I still got a headache!"

"Psychosomatic," said Cheungy, teasingly dismissive. "All in the mind."

~~~

Angie

The next day I sat down in the public gallery. The judge gave me a speculative look, and I could see the jury frowning. Now that I had given my evidence, I was immune to oppression by Digby. I saw him looking at me from time to time, but his face said nothing. Though sometimes I thought he might actually be enjoying this in a perverse sort of way.

That morning it was about how my baby's DNA sample was taken, how Digby had been arrested and how his DNA showed (in combination with mine) that he was unequivocally the father of my baby.

~~~

After lunch the court was reconvened, but before the jury were recalled, the judge spoke to the barristers. "I've had a note from the jury. Almost always happens in this sort of case. The question is, how did the police come by Mr Jamieson's DNA to get a match? Well, of course, he was arrested on another matter, a separate matter which has no bearing on the case. If you're both happy with that, then I shall tell the Jury that, and that they must only consider the evidence that the prosecution present in this trial."

I bit my lips, wondering what else Digby had done to be arrested. And why shouldn't the jury know what a worm he is? Might help them make their mind up against him.

Digby was making frantic signals to his solicitor, who turned, saw, and hissed at the barrister. "Might I have a moment, Your Honour?" There was a hurried whispered discussion. The barrister appeared to consider something and agree. He turned to the Judge.

"Your Honour, Mr Jamieson has pointed out that without information, people's imaginations can magnify things. He feels that the reason for his arrest is a minor matter, but that the jury might speculate upon it and think it something major, and therefore prejudicial. It might be fairer to admit what he was arrested for that first time."

The judge looked at the prosecutor who nodded. "That seems sensible, Your Honour, since the question has been raised."

When the jury had filed back in, the judge told them that Digby Jamieson had been arrested under Section 5 of the Public Order Act and for possession of a spliff of herbal cannabis, for which he had been cautioned and released.

Trivial, then. More fool him, getting himself nicked when he knew the police had the baby's DNA on file. It seemed like divine justice to me.

Rolfe went through the interview with Digby, the one he'd given when they arrested him for my rape, the one which they'd read to me when they had invited me down the police station. The one where he'd lied. Rolfe read her parts, and the prosecutor read his replies.

The jury turned their eyes on me. I brazened their looks, glad I hadn't sneaked off. But I could say nothing to his lies.

Alderton and the prosecuting barrister read out the statement Kim had made, explaining when she had made it, that is, on the day of Digby's arrest. But they also read out the statement I had made, refuting what Digby and Kim had said, pointing out that I had told Digby that the police had taken the baby's DNA.

I knew the truth, but would the jury believe me?

~~~

288

The defence barrister called Digby to the stand. He swore on the Bible to tell the truth, the liar.

"Did you have sexual intercourse with Ms X on that Friday 17th December?"

"Yes, I did," he said calmly, casting me a bland glance.

"Why?"

"She wanted to have a baby. My sister and Ms X wanted a baby."

"Did she enjoy it?"

"Yes. Seemed to."

"Where did you have sex?"

"At Steve Hasset's. He's a friend of mine. I sometimes house-sit for him."

"Did Ms X struggle at all, or in any way show her reluctance to have sex with you?"

"Well, no, that's what surprised me a bit at first, since she was Kim's lover and had told Kim she wasn't bisexual. She came on strong, said she'd always fancied me because I remind her so much of Kim."

"And you had sex?"

"Yes."

"Was she drunk?"

"We'd had a couple, but she wasn't drunk, no. Got drunk afterwards though."

"Why you? Why were you the 'sperm donor' as it were?"

"Because Kim is who she really wanted the baby by. I'm the nearest we could get to Kim being the father."

"Why didn't you use artificial insemination?"

"Thought sex would work better, and I didn't want to masturbate to get the sperm because it's a sin. Kim wasn't too happy, but it was a means to an end. Ms X... well, I reckon she was secretly looking forward to it."

Lie after lie he gave, so plausible.

"This baby was a wanted pregnancy, then?"

"Yes. Until Ms X hit Kim. She'd got a bit aggressive with Kim anyway, once she was pregnant. Seemed to change. Frightened Kim, so Kim said she was leaving. They had a huge row, and A... Ms X said she was going to abort the baby."

"When did you first find out Ms X was pregnant?"

"Oh, just after Christmas. Pleased as punch, they were. First try, scored."

I was staggered by the lie, so easily said, so convincing. The prosecutor asked Digby why I hadn't been to the doctor's earlier if I was so pleased about being pregnant. Seemed illogical that I should risk the baby and myself by not going. But he said that I hated going to the doctor's, so had avoided doing so until I wanted a termination.

So the jury now thought that Kim and I had rowed before I went to see Dr T, and had gone for a termination. Perhaps they even thought I'd play-acted about the rape. But surely not. 'Unplanned pregnancy.' 'Father unknown.' That was what Dr Thomas had put in his notes.

I could see Digby squirming at one pertinent question. "Why do you think Ms X didn't tell the police it was you straight away, when she first reported that she suspected she'd been raped? If it was, as you say, an attempt at revenge to report you for rape, she'd have named you at the time, not waited on the remote off-chance that you would be arrested for some other matter."

The unassailable argument. It wasn't revenge. It couldn't be. Surely the Jury could see that?

Digby shrugged. "She was a bit off her head at the time. Maybe she didn't know she hadn't."

"Ms X makes an allegation of rape by person unknown. Then months afterwards the police find a match, and you then say it wasn't rape. If it was revenge, she would have told the police who had done it when she reported it, had she known."

"I don't know what was going on inside that woman's head at the time. Maybe she just wanted to report it as rape, but didn't want to bring me into it, just have it as a weapon against me, to force Kim to go back to her — she kept trying to get her back with her. And then, when I was matched as the father, she decided to carry on with the farce. Once she'd made the allegation she'd look an idiot if she'd withdrawn it. She'd have got into trouble for it."

Wriggle, Digby wriggle.

~~~

When court finished for the day, I hid in the loos and phoned Sally. A little later they phoned back to say they were in the car park, and to be careful as the press were there again. I slid past even more carefully this time, with a baseball cap to partially hide behind.

Chapter 41

Kirsty

"Hi Mum," yelled Kirsty, as her mother walked through the front door. Her mother kicked her shoes off, padded into the living room and flopped onto the sofa.

"I'm so ffflipping tired. Get us a coffee, Sweetie. I've just about had it."

"The kettle's just boiled. And I've got tea ready, though it's only salad and pasta 'cos I didn't know when you'd get home." Her mother's grateful expression pulled a rush of emotion from Kirsty. She brought back a mug of coffee. "I've put the pasta on. Bad day?"

"Not the best. I was in court this morning. Your line manager. Soon to be ex manager, I hope. When he goes down. If he goes down."

"Mum, look, what did he do? Only you've never said, except that it was rape and just warned me away from him. Could he really get away with it?"

Kirsty blushed under her mother's lengthy scrutiny.

Her mother sighed, decision spilling out with her breath. "OK, I'll tell you. Though I'd rather you didn't discuss it. It's sort of public knowledge now. Though the victim must always remain anonymous. You know that, don't you? You let that slip and you could go to prison for contempt of court. Basically, Ms X came to me with a complaint of rape. She couldn't remember what happened because she thinks she was drugged. The bizarre thing is she didn't know she was pregnant until a long way down the line because she's a lesbian and never had sex with a man. Or so she thought, until she found herself pregnant. We took DNA samples from the baby when it arrived. Nothing matched, so he wasn't a known offender. Then we arrested Digby, and you were there, my Sweetie, weren't you? And his DNA matched the baby. So he'd drugged this Ms X and raped her. Allegedly."

"Well, then he's guilty as hell. No wonder you were so freaky about drinks spiking and me working there. I wish you'd said."

"It's difficult, Sweetie. He's supposed to be innocent until proven guilty. But I'm sure he's guilty."

"So why didn't he just plead guilty? They get less if they plead guilty early, don't they?"

"Ah. His defence is that it was consented to, because his sister was this woman's lover and they wanted a baby between them."

Kirsty bridled with the old loyalty. "Well. Maybe that's right."

He mother shook her head over her coffee. "No. I have an instinct for these things. Though not always. The police are sometimes used as a means of revenge, which makes me so angry for the real victims. One girl alleged rape by her boyfriend. Fortunately for him, he was drinking in a bar the other side of town at the time of the alleged assault, and that bar happened to have CCTV cameras which clearly picked him out. It was just a malicious allegation to get him done because he split with her. If it hadn't been for the CCTV, he'd have ended up in court, because she was very, very convincing. We did her for perverting the course of justice. Don't often do that in case it puts the real victims off from coming forward. But that was just malicious.

"Back to why I think Ms X is telling the truth: If you were aiming to fall pregnant, and your periods stopped, you'd go to the doctor's straight away, wouldn't you, not wait 7 months, because you'd want the best in medical care for your baby."

"Is the victim someone I know?"

"Nope. And anyhow, I can't say."

"Will they find him guilty?"

"I hope so, oh, I really hope so."

"Me too, actually," said Kirsty. "I don't like working for him. Did at first. Had a sort of crush on him. But he's a bit of a perv."

"Umn, so you said before. And that's what worries me. Now look, I'll tell you this for your own protection, because he might get off, in which case you will be working for him still. We have no evidence but it's possible, just possible that Ms X isn't his only victim. Now look, you mustn't say, or even let slip to someone like Jordan."

It was as if her mother had thrown a jug of water over her. "You mean... Jordan and Trish? But I thought you suspect Tom of that?"

"There. Is. No. Evidence. If you repeat either suspicion, I could be in serious trouble. But I'm tired of just giving you hints about taking care of your drinks etc, you saying, 'OK OK,' and then finding it's not OK. So I'll spell it out. We have several reports of date rape type offences. All of them reported too late for any evidence, except for Ms X's where the evidence is the baby. We can't prove anything until he offends again. In other words, if he's acquitted of this there has to be another victim who, this time, has enough wits to come forward before the evidence has vanished. That's why I get so upset and frustrated sometimes. Because sometimes we are forced to let the offender go, knowing he may well offend again, that he will offend again. And there is nothing I can do about it."

"Is it Jimbo, then, the serial rapist?"

"We don't know. He has certain characteristics like a serial offender. But we've no hard evidence. And we have got other suspects in the frame. Like Tom as you said, but not just Tom. People who have either been caught using the drugs, or have behaved in a rather dodgy fashion, if not worse. No evidence. But someone's offending, someone around there is a predator. That's why I get so twitchy."

~~~

Angie

On Wednesday, John and Sally arrived at my house half an hour earlier than I'd expected. I was still in my dressing gown, wrapped up from a shower. I saw them draw up in the car and dressed so hurriedly that my clothes snagged on my damp body. We sat down on the lounge over coffee, whilst I read the papers they brought with them. "Love-Child Defence" was one headline. And, "'Rape' allegations thrown into doubt," was another. They didn't actually identify me, nor did they identify Digby or Kim, because the judge had said my anonymity was paramount, and that identification of either of them could have hinted at my identity. It all seemed a bit futile, though, because Digby had blabbed to all our friends, way before the trial, and turned them all against me. I read the reports. They seemed constrained by the anonymity issue. 'A forty-eight-year-old woman'. But slanted against me. Maybe it was just me being oversensitive. I was impotent, though, because I couldn't set the record straight. There also seemed to be a lot more detail in the reports than was strictly necessary, so those who knew me would now know all these little details.

"Sorry to make you cry," said John awkwardly. "Only we thought you ought to know. Before you went. Perhaps you'd better not go today."

"Look... they said I said I can't really remember what happened. And that I don't trust doctors." I read on. They were careful, oh so careful not to identify me, but those who mattered would know who it was. My ex-friends. The reporter said how I couldn't even remember what my lover had given me for Christmas, or even what I'd given her, the woman I wished to spend the rest of my life with. Perhaps start a family with. The implications were there, hidden but brutal. They didn't exactly call me a liar. They didn't exactly say I'd used the criminal justice system so revenge myself on Kim and Digby. But I read between the lines. And so would everyone else. Including, perhaps, the Jury.

~~~

The prosecutor complained before the Jury were called in. The Judge was frightening in his anger. Cold. Strict. He imposed reporting restrictions until the trial was over. He told the reporters they'd come close to committing a criminal offence. The reporters sat like scolded children in the front row of the public gallery. I was glad to see them looking so chastened.

The Jury were called in. The judge asked them if any had read the morning papers, but none of them had, or at least, none of them admitted to it.

The media were allowed to stay but were not allowed to report anything until the trial was over. I let my eyes bore into their backs, hating them.

~~~

When Kim gave her evidence, the Jury could see the family resemblance. She'd emphasised it by wearing clothes similar to Digby's. It struck me as a calculated move, and it angered me.

But her lies angered me more. She told the court how we'd planned the pregnancy. How we'd decided our love for each other should be sealed with a family. How we'd intended to make the commitment as soon as the law had changed. (Not now, of course, not after the split.) How I'd changed once I was carrying the baby, bullied her. Mood swings. Violent. She lied about the row, saying we'd rowed when she said she was leaving, and how I'd said I would abort the baby just to spite her. Only it was too late.

She lied. But I suppose I can understand why she lied. Blood's thicker than water. Blood will out. She loved her brother more than she loved me, even though he raped me.

Every so often she would look at me with a strange expression. I remembered her doubts early on, thinking I was bi, I remembered that Digby had lied to her, told her I wanted his baby. She knew she was lying about it being pre-planned with her, but perhaps she felt it was near enough the truth to be true.

When the prosecutor came to cross-examine her, he read out her statement given to DC Rolfe. Nowhere did she mention it was a pre-planned pregnancy. Gotcha, I thought. If it had been pre-planned like they said, she would have said so straight away.

"I put it to you that you were telling the truth in that statement, that you believed Ms X was not bisexual and had always been faithful to you until that point when you found out she was pregnant, and then doubts crept in, sown by your brother. I put it to you that this story about the longed-for baby is a lie fabricated to protect your brother."

"No, no. Of course I knew Digs was the father, but she was alleging rape, even though she never said who. I was scared for him. Why mention it to the police then? It would only complicate things. I didn't want Digs arrested for rape. I hoped she'd drop the allegations, stop being so vicious, start loving me again." Kim sniffed, looked directly at me. "But she didn't."

"But it was you who left her."

"She got violent. And I felt betrayed."

"Betrayed? Why?" The prosecutor was like a terrier on a rat.

Kim prevaricated for a minute, then whispered. "I started to think she was bi, that she had it away with lots of men when my back was turned. Digs had said so before then, like when we first started going out. But I didn't believe him until... until she wanted to have his baby." Her eyes locked with mine across courtroom. I was puzzled to see the light of truth in them. She really believed it.

But she lied, and she knew she was lying about us wanting the baby together. Surely?

When she had given her evidence and was dismissed, she came and sat in the public gallery, nowhere near me, between her mother and the same gorgeous woman I'd seen comforting her after our encounter near the pub.

Steve told them he let Digby use his flat, sometimes, and his car, a Lotus Esprite, and had been away that weekend. Well, could be true. Heck, it could be where...

Moira told the court about showing off her baby in the Singing Kettle. And she said she remembered me saying how I wished I could have a baby. She was adamant about it. But I know that's not true.

~~~

Suzy

First thing Thursday morning, Galchester nick had a rather shy but agitated visitor. Suzy (in early before court) looked down at the baby in the pushchair, a comely infant, all giggles and curls, a pleasing shade of brown. "Come through," Suzy said, holding the door for the girl pushing the baby. She led the girl through to an interview room, and suggested she sit. The chair was comfortable, designed to put people at ease, but this girl was uneasy, furtive. Her blush was barely discernible beneath her dark skin. Lynne arrived with a smile.

"You wanted to tell us something?" Suzy prompted the girl.

The girl just burst into tears.

Five minutes later, they got the name from the girl. Toni Wilson. Age 19, living with her mother since she'd split with her boyfriend. More tears.

"It's like this," said Toni, when she was all cried out. "I fell for Garston here a year and a half ago. Me'n Trev were well pleased. Trev asked me to live with him. We were happy. Very happy. Then Garston was born. He was very pale, like they often are, but he never got no darker, and Trev said he wasn't no kid of his. Things got bad and he chucked me out, so I went back to me Mum's. And all the time I was thinking like how it wasn't fair n' all because I never had sex with nobody but my Trev.

"Then I was reading the local daily paper about Mr Y and the rape trial. And they said as how they couldn't identify him in case it identified Ms X, but I know him. My ex-boss down at the Pizza factory. I remember 'cos his name was in the papers way back saying he'd been remanded in custody for rape. And

299

I said to my Mum, 'Look, there's that geezer I used to work with. Bit of a perv, like, what goes around comes around. He tried it on with me a few times, but I told him where to get off.'" Toni caught Suzy's eyes with an earnest look. "He had tried it on with me, way too full on and I kneed him in the nuts and told him if he touched me again I'd report him for sexual harassment.

"I read as how that Ms X says he drugged her, like, all unknowing, and gave her a baby she didn't know nothing about till she was too far gone. And I got to thinking..." Toni's eyes fell on the baby, who was happily gurgling. "Gars looks nothing like my Trev. And he's not really black, is he? But Trev is. Black as me. I know it doesn't always pan out that way, and they can be paler than you think they should be, it's just that Trev swears Gars isn't his kid. And now I wonder if he's right, and maybe Jimbo did the same to me as Ms X to get me back for kneeing his nuts. 'Cos I remember going out with the pizza crowd and getting way too drunk once or twice. Can you test Gars or something?"

Suzy looked at the baby. He was a darling. Long eyelashes guarding sooty eyes, smooth, nut-brown skin folding into creases as he smiled and played and munched on the back of his hand. "Mumumumum."

"Is that wise?" she asked Toni. "I mean, how will you feel about Garston here if you find out he is er... Not Trev's?"

Toni's face fell into confusion, then gelled into indignation. "No, no, don't get me wrong. I love him to bits, me baby. It's just that if Jimbo's done it to her, he might of done it to me, and I want him done for that'n all. He spoilt it between me'n Trev."

"OK," said Suzy. "We'll certainly take cheek swabs, if that's OK with you. But first, can we ask you a few questions..."

Chapter 42

Angie

No mention of the trial in the papers Thursday morning. Good.

Danny told the court she remembered the baby conversation in the Singing Kettle. And how months later Kim had gone to the pub, thin bruises on her face from the slap I'd given her, and told everyone we'd rowed. It sounded bad. The judge asked the defence why they had brought up the bruises since Kim hadn't complained at the time, and it amounted to hearsay evidence. The defence said they felt it important to show that Kim and my relationship had been breaking down. I squirmed in frustration, wanting to jump up and yell that I'd only hit Kim the once, and that until I'd told her I was pregnant, we were happy.

The rest of the in-crowd and Kim and Digby's mother sat in the public gallery, spurning me and the seats nearest to me, whilst lie was piled on falsehood, and the prosecutor struggled to reveal the unreliability of the witnesses.

Why had they lied? All of them? In court? Under oath? Did they hate me so very much?

After lunch came the closing speeches. First from the prosecutor, who emphasised how shocked I'd been when I found out I was pregnant, how unlikely it was that I hadn't gone to the doctors immediately I fell pregnant, had I been trying for a baby. He emphasised my abhorrence of the idea of sex with a man. He said to the jury, "We have heard how Ms X is a lesbian and would never willingly consent to intercourse with a man. She was unaware that she was pregnant until she was 30 weeks pregnant; that is, she didn't attend the doctor's until she was thirty weeks pregnant, because as far as she knew, there was no way she could possibly be pregnant. We have heard how Ms X and Kim Jamieson her lover had a row as soon as Kim heard Ms X was pregnant. Not before that trip to the doctor's, ladies and gentlemen, but as a result of it.

"After carrying a baby of unknown provenance to term, going into labour, having a caesarean section, and suffering all the other unwanted side-effects of pregnancy, Ms X consents to the DNA of the baby being sampled in the hope that one day the father might be found. That is important, Ladies and Gentlemen. If Ms X had known who her attacker was or wanted to implicate Digby Jamieson from a desire for retribution or malice, she would have told the police straight away who the father is. Does she? No. She even blithely tells Digby the child's DNA has been sampled, forewarning him.

"Until recently, has Digby been in trouble? No. Until his arrest for a trivial matter his DNA is not on file. Could Ms X rely on Digby being arrested to be discovered as the father of her child? Of course not. The discovery that he is the father is a fortunate accident resulting from a new arrest, not some contrivance by Ms X to get her own back when her relationship breaks down."

'Good,' I thought. 'Digby can't argue that away. I'd have said he was the father as soon as I reported it, if I'd known.'

"What happened when Ms X was told who the father of her child is? We heard from DC Rolfe and DC Alderton that she is horribly sick. That's how much of a shock it was."

After the prosecutor's closing speech, I knew Digby would be found guilty. His guilt was as obvious. I never consented. He lied to his sister, turned her against me. And she lied for him to protect him. All lies.

But I was disappointed in Moira and Danny. I couldn't understand why they had lied.

~~~

The defence barrister made quite a show of it, playing a role; the part of The Voice of Reason against malicious allegations. "Ladies and Gentlemen, this sort of case is notoriously difficult to call. On the one hand we have the word of a woman who says she was raped and had a baby as a result.

"Digby Jamieson is the father. Of that we have no doubt. What is in doubt is the element of consent. Digby says that he had sexual intercourse with consent, not for pleasure, but to give his sister and Ms X what they wanted. A baby between them, as close a genetic match to Kim Jamieson as is possible.

"We've heard from Kim how things started to go wrong, how Ms X changed during the pregnancy, and how Kim decided to leave. We've heard how Ms X admits she hit Kim that one time when they rowed. Ms X says they rowed after she went to the doctors. Kim says they rowed before, and that Ms X went to the doctors to terminate the pregnancy...."

The barrister paused, sipped some water, then said, "Consent," so loudly I flinched. "Ms X alleges there was no consent, that the alleged rape took place under the influence of drugs, for which we have no corroborative evidence, no doctor's report. Digby has told us that Ms X consented. Kim and he both told us this pregnancy was planned, hoped for.

"We have heard from Moira Stevenson and from Danny Cook that there had been a conversation concerning the desire for a baby in the Singing Kettle. And we heard from Danny that Ms X had assaulted Kim on at least one occasion during her pregnancy; their relationship was breaking down.

303

And when it did, that was when Ms X went to her doctors, Kim and Digby both say, with the intention of terminating the pregnancy. But it was too late to do so.

"How can anyone go for 30 weeks not knowing they are pregnant? The weight gain, the physical changes should, no, must have given the game away."

"One moment," interposed the Judge. "There are cases where people have not known they're pregnant until they give birth."

"Very well Your Honour." The defence solicitor bowed. She turned back to the jury. "Ladies and gentlemen, are you sure that Ms X did not consent to sexual intercourse? Are you sure that her version of events is the correct one? Or did she consent to intercourse to fulfil the need to fall pregnant with the closest genetic match she and her long-term lover Kim could find; Kim's brother Digby?"

The seeds of doubt. I wondered if they'd germinate overnight. Surely logic would prevail? Surely the jury could see through the lies and that I was telling the truth?

~~~

I phoned Peter up that evening to tell her what had happened and to voice something that was troubling me. I told Peter about the incident in the Singing Kettle, how Moira's baby had been passed round for everyone to admire, and how both Danny and Moira had said I'd held the baby and said how gorgeous she was, and how I wanted one. And how they'd remembered other things I had no recollection of. "I can't understand why Danny and Moira lied. They've nothing to gain from lying," I said. "I never said I wanted a baby."

There was a thoughtful silence. "Are Kim and these two good friends?" Peter asked.

"Well, we were all friends." The vision of Moira by the vegetables slapped me in the face. "But I think they saw Kim after we'd split. I think she poisoned them against me, but surely not enough to lie, not perjure themselves in court?"

"Sometimes, mistakenly, people recall a suggestion as a factual memory," said Peter. "In my work I have to be very careful not to evoke false memories. People can be led by suggestion, can become confused. Accepting a suggestion as a fact brings a perceived clarity. It's possible that these two honestly believe the testimony they gave."

Later, thinking about it, I wondered if Kim was the same. Maybe Digby had manipulated her memory, fed her little ideas which grew to be facts to her. Like me being Bi. Like me wanting a baby... Perhaps she wasn't as bad as I thought she was, siding with someone who had raped her lover. Maybe she honestly thought I had seduced him, begged him for a baby, and thought her testimony was a little white lie for the sake of justice. I had a pang of longing, remembering the love we'd had and the happiness we'd shared until Digby spoiled it all. Why? Why? Did he hate me so much? Was he so very jealous he had to rape his beloved sister's lover? What had I done to him to deserve that?

I fell asleep mourning our might-have-beens.

~~~

Kirsty

Thursday afternoon shift at the pizza factory was trundling along quite happily despite being one person short, since Jimbo was in court. But because he wasn't there, people were talking more than normal, and at refreshment break, the conversation turned to him.

"I reckon we'd better get used to working one down," said Tom. "Funny how we all know who it is, yet he has to be Mr Y on the reports."

"Who's Ms X?" asked Janet.

"How should I know?" retorted Tom.

"Well, there you go, said Janet. "That's why. Because she's a les, she's more easy to indentify, and so his indentity is kept secret too... and his sister's. But those who know them must know who they are."

"Usually it's only the victim's name that's kept secret," said Kirsty. "I saw Jimbo's name in the paper when he appeared before the magistrates accused. That was reported then. Must be this judge being extra cautious."

"D'you reckon he did Ellie in as well?" asked Stuart.

"Most likely," said Tom.

"Don't start rumours," said Janet. "From what I gather reading between the lines in the papers, it's a family affair gone wrong somehow, and like Jimbo explained, he had sex with her to give her a baby. She only complained once she and his sister rowed. I reckon he'll get off."

"Anyhow, I thought Tom was in the frame for Ellie... it's what they nicked you for, ain't it?" said Stuart.

"I was just helping them with their enquiries," said Tom. "I've been eliminated."

"Mum said you're only on bail. You're still a sus-pect." Kirsty clamped her lips down on the last word but it escaped anyway.

There was a puzzled silence. Then Tom said, "How does your mum know that if she's a nurse at the hospital?"

"Which hospital?" asked Janet. "Where does your mum work, then Kirsty?"

"Colchester General," Kirsty supplied quickly.

"Which department?"

"Um A&E."

"You're lying," said Tom incredulously. "You fibbed about your Mum. One of the plain-clothes coppers was DC Rolfe. I bet that's your Mum. You've been sent here to spy on us."

"No I haven't. Don't be soft."

"Fucking copper's nark. Could have told you anything and you'd have gone telling tales to mummy," said Stuart.

"Stuart, mind your language," said Janet.

"I suppose she fucking told you all about me 'n Trish," said Jordan.

"No," said Kirsty angrily. "You did that yourself, you and your big mouth. Poor Trish, with a sister like you getting her into a dangerous situation, then dobbing her in to us, just 'cos she did the right thing and told. Mum's not allowed to say anything about her work to me, and she was appalled when I said you'd said about Trish."

"She still told you about me," said Tom.

"Yeah, 'cos I told her you didn't do it, you pillock," said Kirsty fiercely. "God knows why. For all I know you could have done it. Just like you could have done it to Jord here. Let's face it, Mr Condom, you tried to get me drunk so you could have it off with me. I should have listened to my instincts, which say Chav."

"Snob, copper's nark."

"Children, stop this at once. Grow up. Back to work." Janet glared round at all of them. "This is nonsense. Kirsty doesn't gossip like you starlings, she usually keeps schtum. Her mum's not allowed to talk about things so she won't of.

307

Kirsty is not a copper's nark. No wonder she fibbed about her mum being a nurse if that's the way you're going to treat her. No more gossip or I'll report the lot of you."

~~~

When Kirsty got home that night, her mother was ready for bed but watching the news. "Hello Sweetie. Good day? I'm just watching the news to make sure they don't report more than they're allowed about your boss's trial." She turned her face back to the television.

"I want to hand my notice in at the Pizza factory," said Kirsty, and burst into tears.

Her mother jumped up, hugged her. "Sweetie, Sweetie, what's happened?" her mother manoeuvred her onto the sofa, and hugged her whilst Kirsty recounted the horrible row, and how with a tiny slip of the tongue, she had let her mother down. Her mother listened grimly, and said, "Oh dear," in such a dismayed tone, it chastened Kirsty far more than yelling would have done.

"I'm useless," sobbed Kirsty. "You're right. I just had to blab, and when I did, it was too late. I'm no good at anything. I hate myself. I wish I was dead."

"Don't," said her mother, in a dismayed yet forbidding tone. "I saw Ellie dead, ebbed dry on the mud like a bit of flotsam. I had to deal with her distraught family. Never, please never do that to me, wish that on me. Not if you love me. I couldn't bear it." Some tears escaped her mother's eyes, almost unknown, except during her parents' divorce.

Kirsty looked at them in wonder, thought for a minute, then said in a small voice. "No Mum, sorry Mum. I promise."

Chapter 43

Angie

The next day, Friday, the judge did his summing up. He went over the evidence that we had seen, from my testimony and Dr Galton's, to the story Kim and Digby told. He told us what the crime of rape consists of. Penetration, that is, sexual intercourse; well, it was obvious that had happened, from the resulting pregnancy. And Digby admitted he'd had sex with me. A lack of consent on my part. I'd told them I hadn't consented, would never have consented, but Digby and Kim both said I had, and why. A reasonable why. For a baby. And the third element of rape was Digby either knowing I had not consented or didn't care if I'd consented or not. But Digby said I had consented. Kim said the sex was planned for when she went away, in her full knowledge. They both knew, sure that I'd consented. It was a good lie.

The only things telling the jury I hadn't lied were that I hadn't told the police that it was Digby as soon as I complained of rape, my devastation when I heard who it was, and that I hadn't known I was pregnant when I saw Dr Thomas. That showed the illogic of Digs' defence. His was a good lie, but it didn't make sense.

The jury retired to consider their verdict. I went into the cathedral grounds and phoned Sally. "They're out," I said. "I'm a bit worried the jury will believe them not me. I'm going to stay for the rest of the day, just in case they return the verdict before the weekend. If they don't, they'll have to come back on Monday. Oh I hope they find the bugger guilty. He deserves it."

"We'll come over, if you like, and be with you for the verdict."

A rush of gratitude hit me. I hadn't realised just how much I needed someone with me, until they said they would be there for me. OK, the two coppers Rolfe and Alderton would be there, but I could hardly hug them when he went down, now could I?

~~~

Sally and John, and the two coppers met me in the concourse. Digby's fan club was there too, and we all avoided each other as if we were invisible. It was getting on for four thirty when the TV screen outside the court announced that the Jury was returning. We filed in, Digby's mob on one side of the public gallery, John, Sally, myself, Mrs Neutral Suzy Rolfe and sidekick Lynne Alderton beside me.

The last of the jurors filed in, sat down, composed herself. None of them looked at me. None of them looked at Digs. They all looked at the Judge.

The Judge slid his glance over me, halted just for a moment, then back to the jury. He asked the foreman, "Have you reached a unanimous verdict?"

"Yes, Your Honour."

Brittle, pregnant silence.

"Not guilty, Your Honour."

The noise. The cheers. The satisfied looks of contempt at me. The world went black. I can't remember more than a merry-go-round, a mad hurdy-gurdy babble of voices, spinning, spinning. Faces. Cheers, Digby walking free. Kim laughing, laughing with her friends, laughing with her lover, laughing at me. Her mother hugging Kim gleefully, hugging

Digby. Venomous looks at me. The noise. Uproarious. Rejoicing. I alone. Isolated. Sally and John, so far away. The noise, the victorious party drained away. Silence.

"I'm so sorry," said the prosecutor. "I'm so very, very sorry. I don't normally say this. I can't believe it. Please don't repeat this." He blushed and fled. Suzy Rolfe and Lynne Alderton were suddenly in front of me.

"Angie, it's not that the jury didn't believe you, but more that there was enough of a doubt not to convict him. They must be sure... and they weren't. I'm so sorry," said Rolfe. I wanted to slap them both. They must have felt my thought because they flinched and left.

~~~

I staggered into the concourse, with John and Sally, hoping Digs and Kim had gone.

Silence.

We crept down the stairs, hoping the victorious party had vanished. They had. To the Craven Arms, probably, to celebrate.

"Why didn't the jury believe me? Fuck justice," I said out loud.

"You think the verdict's wrong, then?" a woman asked me.

"Of course it's wrong. He's a rapist, and she's a perjurer. Liars. And they've got away with it."

"Angie, she's Press," Sally protested. "Go away," she hissed at the woman between clenched teeth. The woman drifted away, hovering outside a ten-foot exclusion zone.

"I didn't know she's Press," I whispered, a frisson of fear making me shiver. "The papers'll kill me tomorrow."

"They can't. They won't. They're not allowed, remember. All they can say is that Mr Y was acquitted. Let's go."

There was a galloping in my brain. Digby was free, after all he had done to me. Free, when I would have this over me forever. A rape survivor but thought of by the world as a liar and a vindictive old dike. I realised, with a poignant stab, that I hadn't been to the pub since I found out I was pregnant. I had no friends except for Sally and John, and no reason to go out anywhere, and stretch marks and a fat tummy which made me too unsure of myself to find another lover.

I carefully pulled open the court building door; the door to the rest of my life. The news team was there again. It seemed ours wasn't the only verdict returned that afternoon, because the presenter was given his cue then started speaking to the camera. I dashed over. "Justice?" I said. "There is no justice. I was raped. I'm a lesbian and I was raped. But the jury thought I lied. I didn't. He's the liar. He's ruined my life, I get a life sentence of being a so-called rape survivor, yet he gets away scot free."

The presenter looked aghast. There was a muddle of bodies and recriminations. "That went out live," I heard someone say. Then John and Sally were enveloping me in their arms, flinging apologies around, saying I was overwrought from a disappointing verdict. Down the remaining steps, past curious stares from passers-by, round the corner towards the car park, and into the car. I burst into tears. Sally wrestled the seat belt across, snapping it into place.

"I don't know what came over me," I said. A monster was clawing at my throat. A scream bubbled up inside, came out as a near silent squeal of pain.

The street where they live was silent, uncluttered with humanity. Sally jumped out, unlocked the front door, and I

312

was hurried in like a criminal on the run. John gave me a long hug whilst Sally put the kettle on. It was the first really intimate contact with a man since Dr Thomas had examined me. It was a platonic hug, and I didn't mind it. Not at all. I knew what he was saying.

"You must stay with us tonight. I think that's for the best," he said. "Right Sally?"

"Of course."

~~~

Suzy

"Bugger. Bugger. Stupid fucking jury," said Suzy, flinging herself in her chair. "Oh God, I can't believe it."

Cheungy came over with some decent coffee. "So he's out and about, then? Our possible serial rapist. I wish we had some other evidence to nail him with."

"I don't suppose the cheek swab of that baby has come back yet?"

"Pushing our luck, there," said Cheungy, "but I'll phone the lab up and beg. Though I don't think he'll vanish. He has a job and a home, and if he fits the offender profile as we think, he'll feel smug and arrogant about beating the system. He may even feel invincible. I hate to say it, but perhaps we should expect another victim soon. I hope he didn't get his rocks off with Ellie dying, or we could see a nasty new twist in his behaviour... if it was he who killed Ellie."

"Probably more like he lost his stiffy in a panic when she died," said Suzy. "It might have scared the shit out of him like it scared the shit out of Turner. I don't think he meant to kill her. I think it was an accident."

313

"Digby seems to pick victims who have slighted him in some way. Drug and rape them in revenge. Think about it. We have Angie who stole his sister from him… or maybe she pissed him off somehow. We have Stuart the lad who your Kirsty reports teased Digby about his little dick and being a wanker, though that's hearsay; you have the thin walls in the changing rooms where the girls talking could be overheard, and several possible female victims from the pizza factory, and Ellie's Mum, who called him Wee Willy Wanker when he was at school… and Ellie herself who refused his advances…"

"Yes, but we have other possible perpetrators for all these crimes; the teacher who made the GHB and might have used it on Ellie because she was being groomed to be Mrs Turner Mk 3, we have Tom who was texting Ellie those suggestive messages and whose semen was found on her clothing; we have the man who allegedly touched up his daughters in the same estate… it might not be Digby at all. Just because he looks like a serial offender doesn't mean that he is."

"True," agreed Cheungy with a downturn of her lips. "And you're probably right about whoever killed Ellie. It probably wasn't intentional, just a duff batch of GHB. No wonder Turner feels so guilty, and so he should. He as good as killed her with his greedy, criminal behaviour, making and selling that poison, not caring what it was used for."

"And there's Raff, who says he did it, but that doesn't ring true," said Suzy. "Which reminds me; why did you send Lynne to interview him? What's all that about? She was a bit miffed because she has a stinking headache and wanted to go home." She glanced at the clock. It was gone six.

"Raff asked to speak to someone, with his solicitor present. He has something to tell us. I hadn't anyone else to send. Let's hope it's not a wild goose chase. How did Angie Bain take it?"

"Badly, really badly. I thought she was going to slap us. We left her to it, I'm afraid. She was in no mood for reason at that point. She looked a bit mad. I expect she'll blame us."

"Well, you'd better see her sometime over the next couple of days and tell her that convictions must be beyond reasonable doubt, not that we believe she made it up." Cheungy went to phone the forensics lab.

Suzy's mobile went. It was Kirsty. "Yes?" asked Suzy. "Is something wrong? You're at work, aren't you?"

"Yes Mum. It's refs break, and someone was texted to say that Jimbo was acquitted? Is it true?"

"Yes it's true. So you watch your blabbering tongue, will you. I'm working late here tonight since you're at work."

"Why was he acquitted? I thought the case was solid."

"Stupid jury. Not enough evidence, and they obviously didn't understand the logic of the argument that Ms X would have gone to the doctor's sooner. Stupid, stupid juries. You'd almost have to shove a spiked drink in their faces before they'd believe you. I've told you before, rape can be incredibly difficult to prove—so there's no justice for A... his victim Ms X, and see how hard it's going to be to get justice for Ellie? Several suspects, all of whom cast that reasonable doubt over who really dun it. And even if we do find out who killed her, the CPS will probably run it as manslaughter, not murder, because it could have been an accident from a duff batch of drugs, so the killer will get some pathetic sentence even though Ellie is dead and her parents are in hell. Take care and keep your mouth shut.

"And don't go anywhere near Digby because I don't trust him, but I can't do anything about him, not now. See you later, but I don't know what time. I've decided to work late, catch up on paperwork, since you're at work."

When Suzy hung up she groaned. No way could she go home, chill out, relax; not yet. She was far too agitated, still far too angry, and behind with her paperwork.

Besides, she wanted to find out what Lynne had learned from Raff the Derelict.

~~~

Kirsty

"Bye Mum," said Kirsty, and hung up.

"Dobbing to Mummy?" said Stuart as she resumed her seat in the canteen.

"Mind your own fucking business," said Kirsty, regretting half her conversation already, hoping Stuart hadn't overheard it.

"You leave her alone," said Tom. "She's alright really."

Later, whilst dispensing cheese, Kirsty was mulling over the conversation with her mother. So Jimbo was acquitted, yet her mother had been so sure of his guilt. If that was so, perhaps Jimbo was guilty of more than just the one date rape. Think about this logically, she told herself. Either Jimbo is a single event rapist, just with his sister's lover, for whatever reason. Or he's a serial rapist. If he is, then it makes it less likely that Tom is. After all, Tom had wanted to go all the way, but hasn't once tried to drug me after trying it on with the booze. And with Ellie... well, he had no reason to risk a date rape drug, since she was willing enough anyway. So it didn't make sense Tom drugging her.

But then, if she was that willing, maybe Digby knew he didn't need to drug her. But surely Ellie wasn't hoping for sex with dirty old man Digby... unless he was offering something of great value in exchange. Ellie seemed excited, looking forward to it, whatever 'it' was. Maybe he had offered her something else. Like a ride in his Lotus? Or perhaps Digby had something horrible in mind... like anal sex, perhaps, and knew Ellie wouldn't consent to that. Or maybe it wasn't Digby. Maybe it was Tom and his revolting pearl necklaces. No, none of it made sense. Not yet.

~~~

After the shift, Kirsty walked from the building, and turned her mobile back on. A text was waiting for her. Tom hovered behind her, irritatingly looking at her phone as she answered it. She heard him pull in a breath, so she moved away from him to read the text. Astonishingly it said it was from Tom.

Hi Kirsty. It's Jimbo. I was acquitted. I'm having a party and want u to join us for Champagne. U no whr I live. C U soon

"Kirsty... Kirsty, this is important," said Tom. "What was that number... the one who dialled you? Only, that looked like my old phone number, the one that was stolen, the one used to text Ellie. But I'm not sure. All I know is I didn't send it." He pulled his own phone from his pocket. "See?"

Kirsty turned to him, cogwheels in her mind slipping into place until she knew, knew for certain who Ellie's killer was... if that was Tom's number. She showed Tom the number.

"It looks like mine. Now what?" said Tom. "That should let me off the hook."

"I'll phone Mum at work; tell her."

~~~

Angie

I ate the supper Sally cooked without engaging my brain or tasting what was before me. To think would be a disaster. I stared at the tablecloth, vinyl coated. Practical. Homely. Pasta in cheese and bacon sauce. Simple. Easy to eat.

"You can have Drew's room," said Sally. "And I think I've got a new toothbrush somewhere."

Drew's room. Just-post-teenage room. Redolent with testosterone-dictated décor. I helped Sally change the sheets, and slid in early, about nine-ish for want of a better thing to do, a means of hiding from conversation.

Not guilty.

A long darkness.

Not guilty.

I dozed for half an hour, no more, fitful sleep, full of flashback dreams. Not guilty. Smug sneers. Not guilty. My body used, the parasite, the guilt. Not guilty.

Once I started to think again, to feel again, I was surprised that the heat of my anger hadn't set the sheets on fire. But it was a cold anger, bitterly cold, with the clarity that comes from an intense cold. Hard. Unforgiving. Sharp as glass.

I heard Sally and John go to bed about ten o'clock... maybe they were shattered too. The silence grew, feeding my anger. I knew I wouldn't sleep again, so I tiptoed downstairs to the kitchen. I put the kettle on, found a mug, the tea bags, and pulled a drawer or two open in search of a teaspoon.

I found the knives. A set, beautifully stored in a drawer. From little vegetable knife, to whopping cleaver. I hefted it. Too heavy. I picked up the vegetable knife, tickled my wrist with the blade. It whispered over the skin, catching the light. I put it back, quietly. Why give them my life? Would it make

318

people believe me? No. They might even think it a sign that I had lied.

This one, five inches ought to do it. I sat at the table, playing with the knife, drinking tea. Of course, I couldn't use Sally's knife. That would be grossly unfair, as if I'd repaid all her goodness by making her a party to murder. Whose murder? Digby's? Kim's? Mine?

Dangerous thing, cold anger. It doesn't fizzle out. Sally and John, upstairs. Sleeping. Alibis. Sort of.

Chapter 44

Angie

I'd have a hard job arguing that the Papers made me do it, as I hadn't read them before I bought the knife, but it's the truth. They were pivotal. They're why I did it.

I slipped out of Sally's on foot, through the back door, leaving it unlocked and trusting to luck. I walked. It didn't lessen the anger. The supermarket was almost deserted. I felt anonymous in my baseball cap, pulled close over my face. The first thing you come to is the Evening Papers. Headlines. "Not Guilty Verdict on Lesbian Love Child Accused." Love child? In the trolley. "Acquitted! Lesbian Love-Dad." In the trolley. The headlines jeered as I wheeled round to the kitchenware shelves. I scanned the knives, not daring to heft them lest I leave fingerprints, suddenly remembering the unblinking eye of the CCTV monitoring us as we enter. Fortunately, I'd been looking down, unidentifiable in my hat and ubiquitous clothing.

That knife looked the right size, and bloody sharp. Good grip, too. Blade safely out of the way of my fingerprints in a plastic sheath. In the trolley. A chopping board to diffuse suspicions about the knife. In the trolley. Bin bags. Rubber gloves. A small LED torch, ready fitted with batteries. In the trolley.

The clothing section. Black cap, no logo. Dark blue man's hoodie and joggers. New trainers, a size too big, to ensure they fitted, and disguise any footprints. I couldn't argue insanity. I'd thought too well about covering my tracks. It was deliberate. With malice aforethought. Planned.

Thank goodness I don't know the night staff. I nearly paid with plastic. I nearly presented my staff card. I wouldn't look at the CCTV staring down on me.

I went out into the desolate car park. Where now? Digs lived ten miles plus away. How to get there? I walked to my home, put the kettle on, made a coffee, slumped in the lounge and scanned the papers.

The papers dealt with it as if they knew that justice had prevailed; that my vicious lies about a man who had only helped me to achieve what had then been my heart's desire had been thrown out by a sensible jury. They discussed me as if I were a non-entity, that my feelings counted for nothing, the 48-year-old woman who cannot be named for legal reasons. They discussed my outrageous behaviour with the television film crew, and primly said they had still maintained my anonymity despite this outburst where I appeared to waive the right to anonymity.

And they're powerful, with the resources to fight a libel suit. And I was weak. And tired.

And angry.

~~~

Suzy

Lynne found Suzy and Cheungy in the CID room. Her eyes were glittering with savage glee. "Sorry I'm so late, but it was worth it, even though Raff played silly-buggers when it came to interview and took ages to tell us what he wanted to say. I think he enjoyed keeping us dangling. That revolting little git followed the bloke who bought the GHB from him and watched as the girl was poisoned. Raff was, I suspect, hoping to indulge that nasty voyeuristic streak he has. It happened pretty much as Hugh suggested from the scenes of crime data, though the attacker dragged the body to the water on a picnic blanket he'd laid out for the picnic before the rape. The actual picnic spot sounds very secluded from what Raff says...We'll double check with Hugh's scene of crime findings in case Raff is spinning another yarn. Apparently, Ellie met the attacker, and he laid out this blanket, then brought out some alcopops and nibbles. The tape's being transcribed tomorrow, but I thought you'd like to hear this bit..." She took out her notes. "'They were laughing together, smoking skunk, eating, swigging alcopops 'n stuff. He was saying all sorts of things that made her giggle, but I wasn't near enough to hear, and it was getting dark'—Raff looked well pissed off at that, filthy voyeuristic sod. 'She takes her clothes off one by one, and it's getting really exciting. He unzips his trousers and just as he does it, the girl slumps forwards, and the bloke looks round, starts fondling her, puts on a condom. Then he freezes, looks at her face, licks his finger, puts it under her nose, then puts his hand to her neck, and all the time I'm watching, but he starts whimpering, panting like. Starts breathing into her mouth, pushing at her chest, saying Ellie, Ellie, wake up, and crying, and that's when I realise she's a gonner. He stands up, does up his flies, and he's saying, shit shit shit shit in a panicky way. And then he says Oh Ellie I never meant that to happen. Then he looks round, nobody but me around. He drags her to the river on the blanket and tips her in.'" Lynne stopped reading aloud from her notes. "As soon as Raff saw the body hit the water, he ran back to the derelict building to collect his belongings and leave, because he was afraid of being beaten up for supplying the duff GHB. But he can't run fast, old Raff, because he's such a wreck, and he wasn't quick enough. The

322

killer caught up with him as he was leaving the derelict building and gave him a hiding. Raff says he doesn't know who this bloke is, refused to describe him. But I bet that's a lie."

"Interesting," said Cheungy in a satisfied voice. "If we lean on him we might get somewhere with a description. Could well be Digby by the sound of it, but we don't know yet. We also have more information, rushed through by the lab. Digby is the father of the child Garston, ie Toni's little boy. And that wasn't consented to, either. Serial rapist anyone?"

"Are we going to lift him?"

"Oh yes," said Cheungy. "Just as soon as we have a unit or two available. Unfortunately, it's Friday and everyone's busy, so we may have to wait until later, maybe even tomorrow."

"I'd better phone Kirsty, tell her I'll be even later home.... Damn, where is it?" Suzy groped in her pockets, but the phone wasn't there.

"When did you last have it?" asked Lynne, irritatingly helpful.

"I put it down somewhere. Oh, I know... it's in my jacket pocket. Where's my jacket?" It was on the back of her chair. Suzy found her phone. There were twenty missed calls from Kirsty, missed because Suzy had turned it onto vibrate not ring. Her heart clenched. She phoned Kirsty's mobile.

"Muuuuum, you never answer your flipping phone. I've been trying to get through for ages. You listened to my messages?"

"Sorry Sweetie, no. When I saw it was you I just called straight away in a bit of a panic. Where are you?"

"OK, Mum, I'm standing outside Snack-A-Randy's and no-one can hear, but listen, I know who the killer is..." Suzy listened as Kirsty explained about Tom's phone. Suzy glanced at the clock. Getting on for midnight. "What the hell are you doing out at this time of night? Why aren't you at home?"

There was a brief silence, then Kirsty said in a low voice, "I was too scared to go home on my own. Jimbo knows where I live, and I thought, I thought... Mum, shall I go to the party, see if I can trap him or something? Would that help?"

"Oh my dear lord no, what a terrible idea. Go straight home, tell nobody about this. We'll deal with it. And bolt the doors as well as lock them. I'll phone when I get home."

"But Mum, you said we virtually have to shove a bottle of drugged drink under the noses of the jury... I could get that. Show you I'm not a silly little girl; show you I have what it takes to be a copper."

Suzy shut her eyes for a couple of heartbeats. "I said that in the heat of the moment, Sweetie. I didn't mean it. You can't do this, it's too dangerous, you're not trained, and I could get into very serious troubles if you did; understand? Please, please go straight home and don't try any foolish heroics. It's not necessary anyway, we... we're about the deal with him."

Suzy's heart stopped when she heard a masculine voice in the background saying, "They're gonna nick him?"

"Who's that with you?" Bugger, bugger, bugger.

"It's Tom." Bugger.

"Tell him to go straight home too, his home, tell nobody until I say he can. Please... it's important."

"OK, Mum... you tell him."

"Hello?" said the masculine voice. "Is that Kirsty's Mum? It wasn't me, honest. Told you the phone was nicked, and now we know who by. You gonna nick him?"

"Tom, thank you for this. Please trust me; go straight home and don't say anything to anyone."

"OK, it's a deal." The phone went dead.

Suzy phoned it back. "Kirsty, please text me when you get home. You tell Tom to too, please. Tell him to phone me on his landline."

"OK, OK. I promise."

"Please, please go home."

"I said I would." The phone went dead.

Lynne and Cheungy were looking at her with perplexed expressions. "I think we need to move fast," said Suzy. "I think we'd better go in now...." She explained, then said, "If Kirsty is right and Digby used Tom's old phone to try to lure her to his house, I'm worried that Digby's fishing for another victim. If he's approached Kirsty, daughter of the copper who nicked him (remember the vengeance idea) but she hasn't gone, maybe he'll approach someone else, anyone else from work. From what Raff said Digby didn't mean to kill Ellie, but if he is a serial offender, maybe, just maybe he's decided he likes it. And I don't altogether trust Kirsty to go home and not try the foolish heroics, and I certainly don't trust Tom to keep schtum..."

"OK," said Cheungy. "Another worry is that Tom might have sent Kirsty that text as a red herring, putting the blame on Digby. Digby might not have stolen that phone after all. This might be Tom's attempt to deflect suspicion."

"Shit. You're right. Kirsty could be in danger."

"I don't think so, because Tom would most likely have struck as soon as the phone put the blame on Digby, not hung around looking after her while she's too scared to go home. We'll assume it was Digby, but yes, it's urgent. We'll all three of us go, grab a big red key, grab our stab vests and take our asps and spray in case he gets rough. I'll get Control to send anyone they can as soon as they can."

Chapter 45

Angie

I changed into my murder clothing. I put clean clothes to change into as soon as I'd done it. I lined the car with plastic bags.

I arrived in Elversford at just gone midnight. It was raining and the streets were quiet. I parked a couple of streets away, in the old industrial district. I didn't want the noise of the car to alert anyone. Locked the door, and walked near silently, new trainers whispering on the pavement, rubber-gloved hands, torch and knife safely hidden in the hoodie pocket. A big pocket, joining in the front like a muff. I made sure I hadn't touched the knife. Not without gloves.

The chill drizzle made the streets slick and the lamps reflect streaks and dazzles. Sough-sough of oversized trainer feet. Knife heavy with potential. Resolve strong as fire, weak as steel. Rapist Digby. The Jury had failed to give him justice according to the evidence. I would. I'd beat the door down, if necessary. But it probably wouldn't come to that. Break a small pane in the back door, turn of the key, and in. The silent entry. That would be best. Come on him sleeping. Vulnerable. Quicker, that way. One slash should be enough. If I cut his throat, I could make it look like suicide.

Only it wouldn't be murder. It would be justice. He killed my life, my joy, turned me into a baby factory. For some perverted pleasure in raping his sister's lover. Pervert. Dangerous pervert. I would be acting to prevent him from doing anything like that again. Permanently. Or so I told myself, justifying every step.

But really it was cold, hard vengeance I wanted.

Is Digs left or right handed? I couldn't remember, and that might matter if I was going to make it look like suicide.

Please God let him be at home. Maybe he's not at home. Maybe he's at Steve's. That's where Digs said he... And I knew all along that Digs had a key to Steve's place, and Steve's car. Yet I'd forgotten, and I hadn't told the police. They didn't know. Vital information, perhaps. Overlooked. But then, when I'd reported the rape to the police, I hadn't known it was Digby, hadn't known that Steve's place might be where he'd raped me.

Please, God, let Digs be at home.

They'd have a good idea who'd done it, but proving it would be difficult, if I left no trace. So, I must be careful to leave no trace.

I was close, now. Just round the industrial building to the shabby workers' dwellings. The building was high, a fossil from the industrial age, boarded, derelict. Perhaps there were some junkies squatting there. Eyes on me, perhaps? Feet treading yet more silently against that thought. Fear, cold on my neck. Hands slick in the rubber gloves. Mouth dry, heart thrumming. Turn the corner.

The house was in darkness, windows staring blindly at the lamp lit street. Digby's car was parked outside. He must be upstairs asleep then. I slid down the path to the back door and listened against the glass. Nothing. I took the knife out, was about to smash the glass when I realised there was no need. I scraped away at the crumbling putty until the edge of the pane was exposed, then tried to lever the pane out. It wouldn't give, until it split with a crack, the shards shattering on the floor at my feet. The noise cleaved the darkness. I froze, listening until my heart subsided into a bearable beat.

Nothing. I should have run at that point, but I was too angry, too bleak.

I put my hand through the door, unlocked it, pushed it in. The smell of fags and booze hit me. I flicked the torch round the kitchen, picking out the empty bottles, the cans, the ashtrays brimming with crushed butts. The bastard had been celebrating. With any luck he'd be too drunk to resist. I would slit his throat. Then maybe, when the last of his blood was seeping away, I'd tell him just what he'd done to me.

Up the stairs, one at a time, feet placed so carefully close to the walls in case of creaky floorboards. The landing. The door to Digby's room was shut. I carefully grasped the knob, turned slowly, slowly, listening for the sigh of breath but hardly able to hear over the hammering of my heart. Slowly opened the door. Silence, the bed an amorphous blob in the darkness, the quilt humped over his body. I stepped over to it, hearing nothing. I waited, waited, summoning that cold anger, bolstering my hatred. I pulled out the knife. I was going to have to risk the torch to find his throat.

Something downstairs crashed with the sound of splintering wood. "Police, stay where you are." The downstairs lights flicked on, the shadows in the bedroom rising monstrous against the far wall.

I sprang back from the bed expecting Digby to erupt from it, but there was nothing. The bed was empty, unmade, quilt rucked into a heap. Rumpus downstairs, Yells, the sound of smashing glass. Digby's voice screaming, raging.

"Put the bottle down Digby. It's not worth it." Sounded like Rolfe.

Digby was squealing weirdly, "I'll kill ya, kill ya, keep back."

"Watch it Lynne, watch the bottle. Shit."

Moaning hum as something cut the air. A broken bottle? A baton? Sickening thud of metal on flesh. Howls. Crashes.

"Give us your arm, Digby, give it. Get his feet Cheungy. Oh shit, you're bleeding."

Thuds, then yells, gasps and curses from female voices, Rolfe saying, "Digby Jamieson, I'm arresting you on suspicion of rape and murder. And resisting arrest and Wounding. You do not have..."

Rape? Whose? Not mine, surely? And murder? Not Digs. I knew he was capable of sneaky rape, but never murder, surely? That took courage of a sort. I could feel the knife clutched tight in my hand. Murder.

I heard a siren, a roaring van engine, flashing blue lights visible through the thin curtains as it drew up, the thud of footsteps running into the house, the voice of a man—not Digs—talking loudly, sounds of more struggle, thuds, curses now wafting up from the street. The slam of a van door. Then it all went quiet and I realised how stock still I had been standing.

And then I heard the tread on the stairs. I dropped the knife, picked it up, stuffed it in a drawer, shivering, fumbling. The bedroom light went on. I swung round. Suzy Rolfe filled the doorframe. She was wearing a stab vest over her ordinary clothes, was holding a baton, and looked very, very menacing.

I knew from her expression that my guilt was written over my face.

A few heartbeats.

Then she moved back, away from the doorway. "Go. Go now. Quietly. Out the back."

I slipped past her, smelled the fear in her sweat, out through the back door, and into the back garden, still trapped by a police van out the front, blue lights washing silently over the rain-slicked street. I saw neighbours' curtains being lifted, peered round. DC Rolfe came out of the back door, shutting it behind her, then walked round to the front. A policeman in uniform was there, and DC Alderton next to a woman who was clutching a wad of dressing to her arm. "Can you take him to the nick, Pete, then get someone sorted to make the house secure." I head DC Rolfe say. "I'll stay here until that's sorted. Lynne's taking Cheungy to hospital to get her wound stitched up."

The policeman climbed into the van and drove off while Lynne and the other woman walked down the road. Moments later another car engine roared into life and I heard it drive off. Rolfe stared into the darkness where I was lurking, then went back into the house.

The night drifted back into silence. The curtains were dropped. I walked out of the gate as if I had a right to be there. Back to my car, got in, gloves off, slick hands wiped dry down my front. I started the engine up and it seemed horribly loud. Suppose the police stopped me on the off-chance, wanting to know what a car was doing driving around at that hour of the morning? With bin bags all over the seats? I set off for home.

Careful. Speed limit.

Home. I stripped the car of the paraphernalia of crime. I took off the filthy clothing and bunged it in the washing machine. Back into yesterday's clothes. I was too tired to walk back to Sally's so I drove. I parked round the bend from Sally's and hoped they wouldn't see the car.

The back door was still open, so I entered, locked it, tiptoed up the stairs, and slithered under the quilt, wondering why I was so cold, iced up inside.

~~~

330

The sounds of John getting up woke me. They'd done so much for me, both of them. Like family almost. Better than family. They had accepted me for who I am, remained friends, supportive friends, when the world went dark. And I nearly turned them into inadvertent alibis, inadvertent accomplices to murder.

For shame.

I dressed and went downstairs. Sally was just seeing John off. She turned to me with a smile. "John's going shopping. Sleep OK?" Not 'sleep well?' as if she knew that sleeping well would be an impossibility.

"Took me a while to drop off, but once I got to sleep, I slept like a log. I got up after you'd gone to bed and made myself a tea. I hope I didn't disturb you."

"No, didn't hear a thing."

No nocturnal discoveries, then. If I had done it, if the police hadn't arrived when they did, my alibi would have seemed OK. Not brilliant, since they were asleep. But OK. An uneasy feeling crawled through my guts; guilt.

"Sally, I can't thank you enough for the support you've shown me. You've kept me sane. Before, and through the trial. The bastard didn't get what he deserved, and I'm going to have to live with that. I'm going to have to come to terms with it. I think I need some time alone. I have to think what I'm going to do next. I might move away, though I don't know where. Make a fresh start. In case I bump into any of the old crowd. Because, of course, for them, the jury has confirmed that I lied..."

"Not exactly," protested Sally. "I bet they thought your story plausible, but not enough to convict him by. Remember the judge's summing up. 'Beyond reasonable doubt'. Digs had a story that seemed like the truth."

"But it wasn't, Sally. He drugged me. He raped me. He turned my body into a baby-making machine. He made me ugly with stretch marks, he stole my sex life, he killed my future. And I didn't even know it had happened, would never have known except for the baby. That's what makes me so scared. Too scared to go out in company, to relax with people, to trust people again. I think that's the worst of it; the feelings of vulnerability and distrust. I haven't been out socialising since I found out I was pregnant. I thought it was because my friends had all turned against me, but now I think it's more than that. There were times when I…" I remembered the soft sough of the blade across my wrist, the contemplation of ending it all, but I couldn't share that with Sally. She would worry too much. "I understand it now; 'Rape survivor' because that's what I am. I can never go back to how I was before the rape. I can only go on. I don't even know why he did it, just that he did it and he got away with it.

"I'm tired, almost too tired to care just now. But I need to think about my future. Find some way of getting past this. I'll go home, now, if you don't mind, and have a damned good think."

"I'll drive you home, then."

"No. Thanks. I need to walk. To straighten my thoughts."

I hugged her, and she hugged me back, and there was nothing sexual in the gesture. Just gratitude. And love.

Round the corner, I got in the car, feeling shallow and hypocritical.

Chapter 46

Angie

Home. Sanctuary. Coffee. Feet up. Thoughts. Weariness banished by the worries reasserting themselves. What should I do? Just hope everything went back to normal? How likely was that? Move? Where? And I'd need a job.

Not once did I think my criminal behaviour the night before would have repercussions. I think I must have been out of my head.

The doorbell went. It was DC Rolfe. My guts hit the floor. "Can I come in?" she said, assuming the answer was yes. She sat down at my kitchen table, chair swivelled to face me. "Last night, in Elversford. What on Earth did you think you were doing?"

I hadn't sat down with her, and she looked up at me, powerful, from my table, like the Headmistress in her office when I'd been reprimanded.

"Revenge doesn't work, you know," she continued. "If you'd done anything to him, you'd be facing charges. Because we'd know. Same if you'd hurt Kim. Yes, I know she lied in court, and I wish we had the evidence to do her for perjury. But we don't. Not enough. Not yet. Your word against hers. At the moment. But you can't take the law into your own hands even though justice has let you down. You were never meant to be a murderer Angie."

I was empty; everything had been taken away from me, even the chance of vengeance. "What was I meant to be… a wife? A mother? A lover? A daughter?" I asked, voice cracking with grief. "I'm a nothing. I feel so… lost."

Rolfe paused, seemed about to say something, changed her mind. "Don't ever tell anyone you were there and I saw you or I'd end up inside for this; perverting the course of justice."

I couldn't say anything.

"We'll get him this time," continued Rolfe. Her face took on a vindicated, victorious look, banishing the weariness that dragged at it. "And even though he was acquitted of what he did to you, the fact he was arrested for it, and faced trial for it, is admissible nowadays. Wasn't at one time, but bad character can now be used in court if the judge agrees. And double jeopardy doesn't exist anymore; he could be retried for your rape if more evidence came to light..."

I shook my head. "No. I couldn't bear it." As I said it, I felt freer, happier.

"I understand, but we'll get him, one way or another. Let us do our job. Right?"

"He did it again?" I asked. "I heard you arrest him for rape and murder... was it he who murdered the schoolgirl, then? I can't believe he did that. Not Digs."

"If he did—and we're not sure if he did, just suspect that it was him—he never meant to kill her, that was accidental... but never repeat that either. In my mind it's murder because he meant her really serious harm, but that's for a jury to say, not me. As for the rape, I can't tell you the details, but someone came forward. After the news report."

"What, my awful hijacking of the live news report?"

"No, before then. From a newspaper report. Even though none of you were identified in the papers, this person knew who he was, and wondered if he'd done the same to her. And it looks like he has."

"Well, at least some good came of the trial, then. But I was an idiot to do what I did with the TV crew. It's all over the papers... my outburst I mean. And it's done no good, Digby still got away with it. All it's done is mark me out as the mad lesbian woman who accused her lover's brother of rape from spite. This week's shock horror headline."

"And last week's news. People forget, move on. And they don't know who you are."

"My ex-friends. They know. They won't forget."

"And you've no family?"

"What a fool I was, a teenage arrogant fool. I left home after a row about my sexuality. I should have tried to contact them shortly after I left, but I was too angry, too hurt. Once, years later, when I did, the letter came back, marked, 'not known at this address'. I never knew if they'd moved away, or just didn't want to talk to me.

"I've got nothing now. That bastard ruined it all. He took my innocence. Does that seem strange thing to say? For a 48-year-old dike? He stole my love and corrupted her. And when I traded off my pride to pay him back, he took that too." My legs found the other chair, and I sat at last. "Can he lie his way out of this one?"

"I'll make sure he goes down this time, Angie. For a long time. And he'll go on the sex offender's register. I promise." She stood, weariness clutching at her. "It's been a long, long night, and I have to go home, now. I'm shattered. You'd think I'd be used to it by now, but sometimes it gets to me. This sort of thing. And kids." She suddenly looked very bleak, very distant. Then her eyes focused back in the present, her face relaxing slightly. "And there's something else, Angie, something that came out of the media coverage. I don't know how you feel about this. It's sort of why I dropped the question about your family into the conversation. We; Essex police that is, had a phone call from a Mr and Mrs Gregory Bain. Anne Elizabeth and Gregory James Bain. Anne, nee Spooner. They said they recognised you straight away, even though it was only on the News the once, live, and for such a brief moment. They say they wish you well, that they miss you, and your brother Richard is married with grown up kids, Julian and Rebecca. You're an aunty. They've given me a phone number if you want to get in touch." She pulled out a sheet of paper, with the message and the phone number, and put it on the table. "Take care, now. Let us do our job." She stood, saw herself out.

I sat for ages, mind on ball bearings. I looked at the sheet, eyes blurred over the words. Teenage temper. Teenage arrogance born of insecurity. A family whom I abandoned who, it seemed, had never abandoned me. Not quite. There, wanting to contact me, even after all these years. Even after this. It would be difficult. Painful even. Childbirth was painful. Truth was painful. Life was painful. Life wasn't fair. And I was forty-eight, which made them seventy-two.

I made a tea to soothe my throat. Then I picked up the phone and dialled the number. It rang six times and I thought an answer phone would cut in. "Hello." A rich warm voice, the same, even after all this time. Years melted like butter on hot toast.

"Hello Mum," I said.

The end

Blood Will Out is entirely a work of fiction. Although set in Essex, I have changed and fictionalised some of the towns lest I cause inadvertent offence to the inhabitants. I have also created the fictional Rosamundi House in Galchester.

In reality, at the time of publishing this novel, in Essex, there is a specialist care centre for people (both male and female) who have experienced sexual assault, Oakwood Place, on the same site (but set apart from) as Brentwood Community Hospital. The details are to be found on the Essex Police Website.

Oakwood Place is (like the fictional Rosamundi House) a partnership between Essex Police and the National Health Service, and is a Sexual Assault Referral Centre (SARC). A SARC is a safe and confidential specialist centre providing support for sexual assault victims, to minimise long term emotional and physical damage. Every police force in England and Wales should have such a SARC by now, and details ought to be on the relevant police force's website.

In the novel, Angie slipped out of the net for such support, mainly because she felt she didn't need it, even though she did. Sexual assault can have long term detrimental effects. A SARC will offer advice and support, health screening, referral to relevant agencies and a forensic examination service in the immediate period after an assault. The staff are a range of professionals who specialise in caring for victims of sexual assault, supported by police officers who are trained to deal with sexual offences.

Links:-

www.essex.police.uk/be_safe/rape.aspx

www.essex.police.uk/be_safe/rape/oakwood_place.aspx

In this novel, Suzy suggested to Kirsty that she read a booklet "From Report to Court" which is available as a PDF from Rights of Women, a voluntary organisation.

https://www.lifecentre.uk.com/content/uploads/From_Report_to_Court.pdf

Another useful organisation in the UK:-

https://rapecrisis.org.uk/

My listing of these websites should not be seen as an endorsement of my novel by any of these organisations.

Acknowledgements

I have many people to thank for input into this novel. First, as always, my family for putting up with this obsession called writing. Secondly, my writer friends the Scribblers; Nicola Slade for input into the manuscript; Sally Zigmond; Jo Frith; Carol Lucas; and to Elizabeth Lord and Paula Readman for their writerly input and support.

I also need to thank Chris Walters for her information on pregnancy; Howard Neil on his information about how bodies behave in rivers; various members of Police Oracle Website for their answers to my questions (several years ago now); Juliet M, Nelle, and Juliet B for their thoughts on this novel, and Julie Stacey for her brilliant typo-hunting.